TURN U[...]

ISABEL SHARPE

AND

THE WILD CARD
BY
RHONDA NELSON

MILLS & BOON

He wanted Candy...

Candy. Candy's voice. Justin whipped around to stare at his empty doorway.

Then she walked into his room, and he saw immediately that the light tapping footsteps were caused by the same sexy, high-heeled black ankle boots she wore the first time he saw her across the street. With the same leg-enhancing sheer black stockings. But instead of the same black miniskirt, today she wore—

He swallowed convulsively. No skirt at all. Just sheer black panties topped by a red lace garter. Above that a red lace bra trimmed in black, and a red-lipped sultry smile.

"Candy..."

"As sweet as."

She put her foot up on his bed, heel sharp on his navy quilt, calf curving up from the boot to her knee, then diving down again on the slope of her inner thigh. His eyes were held hostage and he was speechless.

"Want a taste?"

There was no such thing as too much Candy...

Dear Reader,

I've had my share of online dating experiences, some fun, some boring, some downright bizarre. I've always thought there was room for a service using the convenience and accessibility of online dating, mixed with the personalization of old-fashioned matchmaking.

Milwaukeedates.com was born, and with it, Marie, its intrepid owner, who is determined to find perfect matches for her female friends and fellow business owners.

In this book, set in Wisconsin's snowy cold February, Candy is looking for a man to help celebrate her first single Valentine's Day in a long time. Coming out of a relationship with a guy who suppressed her true spirit, she is more than ready to be set free, sexually and emotionally, especially by a guy as magnetic as Justin, new in town from sunny southern California, and looking for any way he can to get warm.

Keep looking for those perfect matches!

Isabel Sharpe

www.IsabelSharpe.com

TURN UP THE HEAT

BY
ISABEL SHARPE

All the characters in this book have no existence outside the imagination of
the author, and have no relation whatsoever to anyone bearing the same name
or names. They are not even distantly inspired by any individual known or
unknown to the author, and all the incidents are pure invention.

First published in Great Britain 2012
by Mills & Boon, an imprint of Harlequin (UK) Limited,
Eton House, 18-24 Paradise Road, Richmond, Surrey TW9 1SR

© Muna Shehadi Sill 2011

ISBN: 978 0 263 89364 9

14-0212

Harlequin (UK) policy is to use papers that are natural, renewable and
recyclable products and made from wood grown in sustainable forests. The
logging and manufacturing processes conform to the legal environmental
regulations of the country of origin.

Printed and bound in Spain
by Blackprint CPI, Barcelona

Isabel Sharpe was not born pen in hand like so many of her fellow writers. After she left work to stay home with her first-born son and nearly went out of her mind, she started writing. After more than twenty novels—along with another son—Isabel is more than happy with her choice. She loves hearing from readers. Write to her at www.IsabelSharpe.com

To sweet baby Alice,
who is such a welcome addition

Prologue

"IF YOU ASK ME, which I know you didn't, you are ready to date again, Candy." Marie nodded vigorously, looking around the table for confirmation from Kim and Darcy. The four of them were sitting together, as usual, at the every-third-Wednesday monthly breakfast meeting of Women in Power, Milwaukee's organization of women business owners, held in a seventh-floor meeting room at the elegant Pfister hotel. "It's January, the new year, time for a fresh start."

"I don't know." Candy laughed nervously. She had a fresh girl-next-door beauty: heart-shaped face, long chestnut hair, wide-spaced light brown eyes and a generous, smile-prone mouth. If she put up an Available sign, men would kill each other getting in line. "I don't feel ready."

"You are, honey." Marie laid her hand on Candy's forearm. Candy had dated Chuck, the world's biggest wet blanket, for five years before he had dumped her the previous February. "Trust me. I not only have a degree in psychology, but I am psychic. I had a vision."

"Huh?" Candy looked startled.

"Wait, really?" asked Kim.

Darcy snorted. "Be serious."

"Okay, not psychic, but certainly all-knowing." Marie lifted her chin in mock outrage. "You should show respect for the wisdom of your elders."

"Oh, what, you're two years older than I am?" Darcy looked skeptical, as usual. "All of thirty-four?"

"Thirty-nine. Practically old enough to be your grandmother." No, not quite that old, but Marie felt like a seasoned warrior, having been married ten years and divorced five, while the other three women at the table had never married and were currently single. "I know what I'm talking about. Candy should be out there dating, and she has the perfect resource in me to get started."

"That's for sure." Sweet, shy Kim Charlotte Horton, the blonde of the group, stifled a yawn, striking blue eyes bleary from her being up all night to meet a particularly tough deadline for her struggling one-woman company, Charlotte's Web Design. "You *are* the matchmaking queen."

Marie agreed cheerfully. After her marriage had tanked and her online dating efforts met with no success, she became determined to create a site that didn't just take people's money and then make them do all the work. In five years, her personalized service, Milwaukeedates.com, had gone from the beginning of an idea to one of Women in Power's Best Success Stories the previous year. Marie was happier than she ever thought would be possible again.

"I've considered it." Candy nodded yes to the waitress's pot of coffee and added two packets of sugar and two creamers to her refill. "At least I got that far."

"Good first step." Marie nodded her approval. Kim looked wistful. Darcy scowled.

Marie was content waiting for her own second chance at love, but she was determined to find that first chance for her friends. In fact, she'd made the three at this table her New Year's Resolution. Each of these smart, fabulous women had so much to offer, and each deserved as much in return. "Candy, you do not want to let that first anniversary of being single go by without being out there looking for someone else. It's a matter of pride."

"When did Chuck break up with you? There was something horrible about it, that's all I remember." Kim wrinkled her nose. "But then I can barely remember my own name this morning."

"Last February, on Valentine's Day, the jerk." Darcy narrowed dark eyes over her black coffee. "Candy planned a fabulous meal, made herself an incredible dress, decorated the dining room and her bedroom to the hilt, then Chuck slunk in and smashed her heart. So typically thoughtful of his gender."

Marie sighed resignedly. Darcy, who could pass for a short-haired Catherine Zeta-Jones, was the work-obsessed proprietor of one of Milwaukee's hottest new restaurants, Gladiolas, and would be Marie's biggest matchmaking challenge, no question.

"How could I forget *that* charming story?" Kim made a sound of disgust. "The oinker."

"Aw, he wasn't so bad." Candy moved uneasily. "It was my fault it all went wrong that night. The breakup had been written on the wall for a while. I just refused to read it."

Darcy blew a raspberry. "Stop beating yourself up for something *he* did."

"Thanks, Darcy, but…" Candy shrugged. "Every relationship is a two-way street."

"From what I see, every relationship is a one-way street," Darcy said. "The guy's way."

Marie groaned silently. As she'd thought, Darcy would be her biggest challenge, though she'd keep at her. Kim, she'd wait to match until her company seemed on firmer ground and her financial worries cleared. "In any case, Candy, if you let me help you I guarantee this Valentine's Day will be a whole lot better than the last one."

"Not that it would take much," Darcy muttered.

"That's for sure." Kim drained her third cup of coffee. "You could scoop dog poo and have a better time."

Candy smiled wanly, biting her lip, eyes distant. Marie's instinct kicked in: She was thinking about Chuck, and not the way the three of them wanted her to be thinking about him. The last couple of times Marie and Candy had had lunch, Candy was still bringing his name up suspiciously often. The best way to evict that worthless lump from her heart was to replace him with someone new.

"Valentine's Day is cursed in our family." Candy gestured with her muffin. "My dad either forgot or the restaurant he was going to take Mom to burned down or the present he ordered arrived broken. My best friend Abigail planned a Valentine's Day wedding, which her fiancé canceled. Chuck didn't believe the calendar should dictate when he expressed love for someone, so it was usually up to me how we celebrated, or if we bothered. Most of the time I didn't bother. It is overhyped."

Marie leaned toward Candy. "Would you turn down flowers and candy and a declaration of undying love from a man on his knees in a fabulous restaurant just because of the date?"

Candy's cheeks grew pink; her eyes shone. "Not on your life. In fact, I admit—guiltily—that exact scenario has been my proposal fantasy since I was a girl."

"Come see me. It's time." Marie straightened and picked up the quarter of a cheese Danish she'd been determined to leave uneaten on her plate. "February is around the corner and we want you waist-high in roses and chocolate on the fourteenth."

"That's only a month from now."

"You can find someone in a day if he's right." She took a guilty bite of the rich pastry—by now she knew better than to make dieting any part of her New Year's resolutions. "And that's where Milwaukeedates comes in. Matching clients shouldn't be the job of some software program that doesn't take human variation or taste into account. I work with each—"

"Marie." Kim grinned at her. "You are sounding like your commercial."

Candy snickered. "Yeah, I was looking around for the radio."

"Okay, okay." Marie brushed crumbs off her fingers and held up her hands. "But no apologies. I'm selling the real thing."

"Ha!" Darcy shook her head in mock disdain. "You're selling imprisonment, forced labor and a lifelong descent into—"

"Yeah, yeah, yeah." Marie waved the comments away while pulling out her iPhone. She was sure Darcy's posturing was more about self-protection than conviction. "Candy, it won't cost you anything to come in and talk. Are you hosting any events tomorrow?"

Candy dug out her BlackBerry, an obvious ploy to buy time. In her line of work—party and event planning—she had to know what she was doing every day down to the last hour or she'd be sunk. "Well, no, nothing scheduled, but I have to prepare for a tea party on—"

"Tomorrow." Marie pounced. "Ten o'clock?"

Candy turned helplessly to Darcy and Kim, the excitement in her eyes giving her away. "Am I really going to do this?"

"Looks that way to me," Darcy said drily.

"Sure, why not?" Kim squeezed her shoulder. "You were smart to give yourself a year to get over Chuck. Now I agree with Marie, it's time to move on. Remember, 'Why leave meeting the right person to chance?'"

Darcy chuckled and joined in for the rest of Marie's slogan. "'Leave it to Milwaukeedates.com!'"

"Well?" Marie tilted her head, gave Candy a coaxing smile. "How about it?"

Candy attempted an exasperated sigh, entered Marie's

name in her BlackBerry, then held up the screen. "How does that look?"

Marie patted her friend on the arm, hiding the extent of her triumphant satisfaction. "Like you're on the way to finding new love."

1

CANDY PULLED INTO THE parking lot of Marie's office building at 9:59 a.m. She'd spent the last hour with a jittery administrative assistant organizing an after-work surprise birthday party for her boss, the CEO of the company. She was the type of person who made Candy wish for patience pills: an anxious perfectionist worrywart. "Are you *sure* they spelled his name right on the cake?" No, Candy was sure they hadn't, and she was thrilled because she loved doing a terrible job, which was why she was so much in demand.

Some people.

She picked up her briefcase containing a file of notes and Milwaukeedates.com paperwork filled in the night before, admittedly at the last minute. She'd popped a bowl of popcorn and settled down with a glass of wine to dull her nerves over this whole process. Then she'd been faced with trying to figure out how to represent her entire personality for an online profile in one paragraph, and how to summarize what qualities she wanted in a guy in another paragraph, all the while sounding witty and sexy and fun and appealing, yet honest and substantive.

Right.

Popcorn gone, bottle of wine half-empty, Candy had given

up in exasperation. She had a personality as varied as the parties she loved to plan: whimsical, prim, raunchy—it ran the gamut. How to distill that into a neat sound bite without sounding as if she had multiple-personality disorder?

Exhausted and defeated, she'd finally decided problems like this were what she'd be paying Marie to handle, so she'd gone to bed and dreamed of marrying a guy with six heads.

Oh, baby.

Out into the frigid air of January, the harshest month of winter, though March won for the most wearing, Candy crossed an icy patch in the parking lot with the short, choppy steps people in winter states adopted to keep forward momentum to a minimum. Her breath sent mist streaming into the crisp, dry air, which swallowed the moisture gratefully. She was nervous, not entirely in a good way.

She couldn't let go of the feeling that she was cheating on Chuck, which was ridiculous because he'd left her to pursue someone else, someone he claimed matched him better, which had been the most bewildering part of the breakup. Candy didn't know any other couple that operated in such perfect unison. She and Chuck were so alike, and their minds ran in such complementary directions. She'd felt completely understood and accepted for the first time in her life.

Not that they never fought or disagreed—if couples never fought they were either suppressing emotions or had nothing to say to each other in the first place—but in everything that mattered, the big things, the values, what they wanted and expected from a relationship, on all those things they matched better than she ever could have imagined.

On top of that solid foundation, they shared a sense of humor, taste in movies, food and books, and their sex life was good, too. In short, Chuck never stopped being interesting, sexy and exciting to her; she lit up like a lightbulb every time she saw his face, yes, even five years later. How could she hope to find that again? How could he have let it go?

Most people recommended a year for recovery. Hers had been hell, but she was nearly through it. Maybe taking this first step would be the best way to banish her fear that she wasn't ready, and her deeper fear that she'd never be able to remove Chuck entirely from her heart. When you loved someone that completely, gave yourself over, body and soul…

Yes. But. Chuck was with Kate now, living in her house in Racine, as much as that still managed to hurt, and Candy refused to stay stuck mooning over what wasn't possible.

Plus, Marie's point about Valentine's Day was valid. Candy certainly didn't want to spend the day alone, reliving the hell of the previous year. And being part of a lame-duck collection of single women that night didn't appeal either. She wanted a date. A fun one, if not a really special one.

So.

She entered the warm building gratefully, stomped snow off her boots onto the mat and turned down the hall to Marie's office. For the first three years Marie had operated Milwaukeedates.com out of her home, but she'd felt strongly that an office would up her professional cachet, so when the business started doing well she'd leased space downtown on Water Street, a gamble that had paid off.

Candy unwrapped the floral wool scarf from her neck, took off her black mittens—maybe she was old for mittens, but nothing kept her fingers warmer—and smiled at Marie's receptionist. "Hi, Jane."

"Hey, there." Jane grinned, headset perched on top of her red curls, startling blue eyes blinking behind narrow black-framed glasses. "Marie's in her office, go on in. If you want tea or coffee help yourself."

"Thanks." She crossed to the counter where Marie had set up a generous selection of teas and coffees, regular, decaf and herbal, and poured steaming water over a fragrant orange-spice tea bag.

Behind her, the ring of the phone, then Jane's voice: "Milwaukeedates.com, how may I help you?"

A current client? A prospective client? Maybe even the guy Candy would end up with. Would she be out with him on Valentine's Day?

Stomach churning with a mixture of excitement and dread, she strode to Marie's office, knocked and pushed the already ajar door open. The space managed to be professional and cozy, much like Marie herself. Floor-to-ceiling bookshelves, occasional books turned face-out, deliberately empty spaces on the shelves filled with plants, pottery or sculpture. Over-size chairs in warm brown tones, a burgundy-shaded Oriental rug.

Behind her desk, on the phone and beckoning Candy in, Marie stood in a fabulous teal suit whose cut elegantly camouflaged her extra pounds and deemphasized her short stature. She'd recently started coloring her hair a subtle auburn, which flattered her still-smooth skin and complemented her hazel eyes, today embellished by soft black liner and subtle shadowing. Marie was a lovely, warm person with a core of strength and determination which had gotten her through her stinking husband's betrayal and earned her every bit of her subsequent success.

Candy wanted to be her when she grew up.

"I completely understand, yes. And how did he react when you told him how you felt?" She smiled apologetically at Candy and gestured to the chair in front of her desk "I see. And how did *that* make you feel?"

Candy sank into the cushy chair and arranged a couple of the bright pillows behind her back. The office was deliciously warm and smelled of lavender and orange spice, the perfect antidote to the frozen gray outside. Candy dipped her tea bag a few times and tried vainly to relax. Since her breakup with Chuck, in an attempt to mitigate the crushing grief, she'd thrown herself into work, dragged herself out of the house as often as possible, gone dancing, taken a cruise with her best friend, Abigail, traveled down to Chicago several times…and somehow she hadn't managed to slow down again. Not like when she was dating Chuck and was blissfully content with evenings at home watching TV, weekends spent sleeping late, staying in bed later and puttering around the house.

She kept the pleasant look on her face and sipped hot, comforting tea, telling herself the past was past and she was here in hopes of starting her future—romantically speaking.

"Right. I understand. Well, I'm sorry it didn't work out, but you have the date next week to look forward to…" Marie bent to hit buttons on her computer and scanned the screen. "With Ted. Yes. Okay, talk to you later. Take care. Bye."

She punched off her phone. "That woman has gone out with and found something horribly wrong with practically every guy on our site. During our interview I thought she seemed a little wound-up, but I didn't see this coming. She needs about a year's worth of therapy, not a relationship."

"Oof. Sorry." Maybe Candy needed that, too. Or maybe she just needed another excuse to delay this moment.

"Anyway, this isn't about her." Marie came out from behind her desk and perched on the edge, beaming. "This is your time. We are going to find you someone absolutely fabulous. How did you do on the sheets I had you fill out?"

"Dismally."

"Hmm." She held out her hand. "Let me see."

Candy pulled the papers from her briefcase. "I couldn't decide between answers. I think I checked all the options practically every single time. Do I like staying home or going out? Yes. Do I like old movies or contemporary? Yes. Do I like restaurants, bars, clubs, movies, museums or lectures for a favorite night out? Yes. What is more important, career or family? Both. And on and on. I'm hopeless."

"Hopeless?" Marie took the papers. "Let's call you well-rounded. Adventurous, open-minded, cosmopolitan."

Candy conceded the point. "Yes, better term than *hope-less*. But when I got to the introductory paragraph I splintered completely. I felt I could put up four different profiles."

Marie looked up from the papers. "What would you call those profiles? I mean if you had to classify them. What would those four different parts of you be?"

Candy blinked. She'd expected Marie to laugh, not put on her psychologist hat. "Well. One part of me is playful. Like a kid. The part that dresses up as Sally the Silly Fairy at kids' birthday parties. So one part I'd call goofy."

Marie reached back for a pad and pen and started writing. "Child at heart. Go on."

"Let's see." Candy sipped her tea, considering. "Another would be the part of me that likes to read, to do crossword puzzles, jigsaw puzzles, play Scrabble, to curl up in front of a fire with a glass of wine and a good book I can later discuss, to take classes in things I'd like to know more about. Call her…the Professor."

"Professor." Marie wrote it down. "I like that. Next?"

"Next…is the ambitious side of me, the part that loves organizing, planning, waking up every day knowing what I want to accomplish and knowing I will do it. Continually conquering challenges, beating back problems, making sure everything flows smoothly." She frowned, trying to come up with a title. "Battle-ax?"

Marie pursed her lips disapprovingly. "Superwoman."

"Superwoman!" Candy laughed. "That works, too."

"Is that it?"

"Well…no." Candy felt herself blushing and held the cup of tea close to her face. "There's one more."

Marie's eyebrow raised. "Ye-e-es?"

"It's the smallest part. I'm not even sure it really is a part of me, maybe just a fantasy."

"I'm listening."

"The part that would like to get dressed up for an absurdly

expensive restaurant, to travel to Paris, Monaco, ski the Alps. To wear hot lingerie every day, and have the confidence to seduce a stranger in a bar merely by giving him the right look."

"Hmm, yes." Marie eyed Candy speculatively. "I can see her in you, but I don't think you've indulged her yet. Chuck sure didn't let you."

Candy's mouth dropped. "Didn't *let* me? What do you mean? Chuck was very supportive of whatever I wanted to do and whomever I wanted to be."

For one unbearable moment Marie just watched her, and Candy started feeling anxious as well as angry.

"Yes, sorry. I crossed the line."

Candy let out the breath she'd been holding. She had to keep reminding herself that her girlfriends judged Chuck unfairly, probably out of loyalty because he'd hurt her so badly. She didn't have much nice to say about Marie's ex-husband Grant, either, after he'd left her for some bimbo barely old enough to drink. "It's okay. I guess Chuck is still a raw topic. I'm not even sure I should be here. How can I fall for another guy when this one is still so special to me?"

"Oh, honey. I know how hard this is." Marie capped her pen, face radiating gentle sympathy. "Of course I don't want to push you to do anything you don't want to. But I think this is the right time and the right way. I guess I'll have to ask you to trust me."

"I do." She drank more tea to keep herself from breaking down and bawling. "I do trust you. I'm just a little…"

"Conflicted?" Marie smiled warmly. "I went through the exact same thing after my marriage broke up and I was looking to date again. I had to force myself the first few times. Then it got easier."

"But you never found anyone."

"No. But looking did me a lot of good, made me realize that Grant not wanting me anymore didn't mean no one did.

And besides." Her smile turned wicked. "I didn't have Milwaukeedates, and you do."

Candy laughed. "Of course."

"So." Marie uncapped her pen again and poised it over the pad. "Let's call the fourth one Sexy Glamour Girl."

"Okay." Candy finished her tea, stronger already. Marie was really good at her job. "So that's me. How do I put all that together in a couple of paragraphs?"

Marie sat, eyes narrowed in contemplation, tapping her chin with a professionally manicured fingertip. "I have an idea. Kind of a wild idea, but…"

"I'm all ears."

"Why don't you make four profiles?"

Candy let out a startled laugh. *"Four?"*

"I know, crazy, right? I'm thinking of it as an experiment to see which part of you men respond to the most. See which part you enjoy bringing to the foreground the most. It would actually be fascinating from a psychological standpoint."

"I'm…I…I'm…" She made herself breathe. "I'm stammering apparently."

"Take your time."

"Would that be fair to the guys I was seeing? If I'm not really being me?"

"But you *are* being you." Marie pushed herself off the desk, headed behind it and opened a file drawer. "It's not like you're changing any part of yourself, just emphasizing one in each case. If the guy's got half a brain he won't think he knows you entirely because of how you present yourself on the site."

"I don't know, Marie." Candy was getting excited even as her sensible self told her there had to be disastrous aspects to this plan that she couldn't see yet.

"This will give you a chance to explore certain parts of yourself that might have been…" Marie circled her hand, coaxing out her next word. "Underappreciated."

Candy put her hands to her temples, ignoring the second unreasonable jab at Chuck. "I need to think this through."

"Of course." Marie pulled out several sheets from a folder. "I have four sets of profile sheets here, one for each of you. You'll probably fill them out in half an hour this time."

"I haven't said I'd do it." She was turning the idea over and over. Instinct was telling her she was going to say yes, but common sense wouldn't let her yet. *Four different women?*

"Filling these out doesn't commit you." Marie held the papers across the desk. "You'll have a blast, especially given your talent for performing."

"I haven't been on stage in years." Candy heard the laugh beginning in her voice. She never would have considered doing anything this impulsive and stupid if Chuck were around. He'd be here to tell her she was going off half-cocked again, not thinking through the pros and cons, not making a list and approaching the problem calmly and logically.

But Chuck wasn't here.

"Maybe not on stage, but whenever you manage your events you're performing in a way." Marie shook the papers insistently toward Candy, who gave in and took them. "Plus, even though this is hardly scientific, I'd be curious about the results. Who knows, you might help me help other people decide how to present themselves, too. Oh, and you'd only have to pay regular fees. The three extras would be on the house."

Candy slid the papers absently into her briefcase. "What if a guy recognized the other three of me when he's looking through profiles?"

Marie smiled. "Pardon me, but my experience has been that while men are visual creatures when it comes to the opposite sex, they're more likely to take in an impression of a woman than focus on her features. You probably haven't spent much time browsing other sites, but I'm constantly having to tell men on ours not to submit long-distance pictures of themselves in sunglasses."

"Why not?"

"Women want to see eyes, read faces. Men are okay with the bigger picture, shall we say." She gave Candy a critical once-over. "We can do your hair and makeup differently for each, glasses for one profile, your contacts for another. And since most clients view primarily the profiles I suggest to them, it probably won't even be an issue. If it is, who cares? We'll explain. Not like we're breaking a law."

"True…" Candy shut her briefcase, excitement still bubbling away inside her. It did sound fun. More than that, appearing as a caricature of one part of herself felt more like a game and less like a risk, more like a dare than a date. Most importantly, this didn't make it seem as if she was finally giving up hope that Chuck would come to his senses and want her back.

"Well? You're grinning, that has to be a good sign."

"I'll do it." She finished her tea and stood, feeling giddy and fizzy, better than she had in a long time. "I'll really do it."

Marie broke into a wide triumphant grin. "Candy, honey, get ready for some serious dating fun."

2

JUSTIN PULLED ON his thermal jacket, thrust his hands into puffy black gloves and stepped into boots that promised to keep his feet warm and dry through whatever winter could offer. So far it had offered a lot. Very generous was winter here in Wisconsin. Not much in common with the last thirty winters of his life spent in San Diego. When he'd announced his plans to move to Milwaukee, his friends all got the same bewildered look in their eyes. *Dude, what are you smoking?* They'd predicted he'd last through January then come shivering back to sunny California.

So far he was holding strong, but days like this…

He peered through the back window at the outdoor thermometer the previous owners left with the house, which he could barely see. Five-thirty and nearly dark. And this was better than it had been in December, when it had started to get dark an hour earlier.

The temperature registered…eighteen? Sorry, but that wasn't enough degrees for him. Who was responsible? Who could come to the state and fix it? Shouldn't spring have started by now? Near the end of January? He was certainly ready.

He braced himself and opened the door, cringing at the

blast of air that attacked him as if he were naked. The day before had been miraculously warmer, enough to melt the snow on his roof, which meant that as temperatures dropped again, his gutters became icicle hangers and his driveway a skating rink.

Yes, he had moved here on purpose.

He closed his eyes, briefly picturing palm trees, sunshine—he'd seen the sun maybe ten times during the three months he'd been here—sandy beaches, waves made for surfing.

No point torturing himself. He started on the perilous journey toward his garage for a bag of salt, reminding himself that he owned this spacious two-thousand-square-foot house with full basement, instead of the cramped two-bedroom he'd sold in Solana Beach, his hometown on the California coast. Point in Wisconsin's favor, they were practically giving houses away here. He'd jumped on this one, a typically midwestern brick bungalow on a quiet street in Shorewood, just north of the city of Milwaukee, and made enough profit on the sale of his old house not only to buy the place with cash, but to allow himself time to settle in and write the first book in what could turn out to be a very profitable series with Troy, his closest friend from college.

Justin hadn't been planning to move, but the coauthoring book deal from Troy and the amount of work they'd need to do together, coupled with the nasty break-up of a relationship, had certainly planted the seed. It wasn't until his new neighbor, out of the blue, made a very generous offer to purchase his house that Justin started to view the idea seriously. In the end, it almost seemed as if the fates were pointing him here.

The fates clearly had a high tolerance for cold.

He made it to the garage, no falls or bruises, all bones intact, hefted the bag of salt and managed to work out a method of sprinkling and shuffling carefully forward at the same time, ice crackling under the mineral assault. If he was lucky, he could get the car over this and onto the street without smashing into anything. Snow driving and Justin were only just getting acquainted.

At the end of the driveway he'd turned and started on the sidewalk when a movement across the street caught his eye. His neighbor, whatever her name was, had emerged from her house into the strong beam of her back-door light, and was sauntering toward her car, a bright red minivan parked on the street. He'd seen her through the window a couple of times, but meeting people on a block where no one was ever outside unless he or she was pushing a roaring snowblower had proved complicated.

This woman intrigued him. Not just because she was young, attractive and he hadn't happened to see a guy attached to her, but because, unless she was one of twins or triplets, every time he'd seen her in the past week she'd been sporting a completely different look. Not just different clothes, but hair, accessory styles, even her movements. The first time he'd noticed the change from her usual casual outfit and aura, she'd been striding aggressively toward her car in a pantsuit masculine enough that he could have worn it, no coat, hair in a severe bun, eyes imprisoned by thick, dark-framed glasses. The second time, late one evening, she'd been taking out her trash at the same time he was watering plants in his living room—plants he'd bought to remind himself that not every living thing had died in October. That time, Mysterious Neighbor wore unobtrusive rimless glasses and had her hair in a soft, long braid, exposing chunky gold earrings. On her slender body a bulky hip-length cream sweater hung over casual tan pants and sensible brown shoes. She'd moved in slow dreamy steps, a book tucked under her arm.

Tonight? Whew.

Dark hair hanging sexily loose past her shoulders, tight black miniskirt, fabulous legs in sheer black stockings, which happened to be one of his favorite looks. His gaze followed those shapely legs downward into black lace-up stiletto ankle boots. Under her gaping long black sweater—she must be part Siberian not to be wearing a coat—a purple clingy top dropped low enough to make him yearn for a two-scoop ice cream sundae in spite of the cold. Delicate silver earrings, a silver bracelet, rings on her fingers—bells on her toes?

He realized he was gaping and gave what he hoped was a friendly and neighborly wave, which was all they'd exchanged so far. Her answering smile reached across the street and practically pushed him off his feet.

Whoa.

He crossed, almost forgetting to check for cars, took off his right glove and offered to shake with frozen fingers. "Hi there. I'm Justin."

Her fingers, extracted from black leather and lace, were warm. "I'm Candy."

He was about to say, *yes you are,* when it occurred to him what could be a fun compliment from someone she trusted would sound slimy coming from a stranger. "Nice to meet you, Candy…"

"Graham."

"Candy-gram?"

She shrugged, smiling wryly. "Dad had a weird sense of humor. My real name is Catherine. I've tried to switch to the full name, but…"

He knew this one. "But everyone has always called you Candy, and using another name would be like throwing part of yourself away."

Her turn to gape at him, but unfortunately not because he was the hottest thing she'd seen all winter long as had been the situation when he was doing it. "How did you know?"

"My last name is Case."

"Case?"

"Justin…"

"Justin Case." She cringed, where every other person who made the connection burst out laughing. "Oof. Sorry."

"Thanks." He was distracted by the way her full curving lips were colored a plummy shade that complemented her top. She parted those lips and her breath emerged, a soft white cloud in the dim light. He had a sudden and urgent desire to kiss her, and when he lifted his gaze to her eyes and felt the earthquake shock of attraction, he almost did.

Almost. "Uh, yeah, my dad was quite the jokester, too."

"Apparently." She broke the eye contact, glancing across the street at his house. "Well, welcome to the neighborhood, Justin Case. How long have you been here?"

"Since November." He put his glove back on, crossed his arms over his chest. She had dynamite eyes, lashes long but not fake-looking; subtle liner and smoky brown shadow made them large and smoldering, yet he had the feeling that when she wasn't dressed and made-up in one of her guises, she'd look farm-girl sweet. Nothing turned him on more than the combination of heat and innocence. He wanted to ask if she was seeing anyone, and how she'd feel about staying indoors with him for the rest of this miserable season. "Pretty serious cold here today, huh."

"Today?" She blinked at him.

"My thermometer said eighteen. Brutal!" He shook his head, taken aback when she looked puzzled. "For this time of year, I mean."

"You're not from Wisconsin, are you."

"Uh. Southern California?"

She smirked. "That explains it. Eighteen is a pretty normal temperature. This winter has actually been really mild. We usually go subzero in January."

He shuddered. Were there flights out of Milwaukee to anywhere warm leaving this afternoon?

"It's not that bad." She shifted on the sidewalk, gesturing with her hands in her pockets; her sweater gaped and he got a very nice eyeful. She wasn't tall—he was six-one and she came up to his chin in those incredible boots—but perfectly proportioned. If anything could warm him up... "What made you move here, Justin?"

"A book contract." His teeth started to chatter; he wondered if she'd think he was making a move on her if he invited her to continue their conversation inside.

"No, kidding! What about?"

"An interactive how-to computer manual. There will be a disk with the book, and an e-version. In the ebooks, readers will be able to click links to pursue subjects further, see short animated demos or try out software screens. We're trying to duplicate a classroom experience. A friend pitched the idea to our publisher. He's the computer guy. I'm the writer." Could she tell his sentences were getting shorter and shorter as his body started to want to shake in earnest? It took more and more energy to hold still. Not macho to start violent trembling. "If it flies they'll want a whole series."

"No kidding! That is most excellent. Did you write in California? Where were you from exactly? I have a friend in L.A." Her conversation tumbled out, as if she'd been holding back before.

"I'm from Solana Beach, outside San Diego. Yes, I wrote, technical manuals for a scientific engineering company."

"Oh, wow. That sounds so..." She faltered.

"Unbelievably exciting? Universe-altering, in fact?"

"Of course." She tipped her head, smiling again, hair hanging in a shiny curtain behind her right ear. If he wasn't about to turn into Frosty the Snowman, he'd really enjoy being on the receiving end of that deep-brown gaze, imagining what else she might find unbelievably exciting.

But he *was* about to turn into Frosty the Snowman.

"Listen, I know you natives consider this a balmy day in paradise, but I am about to start dropping limbs. Would you like to bring this conversation over to my house? I have coffee on, though at this point I'm thinking of bathing in it."

She laughed. "I'd love to, but I have a...date."

"Yeah, okay." He was surprised to be so disappointed. But of course a woman like this would have a boyfriend, or guys all over her. Guys who'd walk around on a day like today in shorts, shirtless and not even have their balls retract. His were somewhere up near where they'd been the day he was born. "I should have figured with you so dressed up."

"I don't always dress like this."

He almost said "No kidding" but didn't want her thinking—okay, knowing—that he'd taken a somewhat voyeur-type interest in her and was already curious about her abrupt changes in style. "Too bad."

She smiled, and under her sex-aura he thought he detected shyness. "Thank you."

"You…go on a lot of dates?"

"Recently, yes."

He took a step back. He really liked the look of this woman, the way she smiled so often, and the sensual energy she emitted, but he wasn't the type to stand in a testosterone line. Angie, his ex-girlfriend, was like that. A man-magnet, who was a lot better at attracting than at repelling, for which she was unapologetic, to say the least. She was one of the reasons he'd done more than just consider cutting ties to his home state.

"I joined a dating site."

"Yeah?" He stopped moving back. That would explain all the dates—easy access to a pool of single guys. But not the variety of outfits. "How's that working?"

"Not bad. Not great." She laughed. "Sometimes I don't know if it's such a good idea."

He nodded, not really understanding. For someone who didn't think it was a good idea, she sure put a lot of effort into transforming herself.

"My friend owns the site. Milwaukeedates.com. It's…sort of a favor to her."

"Really." Now that was interesting. She was going on dates

to help out a friend, not to find someone? What about the women who signed up legitimately at the website? What about the poor men who thought they were on a real date and had a chance with her? "The company isn't doing well? Needs more women?"

"Oh." She dropped her eyes, clearly flustered. "No, she… No, it's doing very well. In fact, Marie won a Best Success Stories award last year from Women in Power, a local organization of female business owners. I belong, too."

"Good for her." His reporter instinct started humming. Something was making this appetizing Candy-gram pretty uncomfortable. After graduating with a degree in journalism from the University of Southern California, Justin made most of his money through his technical-writing job, but kept his hand in investigative reporting simply because he loved it. "What do you do?"

"I have my own event-planning company. We do kids' parties, adult parties, corporate events, whatever anyone needs."

"What a great job."

"I enjoy it a lot."

His mind was still spinning. Bob Rondell, longtime friend and ex-roommate, a good-looking successful guy who loved conspiracy theories, had one about a dating site he'd joined in San Diego. He was convinced the company employed hot women, put up their profiles, and had them show up on two or three chaste dates per new enrollee, to boost the site's cachet and to keep the men eagerly paying steep monthly dues in case the next date worked out better. At the time Justin had chalked up the theory to Bob's bruised ego.

But…he'd heard other rumors of deceptive practices on dating sites. It could happen. Justin had learned to trust his instinct when it told him something was worth probing further. Just not here, now, with his ears on fire, his nose running and his toes going numb.

"Well, enjoy your date."

She looked rueful. "Coffee in your kitchen sounds more fun."

"The offer stands for another time." He backed into the street a few steps, keeping their eye contact going, and then turned and did everything he could to amble casually up to his back door when every frozen cell in his body was begging him to run as fast as he safely could.

Was it spring yet?

Inside, still enjoying the mental picture of Candy's body beckoning in purple and black, but feeling bad for the guy she was to meet with all the excitement of someone facing jail time, he let himself warm up for a few minutes, turning over the meager facts. Nothing substantial to go on. But… an article exposing fraud of any type was always fascinating to readers, and it wouldn't do any harm for him to check further.

He hauled out his phone and dialed Bob in California with fingers still clumsy from the chill. Would he ever get used to winter in this place? He missed surfing the most. Maybe he should take up cross-country skiing. Supposed to be a good enough workout that you didn't mind so much being flash-frozen.

"Bob, hey, it's Justin. What's going on?"

"Sitting on my balcony in a swimsuit, getting some sun, enjoying a good book and a beer. You?"

Justin made a noise of disgust. "Up to my testes in ice."

"Ha! Dude, I knew you'd get hammered there. Serious winter. Come home, the living is still easy."

"Nah, I like it so far. Except for the cold."

"Right, and that's only a mere eight months of the year. I lived in Boston and nearly died. Wisconsin is worse."

"Don't need to hear it, I'm living it."

"I'm telling you… How's the book coming with Troy?"

"We've made a good start."

"Yeah? I can't picture the two of you doing anything but goofing around drinking beer."

"We're working. We have deadlines, we have to." He put icy fingers under his arm to try to thaw them. "Listen, are you still signed up at that dating site?"

"CalDates? No-ho-ho-ho." He chuckled out the syllables. "Waste of good money. I told you my theory."

"That's why I'm calling." He outlined the situation with Candy, her odd behavior and his completely unfounded suspicions.

"One question. Is she hot?"

"Let's just say hers is the only house on the block without snow."

Bob snorted. "Then yes. I bet you anything she's working for this friend of hers who owns the site. Probably whoever comes in, he's matched up with her in whatever disguise he seems to want, and bingo, she walks in and he's thinking 'look at this chick, this is the site for me!' Then she disappears after a couple of dates. 'It's not you, it's me. No, really.'

"After that, he keeps striking out, but the memory of that first hot woman keeps him renewing the charges. I'm telling you, men are simple. Lonely men are even simpler. 'Do I have a hope of getting laid again someday? I'll keep paying.'"

Justin made a noncommital sound and switched his hands so the other one could have hope of getting feeling back. He wasn't sure he liked hearing men classified as simpletons, though he admitted one glance at Candy dressed the way she was today, and he'd been having some pretty simple thoughts: *Me want that.*

"You know they did some study of chickens pecking at levers. One group always got food when it pecked. Pretty soon those birds got full and stopped. One group never got food from pecking. They gave up, too, pretty quick. The third group sometimes got food, sometimes didn't. Those guys never stopped pecking. See what I mean?"

"Uh…"

"Dude, men are the same. Give us a little hope, a few dates with a fantasy babe, and we'll keep trying forever. It's brilliant when you stop to think about it."

"Brilliant." He was even more uncomfortable now. The chicken story was a little close to home when he thought about his relationship with Angie. For every week she was horrible to him, there was one he was in, and yeah, he kept pecking that lever for way too long. "Well, thanks, I'll stay in touch."

"You do that. And visit. You'll crack by March at the latest. Government there will be handing out free straitjackets by the end of the month, I'm telling you."

"We'll see." Justin said goodbye and hung up, chuckling and shaking his head. Bob the Man. Full of it, on many levels.

However, as much as Justin was skeptical of his friend's theory, it wouldn't hurt to check out Milwaukeedates.com. He missed the journalistic rush of adrenaline as worthwhile stories emerged under his digging, and would like to keep that part of his career going in Milwaukee. Uncovering a dating-site scam wouldn't earn him a Pulitzer, but it could be a solid foot in the door in this new city. Once he got enough details and felt a story was possible he could put together a proposal and see who bit.

Only one problem as far as he could see.

If he was investigating Ms. Graham's involvement, he couldn't ask her out with anything more in mind than coffee and information. While where she was concerned, his mind was full of a whole lot more than that.

3

CANDY GOT INTO HER CAR and slammed the door, trying not to stare at Justin's very nicely put-together body making its way cautiously over his icy driveway. Oh, my goodness. She hadn't been affected that much by a man in…well not since she'd met Chuck in her senior year at University of Wisconsin Stevens Point. He'd sat behind her in their British Novel class and kicked the back of her chair until she got so annoyed she'd turned around to tell him to knock it off—and encountered the world's most winning grin and a note waved in her direction: *I just fell in love with the back of your head. Meet me for coffee after class?*

She had, coffee that lasted through her free hour, her Entrepreneurship class, too much homework time, dinner and the next five wonderful years. During all that time, and in the last year of horrible grief, Candy had hardly looked at another man.

Oh. Well. There was that guy she'd met at the bachelor party she organized last year. And the father of the little girl who had the Barbie birthday party a couple of years before that. And the cute guy who helped her ver-r-ry attentively at Best Buy when she was getting Chuck a new TV for his birthday.

But those men were either spoken for, or she was, so she'd been friendly, and left it at that. Now, gulp, she was free. And if Justin had recently moved, maybe there wasn't a girlfriend in the picture, unless he'd left one on the beach in California.

Candy turned on the engine, shivering—not from eighteen degrees as much as from Justin. Maybe he was only being neighborly, but her female instincts told her he'd been more than that; the excitement of possibilities had been buzzing in the air between them. Look how she'd jumped to make it seem the whole multiple-dates thing was just a favor to Marie. Candy hadn't wanted him thinking she was desperate for a man, but obviously she'd also wanted him to know she hadn't been swept away by anyone yet. Hint, hint.

She wanted to cancel her date tonight with Ralph, knock on Justin's door and see what talking to him felt like, even though common sense told her this was a temporary thrill. No matter how wonderful Justin turned out to be, odds were he'd end up just a friend in the long run.

Though, mmm, the idea of what could happen in the short run was enticing. Maybe Justin would turn out to be the person Marie prescribed to banish Candy's ghosts of Valentine's Day romantic failure.

Oof. *Pull back, girl.* She was getting ahead of herself, which was a good trait when she was planning an event and imagining everything that could go right or wrong, but not so good when she bulldozed ahead, making assumptions and decisions based on factors she couldn't control. After all, Justin said he wanted her to come over because he was cold, maybe that was all there was to it.

And romance with a neighbor could be complicated. Candy had inherited her late grandmother's house here in Shorewood four years ago, bless Grandma, which meant Candy had been able to put her savings toward starting up the party business. But it also meant she wasn't ever planning to move. Having an ex-boyfriend across the street could be awkward.

One other uneasy thought: Candy had waved hello to Justin a few times, but today was the first time he'd approached, when she was dressed like the kind of person she wasn't. If that was all that attracted him, they had little hope of hitting it off. Her usual look—sweats and fuzzy slippers, glasses and no makeup—would make him run.

There. Reality was much more reliable than fantasy, as Chuck always had to remind her. Tonight, she'd simply celebrate that she wasn't going to spend the rest of her life with a dormant sex drive, since seeing Justin had woken her hormones from hibernation in a big hurry.

Baby steps toward healing, maybe, but forward motion was the only way Candy would get there.

She pulled out onto Prospect Street and headed for Harry's Bar and Grill on Oakland. Tonight she was meeting Ralph Stodges who apparently liked his women dressed to seduce, since Marie had matched him up with Sexy Glamour Girl. Despite Candy's initial misgivings, dating as different types had so far been the perfect way to ease into the concept of new romance with an appropriate sense of fun.

Her first date, as Superwoman—coffee at Alterra by the Lake—had been…interesting. Frank was good-looking and intelligent, but seemed to feel challenged, and kept trying to prove he knew more about pretty much every topic that came up. Tedious, but she'd enjoyed indulging her sense of power and smarts even if she did have to wear that god-awful severe suit.

Her next date—lunch at The Knick as the Professor—was much more fun, probably because that personality came most naturally. Certainly more natural than the one she was trying out tonight. Sam had been thoughtful, interesting and funny, though there was a decided lack of sizzle between them.

Fine by her. She needed to enjoy this experimentation and continue the process of accepting that she and Chuck weren't going to end up together forever. Admittedly, there were times, home alone in bed, when she still had hope he'd come back, and still times she thought resuming a dating life was a mistake, that she was merely looking for second-best after she'd already had the love of her life. What was the point?

Maybe the point was that second-best would turn out to be better than nothing? She should count herself lucky that she'd loved so deeply. Many people never did.

Somehow that didn't make her feel much better.

Her late arrival at the bar was made later when it took ten minutes circling blocks before she found a place to park. Then she couldn't resist calling her best friend since fourth grade, Abigail Glucklich, because God forbid anything should happen the two of them didn't share immediately.

"It's quarter after six, you're supposed to be on your date. Why are you calling me? Is Ralph horrible?"

"I haven't met him yet." She got out, locked the car and started toward the bar.

"Losing your nerve? You were a mess when we were picking outfits, no matter how often I told you how gorgeous you were."

Candy grinned. Abigail had provided clothes, shoes, makeup and advice to bring Sexy Glamour Girl to life, since Candy's wardrobe definitely wouldn't suit. And yes, Candy had been squirmingly uncomfortable no matter what the mirror said. She kept hearing Chuck's voice assuring her she was pretty and sexy without artificial trappings. "No, not losing my nerve."

"Then…?"

"I met a guy." Her voice turned girlish and giggly without her permission.

"What?" Abigail's normal sleepy tone rose an octave. "Where? How? When?"

"Just now. My neighbor across the street."

"The Bakers' old house?"

"That's the one."

"What happened? You went over and jumped in bed with him?"

"I said I *met* him. As in 'Hi, how are you, I'm Candy.'"

"Oh." She sounded disappointed. That was Abigail. In Candy's place she would have accepted Justin's invitation for coffee and made sure they drank it in the bedroom, leaving poor Ralph at Harry's glancing at his watch, wondering what had happened to his date. "What is so momentous about meeting your neighbor? Though of course I can guess."

"He's gorgeous."

"Now we're talking."

"And from what I can tell, available."

"Even better."

"So what do I do next?"

"Take him cookies."

Candy stopped on the sidewalk and burst out laughing. "Do what now?"

"Cookies. A plate of homemade cookies says, 'Hello and welcome to the neighborhood. I'm Candy and I can bake. What's more, in bed I can *cook*. Let's get married.'"

Candy snorted and kept walking. "Oh, that's subtle."

"That's how I got Ron. All the other women after him dressed like bimbos and acted as if all they brought to the table was sex and permission for him to spend millions on them. On our first date, I brought to the table a bag of sugar-oatmeal cookies I baked. He never saw what hit him."

"True enough."

Abigail had grown up in West Allis, one of five boisterous siblings in a house without enough love or money, and had decided the latter was more important, therefore she got herself engaged to the first gazillionaire she could find. He ducked out—the infamous Valentine's Day non-wedding—but she married the next one, Ron Glucklich. They lived in a mansion overlooking Lake Michigan with a three-car garage the size of Candy's house. Until the start of her pregnancy four months earlier, Abigail was always rushing off to this or that country, resort, beach, et al, and was hardly ever around long enough for her house to feel like home, at least as Candy saw it. Now that Abigail had finally stopped throwing up, she and Ron would be off again soon, to Jamaica. Candy wouldn't want her life for anything.

Okay, maybe for a month. Or two. Abigail didn't have to dress up and pretend to be Sexy Glamour Girl, she lived it.

"Where are you?"

"On my way to meet Ralph." She stopped outside the restaurant entrance. "I'm here, in fact. He's probably thinking by now that I'm not going to show."

"My, my, you are certainly rolling in men." Abigail sounded wistful. "Those were the days."

"Like you'd trade what you have now?" She snorted. Though there were times Candy suspected Abigail missed having the kind of love Candy had found with Chuck, she and Ron got along well and were both thrilled about the coming baby. "I'll let you know how it goes. What are you doing tonight?"

"Ron's traveling. I'm going to hang out, watch TV and try not to eat Reese's Peanut Butter Cups. Those miniature ones are so cute you think they don't count, then you reach the end of the bag and realize that's a whole day's allotment of calories and none of them were good for the little one." She let out a groan of exasperation that couldn't hide her joy. "This baby-making is a major responsibility."

"Worth it, though?"

"Oh, yeah." She sighed blissfully. "The little nugget has me already. I'm a goner."

"I knew that about you." Candy grinned over a twinge of envy. Abigail was finally looking out for someone other than herself. That was worth grinning over. The envy…well, Candy had thought that by now she and Chuck would be married and starting a family, too.

"So go. Have fun. I'll fret about calories and you have wild sex."

"We'll see."

"Oh, and I was serious about baking Neighbor Guy cookies, Candy. Make those chocolate chunk ones I nearly gained forty pounds on once I stopped wanting to throw up every hour. He'll fall like bricks."

"Will do."

"And call me the second you're done with the Ralph-date. If he doesn't get a stiffy at the sight of you, he's gay."

Candy giggled. "Thanks, Abby. I promise I'll call right away."

She clicked off the phone, tucked it in her bag, and felt suddenly faint with nerves. She'd have to walk into a bar full of people who would take one look and make all kinds of assumptions about her character. Same for the other dates, yes, but this character seemed so false...

She squared her shoulders and strode into the bar, trying to act as confident and sexual as she knew she looked. No backing out now.

Inside, she gritted her teeth against the rush of warmth and noise, and made herself look around. Ralph was pretty hot in his picture, though Marie said he'd put on a few pounds.

A huge man lumbered toward her. Much taller than she expected. A regular elephant bull. He'd put on, yes, a few pounds. No, several pounds. And shaved his head. And added an earring. And grown one of those soul patches which made Candy itch for a razor. He looked like David Draiman, the lead singer of the band Disturbed, minus the giant, scary lip ring. "Candy?"

"Yes. Ralph. Hi." She stuck out her hand with a bright smile, forgetting she was supposed to smolder, then tried to smolder, but probably looked like she had something in her eye.

This was a mistake. What had been natural with Abigail,

and even with Justin, was foreign and ridiculous with this intimidating mountain of a person. A person she didn't know, a person to whom she was broadcasting messages about herself that weren't true.

"Well, we-e-ell." He gave her a long, slow once-over that was like getting rubbed with used engine oil. "You are one very hot woman. Am I in luck or what?"

What. Candy kept her smile going, tried to arrange her body in a suitably seductive pose, feeling naked, a ludicrous pretender.

She wanted to go home, change into sweats, bake those cookies, deliver them to Justin and spend the evening consuming them in his kitchen over coffee and conversation. What kind of sex kitten did that make her?

Not one. By the end of this evening Ralph would find that out. And who knew what Justin would say to the cookies if they were delivered by a woman in baggy fleece?

Candy should have listened to Chuck who knew her better than she knew herself. Sexy Glamour Girl was only part of her personality in her dreams.

MARIE WALKED DOWN THE STAIRS into the Cellar at Roots Restaurant, her favorite after-work place for a drink and occasionally a reasonably priced and excellent dinner. The restaurant was located in the up-and-coming Brewers Hill neighborhood where Marie had bought a small fixer-upper Victorian. She'd hired a friend to do renovations on the cheap, resulting in a cozy, colorful home that said "Marie" everywhere one looked, and which Marie adored. She and her ex-husband, Grant, had lived in a beautiful Tudor in Whitefish Bay on the east side by the lake, a place she'd decorated the way she thought a wife should decorate a house for her husband. After the divorce, while she'd wanted to stay in Milwaukee where she'd lived all her life, she needed to live somewhere that felt like a new start. Here in Brewers Hill, she wasn't constantly running into Grant or his new hot-young-babe wife, nor did she risk encountering mutual friends with their tsk-tsk sympathy. This part of the city had come to feel like hers.

"Hey, Marie, how are you doing this evening? What'll it be today?"

"I'm fine, Joe." She sat in a tall chair at the long wooden bar set under a dimly lit canopy of tangled brown metal, evoking roots, for obvious reasons, and grinned at the handsome young bartender with the eyes of a doe, the mouth of a young girl and the body of an Olympic swimmer. "Let me see. How about a Prufrock tonight?"

"You got it." He grabbed the bottle of pear vodka which he'd mix with gin, chartreuse and a splash of sour mix at lightning speed. Cellar cocktails were inventive and changed with the seasons. Never a dull moment.

Marie looked around the room, white lights strung in a scattered pattern from the bar overhang, early patrons sitting at some of the tables already, many more to come soon she knew.

"Here you go, one Prufrock."

"Thanks, Joe." She unfolded the *Milwaukee Journal-Sentinel*, dreading the world's depressing news, and took a sip of the icy liquid, fruity and not too sweet. Mmm. Her favorite way to unwind at the end of a long day, especially at the end of a long week. Sometimes a lonely person came in, a close or distant neighbor, or someone needing escape to a place with delicious food, great service and a restful view over the Milwaukee River to the city skyline. If that person was in the mood to chat, Marie would have company. Sometimes during the week Joe wasn't too busy and she'd talk to him—or listen more like it—but most of the time she enjoyed sitting in the bustle of a thriving business within walking distance of her house, indulging in a pleasant buffer between the hectic work day and the emptiness of her home.

She'd adjusted pretty quickly to not being married, but

going home to an empty house—even an empty house she adored—still felt hollow and unsatisfying, though after the trauma of her divorce, and the initial joy of her subsequent freedom, she wasn't looking for a replacement husband yet. If she weren't violently allergic, she'd get a pet. Pets loved you no matter what, didn't criticize, were always supportive, and never left you for a younger version.

Halfway through her drink, while Marie skimmed articles in the business section, a dark suit sat down three chairs away.

That guy. He was here often when she was, more predictably on Fridays. She peeked around her paper for the enjoyment of a surreptitious eyeful. He was delicious. Mid-forties, classically handsome, solidly built, with short salt-and-pepper hair and dark brown eyes, very George Clooney-esque. Sometimes he came alone, sometimes with a woman—seldom the same one twice. Many times he didn't leave alone, even if he came in that way. Women fell with such regularity that Marie found herself tempted to interview him and find out how he worked. She imagined he lived somewhere in Brewers Hill, though she'd never bumped into him anywhere but here.

She'd love to sign the guy up for her site, put his picture on the home page, *Look what you can find here,* but clearly he didn't need help finding company. And if his behavior was anything to go by, he was more into quantity than quality, which wasn't the type of man she'd foist on anyone looking to date seriously. Like Candy, who insisted she was out there for fun, but wasn't, not really. Marie hoped she was having fun with Ralph tonight.

Another sip of her drink and she sat, considering. How about matching this man with someone who wasn't looking to date seriously? Like Darcy? He could be the lure Marie needed to get Darcy to take a first step toward admitting she wanted a serious relationship, too. She was much more firmly in denial than Candy. One way or another Marie would wear down her defenses. After all, the urge to merge was basic human nature, no matter what the level of commitment. Though clearly this clone of George Clooney—George Cloney?—was more about urge than long-term merge. At least until he met the right woman.

He glanced her way, glanced again. Marie hid back behind her paper. He was so fun to observe, she didn't want to speak to him. Especially because they were often here at the same time; if they started now, one or the other would always feel obligated to make conversation in the future. Sooner or later on any particular day, some sweet young 'un would walk in on them chatting, and he'd excuse himself and move on to those greener pastures. Marie could do without that humiliation, thanks very much. Once with Grant was plenty.

But one of these days she wanted to be close enough that she could at least hear his pitch. Though his targets didn't always leave with him, Marie had never seen a woman respond with anything but smiles and a readiness to talk, even briefly. Was he able to read body language with uncanny accuracy or did he have some deep instinct for who would match him, even for a few hours? How did he know which women to approach and which to leave alone? When to move in and when to move on? When to sit tight and wait until the prey approached him?

The guy was a master, and as someone for whom matching people was an obsession, Marie was shamelessly fascinated.

Maybe there was something more to her interest. Something personal. He did remind her of Grant: his confidence, his certainty in what he wanted and that he would get it. Grant had swept Marie off her feet the same way. He'd walked into the hotel bar where she was waitressing her senior year, having returned to UW–Madison after four years of active duty in the navy, to have a drink with the director of the ROTC program, with whom he'd kept in touch.

One glance at Marie and he'd turned on the charm, overwhelming her with his interest, insisting he take her out, then taking every opportunity to visit until she graduated. When she got a job in Milwaukee, where he'd also settled, it had seemed like fate. Now she thought any woman would have done for him at that stage. That was how Grant operated. Back from duty, time to get a wife, here's one, good, check that off, next task on the to-do list…

And then, somehow, ten years later, his checklist included having an affair with a girl young enough to be their daughter. Ironic since they hadn't been able to have children, and Grant hadn't wanted to adopt. In retrospect, just as well. Who wanted to put a kid through an unpleasant divorce? Not that there was any other kind.

Fifteen minutes later, whaddya know, two women walked in, late twenties, dressed to be noticed. A casual observer wouldn't have picked up on the way Mr. Cloney minutely adjusted himself on his chair for the best view. Marie wasn't a casual observer. She waited, with all the patience and concentration of a naturalist studying animal behavior in the wild.

The women ordered drinks, spoke in loud voices, squealed with laughter. One glanced behind her friend at George, glanced again, then a third time. He appeared not to register her interest, taking a leisurely sip of his martini, of which he never had more than two in an evening, at least that Marie had seen.

He was implacably cool, yet, when he chatted up his prey there had to be warmth, or he wouldn't do so well. You could fool some of the women some of the time…

The girl with her back to Mr. Cloney gave him a shy smile over her shoulder.

"Hello." His deep voice carried. No stupid line, nothing suggestive in his tone, just a friendly greeting, acknowledging her smile.

"Hi." The blonde's blush was visible even in the low, warm light. "I'm Jill."

The brunette swivelled to face him, giggling silently. "I'm Maura."

"Hi, Maura. Hi, Jill. I'm Quinn."

Quinn. Marie nodded. She loved that name.

The girls put their heads together; the blonde nodded.

"What are you drinking, Quinn?" Tipping her head coyly, the brunette extended her arm toward him, let her hand rest on the bar.

"Gin martini. Extra dry with a twist."

"Join us? We'll buy your next one."

"Only if I can buy both of yours."

Marie had to stifle laughter. Nothing scintillating in that conversation. Nothing cute, nothing enticing, no showmanship, and yet…Quinn was in once again.

He got up, moved closer, left one seat between him and the brunette, not crowding them, keeping his own space to himself. Brilliant. He struck up a conversation Marie wished she could hear, but she'd bet it was casual get-to-know-you chitchat. Where do you work, where do you live, how about them Packers/Brewers/Bucks, and will winter ever end?

The closer she got to the bottom of her drink, the more convinced she was that this man would be perfect for Darcy. Too smooth, too polished for Kim. Kim would do better with a sweet boy-next-door type. Once Candy figured out who she was and what she wanted, her guy would come along, too, someone earnest and kind, harboring an inner wild child. But Darcy needed someone with as much confidence as she had. Someone who'd let her be herself, but would never let her walk all over him.

Marie dug her cell out of her bag and dialed, knowing Darcy was at Gladiolas and wouldn't pick up. Better that way. If she spoke to her, Darcy would blow off the suggestion.

But if Marie left a message to work on Darcy's subconscious before she brought it up again in person…maybe.

Marie grinned, waiting for voice mail to pick up.

Darned if she wasn't as big an operator as Mr. Quinn.

4

"HI, JUSTIN, NICE TO MEET YOU. Come on in."

Justin shook Marie's hand, impressed by her grip. She wasn't what he'd expected. Her rich voice on the phone had him imagining a broad-shouldered Amazon, not this intriguing mix of elfin and elegant. Small, plump, with short auburn hair and scattered bangs above hazel eyes emphasized tastefully with makeup. She wore a stylish reddish-brown suit with a silk scarf of beige, orange and yellow, the colors combining to evoke pictures of a New England fall.

"Nice to meet you, too." He stood looking around, hands in his pockets, portrait of a brand-new dating client nervously ready to put his ego on the line. He hoped the act was convincing. "Great office. Very inviting."

"I'm pleased you noticed." She leaned over her desk to make a quick note in a folder—that he appreciated decor?—and gestured to one of the two chairs in front of her desk. "Have a seat."

"Thanks." He dropped into the comfortable chair, rubbing his hands along his thighs, poor ill-at-ease dude who could barely handle the stress of putting himself out there. "So, how do we do this?"

He was having fun already. Not that he wanted the lovely

Marie and the even-more-lovely Candy to be involved in anything shady, but it was great to be back to the rush of an investigation. Writing the computer book with Troy was a good idea, a great career move, satisfying in many ways, but not exactly a thrill ride.

"We 'do this' any way that makes you comfortable, Justin. You and I can talk, or you can fill out paperwork, or we can fill it out together. What do you think?"

"Well…" He shrugged lamely. "I'm okay talking."

"Good." She dimpled a smile, and instead of taking the Interviewer Seat behind her desk, came around and settled into the chair next to him. "That's the way I like getting to know our clients, too."

"Do I tell you my life story?"

"I've got some of it here." She opened his folder; he could see part of the form he'd completed online with basic information—name, address, marital status, brief romantic history. "You're straight, college educated, nonsmoker, never married but coming off a relationship in California. Would you mind talking about it with me?"

Oof. He hadn't planned on this. "No, not at all."

"How serious was it?"

"More for me than for her." He couldn't help the bitterness seeping into his voice. "When a job came open in Milwaukee I knew it was time to cut ties and go."

"You're a writer…"

"I was a journalism major, did technical writing and some reporting on the side in California. Now I'm writing a non-fiction book with a friend and hoping to get back into the print-media business as well."

"Interesting career." She made a note. Rating him on the Great Catch vs. Loser scale? "How long have you been single, Justin?"

"Oh…" He rubbed his hands together, not having to fake the nerves and reluctance any more. *Single?* Calculations were hard, since as a couple he and Angie had been on-and-off and off-and-on for the better part of a year since he'd met her at a friend's beach party. Finally last fall he'd left her apartment swearing it was over for good that time, and though he got suckered into one more night with her—saying no to sex with Angie was a skill he took a while to master—he'd never felt the same way about her again. You could only kick a dog so many times. "About five months."

"Five months." Marie was watching him carefully, probably taking in more signals than he knew he was sending. He unclenched his hands, which he hadn't noticed were fisted until Marie glanced at them. Bizarre interview, both of them talking on one level while searching for a deeper, possibly contradictory story lurking underneath. "And you feel ready to move on?"

"I *am* ready to move on." That much he could state firmly and with absolute honesty.

"Good to hear." Another note in his folder. "Are you comfortable talking about why the relationship didn't work out?"

"You don't pull punches."

"No, I don't." She leaned toward him, eyes earnest. "This is what sets Milwaukeedates.com apart from other sites. I want my clients to find partners who can give them what they need. If you don't understand what you need, or keep reliving destructive patterns by choosing and discarding the same type of person, you're going to have trouble finding happy-ever-after. The best way to ensure future romantic success is to dig into the whys and whats of past relationships and sort those out before you meet someone new. This is why I always ask this question, even though it can be difficult and emotional to answer. That said, if you're not comfortable with it, that's entirely fine."

Justin nodded as if he were considering her words, keeping his face blank while internal chemistry urged him to run far and fast. He'd thought he'd be able to walk into Marie's office, answer a few superficial questions, gather some evidence as to whether she threw Candy at every first-timer, then get out. He wasn't expecting to have to eviscerate himself and lay his entrails out for her inspection.

"The relationship didn't work because…" He couldn't say *she was a man-eater and I was dinner,* because it was more complicated than that. Angie had been a beautiful, sexual, vulnerable mess. *She was a cheater and I was a sap* didn't work either. He needed a more balanced and less angry sound bite. "I was willing to commit to an exclusive dating arrangement and she wasn't."

"She was seeing other men."

"Compulsively." Justin resettled in the chair, beginning to perspire. He'd thought *he'd* be doing the investigating here.

"You think her behavior was beyond her control?"

"No. But it was her way of coping with baggage and avoiding commitment. She was trying to fill a black hole of need for reassurance that she was desirable and worthy of love."

Marie sent him a sympathetic look that stopped short of pity. "It sounds as if you have a good handle on the dynamic. How long did you date her?"

He gritted his teeth. "Nearly a year."

"Was she dating other men that whole time?" Marie asked the question as if she wanted to know what was available for lunch, while he was using all forces at his disposal not to writhe too obviously.

"I knew of one at the beginning. One at the end. I strongly suspect there were others. Flirtations certainly."

Marie pressed her lips together and let the silence settle for several seconds. Letting him relax? Building more tension? "Did you think that by staying with her you could save her, Justin? Fix her?"

There it was, the sucker punch. He hated being dragged

through this Dr. Phil torture. "I hoped...that what we had would be enough, yeah."

Marie let more time go by. Which probably meant he had another killer question to look forward to. He relaxed his diaphragm, made sure his hands stayed open.

"Do you think there was something you could have done differently that would have affected the relationship's outcome?"

Boom. Marie knew her stuff. He felt like squirming in his chair, the schoolboy asked the tough question in front of the class, wanting to avoid answering at all costs. But he'd come this far; he had to fight on to the payoff—when he was matched up with Candy...or not.

He forced himself to consider her question seriously, to think back carefully through a jumble of hot nights, cold mornings, laughter, heartache, jealousy, passion...

"No." He laced his fingers together, resting his forearms on his thighs, not sure his current relief was from coming up with an answer, or from finding a truth that freed something inside him. "No, I don't think anything I could have done would have made us right for each other."

"It doesn't sound as if she was willing to stop and look at her behavior."

"It was all she knew how to be." He tried to grin, but his voice cracked, and only half his mouth seemed able to function. He'd spent months brooding over this relationship, and in ten minutes Marie had gotten to the essence of why he was right to leave it behind.

"Looking forward now." Her voice was gentle. "You are searching for someone who knows herself."

"Yes."

"Someone who wants a serious relationship?"

"Not necessarily." Justin rubbed his forehead. He'd never been this rattled in an undercover situation. He'd met with bank vice presidents, calmly requesting loans with collateral he didn't have. He'd visited hospitals and funeral homes, pretending to be a grieving relative. He'd shadowed people, staked out homes and businesses, eavesdropped on conversations, rifled through private filing cabinets—all with more poise and cool than he was able to summon talking about women. "I mean I'm not looking to get married…"

"Why not?" The question was sincere, not challenging.

"Well, not soon."

"Even if you meet the right person?"

"Uh…yeah, if she's the right person. I guess." He wanted either to laugh or bellow in frustration. He'd lost track of which were honest answers and which he'd decided to give when planning this meeting. "I'm not against getting married in the big picture. It's just not on my radar right now."

Marie made a note. "So you're looking to meet someone, with the possibility of marriage down the road."

"Yeah. Sure. If it seems right." *Marriage?* He'd come in looking for a piece of Candy and was being offered a whole cake.

"What would she be like, this person?"

Finally. Solid ground. He'd prepared for this. "Someone honest. No head games."

"Is appearance important to you?"

"Some. But it's what's inside that really counts, right?" He wanted to cringe at his Boy Scout sweetness.

"We can't help being attracted to some looks and turned off by others."

"Well, yeah. I mean, I am a guy." He shrugged as if it were the most obvious conclusion in the world. "I do want a woman who cares about her appearance."

Marie nodded. "Understood. Beyond the facade, do you want a risk-taker? A homebody? What type?"

"A little of each. Someone happy to be alive, someone who throws herself into each day, who's grateful for what she has but works hard to get more. A woman comfortable with her body, with a healthy attitude toward sex."

"'Healthy' meaning…"

"Uninhibited. With a good appetite." He winked, again covering his discomfort. The best way not to get caught in a lie was to tell as much truth as possible, but as he kept talking about what he wanted, he kept seeing Candy's face, not merely as a target of this investigation, and kept having to tamp down excitement he hadn't felt in a while.

Which was nuts. He didn't know Candy at all. She could be a prime manipulator, using men to pad her friend's coffers and her own. He was out of his element, that was all—displaced from his old home, not yet comfortable in his new one. Of course he'd latch on to someone he could conceivably belong with because belonging was something everyone wanted. Because he'd never belonged with Angie, no matter how much he wanted her or how much he tried.

Half an hour later, hallelujah, Marie finally closed her folder, apparently out of questions, leaving Justin drained, as if she'd sucked out several pounds of his self. No wonder they called psychologists shrinks. "What do you think, Marie, is there hope?"

"Absolutely. Come see." She reached eagerly for her laptop, eyes dancing. He stood next to her, found himself oddly nervous as she logged on to the Milwaukeedates.com site. "You'll have your own username and password to look through profiles, but I always start people off with a suggested match since I know my clientele pretty well. Someone came to mind when you were talking, and I thought you'd like to see her."

"Sure." Here it came, the moment of at least partial truth. Had someone really "come to mind" or was she offering Candy to all strangers?

"She's fun, energetic, but a good solid person underneath. Like you, she had a serious relationship that didn't work out, and while she wants marriage, right now she's more interested in easing back into dating than in going for the perfect fit first try. However, I guarantee if you hit it off, you'll find she's strictly a one-man woman." She pressed a few more keys. "Let me pull up her profile."

He held his breath. Five…four…three…two…one—

Candy. Dressed up the way she'd been the other night, the seductress. Not proof yet, but another hint that all wasn't on the up-and-up at Milwaukeedates.com. If he hadn't said sexually uninhibited, he might have gotten the version of her with the braid and the sensible shoes. If he said he liked strong women, he could have been standing here looking at her picture in that overly masculine suit.

Instead of triumph, he could only manage grim satisfaction mixed with disappointment. Apparently he hadn't acknowledged the part of him that wanted Candy and Marie and this entire operation to be clean. Because…? He didn't want to explore further.

"What do you think?" Marie twisted to look at him. Justin had apparently missed the window for a normal response to the image.

"She's gorgeous." He gestured toward the screen, back on script. "You're not going to believe this, but she lives across the street from me."

Marie's face fell. "Oh, I am sorry. I usually check addresses. I'll just—"

"It's fine." No way would he let Marie back out of this now that he'd gotten her where he wanted. He reached over and hit a button to enlarge the image. Candy's sexy smiling face filled the laptop screen. Sweet-hot innocence? Or a devious diva preying on the lonely for profit? He wanted to find out, more than was professionally appropriate. "In fact, it's no problem at all. I've been wanting to get to know Candy a lot better."

5

CANDY SAT ON HER KITCHEN STOOL, staring at the bird clock Grandma had bought a few years before she died, the one that made different bird sounds every hour. It was three minutes to mourning dove, when Justin would pick her up for their date. Guess what, she hadn't had to bake him cookies after all; he'd called all by himself.

It did seem a little odd that he'd sign up for Milwaukee-dates.com to invite her to dinner when he could have asked her on the block, but maybe he wanted other female options. Maybe he hadn't really thought of her as dating material until Marie shoved her in front of his face. Maybe he still didn't, but Marie had threatened him with certain death if he didn't go out with her.

Who knew? She didn't. She didn't even care right now.

Before her other dates, Forceful Frank and Sweet Sam and Randy Ralph, she'd been upbeat, excited, filled with a sense of purpose and fun, giggling the whole time she got dressed as whatever person she'd be for that night.

Tonight she'd started off okay, but on her way to the borrowed clothes hanging in her closet, she'd bumped her bedside table and knocked over the silver-framed picture of her and Chuck. Putting it right, she'd made the mistake of stopping to look at the snapshot. Chuck hadn't liked being photographed so it was a rare example, slightly out of focus, taken by Abigail at a Brewers' game. Chuck, in the act of rising from his seat after a huge line drive toward right field, arms in the air already celebrating the home run, mouth open in a victory roar Candy could still hear in her imagination. Next to him sat Candy, hands on their way to clapping, laughing up at his joy.

She missed him. Thinking about Chuck had made the game of Who Shall I Be Tonight? seem silly and shallow. Candy should be going out with someone who'd be into her no matter what she looked like.

Tonight she'd wanted to dress as a different character for Justin, maybe try out Child at Heart, but Marie said she'd shown him the Sexy Glamour Girl profile at Milwaukeedates. com, and what he saw should be what he got. Truth in advertising. On subsequent dates Candy could tone down her appearance if she wanted.

Yeah, okay.

Eventually Candy had roused herself from staring mournfully at the photograph and made it to her closet for the evening's outfit. She'd tried to enjoy stepping into the little red skirt Abigail wouldn't be able to fit into again for many more months, tried to grin while brushing her hair into a side part so she could execute the perfect mane-over-the-shoulder toss, tried to giggle while adjusting her boob-crusher of a bra under the scoop-neck stretchy white top. But by the time she stepped into what Abigail called her "ho shoes," bright red, open-toe with silver stiletto heels, which would undoubtedly do their best to pinch and freeze Candy's feet, Candy was completely out of fun.

Now, slumped at the kitchen counter in her Sexy Glamour Girl finery, ready to go out with another guy she didn't belong with, she felt like a first-grader in a beauty pageant: ludicrously made over into someone she wasn't meant to be.

Why had she thought this was a good idea?

She let her chin drop into her hand, leg swinging back and forth, bumping the stool next to hers. Bump. Bump. Bump. One minute to mourning dove.

Maybe she should call Abigail. Except Abigail was escaping winter in Jamaica at the moment and probably wouldn't appreciate having some fabulous dinner interrupted by Candy whining about an ex-boyfriend she should have gotten over by now. Or so people said—mostly Abigail, who was as sentimental about past relationships as a stapler.

Bump. Bump. Bump.

The sad strains of the mourning dove filled the quiet kitchen. Whoo-ee ooh-ooh-ooh. Whoo-ee ooh-ooh-*ding-dong*.

Justin. She moved to jerk her feet off the rungs of the stool, caught a heel, and barely managed to slam fingers on the counter before she fell on her face.

Darn it. She pressed a hand to her heart, trying to calm its thumping, trying to swallow a silly rush of poor-me tears. He was here; she'd have to make the best of the evening.

"Coming." She tap-tapped to the front of the house, pulling on her black sweater-coat, wishing she were wearing sweats and sneakers. Deep breath and she opened the door, determinedly bright smile superglued to her face. "Hi, Justin."

She'd been planning to say more. A comment about how he was so perfectly on time. A comment about how he'd picked truly decent weather for their date, below freezing and dry. Maybe a simple "nice to see you."

None of it came out. Somehow since she'd last seen him, Candy's face-recall powers had turned Justin ordinary. She'd dulled his eyes to flat brown, softened his lean, masculine face, over-neatened his hair, grown his nose too large.

Surprise attraction punched her in the solar plexus; it was hard to breathe and harder to look into those eyes. Deep, lively, gaze-into-your soul eyes, boyish and Bambi, rugged and Rambo all at the same time. The kind that could get her to do to anything with one blink.

How could she have forgotten?

"You look very, very nice, Candy Graham."

She pulled herself together. Sexy Glamour Girl wasn't rattled by anything as mundane as killer eyes. "You look very nice, too, Justin Case. And you're very on time."

"No, I'm early."

"Really?" Candy turned to lock the door. "My clock said exactly seven."

"Mom said every woman needs five to ten extra minutes to fuss. She taught me never to show up exactly on time for a date."

"Ah." Candy pocketed her key, wondering if she should have played "not-ready-yet" when he rang the bell. Sexy Glamour Girls probably loved to keep their men on tenterhooks. "Why didn't you wait ten more minutes?"

"Actually…" He glanced from her hooker shoes back up to her eyes, stopping infinitesimally at the inflated wonders she barely recognized as her own breasts. "I couldn't."

"Couldn't…"

"Wait." He smiled a slow smile, which made Candy wish she hadn't locked the door yet so she could turn away now to hide her pleasure and confusion.

Instead, she hid it under an attempt at a smoldery smile, suddenly less reluctant to tackle the evening as an overpumped sex goddess. "It's fine that you were 'early.' I was ready."

"You were." He gestured to the shiny red sedan in her driveway, engine still running. "Shall we?"

"Sure." She moved forward; a sharp wind gust flung stinging crystals at them from a nearby snowdrift. Justin immediately crossed behind her, taking the wintry surprise attack on himself.

Considering it probably felt like icicles flung from a catapult to him and a cold tickle to her, he was very gallant. Chuck hadn't been into the whole protect-the-woman thing. Candy hadn't minded—women could take care of themselves, thank you very much—but this, yes, was nice.

"Thank you, Justin. The wind can get pretty frisky."

"So I've learned." He came around and opened her door, stayed to help her in, which she thought at first was overkill, but the combination of ridiculous heels and a teeny skirt did make getting into a vehicle dicey business, and she ended up grateful for his hand.

His car, some manly sport model, was heated to the point where most of the moisture had left her throat by the time he closed his door. "You must be looking forward to experiencing a Wisconsin summer."

"I hear it gets humid."

She shrugged. "More than San Diego. Less than Florida. It's all relative."

"True." He backed out of her driveway, avoiding the snow-banks crowding either side, and headed south toward Capitol Drive. "I'm *really* looking forward to spring, though. My first."

"Your first! You'll love it." The idea of someone being introduced to spring lifted her spirits. "It's indescribable."

"Try me anyway." He tuned the radio to Milwaukee's jazz station, WJZI, and a gruff saxophone solo filled the car with musical color.

"The crocuses show up first, purple and yellow miracles after so much white and gray. Birds are suddenly in everywhere. You hear them singing even though the temperature hasn't changed yet, and you have no idea how they know it's time. Daffodils come next, and tulips. Those first inches of green pushing through the earth are enough to bring tears to your eyes. And the smell…" She leaned back in her seat, stretched her arms forward and took in a long, searing breath of overheated air, eyes flying open when the car veered to one side and back.

"Sorry. Sorry." He turned right on North Lake Drive, which meandered along Lake Michigan toward downtown. "You were saying?"

"Oh. Yes." She released her two-handed grip on the dashboard. "Smells that were frozen all winter thaw, scents of earth and grass and wind. The air softens into a caress instead of a razor slice. It's wonderful."

"Wow." He glanced at her. "I can't wait to see and hear and smell all that."

"You will." She wasn't sure her description of the season was very Sexy Glamour Girl, but she'd gotten carried away wanting to communicate how special it was. Justin hadn't seemed to care that she'd abandoned the I'm-so-hot act. Clearly he had more depth than Randy Ralph who'd gotten itchy whenever a sentence lacked a double entendre he could guffaw over.

By the time they were opposite the Milwaukee yacht club, however, she was hot in an entirely literal way, and finally gave in, stripping off her sweater coat, exposing more thoroughly the Boobs of Wonder. "You like it really hot, don't you, Justin?"

The car veered again; he swore under his breath. "Sorry. Uh. I'm really sorry."

"Ice?" She peered at the road, which looked clear and dry in the headlights.

"No, no." He shook his head, chuckling. "Not ice. Mild brain malfunction."

"Ah." She studied him in concern. Had he been drinking? "You okay?"

"I'm fine. Really." He met her eyes, his slightly sheepish. "Before, when you stretched back with your eyes closed, I was, um, watching you instead of the road. And just now when you took off your sweater and asked me if I liked it hot…"

If Candy's cheeks weren't already flushed from inferno-car, they'd definitely be so now. She attempted a sensually nonchalant pose, but Justin grinned wickedly and she couldn't help laughing, glad when he laughed with her. "Where are we going for dinner?"

"Cempazuchi. You ever been?"

"No, but I've heard raves. I love Mexican food."

"This is Mexican from the state of Oaxaca, way south on the Pacific coast, nearly to Guatemala. Supposed to be the closest I'll get to Southern California here in town."

"Or to Mexico."

"Or to Mexico." He laughed again, easily, relaxed and California laid-back; his attitude made her calmer. "Troy swears by it."

"Troy is your book-mate?"

"My roommate in college, now we're writing the book together, yeah."

She tried to imagine Justin as a student. Had he been the party type? The serious scholar type? She'd guess somewhere in between. "Must be nice knowing someone in a new town."

"It is. He grew up here, so he has lots of friends and knows the city inside out. The perfect introduction to Milwaukee, and a good starting place for building my own life."

"You're planning to settle here?" For some reason she felt hopeful.

"I'll stay while we're writing obviously, then see how the book does, whether the publisher will want more in the series. Troy seems to think there will be more contracts coming, and I'm optimistic enough to have bought the house. But by that time I should have a good feel for how Milwaukee fits me."

"How is it doing so far? Besides freezing you?"

"Not bad." He turned away from the lake toward North Farwell Avenue. "Except for college in L.A., I've always lived in San Diego. I don't know if anywhere else can feel like home."

She felt wistful for him. "I hear you. I've lived in Milwaukee all my life, minus five years in Stevens Point, where the University of Wisconsin has a campus."

"Did you do a five-year B.A. or get a master's?"

"Neither. I hung around with a secretary job, trying to figure out what I wanted to do with my life. My then-boyfriend was a year younger, so I stayed until he graduated." She cleared her throat, hoping Justin hadn't noticed her voice thickening. "Then my grandmother died and left me the house in Shorewood, so we moved in."

"And figured out what you wanted."

"I did."

"Yes to the career, no to the boyfriend?"

She sighed. Sexy Glamour Girl would be a serial heartbreaker, but Candy didn't have it in her to lie about Chuck. "The breakup was his idea."

"I'm sorry." He slowed as they approached Brady Street. "I know how that feels."

"From recent experience?"

"Pretty recent, yes. It doesn't feel good."

She nodded, not trusting herself to speak. No, it never felt good, and sometimes it seemed it never would again.

"When do I get to come to one of your parties?"

"Well…" Candy forced herself back to life, appreciating his change of subject. "I'm doing an engagement party tomorrow, a bachelorette party Saturday and a formal tea Sunday. Would you like to go to that? Finger sandwiches and tiny crumpets?"

"Uh, gee." He cringed comically. "You know, it happens that my white gloves are at the cleaners."

She was even able to giggle. "Why don't you hire me for a party and come to that one?"

"There's an idea. Hey, help me look for parking." He scanned the street on either side. "How about a book-launch party?"

Candy blinked. A guy who could park and talk at the same

time? Chuck always went grouchy and silent. "Absolutely a book-launch party."

"What would you do?"

"Let's see…a book-shaped cake, of course, topped by an edible photo of your cover. Around the room, fake quotes from famous authors extolling your work, Shakespeare, Dante, Mark Twain, Ernest Hemingway. Then small bites, spelled *bytes* because it's a computer book. Tiny pizzas that look like CDs, little square sandwiches with letters on them arranged to look like a computer keyboard. Then we could have licorice cables connecting—" She turned from looking for parking. "What is so funny? Wait, look there, someone's leaving a space."

"Across from the restaurant? Toto, we are not in San Diego anymore." He pulled behind the exiting car and turned on his blinker. "Have you done one before? A book party?"

"No. It would be fun though."

He turned toward her, and in the dim car his eyes were even more powerful than they'd been at her front door. Or maybe she was just in a better frame of mind to notice. "I'm amazed. All those ideas poured out of you, all great ideas, and you didn't even have to stop and think."

"Oh." Candy shrugged self-consciously. Brainstorming party ideas didn't seem amazing to her. "It's how my mind works."

"Remarkable."

"If you say so."

"I do." He pulled the car forward and gave a deep sigh. "Oh, boy. Parallel parking on a first date, a serious test of my manhood. Will you still respect me if I mess up?"

She pressed her lips together, shaking her head regretfully. "I don't know, Justin. A guy who can't parallel park…"

"Uh-oh. Wish me luck." He backed in at the perfect angle, maneuvered parallel to the curb and gave her such a cocky look she burst out in giggles and high-fived him. If Justin could make parking fun she was going to have a good evening no matter what. In fact, he seemed to be exactly what she needed—a low-key, funny guy she could enjoy without getting bogged down in expectations. This date could go a long way toward making her feel she had a chance to belong in the romantic world again someday.

"You are The Man."

"I am." He turned off the engine and winked at her. "Now that's settled, let's go eat."

Cempazuchi was bright and colorful, walls painted rich shades of red, yellow and blue to match bold floor tiles of the same three colors. Decorations hung on the walls: papier-mâché masks, woven hangings, demon heads and Day of the Dead skulls. Bold Mexican rhythms played through the speakers, making Candy's feet itch to dance. The place looked like a cross between a funky art house and an elementary school. She loved it.

Almost as soon as they were seated at a table next to a cheerful wall mural of a woman tucking a bottle of booze into the saddlebag of an appreciative cowboy, a basket of thin, crisp tortilla chips showed up alongside two types of salsa that their efficient waitress explained were house-made: one dark red and complex with chili heat, the other rich with a spiced peanut flavor. Candy could have made a meal of those alone. They ordered margaritas, which arrived on the rocks, strong and fresh with real lime juice—no premixed base here. Within four sips, she was feeling a buzz that was not caused exclusively by tequila.

"So, Candy, how long have you been on Milwaukee-dates?"

She put down her margarita carefully. He sounded odd when he asked that. Or maybe it was the way he switched gears from laid-back California to focused New York. What was up with that? "Only a couple of weeks."

"It's wild, isn't it? I was kicking around looking at profiles the other night."

Her smile felt tight. Why shouldn't he look around? That's what he'd paid for. She'd gone out with three guys already, it was natural. "Shopping for humans."

"Strange, but practical." Was he looking at her more searchingly or was she imagining it? "I saw this one woman who looked enough like you to be a twin."

Dread soured her stomach. "Really?"

"Yeah, it was striking. Do you have a sister?" He was smiling, jovial. She couldn't tell if the tension between them was coming from him, her, or both.

"Only brothers." She could barely get her lips to move. She wasn't a liar, and this felt like lying, to a guy she liked and wanted to trust her.

"Funny." He seemed genuinely unconcerned; she felt like she'd been force-fed rocks. "I could have sworn she'd turn out to be related to you."

"Nope." She couldn't tell him. Not yet.

"You signed up as a favor to your friend, huh?"

She picked up a chip, trying to decide which dip to choose this time. "Not really."

"You said you were dating around as a favor to Marie."

"Oh, no, well…" Damn. She dipped the chip in the hotter salsa and shoved it into her mouth, stalling while she collected herself. She'd only said that about Marie to downplay her involvement. "I'm definitely dating to find someone."

"So the favor part…" He waited expectantly.

"I didn't sign up anywhere else. I'm not trying to meet men any other way, hanging out in bars or anything." As if she would. "I want to help Marie."

"I thought you said her company was doing really well."

"It is." She frowned at him. "Is this some kind of interview?"

"Sure." He grinned and relaxed against the back of his chair. "Aren't all dates?"

Candy shrugged noncommittally and picked up her drink again. Had she imagined the weirdness? "I guess they are."

"Applying for the position of boyfriend or girlfriend, checking out the applicant's qualifications, doing background checks—"

"Sizing up the staff."

His eyebrow arched. "How big do you think mine is?"

"Mmph." Candy's sip of margarita barely stayed in her mouth.

"Sorry." His easy smile melted most of her worries. She'd probably created the awkwardness with her guilt, while he was just making small talk. But this was a warning sign, one she should take seriously. She'd talk to Marie first chance she got. She didn't want to hurt anyone or reflect badly on Milwaukeedates.com.

The waitress came by and took their dinner order, offering recommendations, steering them toward dishes that might suit their tastes. Candy ordered a tortilla soup that arrived brimming with chicken and vegetables flavored with lime. Heaven. Justin had seviche, seafood marinated in lime juice whose acids essentially cooked the fish, served in a stemmed glass. The taste he offered was fresh, clean and salty with a subtle chili kick. Next time she was ordering that. And the soup again. And margaritas. And the peanut salsa, served in a bucket.

Justin forked up his next bite. "Since you grew up here, you have a lot of friends still around?"

"I do. From high school and a few from college. And Abigail."

"Abigail…"

"My best friend since fourth grade. She's nothing like me, but we've stayed close."

"Different how?"

"For one thing, she is model-gorgeous. And has this incredible body, and sex appeal that that—"

"Candy." His seafood stopped halfway to his mouth; he was looking at her intently.

"Huh?"

"Do you, in fact, have mirrors in your house?"

"Mirrors?" She stared at him blankly. "Uh, yes?"

"Did you happen to look in one of these mirrors before I picked you up?"

"Oh, no." She brushed under her nose, put a hand to her hair, ran her tongue over her teeth. "What is it? What did I miss?"

He put his fork down. "Either Abigail is a freak of nature or your ideas of gorgeous and sex-appeal are completely off."

"I don't understand."

"Seriously? This isn't an act?"

"Justin, if you don't tell me what you're talking about I'll…" The only thing she could think of involved attacking him somehow and that seemed like more fun than punishment.

"You'll what?"

"I don't know, I'm not the violent type. But something truly evil."

"Here's a clue. If you're the absolute opposite of Abigail then she should be toothless, drooling and six hundred pounds, with foul body odor."

She blinked at him. He was right. She did have mirrors at her house. She'd peered into several tonight and had seen Sexy Glamour Girl's reflection and knew she looked good, and therefore what she was saying didn't make any sense. Justin probably thought she was fishing for compliments, though he'd responded sincerely.

All she could say was that this vision before him wasn't her. This was clothes and makeup. Abigail…well being near her could make Miss America insecure. "Thank you. You have to meet Abigail to know what I mean."

"I don't need to meet Abigail. I have no idea how you could have reached your ripe, young age and not have a clue how hot you are. What was wrong with your boyfriend?"

Candy bristled, about to say "absolutely nothing," but that wasn't a great thing to say on a date. "He was—"

Justin held up his hand. "Rhetorical question. I'm not asking you to defend him. And I'm sorry I derailed your answer to my question."

"No, don't…it's fine." She hardly knew what to say. He had identified the problem, apologized and wanted to move on. Men she knew always bogged down the conversation with their need to be right.

"Before I interrupted to comment on your devastating appearance, you were saying Abigail is your opposite."

Candy forced her brain back on track, still confused, but glowing from his compliments. "Abby grew up poor in a house full of brothers and sisters. When she realized college wasn't for her and that her job prospects weren't incredible, she decided to hell with happy ever after, and went looking for money. She married obscenely rich."

"If you're her opposite, then you're looking for true love with a soul mate, wallet be damned."

"Yes." She expected him to make fun, but he waited calmly for more of her answer. "I found him once. Seems greedy to ask lightning to strike twice. But bottom line, yes, love is more important to me in a relationship than money."

"Good for you."

She finished her soup, strangely shy. "How about you? Have you ever been… Have you ever found it?"

"True love with a soul mate?" He shook his head. "Not me. I came close a couple of times, thought I was there when I was in it, but in retrospect, no cigar. I'm not like Abigail either, though. I'm still hoping."

Candy nodded and finished the rest of her margarita, wondering if the woman who hurt him was the one he thought he loved, but reluctant to pursue the conversation. It didn't feel right talking about forever-after on a first date.

"Ready for another?"

"They're strong…"

"I'm driving."

"Okay, you convinced me."

He laughed, and she was struck by how easy it could become to talk to him about pretty much any topic. He seemed to take everything in stride: superficial, personal, bittersweet or funny.

"What do you do when you're not throwing parties and driving men to distraction all over Milwaukee?" He signaled to the waitress just leaving the next table.

"Ha!" Candy gestured dismissively. "Thank you, but I don't really do the distraction thing that much."

"No?" He clasped his hands on the table, eyes engulfing her. "You're doing it right now."

Her mouth hung open in dopey surprise, thrills shooting through her. Sometimes when men flirted she felt cornered and defensive, like with Ralph. But not this time. Not at all.

She just hoped his attentiveness wasn't primarily due to her bra's aerodynamic expertise. She'd like to think he had more depth than that, and that she had more appeal than enhanced cleavage.

"Hi there, can I get you something? Another drink?"

Justin turned to the waitress, leaving Candy alone in her hormonal muddle. "We'll have two more margaritas, thanks."

"Right away." She collected their plates and empty glasses. "How was everything?"

"Fine. Delicious." He held his polite smile until she was out of range, then leaned forward confidentially. "What would happen if you really told her how *everything* was? Life, school, job, love life, town, country, planet…"

Candy giggled, buzzing nicely on tequila, glad the moment

of intensity that had hijacked her cool was over. The flirting that practically knocked her over could merely be a reflexive habit with him, as it was with plenty of men. One thing about Chuck, he never said anything he didn't mean, but that trait was rare, she knew.

"Where were we?" He put his forearms back on the table. "I think I was complimenting you."

"Outrageously. But you also asked about my hobbies."

"Right." He gestured a go-ahead. "Tell all."

"I paint some, I design and sew clothes and costumes, I love watching movies, hanging out with friends, skiing downhill and cross-country, going dancing, out to eat, comedy clubs, concerts, jazz clubs…what is so funny?"

"A couch potato, huh?"

"Oh." She pursed her lips. "I love staying home, too. I mean that's what I used to do most nights when Chuck and I were together."

"Why, with all those things you enjoy?"

Hmm. How could she explain how she and Chuck completed each other? She hadn't needed to be out doing something every night.

"I guess maybe I started to enjoy those things more after we broke up." That wasn't right. She had indulged her hobbies in college, too, before she and Chuck started dating. The truth was she'd thrown herself back into frenetic activity after the breakup because if she stayed home she'd have gone completely out of her mind missing him.

"I get it. *He* was the couch potato."

"No, no, we did plenty of stuff together. Parties, out to eat, out dancing." She usually had to coax Chuck to go anywhere, but he always did because he knew it would make her happy. And since staying home made him happy, that was okay with her, too. "It's just that after he left, I was… I don't know, it's complicated."

"Here you go." The waitress put down their second drinks. "I'll bring your food out right away."

"Thanks." Justin clinked glasses with Candy. "Here's to surviving breakups in whatever way works."

She nodded, oddly moved. He understood what she felt, and also got that she didn't want to talk it through any further. "What do you do when you're not writing?"

"Ah." He put his drink down, rubbed his hands together. "That's easy. I surf, hang out at the beach with friends, sit in the sun and read, play with my band at a local park…"

Her uneasiness dissolved into laughter. "Uh-oh."

"Time for some new hobbies, ya think?" He frowned off into space. "I've shivered a lot, that's been fun."

"You'll be native before you know it." She smiled sympathetically. "It takes time to put down roots in a new city. I had no problem in college, but that extra year in Stevens Point, after most of my friends had graduated, with Chuck still studying, I felt cut adrift. It was great to come back home."

"Tell me." He leaned forward again; on cue, her insides went a little nuts. "What city would you live in if the world was your oyster?"

"Wait." She pretended outrage. "It's not?"

"It should be, but…"

Candy paused, organizing her thoughts. "The midwest fits me. Milwaukee is a good-size city, not too big, not too small. There's a lot going on."

"Here you are." The waitress put down their plates, a steaming *mole negro* over turkey for Justin and three duck tacos on soft blue-corn tortillas served with a bowl of tropical fruit salsa for her.

"I think you'd like Southern California."

She thanked the waitress and folded a tortilla over the moist filling. "Why do you say that?"

"There's a sunny, laid-back energy there that you'd fit into.

And sun. And it's sunny. Because the sun shines there. Which it doesn't here. Ever."

She could hardly swallow from the giggles. "Okay, okay, Wisconsin is sun-challenged in the winter."

"Ya think? How are your tacos?"

"Mmm." She rolled her eyes orgasmically. "Perfect. How's yours?"

"Here. Pass your plate. Or hell, just eat this." He cut a bite and held it out to her. She didn't hesitate, leaned over and closed her mouth over the tines of his fork. Rich, complicated flavors burst over her tongue.

"Oh, my goodness. I will never be able to eat Tex-Mex again."

He grinned triumphantly. "You would definitely like Southern California."

"No, not me." She put her hand to her chest, forgetting about the push-up bra and for a horrified second she had no idea what she was touching.

"Why not?"

"Because we midwesterners don't adapt well to paradise. Don't you listen to Garrison Keillor?"

He laughed, loud and free, and she felt herself going giddy, and not just because the margaritas were killer-strong. By the time they finished the excellent meal he insisted on paying for and made their way back to his car, Candy was floating even higher. She'd had a great time. Justin was an amazing guy— handsome, funny, sexy. Maybe he even believed in Valentine's Day, roses and chocolate, restaurant dinners and proposals on bended knee.

No. There must be something wrong with him. There *had* to be something. He was thoughtless, that was it. Self-absorbed. He wanted a woman who would worship him. Or no, he was charming as hell during courtship, but after commitment, he'd say okay, that's all the effort I'm putting out for you, then he'd sit back and wait to be served. Or no, as soon as he was out of sight he'd be exactly this charming and flirtatious with whatever other women came along. After all, he'd signed up on Marie's site. Who knew how many other dates he had lined up?

Hmm. She could call Marie and ask, but Marie would probably cite client confidentiality and not tell her. Candy was left to find out about him on her own.

The night was clear, a rare event in January, and when Justin's man-car turned back onto Prospect, the moon was shining brilliantly over the tree line, not quite full but on its way. A beautiful accent to a wonderful evening, which Candy didn't want to end yet, but she couldn't think of a way to ask him to her house for coffee and cookies without making it sound like, "Hey, let's get naked!"

The drawback of dressing like someone who did that at the drop of her skirt.

Justin pulled into his own driveway. "I'll walk you home."

She shook her head, as if it were the silliest thing she'd ever heard, while her brain was thinking an involuntary *Oh, how sweet!* "All fifty yards?"

"Lots could happen in those fifty yards. Mugging, dog attack, frostbite…"

It was on the tip of her tongue to say, "no, no, it's fifty yards, I'll be fine," which she'd always done when Chuck offered his mostly symbolic gallantries, but this time she stopped herself. She'd let Justin walk her home. Maybe she'd even find some platonic way to ask him in.

Fifty yards turned out to be long. Neither of them seemed to be able to think of anything to say beyond an artificially extended conversation about the moon. The farther they got along her driveway, the more of Candy's bubbles burst. How many times had she walked this path to the back door, chatting easily with Chuck after an evening out? Knowing that within seconds they'd be inside together, comfortably at home.

By the time they reached her door, she knew she couldn't invite Justin in, even for cookies. It was still too soon to switch men.

"Candy, I had a great time."

"Me, too." She summoned a smile, which he returned, holding her gaze a beat too long, which brought on the horribly awkward moment where they were both thinking about first kisses and whether one would or should happen tonight. She hated that moment.

"Well, good night." She stuck out her hand at the same time he bent forward, so she ended up jabbing him in the chest while his lips missed hers and landed on her nose.

Oh, God. Such a nice evening, then she'd gotten all morose and botched the kiss for him—though it was nice he'd wanted to give her one. Now he'd walk away and she'd go inside by herself and start brooding all over again, full circle to the mood she was in before he showed up.

"That didn't work too well, Candy." He was frowning, hands on his hips, not shivering, even though the temperature had dropped, probably into the upper teens. "First-date good-nights are even harder than parallel parking."

Instead of saying something to help him diffuse the situation, she came out with a cross between an embarrassed laugh and unintelligible words, which made her sound like an alien under torture.

Help.

"I want to kiss you again." He spoke with awe, as if he hadn't expected to want to kiss her the first time, and really thought he shouldn't be kissing her again, but he couldn't help himself. The combination was very, very sexy.

A touch of spring started thawing the winter of her discontent.

"But hold still this time." His eyes warmed with amusement, his lips curved, lips that were firm, masculine and very tempting.

"I promise," she whispered.

He leaned in, hesitated a millimeter from her mouth, which tingled in anticipation. She closed her eyes, past caring what Sexy Glamour Girl should do.

The kiss was soft and sweet, over too soon, but left its mark with a quicksilver trail down her chest to where really good kisses should go. She stood still, savoring, knowing she needed to open her eyes and say, "Well, thanks again for a great evening" and go inside.

But when her eyes had made it open and she'd gathered herself to step back, Justin made a deep, male sound halfway between a sigh and a growl and kissed her again. More than once. Serious kisses, deep and seductive, his solid arms holding her tightly.

Candy gave in and let instinct take over. It told her to kiss him back, slide her hands under his jacket to explore his back and shoulders, and to press her body against his, all of which felt unfamiliar with him, but pretty wonderful. Pretty damn wonderful.

Then an even more primal instinct started begging to be heard, one which involved inviting Justin in as planned. Only not for coffee. Or cookies.

Immediately, Candy started coming up with reasons why that wasn't a good idea. The new upstart instinct just as immediately told her to stop being a chicken-hearted moron and do it.

Justin pulled back, rested his forehead against hers, breath unsteady. "Wow. I didn't expect… Candy, that took me totally by surprise."

She clung to him, fingers pressing into the hard muscles of his upper arms, heart pumping as if she'd been running sprints. "Me, too."

"It was nice." He chuckled wryly. "Nice. Like eternal bliss is 'nice.'"

"Really nice?"

"Really nice." His eyes were so bright she half expected to find circles of light on her own face if she looked in a mirror. She'd bet hers were doing the same. "Candy, I'd like to come in. For coffee or…something."

So simple. One little word. *Sure.* Sexy Glamour Girl would do this without blinking. He'd come in, they'd have coffee, cookies, he'd kiss her again and they'd go upstairs and make hay until the sun shone.

So simple. *Sure.*

Candy opened her mouth. "No. I'm sorry."

She felt as surprised, then disappointed as he looked. She simply couldn't do it. No matter how passionately she'd kissed him, and no matter what he thought she was trying to convey, Candy wasn't Sexy Glamour Girl. She couldn't invite Justin into a house she'd been carnal in so many times, in so many rooms, with someone else she'd loved so deeply.

"Okay. I should get going. Thanks, this was great."

Oh, no. Now he was becoming distant. And she was becoming miserable. She knew she had to get over Chuck sometime, and Justin was the only man she'd met in the last year that made her think she actually wanted to.

But not this. Not yet.

Justin backed up a couple of steps. "Thanks for the date, Candy."

"No, thank you. Dinner was wonderful." She pasted on a happy, happy smile. That was it? She wouldn't screw him so he was done with her?

The familiar pain and panic of loneliness and rejection threatened.

Candy fought back. She was *not* going to dissolve again into self-pity, not around this man, not around anyone ever again. Sexy Glamour Girl would not care a fig if a guy suddenly blew her off, because with a flick of her manicured finger she could beckon the next, since they were lined up around the corner like taxis at a stand. In fact, if Justin left tonight with no mention of seeing her again, that would be completely, *completely…*

Horrible.

"Good night." He was already turning to go. "See you around the block."

She gave a brisk, cheery wave, clenching her teeth, unlocked her door, pushed inside, slammed it behind her and let the tears go. Only a few. Only for a bit. There would be others, plenty of them before there could be none. In her dating life this was A Beginning, another baby-step part of getting over Chuck and moving on. This was not anything like The End.

No matter how much it felt like it.

6

"SPAM, SPAM, SPAM, SPAM. I feel like I'm starring in the *Monty Python* sketch." Justin pitched his voice into a shrill falsetto. "'Have you got anything without Spam in it?' Only I'm talking email, not breakfast."

"Ha. Funny." Troy slumped back on his couch, pushing at his dark curling hair with both hands, eyes narrowed by fatigue. They'd been working since noon in Troy's living room, Troy fussing over the chapter on peripherals, Justin finishing the chapter on email. "Put that in somehow."

"I'm sure it's been done."

"Not by us."

"True." Justin stretched his arms over his head and yawned. "How's the printer hookup demo going?"

"It needs a break and so do I." Troy set his laptop onto his antique coffee table, already littered with pads, notes and reference books. His house was modest, but in a nice area of Whitefish Bay near the lake, furnished with care by his interior-designer mom. His day job as the tech guy of a local IT firm meant he wasn't hurting for cash, and the generous advance for their book didn't cause pain either. Troy picked up an empty coffee mug. "Caffeine or alcohol?"

"Dude, if I have a beer, I won't be getting back to work."

"We've done enough."

"Enough?" Justin quirked an eyebrow. "It's not even midnight yet. And I'm starting to have some serious doubts about the way we've set up this spam chapter."

"I know, I know. Something's not right. I can't get my brain to work today."

Justin nodded. He'd noticed. Like when Troy had served their first cup of coffee with a healthy splash of orange juice instead of half and half. "What's going on?"

"I slept like crap."

"Yeah?" He hadn't slept well himself. Candy had his brain in a stranglehold. "Noisy neighbors? Too many burgers before bed?"

"Debby called last night."

Justin set his jaw so he wouldn't let loose any of the words gathering in his throat. Few things pissed him off like women who threw men away, then wouldn't let them go. His ex-girlfriend Angie had been the gold medalist of that maneuver, but Debby could easily win silver. "And how is the Divine Ms. D?"

"She misses me." Troy laughed bitterly, got up from the couch and stalked into the kitchen, followed immediately by his golden-brown chow mix, Dylan, and by Justin.

"Let me guess. Her latest man-victim didn't work out."

"Bingo." Troy yanked open his stainless refrigerator door and grabbed two bottles of Bass Ale. Dylan's tail wagged.

"You've got to admit she's consistent." Justin reached for his bottle, which Troy slid across the kitchen island. "Every time she's single, you are irresistible until the next idiot comes along."

"I told her not to call me anymore."

"You told her that last time, too, man." He saluted Troy with his beer and took a long, cold swig. "Don't you check caller ID?"

"Yeah." Troy looked sheepish. "I almost didn't answer."

"*Almost* doesn't win the prize."

"I know, I know." He shook his head disgustedly. "Everyone has something he's stupid about. She's mine."

"I finally got rid of Angie." Justin took a guilty sip of beer. Yeah, he'd escaped that frying pan, only to find himself playing with Candy's fire.

"But you had to move halfway across the country to do it." Troy took down a bag of corn chips from the cabinet next to his granite sink and ripped it open. Dylan's nails clicked excitedly on the faux-hardwood floor.

"Almost true." Too true. After breaking up with Angie, Justin had succumbed to her seduction one night, managed to stay strong and send her away on another night, swearing he'd never let her close again, but Troy's offer had represented an opportunity to leave temptation in his dust.

"'*Almost* doesn't win the prize.'" Troy crunched a handful of corn chips, reached for another, cheerfully inhaling calories his triathlon-trained body wouldn't even notice. "Debby lives ten miles away and works only two miles away."

"We should have swapped houses. Me here, you in California."

Troy passed the chips to Justin. "What is it about women like that? They take possession of our brains."

"Not all men. Just men like us."

"Well, that's depressing." He went back to the refrigerator and stared at the contents alongside Dylan. "How come there's no book called *Men Who Love Too Much?*"

"What guy would admit it?"

"Good point." Troy rummaged in the meat drawer, pulled out some summer sausage and sharp cheddar. "Hey, didn't you have a date last night?"

"Research."

"Oh, by the way, I called Brian, my friend at the *Journal-Sentinel.* He'll feel his boss out on your dating-site scandal, and if there's interest, he'll put you in touch." Troy pulled a serrated knife and a cutting board from a drawer next to his dishwasher. "What did you find out from Candy?"

"Inconclusive." Her initial answers hadn't done anything to allay or confirm Justin's suspicions, and then under the influence of tequila and Candy, he'd found himself having more and more fun and caring less and less about the story until he'd dropped it entirely from the evening's agenda. What kind of professional journalist did that make him?

A pretty lame one. If he wanted to land that first freelance gig in Milwaukee he'd need to push harder, not let her get away with a few evasive answers.

"Guess you'll have to take her out again, huh?" Troy smirked, cutting the sausage into thick slices. Dylan let out a muted moan. "Tough job."

"I don't know if that's such a good idea."

"No?" Troy looked at him sharply. "Why, she's scary?"

That was an understatement, but not the way Troy meant it. "More like dangerous."

"Uh-oh. You like her."

"I shouldn't mix dating with an investigation. For her sake, too, though she seems like she could handle herself in any situation."

"You *really* like her."

Irritation flashed, which Justin knew from growing up with a psychiatrist mother meant Troy had hit a nerve. Justin wasn't going there. Not willingly. "But *you're* not investigating her, Troy. Why don't you sign up on Milwaukeedates.com and see if Marie matches you up with Candy, too?"

"*Me* go out with her?" Troy eyed him suspiciously.

"Sure, why not?" Justin found himself gritting his teeth. He could think of many ideas why not, but at least Troy was a known quantity who wouldn't put moves on a woman he knew Justin was…intrigued by. Whereas, who knew where Candy was tonight and with whom, as which personality?

He loosened his jaw. What Candy did with her time

shouldn't bother him. Not after a single date. Justin had already fallen into the trap of mistaking one really good time for the beginning of stronger feelings; he'd already wasted pride and energy chasing after a woman who couldn't be caught by one man for any length of time. He wasn't ever doing that again. If nothing else, the sickening sight of Candy in four completely different profiles up on the Milwaukeedates site should have been enough to cure him of any attraction. What game did she think she was playing?

She played it well. She played *him* well. But there was a name for women who dated around professionally, and it wasn't Happy Ever After.

And yet, there seemed to be a core of sincerity and humility under Candy's fire and sexuality, which Angie had been missing.

"Are you kidding? Me sign up for online dating?" Troy held the knife up, ready to start slicing cheese. "I'd rather sign up for a colonoscopy. At least the medical technicians are honest about what they're going to do to you."

Justin rolled his eyes. "Two reasons. One, you'll help me test my theory about the place, and two, it will give you something better to do than sit around wanting to kill yourself over Debby."

Troy snorted, piling slices of cheese onto slices of summer sausage. Good Wisconsin food—a miracle any resident made it past the age of fifty. "I have a better idea. Have people over one night. I'll invite a few friends, you can invite Candy, and I'll chat her up and see if I can spot any BS."

"Why are you a better judge?"

Troy sent him a look. "Because my brain won't have lodged behind my zipper the way yours obviously did last night."

Justin couldn't argue. Not only had he ditched trying to research the story, but when Candy had lingered in her driveway at good-night time, those incredible brown eyes so sensual and expectant…what could he do?

Yeah, what? Maybe shake the hand she offered and leave it there? But around a sexy, beautiful woman, he'd turned into typical putty. He had to kiss her. But only once, one good-night kiss and that was it.

Right.

Even then, he could have stayed out of serious trouble if the run-of-the-mill peck on the lips he anticipated hadn't turned out to be so soft and so sweet.

Even *then,* he might have had the strength to leave if she hadn't stayed still, eyes closed, full lips parted, practically begging him to kiss her again. Even her breasts seem to be reaching for him. What kind of man could walk away from that?

One who could control himself around women hot enough to bring spring to an entire city. Thank God she'd put the brakes on when, in hormone-induced insanity, he'd invited himself over. Though fantasies about what "coffee" with her would have been like kept him awake most of the night more effectively than the real thing.

"Hello? Anyone home?" Troy was waving a salami/cheese stack at him. "Too much Candy before bedtime?"

"Ha ha. I was thinking over your plan. To have a party."

"Oh, yeah, right." Troy nodded in exaggerated agreement. "That's exactly what it looked like you were thinking about. 'I *lo-o-ve* Troy's plan. I *re-e-e-eally* love Troy's plan. I am *so-o-o* hot over Troy's plan, that I can't even keep my mind on—'"

He broke off laughing, dodging cheese Justin hurled at him.

"Okay, Troy. I *lo-o-ve* your plan. What night works for you?"

Troy picked up the cheese from his spotless floor and tossed it to Dylan, who caught it in his mouth. "Gee, I'll check my busy social schedule and get back to you. Pick any night, dude. Friday, Saturday, Sunday, Monday—"

"How about Wednesday?" Four more days. In the meantime, when he wasn't working on the book, he'd keep trying to convince Troy to sign up for Milwaukeedates.com. And he'd check out more online profiles to see if any other women appeared to have more than one version of themselves available, maybe contact some of the men on the site to see what their experiences had been so far.

Wednesday when he saw Candy again, he'd be safely surrounded by other people so he could keep his brain out of his pants, as Troy politely put it, and see how she behaved, maybe get Troy to ask her more about this "favor" to Marie she was reluctant to discuss with him, see if she'd try to sign Troy up for the site, or if she mentioned other friends who might be involved.

In short: he'd focus on the story, not on the woman.

Simple, right?

Sure. Like running one of Troy's triathlons. He'd lace up his discount-store sneakers and go.

MARIE SAT IN HER USUAL SPOT in the Roots Cellar; the only patron at the bar that early, though a few of the tables were occupied. She was enjoying one of those delicious early signs that spring was actually going to show up some month—daylight still in evidence through the glass wall at the far end of the room. Milwaukee's skyline across the river, modest by big-city standards but beautiful to her native gaze, remained visible. Could warmer temperatures and melted snow be far behind?

Unfortunately, yes, they could.

Her cell rang; she took a hurried sip of her martini—gin with a twist in honor of Quinn's favorite—before she dug out her phone. Invariably a call at this hour, shortly after five, meant trouble at the office. Friends knew to call later in the evening when Marie had had time to shake off the day's pressures and relax.

It was Candy.

"Hey, woman." She smiled with relief. Even if Candy was calling with a problem, she'd be reasonable about any proposed solution, unlike some of Marie's pricklier clients. "How was your date with Justin last night? I've been dying to know of course, but didn't want to be nosy. Or at least admit how nosy I am."

"It was… Oh, gosh."

Marie's left eyebrow rose. Oh, gosh? Was that bliss or anguish? Funny how sometimes there seemed to be a fine line. "Good 'oh, gosh' or bad 'oh, gosh'?"

"Both 'oh, gosh.'"

"'Oh, gosh' indeed." Marie frowned at her Roots napkin. Candy had to be really rattled not to launch into her usual chatter. "Tell me more."

"Well." She sighed. "I mean it was great. He was great. But then at the end he wanted…he kissed me, really, really, and then he left after no."

Marie narrowed her eyes, trying to make heads or tails of that one. A great time followed by a good-night kiss? Sounded like first-date perfection to her.

"Okay, but—" In her peripheral vision she saw Quinn reaching the bottom of the stairs, in jeans today with a casual shirt. Second time she'd seen him in as many visits. If he sat at the bar as he usually did, they'd be the only two there. She forced her attention back to Candy. "I'm missing the bad 'oh, gosh.'"

"The leaving part."

"You didn't want him to leave? The date wasn't over?"

"He invited himself in. I almost said yes."

Marie's eyes shot wide; she let out a blast of laughter. "Way to go, Candy!"

"But I didn't. And he left."

Marie couldn't stop grinning. She'd suffered watching Candy clinging to a relationship with Drippy Chuck, trying to please him by tamping down every fabulous internal fire she had. After the breakup, Marie worried Candy would never get over him, or worse, that Chuck's next victim would rebel against his control, he'd come oozing around again and suck Candy back into the suffocating safety of being what he wanted her to be.

Having escaped her own disastrous marriage, Marie had no trouble recognizing guys who wanted their girlfriends/spouses only as reflections of their own self-perceived glory. Which was one reason Quinn intrigued her. Instinct kept telling her he didn't quite fit the mold. "What matters is you considered having sex with someone. Even better, you wanted to. At the same time, you recognized it was probably too soon with this guy and you stood your ground. I am so proud of you."

"Oh." Candy sounded doubtful. "I didn't think about it that way."

A few chairs down from her, Quinn sat and greeted Joe the bartender. Marie couldn't *not* notice him; he had that kind of magnetism. Same as Darcy. The two of them would spontaneously combust just being in the same room.

"There are all kinds of reasons he could have left abruptly. Doesn't necessarily mean he doesn't want to see you again. Maybe he was embarrassed, or reliving some other rejection. Remember he put himself out there asking to come in."

Quinn's head swivelled toward her; Marie bit her lip, reminding herself to speak more quietly. Candy wouldn't want her date discussed all over town.

"He didn't mention seeing me again."

"How did the rest of the date go?"

"Fabulous." Candy sounded distinctly dreamy. *Take that, Chuck.* "We had such a good time."

"Did he flirt?"

"Yes, but not insistently. I mean I was surprised when he asked to come in. I think he was, too, actually."

"Good." Marie nodded firmly at her drink. All good news. The "oh, gosh" belonged in the positive column.

"Oh, but at one point he said he'd been online and saw another woman who looked enough like me to be a twin. I nearly passed out."

Marie made a dismissive noise. "None of his business."

"But I felt really dishonest and kind of creepy."

"You are approaching the dates with him honestly, right? Open to whatever feelings develop?"

"I guess…"

Marie rolled her eyes. Candy was practically climbing into the phone tonight after being ho-hum about all her other dates, and she still wouldn't admit how much meeting Justin excited her. Damn the Chuck Syndrome. "You're being honest in all the ways that concern him. As for him leaving abruptly last night, put yourself in his place. He's in a new town, maybe he left a girlfriend behind…"

She paused, hoping Justin had filled Candy in so Marie could mention the relationship without breaching client confidentiality.

"He implied a woman had dumped him recently."

"There you go. We'll assume he had a tough ending to a tough relationship. Last night he had a great time with you, but maybe he went further than he meant to, or maybe he felt particularly vulnerable to rejection. Either way, when you refused him he was off balance. Hard to keep cool when you're crazy hot for someone."

Candy giggled. "He did seem into the kissing."

"I'll bet he had wood the size of the Washington Monument."

Quinn glanced over sharply. Marie cursed silently and lowered her voice further. His hearing was entirely too good.

"Give the guy a break and don't assume you know what he's feeling. I bet he'll call. Or if he doesn't right away, after a while you can call him, or do something completely neighborly and unthreatening like…I don't know, take over brownies to welcome him to the block. Something like that."

Candy snorted. "What is it with the baking? Abigail said the same thing."

"Way to a man's heart. Stomach, then zipper."

Quinn chuckled. Marie turned and met his eyes, sending a firm butt-out message. Did the guy have bionic hearing? To her shock, he winked, which completely ruined her indignation because she blushed hydrant-red, impossible to hide with her fair skin. Score one for bionic hearing.

"This whole dating thing is so confusing. Everything was easy with Chuck."

Marie turned deliberately away from Mr. Hottie. Yes, easy with Chuck because Candy didn't have to—or wasn't given the chance to—think for herself.

"I understand. But if you can stand a little advice from Auntie Marie, remember, this is only the first guy you're attracted to after Chuck, and there are lots and lots of fish swimming around Milwaukee. Take your time, date around, get a feel for what's out there, how different men behave toward you and toward your various personalities. You have the power to choose the one you want, remembering that what seems familiar may not always be good for you, and that hormones aren't the best judge of a mate, either. You deserve some pure fun after what you went through last year, so concentrate on lightening up and flying free for a while."

"I will." The smile was back in Candy's voice, which had been uncharacteristically flat without it. "I feel much better. I've been sitting here a complete mess, and now I'm ready to work on penis-shaped cookies for the bachelorette party tomorrow."

"See? That was all you needed, to work on—" She peeked at Quinn, who was staring unconcernedly ahead, but could probably hear her eyelashes when she blinked "—those cookies. I bet you anything he'll call. But if he doesn't, it's not the end of the world. You'll go on to lure many more men into your…life."

"Thank you." Candy seemed to be melting with relief. "I so needed to hear all that. I almost feel sane again."

"No problem, honey. Take care." She clicked off the phone and tucked it into her purse, feeling awkward now that her illusion of privacy had been breached by the interaction with Quinn. Expectation hung in the air that something about that brief connection needed to be acknowledged. Maybe it would be a good idea to start chatting, feel him out to see if he'd be as good for Darcy as Marie suspected.

"I'm sorry for eavesdropping. I wasn't trying to, but a few key words jumped out."

Ta da. Marie had been saved the trouble of an opening, though she was well aware that if a babe had been around, his opening shot would not have been lobbed to Marie.

"Hard not to hear when it's so quiet tonight." *And when you have the hearing power of a cat.* She smiled her professional smile, the one she used to welcome prospective clients.

He moved one seat closer and leaned toward her, holding out his hand. "Quinn Peters. I've seen you here a few times."

"Marie Hewitt." She shook his hand. *Peters.* She liked the name. Quinn and Darcy Peters. Very nice. Though before she found a way to trick Darcy into a meeting, she'd have to get at something deeper than his need to chat up younger women. "Yes, I love this place. Great atmosphere, drinks and food."

"You live nearby?"

"Not far. You?"

"Not far." He raised his glass toward hers. "I see you have excellent taste in beverages."

"Thank you. Though I only drink gin when the mood strikes."

He gazed at her as if she was the most fascinating person

he'd encountered all week. "What mood makes Marie crave a martini?"

Oh, he was good. An innocent question, asked in a perfectly straightforward manner, but with a deep seductive voice and vivid brown eyes full of mischief. Even Darcy would have a hard time resisting, and she could resist almost anything. With the bizarre and compulsive exception of potato chips.

"Exhaustion." She smiled demurely. He wasn't going to get her flirting; with women his own age, he was doubtless just going through the motions. "Long tough day."

"What's your business? Or your pleasure?"

Marie kept a straight face. "I own a dot-com company. You?"

"I'm an investor."

"Stock market?" She hoped not. Adrenaline junkies made draining partners, and Darcy needed ballast in her life.

"Businesses."

Perfect. A private-equity investor. That would explain the expensive suit some days and jeans the next, plus his presence in the bar at hours when most working stiffs were scrambling to finish late days at the office or still commuting. Marie could assume he was independently wealthy, great for Darcy whose restaurant was currently booming, but with the whims of customers, tastes and trends, that could change all too easily.

"Are you a Milwaukee native?" She sipped her drink, appearing unconcerned whether he answered or not. She needed to walk a line, finding out as much as possible without padding his ego by seeming interested in him herself.

"Born and bred."

"You don't sound like one."

"Mom was Canadian, Dad is from Chicago. I inherited their lack of accent."

"So you did." Over his shoulder she saw a trio of dark-haired thirtysomething women dressed to kill coming down the stairs. If they sat at the bar, she wouldn't have much more time to dig into Quinn; she'd have to wait until she could catch him alone again, and who knew how long that would take.

"Where did you grow up, Marie?"

"Glendale. UW–Madison for college, then back here. A real Wisconsin girl."

The women settled on the other side of Quinn. He glanced over and obviously did his charm thing, because all three broke into wide smiles.

Irritation prickled Marie. Had he even heard her?

She took a calming breath, telling herself that this man and his young women had nothing to do with her ex and his young woman, and nothing to do with her.

Quinn turned back. "UW–Madison, huh. What did you study?"

"Psychology." He'd heard. Point in his favor. But if he stayed true to form, he wouldn't want to talk to her much longer. She'd need to find out as much as she could, then find a graceful way to release him for the evening's pursuit.

"What kind of dot-com does a psych major start up?"

"Milwaukeedates.com." The familiar combination of pride and vulnerability flooded her. Pride at what she'd accomplished, vulnerability from many married years of being told she wouldn't accomplish anything. "The city's finest dating service. Are you single?"

If she could get him to sign up, it would be all the easier to send him on a date with Darcy. Once Darcy saw his picture— well, who could say no to George Clooney?

"I am single, yes." Bitterness tugged at his voice and the corners of his smile. Aha. Burned? That would explain the current trend of romantic channel-surfing. More importantly, it would mean he'd been able to love at least once, and could be able to do so again with the right woman.

"Are you interested in signing up? I screen all my clients personally."

"So I'd be screened by you personally." He quirked an eyebrow. "That sounds pretty tempting."

She refused to blush this time. "I was referring to any woman you'd be dating, but yes, we'd have an appointment to talk before you could look over profiles."

"Hmm." He lifted his glass, looking at her over the rim as he drank. "Are you a client on the site?"

She wished he'd cut the reflex flirting; it was a waste of energy for both of them. "Of course not."

"Too bad."

"I'm sure I could set you up successfully." She sent him a saccharine grin, unable to resist a dig on behalf of women in their prime. "Though you seem to do fine on your own."

He nearly spat out his sip. "You've been keeping track?"

She shrugged, hiding her satisfaction. So busted. "Analyzing male/female interaction is part of my job."

"And what did your *analysis* of me reveal?"

That you can get laid as often as you want. "That women respond positively to your confidence and friendliness."

"Hmm." He obviously wasn't sure what to make of a woman who was on to his tricks and didn't fall for them. Which would describe Darcy, too. The key to hooking a guy like this was not to behave like all the other women he collected and threw out indiscriminately...to cover his pain? She still hoped that was the reason.

"In fact—" Marie gestured subtly to the women behind him, hiding her contempt this time "—feel free to attend to business now."

His eyes narrowed. "What makes you think I'd rather talk to them?"

She laughed, trying not to sound bitter. *Because they're young and beautiful, I'm just this side of forty and you're a man?* "Just a hunch."

"*Au contraire.* We're both regulars, I'd like to get to know you."

"That's sweet." She resisted rolling her eyes. *Spare me the charity flirt, buddy.* "I have to get going anyway. But it was nice to meet you."

His smile was forced. "Nice to meet you, too, Marie. Hope to see you again."

"I'm sure you will. Have a good night." She threw money on the bar, grabbed her coat and hopped down from the stool, relieved to manage a graceful exit.

Outside the cold air felt wonderful on her overheated cheeks and she blew out a misty breath of release and relief, snuggling into her favorite red coat. The sky above was darkening to navy; fading light still glowed in the west. She forced herself to slow her steps and her need to put distance between herself and what had just happened as quickly as possible.

How long before the post-divorce emotions would leave her alone? Six years wasn't long enough? Ironic if Candy got over her obsession with Drippy Chuck and into a new, healthy relationship before Marie could thoroughly process the betrayal and dissolution of her marriage. Apparently a degree in psychology didn't guarantee you could find answers to all your issues.

One thing was sure. If she was going to move forward with the idea of screening Quinn as a possible match for Darcy, she'd need to erect much larger barriers to protect herself from her past.

7

SNOW. SERIOUS SNOW. Absolutely no one was in the mood for a storm like this in early February, but everyone knew more than to think he or she could escape the month without one. Or two. Or more. Candy was shoveling her front steps in her favorite winter-protection outfit: bulky, fabulously warm boys' size-sixteen snowpants that made the swishy sound she remembered from childhood when she walked, and which made her legs look like overstuffed sausages. Over that, her puffy old down parka, which she'd kept for running the snowblower so her newer coat wouldn't smell like engine fumes, heavy black boots suitable for hiking in the Arctic—not exactly feminine, but they'd never failed to keep her feet warm; a wool scarf wrapped around her neck inside her parka and a fleece scarf wrapped over her head and again around her neck, to make sure no flakes could find their way down her collar. On her hands, thick, waterproof mittens, and *voilà,* her body stayed warm not only from its layers of protection, but also from the exertion of pushing the snowblower and shoveling other areas the machine couldn't reach. Nothing felt as cozy and smug as being out in horrible weather suitably dressed. With the possible exception of being home in bed with a man she loved while the storm went nuts outside.

But she no longer had that option, so why bother torturing herself with the memories? She should instead be looking forward to when she could do it again. Even if it might not be quite the same.

Snow was still falling, but barely; the storm had all but passed. Streetlights had come on, other neighbors were out clearing their driveways and sidewalks, few cars ventured onto the street. It was one of Candy's favorite winter times—clean and peaceful, snow-muted sounds making the block feel small and intimate.

While enjoying this winter wonderland, she was also trying very hard not to peek at Justin's house. Silly, because the effort had become similar to telling someone not to think about an elephant in a sparkly pink tutu. Pretty much impossible. Candy hadn't heard from Justin since their date four days ago, not that she'd expected to. Well, she'd sort of expected to. That is, she'd hoped to. Barring that, she'd at least hoped to bump into him so they could chat without anyone having to pick up a phone. But nothing. Maybe he was away?

He was home. She knew because her thoughts had just conjured him to appear at his front door, blinking like a mole emerging into sunlight. Or a Californian emerging into the vestiges of a Wisconsin snowstorm. Candy reacted rationally and maturely by whirling away to attack the icy mess the city plow thoughtfully deposited at the base of everyone's driveway when it passed.

Ten seconds later, she had the good sense to be embarrassed by her instinctive duck and cover, when she'd been handed the perfect chance for a friendly hello. She straightened resolutely and turned again toward Justin. He appeared to be trying to reach his mailbox from his front door without stepping out into the snow. Was he in bare feet? Socks? Slippers? Didn't he own boots? She couldn't tell. But she could see that he took a big chunk of mail from the box, reaching with one hand, the other clinging to the door behind him. She held her breath, praying he wouldn't fall, half hoping he'd turn and notice her, half hoping he wouldn't.

He did. She knew because his body stiffened, staring in her direction, and she knew because her adrenaline was off and racing. Did he recognize her Michelin Man silhouette?

"Hi, Justin." Her voice was flattened by the snow. She pushed back her scarf and grinned widely. "Isn't it beautiful?"

"It's…something. Definitely, something."

Poor man, born unable to appreciate the majesty of winter. "Do you—"

"Enjoy it." He lifted his arm in salute and backed into the house.

…need help shoveling?

Ouch. She stood staring at his closed front door. He *had* kissed her as if he never wanted to stop, hadn't he? Same guy? Only a few days earlier?

Marie was right. There were lots of other fish in the Milwaukee sea. Candy just wished she hadn't gotten so fixated on this one.

So. It was over. Over! From now on she'd leave Justin Case entirely alone.

THAT WAS NOT HOW HE WANTED his latest encounter with Candy to go.

Justin stared at his armful of mail, brain groggy. When was the last time he'd picked it up? Forget mail, when had he last eaten? Slept? The chapter on email, due at the publisher the next day, had taken over his brain. He and Troy had worried they weren't on the right track, and after consulting each other and their editor, they'd decided to switch format and emphasis. Less on how spammers formulated their pitches and harvested addresses, and more on how to avoid clogged in-boxes, hijacked computers, identity theft and how to deal with those messes if avoidance came too late.

In short, a major rewrite for Justin, and new demos for Troy to work out for the ebook version, new links to finesse. They couldn't afford to make any mistakes now that would snowball—to use an appropriate seasonal metaphor—into later and later deadlines for subsequent chapters.

Which meant he'd needed everything in him just now to keep from running across the street to talk to Candy. That and because he wasn't wearing shoes and would probably lose a few toes in the process.

He missed her. Could he miss someone he barely knew? He didn't get the chance to find out with Angie, because once they spent that first night together at his friend's party—the night they'd met—they were hardly apart. Before Candy, Justin would have said no, not after one date, impossible. Even now he was tempted to respond intellectually, scoff at his emotions and insist he simply missed having a girlfriend, missed the intimacy, missed California, maybe even missed Angie, though he'd like to think he wasn't that masochistic.

The party with Troy had been postponed due to writer's panic. Everything had been postponed due to writer's panic, including any further research on Milwaukeedates.com, though Troy said his friend Brian's boss at the *Journal-Sentinel* had expressed definite interest in whatever Justin turned up. Assuming he could turn up anything.

Once they got this chapter in, scheduling the party would be next on his agenda, and poking around the dating site some more. The faster he got to the bottom of the story, the sooner he could either dismiss Candy as another Angie or ask her out again to follow up on his instinct that she was a whole lot more.

One thing was for sure: he was not going to be such a screwup around her again.

CANDY SMILED AND WAVED at Carl, driving away from her house with a cheerful double toot of his horn. She'd spent the afternoon with him on another Milwaukeedates.com date, this time as Child at Heart. The day after the storm had been fairly mild, and they'd gone to the Milwaukee Zoo, been roared at by lions, sneered at by camels, ignored by rhinos and entertained by apes playing in their indoor "forest." They'd eaten ice cream bars, munched popcorn, drunk hot chocolate and ridden the zoo's miniature coal-burning train around the grounds, waving at visitors. It had been a great date, lots of fun.

His car went around the corner onto Capitol Drive and out of sight. Candy turned to go inside, still determinedly not glancing across the street at the house for which her eyeballs seemed to have developed magnets. She couldn't feel for Carl even a tenth of what she'd felt for Justin. Why the heck not? Was it mere chemistry or something deeper? Marie had wisely cautioned her that hormones weren't the best way to choose a mate. But you had to sizzle at least some.

No sizzle today. None.

Her adolescence had been like this. The boys who liked her she had no use for, and the boys she liked had no use for her. Until Chuck. Their coming together had been effortless and angst-free, the way she always fantasized a relationship starting. From the beginning she understood he was into her, he understood she was into him, and they both moved forward knowing they'd be together until that changed, whether the change came that day, that week, or never.

Inside her house, she peeled off her royal-blue coat, kicked off the red ankle boots she'd tucked floral pants into and dug out her cell. Abigail was back from Jamaica as of last night. Candy needed a girlfriend fix and Abigail would want the latest scoop.

"Hey, you tropical babe, welcome home! How are you feeling? Was it fabulous?"

"Candy! It was totally fabulous, and I'm feeling great. You

absolutely have to go to Jamaica, you would love it. Next time we'll drag you along."

Candy smirked. "Yeah, I can't think of anything more fun than being in a romantic paradise as the third wheel."

"Mr. Right didn't show up while I was gone? What happened with Justin?"

Candy filled her in, a long, rambling cathartic explanation including every detail, the way she and Abigail always communicated. Both had long since learned that leaving any tidbit out would only lead to questions later, so the initial verbal deluge actually saved time in the long run.

By the time she'd finished with the snow-shoveling shut-out from the previous day, Candy already felt better. "And that's where we are. Done. Finished. Totally over!"

"I gave you advice, you ignored me and look what happened."

"I what? What did you say? When?"

"Cookies."

"Oh, come on." She slumped into the chair in her living room which had replaced Chuck's favorite and always looked wrong and out of place as a result. "Is that all anyone can tell me?"

"Since when am I just anyone?"

"Marie said the same thing. Aren't we past the era when women had to prove culinary skills to score romantic points?"

"Candy, dear, you're forgetting what we're dealing with here. *We* might have evolved, but *they* haven't, poor things. Taking him something you made for him is a sweetly personal and totally nonaggressive gesture. If he's skittish or thinks you rejected *him* instead of rejecting first-date sex, or whatever else his issues are, then the next move has to come from you, but it has to be completely nonthreatening."

"Yeah, because I'm so terrifying. And I don't think the next move has to come from me. He's made himself very clear. Do not come around again. Do not pass Go. Do not collect—"

"We're talking about men, here, honey. We have to work to understand them so we can give them what they need, because they have absolutely no clue. Justin might well want you, adore you, be on his way to marrying you, but since he obviously doesn't know that yet, you have to make sure he figures it out in a way that isn't going to scar his ego or kick up any fear."

Candy shook her head, almost feeling sorry for Abigail's husband, who had clearly never had a chance. At the same time…Abigail could be right. Abby had certainly landed the wallet of her dreams mere months after she set her sights on him. "Cookies, huh?"

"Have I ever steered you wrong?"

"How about the time you told me to send Jack Jenkins an anonymous letter saying Candy Graham was hot for him, and he not only found out it was from me, but posted it on the student message board?"

"Ooh." Abigail sucked air guiltily through her teeth. "Right. That wasn't so great. But we're older now and wiser, thank God, and this advice is right on. I promise."

Candy turned to her front window, gazed at Justin's house, thinking about his incredible eyes and smile, his charm and easy flirtation.

Okay, maybe it wasn't *totally* over. Candy would give it one more try.

THAT WAS NOT HOW HE WANTED his latest encounter with Candy to go.

The party had gone well. Most of the guests were gone. Only Troy and Candy lingered in Justin's living room, sipping wine, involved in a discussion. A long discussion. Justin had barely had the chance to speak to her— *Hello, how are you, glad you could make it, may I introduce my friend Troy?* That

about summed it up. A few minutes ago, Troy had nodded
meaningfully to Justin and given a surreptitious thumbs-up,
which hadn't helped Justin at all. Had Troy succeeded in finding evidence of something fishy at Milwaukeedates.com, or
had he succeeded in proving there was nothing to find? The
result would impact Justin's feelings for, and possible relationship with, Candy.

Frustrated and impatient, he strode up to his room to find
the flash drive he'd promised to give his book partner before
he left. He knew where he'd left it: sticking out of the USB hub
behind his laptop. He even knew where its cover was: behind
the speaker. Neither were where they were supposed to be, and
he was positive he hadn't moved them. Had someone been in
his room during the party? He turned papers over on his desk,
searched under the laptop, on the floor, in the wastebasket.
Nothing.

Downstairs the front door opened and closed. Justin swore
under his breath. Candy must have left without saying goodbye, which irritated him even more than not being able to find
something he always kept in the same place. Where was that
flash drive? It held copies of all the chapters he was working
on, and of all his notes. God forbid his laptop crashed without
a current backup.

Footsteps sounded, coming up the stairs. Troy must be
wondering what was taking him so long.

"I can't find the damn thing."

"Find what?"

Candy. Candy's voice. Justin whipped around to stare at
his empty doorway. Now that his brain was focused outside
the room, yes, the footsteps sounded too light to be Troy's,
too tappy to be coming from a man's shoes.

Troy had left without goodbye? Without the flash drive he
knew Justin was upstairs getting for him? Without staying
to report on his impressions of Candy vis-à-vis Milwauke-
edates.com?

She walked into his room, and he saw immediately that the light tapping footsteps were caused by the same sexy, high-heeled black ankle boots she'd worn the first time he saw her across the street. With the same leg-enhancing sheer black stockings. But instead of the same black miniskirt, today she wore—

He swallowed convulsively. No skirt at all. No panties either. A red lace garter, a red lace bra trimmed in black, and a red-lipped sultry smile.

"Candy."

"As sweet as." She put her foot up on his bed, heel sharp on his navy quilt, calf curving up from the boot to her knee, then diving down again on the slope of her inner thigh, ending front and center at the soft pink crevice framed by dark curls that grabbed and held his eyes hostage. "Want a taste?"

His cock reacted at the same time his brain registered something wasn't quite right about this scenario. First the missing drive, Troy leaving without goodbye, Candy in shoes she hadn't been wearing earlier...

"Yes." He barely managed to get the word out. The jeans he'd had on for the party were gone; he had on something he'd never own in a million years: a black satin jockstrap whose material was soft on his balls and shamelessly stretched by his erection. His shirt had disappeared, too. He didn't remember taking anything off.

"Oh, that is much better," Candy whispered. "Much better. Come here."

What was happening? Was she a witch? She'd certainly bewitched him. He walked toward her, not feeling as stupid as he should in an outfit straight from a porn catalog.

"Closer. Closer. There. Now kneel."

He knelt, face an inch from her sex, warm and sweetly fragrant, smelling of woman and roses. She was so beautiful. He opened his mouth to tell her, but she thrust her hips forward, and instead he was inhaling, then tasting, then devouring her sweetness, reacting to her gasps and moans, wanting her to come more than he wanted to himself, even knowing if she came apart in his mouth he'd lose control and probably topple her onto the bed whether she wanted him to or not.

"Oh. *Oh*."

He loved her pleasure, loved the helpless syllables, loved that he was driving her crazy.

Without noise or preamble, two more long, black-stockinged legs appeared in his peripheral vision. Another garter belt, this one black, a firm slender stomach oddly familiar, a black lace bra filled to overflowing with olive-skinned breasts he knew intimately.

Angie. How did she—

"Hi there." Angie murmured the words into Candy's neck, lips leaving lipstick bites on her fair skin. Red-tipped fingers brushed over the lace of Candy's bra, settled, stroked back and forth, then slid inside and cupped the fullness of her breast, making Candy cry out and throw her head back, hair a cascading waterfall.

Then it was Angie who tumbled Candy to the bed, took over where Justin had been. Angie who made Candy come with spasms that practically rocked the house. Angie, who afterward looked back over her shoulder with vicious triumph and laughed, like the bad guy in a bad movie, at Justin, kneeling with the silly satin stretched absurdly out from his body.

Worse, when he shot indignantly to his feet, her hilarity increased; he followed her gaze to discover he was wearing yellow-and-brown argyle knee socks.

Ding dong.

Justin scowled at Angie in anger and confusion. Who did she think she was? And why did she sound like a doorbell?

"Justin, where did you go?" Candy pushed Angie onto the floor, where she crumbled into dust. "Come back to me."

She opened her slender arms. "Please, Justin."

Ding dong.

No, no, no. He didn't want to wake up. *Don't wake up. Not yet.* He wanted onto that bed; he wanted to be with Candy.

Justin's eyes opened; he groaned in disappointment.

Door. Someone at the door.

Troy. They were going to celebrate finishing the chapter this afternoon, and probably long into the night. What time was it? He rolled over and peered at the clock. Four-fifteen. Damn Troy for being early. Five more minutes and Justin could have finished the dream.

He pushed out of bed, rolling his eyes at his boxers, which were nothing like the satin jockstrap—where did that image come from?—but which were about as distended. He was going to have to get a lot further from the picture of Candy with her ankle boot planted on his bed before he'd get his underwear fitting again.

Ding dong.

"*Coming.*" He started downstairs. Stupid to yell; Troy probably couldn't hear him.

At the front door, his erection had calmed enough to be presentable—at least as presentable as he needed to be for Troy. After a good yawn and head-scratch, he pulled open the door.

Then stared openmouthed, his cock not sure whether to shrivel in mortification or rise again like a mighty obelisk.

Not Troy. Of course not.

Candy.

Hadn't he said he was not going to be such a screwup around her again?

CANDY STRODE DOWN HER DRIVEWAY toward Justin's neatly cleared one. She wasn't going to sit home and wonder what their connection was about any longer, nor wonder if and when she'd see him again, or what he was feeling, what he'd been thinking, blablabla. Enough. She was going over to his house on Abigail and Marie's advice, with her ultimate weapon:

rocky-road brownies. Chewy dark-chocolate cake topped for the last five minutes of baking with marshmallows, caramel, melted chocolate and toasted pecans. If he didn't orgasm within a minute of tasting one, there was no hope for him. And if he didn't take this opportunity to talk to her at least in a friendly manner, there was no hope for her.

She rang the doorbell and waited, head held high.

Wait, what if he was some kind of California health freak who wouldn't eat sugar?

Stop, stop that.

A deep, calming breath. The scent of the still-warm brownies rose temptingly. She started humming. If he didn't answer soon she was going to plonk her face into the pan and gorge.

No answer.

She tried the bell again. Waited longer, her calm beginning to fracture.

Wasn't he home? She could leave the pan on his front stoop, but what fun was that? The whole point of coming over was to see him and talk to him, gauge his reaction to—

Wait. She heard something. Had he shouted? Was he there?

Unlocking sounds at the door. Yes. Her heart sped. *Stay calm. Stay calm. Just a neighborly gesture...*

The knob turned. The door swung open.

Whoa.

Justin, wearing light boxers and a T-shirt, hair tousled, jaw stubbled. Oh, my lord, he was stunning, even if he was staring at her in a sort of horror, which she'd definitely rather he wasn't.

How long would she keep being surprised by how hot he was? And by how strongly she reacted? How long before she could greet him without the little kick of excitement in her chest? Okay, big kick. Big enough to impact her breathing.

"Candy...hi."

"Did I wake you?"

"No. No. I was…it was time to get up anyway. I, um, not really. No."

A horrible thought: did he have a woman up there? *Please no.*

"Am I, um, *interrupting* something?"

Her meaning sank in; his eyes widened, he held up his hand. "*No.* Nothing like that. No."

"Okay." She tried not to wilt too obviously into relief, hoping he'd say, "Why, Candy, after the other night I couldn't even *look* at another woman." Fantasy men never had trouble coming up with lines like that. Unfortunately the best lines never occurred to real ones.

"Here." She held the brownies out, certain all of a sudden that her offering was childish overkill. "I haven't officially welcomed you to the block, and I thought you might like these. They're amazing."

Wince. *They're amazing?* Why not start patting herself on the back?

"They look incredible." He took the pan. "Thank you, wow. A lot. Really."

"Sure." She forced a smile, sick and panicking. Why had she thought this was a good idea? Marie and Abigail had forgotten the fact that Justin was a guy. If guys wanted to see women, they called. If not, they didn't. This was not highly complicated. "I thought you'd enjoy them."

"I will. I know I will. They look delicious."

He looked delicious, too, but also clearly and painfully tortured by her presence.

"Okay, then." She backed away a few steps, feeling as if she'd swallowed one of the bricks his house was made of. "See you around."

"Definitely. We'll do…something. Soon."

Something. Soon. She barely managed to keep her bright shiny smile from dulling before she turned and fled.

Message received and understood. If rocky-road brownies weren't enough, and she wasn't enough, then nothing would be enough.

So. It was totally over. Over! From now on she'd leave Justin Case alone.

THAT WAS NOT HOW HE WANTED his latest encounter with Candy to go.

Justin closed the front door and slumped against it. Damn. *Damn.* Could he have handled that any worse? She'd made him brownies. He was still holding them; they smelled fabulous. A sweet, generous gesture—something Angie would never have thought to do in a million years—and how had he reacted? He'd stammered a few awkward words of thanks and spent the rest of the time gaping at her as if she were a stripper who'd made a house call. Real smooth, especially after he'd practically jumped her last time they were together.

He had excuses, but hadn't offered any. The night before he'd been at Troy's house, working. Their brains had given out around 3:00 a.m. and they'd had a few beers to unwind. Justin had been home in bed by 5:00 a.m., was up at 8:00 a.m., finished the chapter and emailed it to Troy for the final check. After a workout and some lunch, he'd been so sleepy he couldn't hold out any longer, he'd gone upstairs for a nap. Then the dream, and then Candy, so beautiful and fresh in real life, on top of the picture of her lingering in his mind: hot, wanton and lace-covered—or rather lace-*un*covered.

In short, he'd lost his cool, feeling thick-headed, bad-breathed, unshowered and entirely unappealing in comparison.

Oh, and still horny.

Great.

He could have invited her in to share the treats. Yeah, his place looked like it belonged to a frat boy the night after a party, but he could have explained he only lived like the typical slob bachelor on tough deadlines.

He could have brought up the postponed get-together with Troy and friends a little more specifically than "Something… soon." With all the other guys she was dating, he didn't want to delay too long. It was not like she was home waiting for his call.

He *should* have decided by now whether he was a potential boyfriend or a reporter so he wouldn't keep sending c'mere/ go away signals.

After he ate a brownie—he inhaled over the pan—or maybe two, he'd call Troy, fix a firm date for the party, yes, *soon,* go immediately over to Candy's place, apologize for being in outer space when she came by, and invite her. The sooner he figured out her story, the sooner he could write their ending, the sooner he could figure out what these feelings meant and the sooner he'd have the chance to make a recent dream come entirely and erotically true.

One thing was for sure: he was not going to be such a screwup around her again.

CANDY GLUMLY PULLED ON her skintight thermal jogging suit. Exercise was the best method she knew of to chase away the blues which had settled heavily an hour ago—not coincidentally right after the brownie disaster. It would be dark soon, but she had to get out and chase a runner's high or she'd bury herself in ice cream and old movies and never see daylight again.

Headband arranged firmly over her ears, gloves protecting her fingers, lip balm on her lips, she gave her running shoes one last check and headed out to do light stretches in the driveway, then started a brisk walk to warm her muscles.

"Hey, there!"

Candy whirled around. Hey, there who? It was a man's shout. A man's shout which sounded like Justin's. A man's shout which sounded like Justin's coming from the direction of Justin's house.

Well. Go figure. It was Justin. Pulling on a coat, jogging down his driveway, grinning at her. Waving eagerly.

Maybe *he* was the one with multiple personality disorder.

"Candy, glad I caught you."

She waited warily as he crossed the street, making sure her stomach was sucked flat, aware of the way her thin suit clung to every inch of her body. Even more aware when his eyes seemed to be discreetly taking in every one of those inches.

"Sorry I was unable to come up with full sentences earlier. I was still half-asleep."

"I thought I woke you. Sorry."

"Don't worry about it. Who sleeps at four in the afternoon? Only me, when I've been up most of the night finishing a chapter."

"Oh, I see." She tried to keep a mental scowl going, but something perky and hopeful had sat up to take notice. Would she never learn to stay off the Justin roller coaster?

"Thanks for the brownies. They were delicious. I ate three already." He was watching her in that measuring way that had turned her inside out so often.

"Glad you enjoyed them."

"I did. Both the brownies and the gesture." He took a slow, easy step toward her, making her tense. When he was close like this, she had to fight the urge to touch him, and she wanted him to touch her, everywhere. Where did this power come from? She didn't trust it. "Troy and I are having a sick-of-winter party on Friday at my house. People are bringing food that reminds them of summer. I was hoping you could come."

"Cute idea." Her head was racing. Did she want to go? Shouldn't she say no? What was she doing Friday? Something...

"Troy's idea. He could probably work for you." He smiled wryly. "Me, I was thinking, 'Yeah. Party. Beer.'"

Candy laughed. *This* was the guy she'd flipped for that first night. Where had he been? "That sounds fun, too."

He grinned and gave her shoulder a gentle nudge that made her want to fling her arms and legs around him and embarrass them both. What had she been saying about staying off the Justin roller coaster? "I hope you can make it, Candy."

"I have to give a fiftieth-anniversary cocktail party that night." She bit her lip, unable to close the door of opportunity completely. "But I'll try to show up afterward. Thanks for inviting me."

"You're welcome." He looked her up and down, this time with less heat than amused horror. "You're really going to run in this weather?"

"Justin..." She shook her head in disgust. "You need to live in the Yukon or something, to find out what real winter is like."

He shuddered. "No, thanks. This is all I can handle."

"This is nothing, this is halfway to spring. One year, for an entire week it never got above ten below."

Justin's eyes bugged out in mock panic. "I think I have somewhere to be that week. Like in my oven."

Candy laughed again, half giddy, half cautious, which added up to confused. "We northerners will thicken your blood eventually. You'll see."

"Have a good run. Hope to see you Friday night." He lifted an arm, walked a few steps backward, then turned toward his house.

Candy had to force herself not to watch him walk the rest of the way home; she turned deliberately and started on her pace. This push-pull thing was driving her crazy. Did he want to be with her or not? Why now and not earlier? Not when she was shoveling, not when she brought over baked goods? In her driveway that first time they met, then on the first date

and now, he'd been adorably attentive. The rest of the time it
was "Candy who?"

Her leg muscles began accepting the rhythm, her lungs
began adjusting to the cold. She relaxed into her stride, going
over the times he'd seemed into her. The times he hadn't. What
could account for the diff—

Oh, no. She stumbled over nothing and had to work hard
to regain her composure. Whenever he flirted or acted sweet,
she was wearing something revealing. He'd been on the block
since November, but hadn't come over to introduce himself
until he saw her wearing the teeny-weeny purple-and-black
outfit on Sexy Glamour Girl's first outing. All was wonderful
on their date when she was dressed to kill; he'd even wanted to
come in. When she'd been shoveling, shaped roughly like the
Pillsbury Doughboy, he'd waved and run. Bringing brownies
earlier today? Jeans and a bulky sweater. Yeah, thanks, gotta
go. But when she put on this second-skin jogging outfit? Here
comes Justin, roaring out of his house, standing close, inviting
her over.

He couldn't be that shallow, could he?

He could, of course he could. Some guys were. Some
women, too. What a waste of a sexy exterior.

But if that were true, that he only wanted one part of her,
there was no way she wanted any part of him. If that were
true it was totally over. Over! From now on she'd leave Justin
Case alone.

She sighed, knowing her attraction had become an obsession she needed to figure out. Knowing she'd go to the party.
But *not* dressed as Sexy Glamour Girl.

Okay. Maybe it wasn't *totally* over. Candy would give it
one more try.

8

THIS TIME THE SICK-OF-WINTER party wasn't a dream. Several of Troy's friends had come, and the weather had cooperated enough that Justin had been able to drag his grill out of the garage and tend to it in the driveway, huddled as close as possible without becoming charred meat himself. Hot dogs, hamburgers and bratwurst, of course—this was Milwaukee after all—frozen corn on the cob, which was grilled and slathered with chipotle butter, green salad, potato salad and a truly scary dish made from strawberry Jell-O, cream cheese, Cool Whip and crushed pretzels, which Justin planned on giving a wide berth. Some things about the midwest he'd never get used to.

By the time people had had their fill of grilled meat and various starches, Candy still hadn't shown. Justin hadn't realized how often he'd been glancing at his watch until Troy sidled up to him and grabbed his wrist. "Dude. She'll either come or not. Chill."

Busted. He shrugged, Mr. Nonchalance. "Just anxious to get this investigation going."

"Uh-huh." Troy slapped him on the back. "I believe you. I do. Really. Fun party, by the way."

"Thanks for supplying the idea and eighty percent of the guests."

Troy chuckled. "No problem."

The bell rang. Justin managed to give the front door a supremely cool look.

"Run." Troy gave him a nudge. "You know you want to."

Justin ambled. But not after giving his smirking friend a look that wouldn't do anything but make Justin feel better.

It was Candy, so beautiful Justin had to remind himself tonight was all about the story. He'd scanned Milwaukeedates profiles online and had found only one other woman who might have a duplicate profile. He'd written to both versions of her, and was trying to get her—or maybe them—to agree to meet him. One seemed willing, one wasn't, which didn't mean much. He'd also contacted a number of men, only a handful of whom were willing to share their experiences. A few of that handful had encountered women they described as extremely hot who lost interest after two or three dates. A couple of those women could have been Candy. Not proof by any means, but not dis-proof either.

"Hey, there." He grinned foolishly. Under her open parka, Candy wore a pretty floral sundress that scooped discreetly at the neck and flared past her knees. Her long, thick hair, the color of cherrywood, hung wavy and loose past her shoulders. Over her eyes, narrow blue-rimmed glasses that were chic and endearing at the same time. In a room of tank tops and shorts, she'd look like an elegant flower garden. "I'm glad you made it."

She smiled and Justin swore his heart skipped a beat. How was he going to get through this? He should have stayed away from alcohol. Even a moderate amount could crumble resolves stronger than his.

"I brought a vanilla ice cream pie." She held up a foil-covered plate. "With coconut crust, topped with blueberries and strawberries, kind of a red white and blue, Fourth of July thing. It should go in the freezer if you're not going to eat it right away."

"We're going to eat it right away. Come on in." He took the pie and draped her coat over the same arm so he could touch the small of her back, encouraging her into the room full of strangers. The perfect host, except her body was warm through the thin, soft material of her dress, and his manners wanted to slip as much as his hand did.

He introduced her around; she was welcomed warmly by Troy's friends who had rapidly become Justin's, too, as the sangria, hard lemonade and Corona beer took hold of everyone's mood. Troy gave Justin a wink over Candy's head and a surreptitious thumbs-up so like the one in Justin's dream that he almost dropped his beer. A lemonade was thrust into Candy's hand, a reggae CD put on the sound system, pies and watermelon were passed, and everyone settled in for a good sugar high. Justin made sure Candy sat near Troy, started them off chatting, then made some excuse to move on, pleased all would go according to plan.

Half an hour later, he was trying desperately to have a conversation with a blonde named Betty or Betsy, while an all-too-large portion of his attention was focused on Troy. What was he finding out? Anything? Nothing?

Candy burst out laughing; Troy grinned sheepishly. Justin gripped his beer. He didn't want them to get along *too* well. He trusted Troy, but stuff happened, and Candy was very... appealing. To use ludicrous understatement.

Justin gave up paying attention to Betty/Betsy and allowed his mind to wander. He'd worried his attraction to Candy came from her resemblance to Angie, not so much in features, but in the way she dressed and moved. But he was still hot for her tonight, dressed sweetly, and hot for her in jeans when she'd brought over the brownies, and hot for her while shoveling, padded in about forty layers of down and fleece—a bundle he could unwrap at leisure. She attracted him on a level he didn't understand yet, one he could only hope wouldn't set him up for more pain.

Another half hour went by. One couple left to relieve a babysitter. Two others left to continue partying at a downtown club. Betty/Betsy gave up on Justin and left, too, as did Troy's best friend from high school, Chad.

Which left Troy, Candy and Justin.

His dream come true.

"Well guys, I'm outta here." Troy offered his hand to Candy. "Really nice to meet you."

"Same here. I enjoyed talking to you. Don't forget Milwaukeedates.com."

Justin's stomach jolted. "You're signing Troy up?"

"Yup." Troy's lips smacked on the *P* while he made deliberate eye contact with Justin. "She thinks the owner has some great and very hot women for me to meet."

"Marie." Candy was beaming. "You met her, Justin. She's great."

"Yup." He smacked the *P* on his *yup,* too, because he was disappointed and a little annoyed. Did she get a signing bonus? A free small appliance for every single guy lured to the site? She must be swimming in toasters and hand-mixers.

"Can I use your bathroom, Justin?"

"Through the hall, to the left." He could barely return her smile.

"Exactly where it is in my house!"

Both men watched her slender form leave the room, skirt swirling around her muscled calves. The bathroom door clicked shut; Justin broke the freeze. "She tried to sign you up."

"She got right down to it." He picked up a couple of empties and put them on a tray on the coffee table. "But I didn't sense any manipulation. Nothing but an honest wish for me to find someone. Either she's clean or she's so good that you need to get away from her *now,* because a woman like that won't even bother spitting out your bones when she's done."

Justin groaned. "Exactly what I'm afraid of. Though it would make the story—"

"I'm not talking about the story."

"I know."

"She's something else, man."

"No kidding."

Troy whistled silently, looking down the hall where Candy had disappeared. "Yup. Send me that Candy-gram a-a-any day of the week, and I'll—"

"O-*kay,* Troy."

He chuckled and punched Justin playfully. "I'm safe. Not so sure about you, though. Be careful."

"I will be." He hoped. He picked up a couple of glasses and an empty pie dish. "You going to sign up?"

"Oh, for—" Troy pulled on his winter jacket, zipped it up to his throat. "Are you going to get on me about that again?"

"What can you lose? I'll pay. You don't even have to date anyone. Just talk to Marie and see who she matches you up with."

"Aw, man." Troy drew his hand down his face, a sure sign he was weakening.

"I'd owe you." *And maybe you can meet someone and get the disease called Debby out of your system.*

"Hey, you have the exact same tile in your bathroom as I do." Candy flowed back into the living room. "We must have had the same builder. 1938?"

Justin nodded curtly. "That's what they tell me."

Candy looked back and forth between the men. "I'm sorry, was I interrupting?"

"Nope." Troy gave her a brilliant grin and headed toward the front door. "I'm just leaving. Justin's on your side, by the way."

"How's that?"

"Wanting me to sign up for Mil-wau-kee-dates." He spat out each syllable with distaste.

"He's a good friend." She stepped closer to Justin; put her hand on his shoulder. It hit him with a combination of thrill and horror that it felt natural to be standing together in his house after a party, saying goodnight to their last guest. Where the hell did that come from?

"I'll think about it." Troy lifted his hand. "Justin, thanks for the good time."

"We should do this after each chapter."

"Deal. Good night." He went out. The door shut after him.

So.

Here they were.

"That was really fun, Justin. I'm sorry I missed so much of the party."

"How was yours?" He started picking up more dirty glasses and plates, needing to keep busy, feeling the thrill and horror again when she started helping as if she lived there, too.

"Dull for me but I think everyone else had a good time."

"I'm glad." He took the loaded tray into the kitchen, not surprised when she followed. "You want another drink?"

"Another hard lemonade would be great. I had a late start. Hey, your kitchen looks like mine, too."

"Yeah?" He fished a lemonade out of the refrigerator, poured himself a glass of water and started loading the dishwasher.

"I liked Troy a lot." Candy leaned on the edge of his kitchen table. Justin had to remind himself she didn't belong there. Had to remind himself that this extraordinary sense of comfortable intimacy might be nothing more than a deliberate fabrication on her part. Another date or two and she could disappear, on to the next new client and sorry it hadn't worked out. "He had some great stories about you."

"We had some pretty wild times. College, you know, the stupid stuff you do…"

"No, actually. I was in bed by nine most nights."

Justin turned to stare at her unblinking sincerity until she finally broke into giggles and he realized she'd been teasing. In any other circumstance he'd love her sense of humor. But the way she'd so effortlessly convinced him she was dead serious made him even more uneasy. He went back to loading the machine, wondering if she planned to stay long.

"I was kidding. I had some wild times, too. It's not really college if you haven't been stupid at least once."

"True."

"But at that football game, did you and Troy really—"

"Yes." He closed up the dishwasher and dried his hands. "We did. Wearing only socks."

"Not on your feet."

"Not on our feet. Want to go sit down?" He didn't know what else to do with her. He couldn't ask her to leave.

Okay, he could. But…

Crap. He didn't want to.

"Sure." She followed him into the living room and disconcerted him by sitting next to him, kicking off her sandals and curling one leg under her, shaking back her hair, then resting her elbow on the back of the couch, gazing through her lenses as if he were a big piece of butter cake with chocolate frosting. "Tell me about your childhood, Justin. What kind of kid were you in grade school?"

He swallowed. This was going to be a long night of sexual torture. "I was pretty average, kind of wild but no police record. Teenaged stuff."

"Were your parents hard on you?"

"My parents divorced when I was eight."

"Oh, I'm sorry." Her forehead crinkled into concern; her eyes conveyed sympathetic warmth. "Was it nasty?"

He laughed shortly. "It wasn't great. Dad had a younger

mistress, Mom found out. That wasn't pretty. Though I didn't understand the whole picture until much later."

"Ugh. I can imagine."

"It worked out in the long run. I lived with Mom after they split. She bought this funky little house in Solana Beach, in a neighborhood of surfers and artists. We probably got closer than we would have otherwise. She never married again, but she's been with Marty for probably ten years now. Dad married Chloe right away and stayed in Rancho Santa Fe. Probably both my parents are doing better than if they'd stayed together. Mom hated the whole gated golf-community thing, and Dad would have been miserable living anywhere less prestigious."

He was nervous. Babbling. Her proximity, the way her hair wound around her shoulder, the way a strand lay on the soft skin of her throat, the way her forward-leaning position made her neckline gape, the tantalizing shadow of her cleavage—all of it made him want to do anything but talk, so he talked in self-defense. It was hard to believe she was fake, hard to hang on to his outrage. When he was with her like this it felt calm, solid and right. More than being with any other girlfriend ever had. Which made no sense. He barely knew her, and what little he knew he might not be able to trust.

"Wow. Your parents went after completely opposite lifestyles. Did that make it hard to figure out who you were?"

Her question stopped him. He had to think before he could answer. "Actually it made it easier. Dad's life was so artificial, so defined by money and show. The people he and Chloe hung out with—all of it was unnatural to me. If my parents had stayed together it might have been harder for me to single that piece out and reject it quite as neatly."

"I see what you mean." She nodded, and he felt she really did understand; she wasn't agreeing with him to be sweet and appealing. He had to keep Troy's words in mind, *Either she's clean or she's so good that you need to get away from her* now.

"What kind of kid were you? Besides beautiful."

She laughed, flushing at his compliment. Could a hard-boiled liar blush that easily? "I was average, too. Unremarkable."

"I doubt that."

"I had a good imagination. My parents were extremely protective which sucked, especially when I got to be a teenager. I was the only girl and the oldest, so double whammy. I escaped by going over to Abigail's where it was too chaotic for her mom and dad to notice who did what, and by escaping into daydreams. And onto the stage." She smiled wistfully. "I wanted to be an actress."

"No kidding." Candy on stage, captivating audience members by disappearing into different characters? It sounded painfully familiar. "A movie star?"

"No, I wanted to be a Broadway actress." Her graceful hand gesture was accompanied by a self-deprecating smirk. "Straight plays or musicals—didn't matter to me. I loved to sing, though I wasn't much of a dancer."

"What did you like most about acting?"

"Getting on stage and leaving myself behind. The satisfaction of working at something I enjoyed and was good at. The camaraderie of the cast. Applause was nice, too."

He was really uncomfortable now. Both because she was talking about her skill at becoming someone she wasn't, and because her movements had taken on a sensual quality, her gaze had became faraway, and the reflective tilt of her head exposed a long, bare curve of skin his lips wanted to taste.

How could he get her out of here?

"Are you doing any theater work now?"

"Only at my parties. I dress according to the theme when the hostess wants me there making sure things run smoothly. I act silly for my kids parties, very prim for the tea parties.

For the bachelor parties…" Her expression changed. "That kind of thing.

"What about the bachelor parties?"

She laughed mischievously, then leaned toward him. He caught her scent. Floral. Jasmine? Lavender? He didn't know. But he could sit here and inhale her all night. "I'll tell you a secret, Justin."

God help him. She was so close, her whisper so intimate. "What's…" He had to clear his throat. "What's that?"

"One time for a bachelor party the woman supposed to jump out of the cake didn't show. So I did it." She pouted seductively. "Pasties, G-string. The works."

He nearly moaned, moved his hips up slowly, then down, trying to ease the pressure as imperceptibly as he could. He had to get off this couch or he was going to slide his hand up her thigh and kiss her until he finally got enough. Which might not be possible.

One problem—he couldn't move.

"I think you're trying to kill me, Candy."

"Kill you?" She looked genuinely puzzled. That had to be an act. How could she not know what she was doing to him? She'd lived with a guy for some years. She was no innocent. "I'm not trying to kill you."

"Then what *are* you trying to do?"

She blinked. Leaned back, flushing. "I thought you'd think it was funny. Since I'm not the type."

"Not what type?"

She looked incredulous. "Not the jump-out-of-the-cake type."

What the hell game was she playing? "Then what type are you?"

"I'm…" She looked blank. "Just me."

He got up from the couch, restless and annoyed. Forget calm and solid and right. She was even more unsettling to be around than Angie. He'd have glimpses of a wonderful, fun and funny woman with real substance, then she'd pull something manipulative and weird like this and he'd be back to square one thinking she was playing him.

Was this the big seduction move? Was that on her schedule? Date number one: Kiss like you mean it but don't let the guy in your house for coffee. Date number two: Drape self seductively over couch and tell story of wearing pasties, then pretend surprise at any sexual connotation. Date number three: Get man to the brink of coming, then tell him you met someone else and sorreee!

"Do you want anything more to drink?"

She shook her head, looking subdued and slightly bewildered. Damn it. Even annoyed with her, he didn't want her to be upset. Along with the self-protective instinct warning him to keep his distance, came a paradoxical need to protect her. From what, he wasn't sure, since she held all the power here.

"How about a tour of the house?"

She swung her legs onto the floor, put her delicate sandals back on. He wasn't a foot-fetish kind of guy, but even her feet were sexy to him. "Okay."

Yeah, he didn't think it was a great idea, either, but it would put them back on a normal footing, and then maybe she'd leave.

She'd seen the kitchen, but admired the art-deco chandelier in his dining room, and exclaimed over his drum set in one of the bedrooms downstairs.

"Can I hear you play?"

"You wouldn't be able to help it. Probably from across the street." He rapped a cymbal. "I'm out of practice now, and drum solos aren't all that fascinating without a band. But if I find one to join I'll invite you."

"Promise?" She smiled coyly.

He nodded and tapped the snare. "Promise. You've admired the bathroom already. Come see upstairs."

He went up ahead of her, not because he was gallant, but to avoid climbing behind her, with that incredible rear end at eye, mouth and hand level. On the second floor, he gestured to each doorway: his bedroom, his office, the bathroom, the closet, thinking this tour might be lame enough that she'd get his message and leave.

"Oh, this is your room." She wandered in, turned to smile at him over her shoulder.

Not lame enough.

She stopped by his bed and his dream came back full force, as clearly as it had the last few nights when he'd conjured it, pumping himself into Candy-induced bliss.

He could have that same bliss now. She was obviously offering.

Why tonight? Why not after their first date when they'd kissed their way to a much more intimate place? Because that was date number one and her Milwaukeedates.com contract didn't allow for sex that soon?

"This is so much like our—I mean *my* bedroom." She made a face. "Sorry, old habits die hard."

He nodded abruptly. *Our bedroom?* She had broken up with that guy, hadn't she?

Of course she had. Crazy thought. And yet…even wondering for a few seconds was a few seconds too many. Justin wasn't going to sleep with a woman he couldn't trust. Done that already, barely survived.

Troy had to get him to the next level. If Justin asked Candy about her role at Milwaukeedates now, she'd deny everything, whether she was innocent or not, and he still wouldn't know the truth.

"You even have your room set up similarly. My dresser is over there." She pointed to his laptop desk. And I had the closet doubled."

He murmured something polite.

"Ooh." She peered at a portrait on top of his bureau. "Is that your mom? She's beautiful."

"Yeah, that's her."

She nodded, then turned her head and met his eyes, perfect lips curved in a half smile. He stopped breathing. She prowled toward him, stopped barely a foot away, head tipped back with a look of sensual intent—and a bit of vulnerability that haunted him. "Thanks for showing me your house, Justin."

"No problem." He should turn away. Go downstairs now, say, *Hey, it was great having you here, Candy,* and make it dead clear she was going back to her own bed. Right away. Alone.

She put her hands to his chest and rose on tiptoe until her lips met his, pressed, clung, opened.

No. Yes. Oh, no. Oh, man. Her mouth was so soft, so sweet; it fitted his perfectly. He stood rigidly, willing himself not to slide his arms around her, not to get greedy caressing the curve of her hip, the swell of her bottom, not to think about the strong thighs under the flowery skirt.

She whispered his name, slid down the front of his body, hooking her hands in his jeans waistband until she was kneeling.

Oh, no. No no no. She rubbed her cheek against his swelling fly, pressed kisses to his straining erection through the too-thick material of his jeans.

Yes. He closed his eyes, gritted his teeth, felt her unsnapping his fly, fingers running up and down his zipper. He groaned, wanting his zipper down, his cock out and in between her lips.

No.

Not until he got to the bottom of who she was and why she was doing this.

He pulled back.

She made a small sound of regret, eyes looking up at him, dark with confusion. "What is it?"

"Candy." He clenched his teeth and pulled her to her feet. What the hell could he say to her? She was undoubtedly asking herself the same question he'd been asking about her in reverse: Why was he willing on their first date and not now? "I, uh, have to get up early and work."

The worst. That was the *worst* thing he could say. Even admitting to a raging STD would be kinder.

"Oh. Right." Her smile was brittle. She stepped back. "Right. Gotcha."

"I'm sorry, that was stupid. The truth is, I'm not—"

"No." She held up her hands. "Don't bother. I understand."

That didn't sound good. It didn't feel good either. He'd tried to be honest, too late maybe, but she hadn't even let him finish. "Understand what?"

She jabbed a finger into his chest. "I know why you won't sleep with me."

Justin perked up at that one. Had she figured out that he was on to her? Was she about to confess? "Tell me. I'm all ears."

"Because I'm wearing this dress."

He could only gape. "The *dress*? What does that have to do with anything?"

"I'm wearing a nice normal dress and glasses, and you won't sleep with me."

"And that makes you angry because…" The part of him that had wanted to protect her was rapidly dissipating. Enough with the games. Had he learned nothing by bending over repeatedly for Angie's boot? "What, it's your get-lucky outfit and I ruined your streak by turning you down?"

"You—" She made a sound of utter disgust, staring at him with an expression that would make Cruella De Vil look like Bambi. "Yes. Exactly. My streak. It's broken and I'll have to start another one with a different ensemble and that *really upsets me*."

"Oh, *no!*" He clutched his chest in exaggerated dismay. "I feel so *terrible!*"

"I am out of here." She thudded past him into the hall, then down the stairs. "Where is my coat?"

He thudded after her, grabbed her parka from the closet and tossed it to her, grateful to have escaped. Every trace of the sweet, seductive innocent was gone. This was Candy at her essence. Hell had no fury like a woman scorned, and he'd seen this exact display of irrational rage when he'd rejected Angie.

Fine. Good riddance. Candy had shown her true colors, and green was his, as in green light to go forward with this article without any hesitation whatsoever.

And when he found hard proof of Ms. Candy pulling this crap on men all over the city, he'd take great delight in making her, Marie and whoever else was involved, into targets of disdain and outrage for the entire city of Milwaukee.

9

MARIE LIFTED HER SHOVEL and dumped another load onto the three-foot-high bank winter had accumulated at the mouth of her driveway. Snow weighed a ton at this time of year with the warmer temperatures, but the overnight flurries had only resulted in an inch of cover, so she couldn't justify starting the blower. Besides, the exercise would do her good—if it didn't give her a heart attack.

She would have started earlier, but Candy had called that morning. Apparently Justin had been blowing hot, then cold, then hotter, then absolute zero, and Candy thought she'd finally figured out why. Marie was disappointed, as she always was when matches didn't work out, but particularly in this case since she'd had such a strong feeling Candy and Justin would enjoy each other enough to start a relationship, at least for a while.

Though she'd found Justin attractive, articulate and interesting, Marie would admit that something about him hadn't quite rung true. He didn't strike her as shallow, as Candy insisted—face it, if women rejected every guy powerfully drawn to females in skimpy clothing, the human species would eventually die out. But Justin had seemed hyper-observant in her office, both of her and of the process, as if she were the one being interviewed instead of him. Since he'd been so charming, and since Marie had found his analysis of the dynamics of his last relationship unusually honest and perceptive, she'd dismissed her reaction. Maybe Candy had gotten some of the same not-quite-right vibes?

In any case, if Candy was truly interested in moving on from Chuck, she wouldn't stay single long, not with that fresh beauty and enthusiasm for life. Darcy, too, could find happiness if she'd slow down long enough to acknowledge her needs. Big "if." She'd never responded to Marie's call about meeting Quinn. As for Kim, her reticence would make her a harder sell because she needed a guy patient enough to coax her out of her shell. Matching her with a sweet, quiet man would be wasting her.

Marie heaved another half shovelful of leaden ice chunks and paused, bending forward to readjust her sore back.

At the lowest point of her stretch, something jabbed her most personal bits from behind. She yelped and spun around to face the dog's apologetic owner, jogging up the block to call off his pervert hound.

Quinn. Looking as surprised to see her as she was to see him, and incredibly hot in navy sweats and a gray sweatshirt.

"Dante, *come*." The dog, which looked to be part golden retriever, part who-knew-what, went obediently; Quinn snapped on his leash. "Hi, Marie. Sorry about that. I had him on the leash earlier for our run, but he still had plenty of sprint in him after I was winding down, so I let him go on ahead."

Marie laughed, more flustered than amused. "Not a problem."

"Is this your house?"

"Yes." She clutched her shovel, wishing he'd move on with Dante. At the bar she was safely anonymous, in control of how long she stayed, whether she spoke to him, how much he knew, how she dressed. Outside today, he had her cornered at her home, unshowered, without makeup, wearing Saturday-morning clothes. Since she'd only seen him while sitting on the high chairs at Roots, she hadn't realized how tall he was. Six-two? Six-three? At five-three, she felt like a child next to him.

"Need some help?" He told Dante to stay and stepped toward her, hand out.

"Oh, no, I'm fine, really."

"Let me." He reached for the shovel. "I did mine already. It's like shoveling bricks."

"Thank you." Marie watched gratefully while he scooped up huge loads as if the dense snow were fresh powder. She couldn't help brief speculation as to what that chest and those shoulders looked like under his loose-fitting sweats. What a head-turning couple he and Darcy would make. Marie could imagine the two of them on a Hollywood red carpet, at a White House dinner, skiing the Alps, cruising the Amazon, having sex in every position known to man, and a few not.

She sighed, but made her face brighten when Quinn finished. "Thank you so much. That was really nice of you."

"Not a problem." He handed the shovel back. "I was about to go get a cup of coffee and a sandwich from Joe's Java. Want to come with me? My treat."

She stared at him, completely taken aback by his offer. "I...look like hell."

Oh, for— She couldn't believe that came out of her mouth. Was she about to turn forty or fourteen?

He grinned. "You look fine to me. No dress code at Joe's last time I checked."

"No, I know." She tried to laugh off her embarrassment. "I'd love to come, thanks. Let me just put the shovel away."

"Sure thing."

She strode down the driveway, trying to compose herself. What did he want? To find out if she had younger sisters? Younger friends? Or was he an extreme extrovert who couldn't stand alone time? Her introvert sister Carrie's first-born was like that. Every second of every waking hour he had to be interacting with someone or he'd fall apart. Marie already felt sorry for Quinn's mother.

The garage door rattled up; she ducked inside and hung the shovel on the rusted hook where it belonged, then gave in to temptation and did a quick check in her car's side mirror to see how bad she looked.

Surprisingly okay. Her cheeks were flushed from exertion, hair not too bad for having been slept on, and her eyes, while smaller and indistinct without their usual mascara and liner, were bright and clear.

Not that she was interested in Quinn, but a woman didn't want to be seen with one of the Seven Male Wonders of the World looking like a refugee.

She headed back down the driveway to where Quinn stood waiting, a tall, relaxed, solid-pack male, Dante sniffing the ground around him. Marie could use this lunch as an opportunity to feel him out on whether he'd be willing to meet Darcy. Maybe Marie could lure him to Gladiolas on some pretense, then call Darcy out to say hello. Or, much simpler, lure Darcy to Roots.

Marie cackled inwardly. *Oh, Mr. Peters. If anyone can shove you out of your manly comfort zone, Darcy can.*

They walked the blocks to Joe's Java, a great neighborhood hole-in-the-wall with fabulous coffee and oversize sandwiches, chatting about uninspiring topics like the recent snowstorm and Dante's penchant for finding smelly, often dead things and bringing them in to hide in his house. Outside the restaurant, Quinn went on to take Dante home, saying he'd meet her back in five minutes. Apparently he lived close by.

Inside Joe's, she took down her parka hood, reveling in the warmth, inhaling the rich coffee smell. A couple had just vacated a tiny table by the counter where Joe's sold take-out and bakery items, so by the time Quinn returned, Marie had relaxed and regrouped. She even admitted to a little cave-woman pride when he crossed directly to her table with a wide smile. Female friends having coffee glanced up, did a comical double take and bent their heads together to discuss the eye-candy addition to their Saturday. Either that or they were wondering what a hunk of beefcake was doing keeping company with a meatball.

A young man with black hair hanging over his forehead and a nose stud that looked like a metal wart came by with a pad and poised pen. Marie ordered a grilled chicken panini with balsamic onions and a side salad, Quinn a roasted veg-etable sandwich with fresh mozzarella and pesto, with a side of waffle fries.

"Are you vegetarian?"

He shrugged. "I find myself eating that way pretty often, but by taste, not conviction."

She was relieved. Darcy was a disciple of the "everything in moderation" school, and would probably prefer a guy who ate the same way. "I have someone I want you to meet."

He looked startled, then recovered quickly. "Always the matchmaker, huh?"

"It's my job."

"Okay. I'll bite. Who is she?"

Marie bit her lip. She'd expected more of a fight and didn't understand why she felt disappointed. "She runs a restaurant on the east side. Beautiful woman, the kind who can walk down the street and make men trip and bump into things."

"But…"

She raised her eyebrows. "But what?"

"If she attracts that much male attention, why are you hav-ing to shop for her?"

The waiter brought coffee in bright, thick, mismatched mugs, which gave Marie a minute to find a reason other than *She thinks men suck.* "The restaurant keeps her pretty busy."

"Workaholic?"

Marie sipped her smooth, rich coffee—more stalling while she chose her words. "She needs someone to remind her how to have fun."

He eyed her with amusement over his mug. "And I strike you as the type who knows how to have fun."

"Yup." She spoke cheerfully, deliberately avoiding the sexy tone he seemed conditioned to set. "Plus you match her in looks. And style. And grace. And athleticism."

"That's quite a list of compliments." He paused while the waiter set their food down and asked the obligatory will-there-be-anything-else question. "What's her issue with relation-ships?"

Damn. He was no dummy. "What do you mean?"

"Everyone has an issue. Baggage. Whatever you want to call it. Especially at our age."

Marie gritted her teeth. She'd put him five years older than she was. "Darcy's younger."

"How much younger?"

"Thirty-two."

"That's plenty old enough."

"Right." Anything over eighteen. She stared down at the enormous sandwich, golden-crusted chicken plump under fragrant caramelized onions, wanting to pour her coffee over his head, and furious with herself for the impulse. *She* was trying to match him up with a younger woman, why was she angry with *him?* Of course she wasn't. She was angry with Grant.

She had to get over this.

"Marie." He leaned into her field of vision. "I meant thirty-two is old enough to have issues."

Marie jerked her head up, mortified. He'd realized not only that she was upset, but why? As a therapist she was trained to be inscrutable. Obviously she'd slipped. "Yes…no, I understood. And yes, Darcy had some difficulties in her past. For one, she grew up in a grim family situation."

A frown wrinkled his forehead. "Abuse?"

"No, but her parents had a toxic marriage and she's had a pretty unsuccessful romantic history, too. She's kind of sour on the whole deal."

"Understandable."

"That is, *she* thinks she is." Marie picked up her sandwich. "My theory is that she's just afraid, and that a strong, patient man can turn her around."

His eyebrow went up. "You think I'm patient?"

"I know you are." She wiped her mouth with a napkin; the sandwich was as messy and delicious as it looked. "I've seen your work."

"My work! So now I'm an artist. A pick-up artist?"

"I didn't say that." She held back a triumphant grin when he mumbled skeptically. "Darcy's my friend. I wouldn't want to introduce her to you if I didn't think you were…"

"Worthy?"

She swallowed an odd thickness in her throat. "A good man."

"Thank you." As before, he accepted the compliment calmly, neither arrogant nor dismissive, but with a touch of amusement that made her rush on.

"A good man possibly soured on the whole deal, too."

"I wouldn't say that." He picked up a fry and ate it thoughtfully. "I haven't given up on getting married again. But it's not an immediate goal, and I won't settle just to get hooked up. I'm willing to wait. And yes, Marie, I want to play a little in the meantime."

"Understood. I'm not judging." Married *again*. He had committed once. Better and better. "You don't want kids."

"Not unless she comes with them."

"She doesn't." Darcy couldn't stomach the idea of giving

up her career, and with the horrendous hours she worked, she didn't think she'd be much of a mother.

"Why are you so concerned with matching her up, Marie?"

"Because deep down it's what she wants, but she won't let herself admit it. I made a New Year's resolution to help her and two other single friends this year."

"Why?"

She put her sandwich down, considering how to answer. "I want people to live fully and richly, to be honest with themselves about who they are and what they need and want. These are three terrific women with a lot to offer the right men. They just need nudging when the time is right."

"What about you? Aren't you looking?"

"No. No. Not me. Not really." She laughed awkwardly. "I mean if Mr. Perfect came along, okay. But no, I've got my hands full—"

"Deciding all your friends need love, but you don't."

"Why are you so concerned with me finding love?"

"Ha. Threw that right back at me, huh."

She returned his smile. "You had it coming."

"I'll let you in on a personal secret." He leaned toward her, pitching his voice to low intimacy. "It's a hot-button issue for me when women take care of everyone around them and not themselves."

"I see." She kept her therapist hat on firmly so she wouldn't break out in goose bumps. "Where did this come from? Your mother? Ex-wife?"

"Mother. And my sister, too, who followed in Mom's footsteps by marrying a man who expects everything and gives nothing."

"And you? What was your ex like?"

He grimaced. "I was so determined not to marry a doormat that I married the opposite, which is just as bad."

"Being aware of the patterns is half the battle. Sounds like you've worked it all out, though." Oh, he was perfect. Darcy needed someone on solid emotional ground to support her while she struggled onto hers. "You must have a good idea of the type of woman you're looking for."

"Somewhat." He quirked an eyebrow humorously. "But then life is full of surprises, isn't it?"

For some reason she started feeling nervous. "Well, I think Darcy is your type, at least judging by—"

"You know what, Marie?" He shoved his chair back and arranged himself comfortably. "I'm sure your friend is great, but—"

"You want me to mind my own business?"

"Nope." He held his coffee up to the waiter for a refill. "I'd rather talk about you."

"Me?" She couldn't hide her surprise, and couldn't stop the rush of pleasure. "What do you want to know about me?"

"Let's see." He added a creamer to his cup and stirred. "I admitted to some of my baggage. What about yours?"

She started playing with the handle of her cup, wondering how he'd react if she told him that men hitting on younger women was her hot-button issue. Probably too much intimacy this early in their…friendship? Was that what they were starting? Or did he only need someone today to watch him eat his sandwich? "I was married for ten years until my husband found someone else. I started my dream career, it's done well, and I'm happier now than I've been in a long time. That's about it."

"Good story. Love, betrayal, pain and a happy ending." His grin contained empathy. "To play you in the movie I'd cast… Julianne Moore."

"Oh, come on."

"I'm serious. Now who should play your ex?"

"How about…" She frowned thoughtfully. "The pig from the movie *Babe?*"

He cracked up, throwing back his head, legs long and loose to one side of their table. She imagined curling up on his lap—imagined *Darcy* curling up on his lap. "Well, Marie, I guess it's good to get to a place where you can laugh about the bad stuff."

"Finally. Yes. Was divorce your idea?"

"Nope." His face shut down; he pulled his chair back in to the table. "I'm not laughing now, am I? Still need work."

Her heart ached for him. "Another man?"

"She married him, then cheated on him and married the third one. Probably only a matter of time before she does it again." He pulled his wallet out of his sweats and slid the check toward himself.

"People like that…" She shook her head, wishing she hadn't brought up his divorce if it made him want to cut their meal short. Or maybe he'd been ready to go anyway. "Sometimes I think therapy should be a requirement for graduating high school."

"A whole country of well-adjusted people?" He extracted cash and stood. "I can't even begin to picture it."

"Me, neither." She waited while he paid, feeling oddly let down. "Thank you for lunch."

"You're very welcome, Marie. You heading back home now?"

"Yes." To an empty house full of waiting chores.

"I'm going the other direction." He opened the door for her, turning up his collar against the wind. "I'm glad I bumped into you today."

"Same here." She started edging back, unaccountably nervous, then made herself hold her ground. "See you at Roots?"

"I'd like to do this again if you're up for it. Maybe make it dinner next time?"

"Oh. Sure. Yes." Her voice came out too high; she found herself nodding frantically. Was he interested in her? A man like this? She took another step back, dangerously giddy.

Stranger things had happened. Maybe he'd finally tired of his bimbos and wanted a woman of substance.

"Good. I enjoy your company."

My God. Was she dreaming? "Same here, Quinn."

"You remind me a lot of my sister."

A burst of pained laughter. Stupid, stupid, stupid even to fantasize. A pudgy, short woman on the verge of middle age catching his attention after he'd been going for nothing but Darcy types?

"Your sister." Her voice cracked. "The doormat?"

"No, no, my other sister. Angela. Very smart. Very funny and fun. You'd like her."

"I'm sure I would." She was nodding too much again. Forget her houseful of chores. She wanted to take her bruised almost-forty-year-old ego home to her warm living room, crush a package of Oreos into a bowl of ReddiWip and eat it with her hands. She was angry at his confident handsome face, and at herself for giving him the power to make her feel worthless. "It's funny you said that, Quinn, because actually you remind me of my brother."

"Yeah?" He was looking at her curiously. Hadn't she sounded sincere? "Well, how about that."

Yeah. How about that. He was still watching her with that measuring look, so she said goodbye, see ya later and turned away, not wanting him to see her face any longer, in case he figured out she was lying.

Quinn Peters did not remind her of her brother, for two reasons. One, the instant she thought he might be attracted to her, the truth had jumped up and shouted itself hoarse. This wasn't about Darcy. He was hot and she wanted him, like every other female on the planet.

And the second reason he couldn't possibly remind her of her brother was much simpler.

She didn't have one.

10

"WHAT THE HECK KIND OF PARTY is this going to be?"

"Valentine's, what did you think?" Candy smirked at Abigail who had emerged from the bathroom wearing a variation of the sexy-Cupid costume Candy had on, only on her long, lean body, and with her model's beauty, the ridiculous getup managed to look almost chic. In deference to her friend's baby bump, Candy had given Abigail the less revealing of the two styles she'd designed. Her client, Josie Abernathy, would arrive momentarily to discuss party details and to choose one of the two looks for her Cupids. For a reason Candy had yet to figure out, Mrs. Abernathy thought it was a cute idea to have scantily dressed females flitting around with trays of cocktail tidbits. Candy had tried every diplomatic means at her disposal to squash the idea, but nothing. She'd even suggested a few males dressed in red-and-white boxers, to keep sexism charges at bay, but Mrs. Abernathy would have none of it. Or, Candy suspected, her husband wouldn't.

"Gee, I guessed Valentine's. But what else, a grope-your-server party? A women-are-nothing-but-objects party?" Abigail gestured to the white micro-miniskirt dotted with red hearts that flared under her red faux-leather lace-up bustier.

"This is revolting. Any guys going to be there in red Speedos or jockstraps?"

"Nope. Just babes bearing hot nibbles." Candy tugged on her red satin bra trimmed with marabou. A red satin miniskirt sat below her waist and connected midthigh via a red lace garter to sheer red stockings.

"Ew." Abigail waved her plastic bow and arrow disgustedly. "Where did you find these people?"

"River Hills."

"Oh, for heaven's sake. All that money and no taste."

"As long as some of that money is coming to me, it's not my problem." Candy adjusted the white feather wings hooked onto Abigail's shoulders. "Ready to go downstairs? She'll be here any second."

"I'd rather hide."

"I know. Wait, I need one more minute." Candy peered in the mirror and fixed onto her head the tiara decorated with rhinestones and red glass hearts. "These are definitely the tackiest outfits I've ever had to make."

"What about the Always-a-Bridesmaid party that woman gave? Those brown-and-green dresses with puffy sleeves and no waists?"

"A true fashion nightmare." Candy gave her hair a final pat and pulled the bra down a little lower to make sure the red heart "tattoo" on her right breast was visible. "But at least those were *supposed* to be horrible."

"Anything more from Justin?" Abigail started downstairs. "Not that you'd dare not tell me if there was."

"Nothing." Candy was startled by the abrupt question and annoyed when her voice thickened. "Which is *fine* by me."

"Uh-huh." Abigail turned at the bottom of the steps and folded her arms across her pregnancy-bountiful chest.

"What?" Now Candy sounded upset and defensive. Why bother trying to pretend? Abigail wouldn't miss a trick.

"Look, I admit he's behaved sort of…erratically. But I still,

I don't know." She frowned, looking absurdly lovely in the ghastly red-and-white costume. "I have a strong feeling this isn't the end. That he's going to show up again."

"Oh, please." Candy took the last few steps down and brushed past her friend, nearly knocking off her wings. "I don't even want to think about it. I have another date tonight at Firefly Café with Sam, the guy I liked so much last time. I'm looking forward now."

"Oh, yeah! I remember Sam! In particular I remember how you could barely stay awake describing the date." Abigail rolled her eyes. "My first dates with Ron, I was flying. I couldn't wait to see him again. And not just because he spent more on me in a month than my family spent on me my entire life. There was this something when we were together, this spark."

Candy knew exactly what she meant. Damn it. "Marie said hormones are a completely unreliable way to choose someone."

"Marie is single." Abigail put a hand to her abdomen, a tender, nurturing gesture Candy wouldn't have expected from her friend only a few months earlier. "I'm just thinking you might have jumped to conclusions about Justin. That there's something going on you need to talk out."

Candy blinked. Had pregnancy softened Abigail's brain? Since when was Ms. Scream Until She Gets Her Way understanding and forgiving toward men? "He ignored me at his party all night. And said no to a blow job after."

Abigail's face stretched into incredulity. "Are you *serious*? You didn't tell me that part. You asked if he wanted one and he *turned you down?*"

"No, but I was on my knees ready to go and he stopped me." Candy heard Mrs. Abernathy's car pulling into her driveway and hurried to the front window. "She's here. Come on. We'll pose by the door and I'll fling it open when she arrives for the big surprise."

Abigail groaned. "This is so embarrassing."

"You'll never see her again." Candy tipped her head seductively, pushed her chest out and positioned one foot in front of the other, making sure her bright red wings were on straight. "Do something like this."

"Oh, for— You look like a mythological hooker."

"Perfect," Candy said wryly. "Though Chuck would have a heart attack."

Abigail blew a long and heartfelt raspberry. "That's what I think about Chuck not wanting you to look sexy."

"It wasn't that." Annoyance made Candy break her pose. "Around him I didn't *need* a Cupid costume to be sexy."

"Come on, Candy. Open your eyes. He didn't want you looking hot so guys wouldn't line up to take you away from him. So he could control you."

"What?" Candy glared at her, that odd panicky feeling boiling again in her stomach. "That is the most ridiculous—"

The doorbell rang.

"Oh, crap. Pose." Candy glanced to make sure Abigail was ready, then pulled sharply on the door so it swung into the room on its own and she had time to get back into position.

Justin. Standing at her door. Holding her pie plate.

His eyes widened to the size of walnuts and started bouncing back and forth, Candy, Abigail, back to Candy, back to Abigail, then came to rest on Candy. "Holy sh—"

"Justin." She blushed fiercely, which ruined her determination to be icy around him, wishing he didn't look so incredibly handsome and virile, because that made it much harder to stay furious with him as he deserved. A traitorously weak part of her threatened to melt into submission at the mere sight of him. She had to remind himself that if he made anything like a move toward reconciliation, it was likely the fact that her breasts were pumped higher than tires on a monster truck, and little of the rest of her had any covering at all. "What were you doing in Mrs. Abernathy's car?"

The second she said the words she realized they were ridiculous. That, the snort from Abigail and the obvious confusion on Justin's face.

"I meant where is Mrs. Abernathy?"

Only slightly less ridiculous.

"Uh." He swallowed convulsively, eyes clearly making a valiant attempt to stay on her face, but not succeeding too well. "Mrs. Who?"

"The car in my driveway."

"Yeah, um. Yeah. I saw her." He swallowed again. "She's in her car. On her phone. You left your plate. Here it is. God, you both look— Whoa."

Candy turned pointedly to Abigail, who wasn't rolling her eyes as she was bloody well supposed to be. In fact she was watching Justin intently. Not even frowning in cynical sisterhood. The betrayal became complete when she held out her hand, smiling the smile that knocked every straight man to his knees, and probably quite a few gay ones, too.

"Hi, Justin. I'm Abigail."

"Nice to meet your—you." He shook her hand, glancing at Candy. "Nice to meet *you*."

Abigail giggled. "Candy's told me a lot about you, Justin."

Candy froze her face into fury. *Abigail!*

"Oh. Well. That's nice." He turned back to Candy. "You going to a Valentine's party tonight?"

"Nope." She lifted her chin, determined to let him know she wouldn't be sitting home pining for him. "I have a dinner date."

"You're going on a dinner date in *that?*" He gestured to her uplifted breasts.

"*No,* not in this." She managed to hang on to her cool, but only barely, because he was standing too close, heating her half-naked body with his gaze, and she was reacting both emotionally and sexually without having given permission for either one. "What do you take me for?"

He met her eyes, looking perplexed. "I'm never quite sure."

Abigail made a sudden movement. They both looked at her.

"The baby?" Candy asked anxiously.

"No, no. It's all good." She smiled at Justin with real friend-liness, which on Abigail looked like "please sleep with me now." Candy wanted to yank off her wings and stomp on them.

"So, Candy, where are you going on this *date?*" He spat the last word out, sounding contemptuous. Or…jealous? Her heart did a funny triple flip.

"Firefly Café in Wauwatosa."

"Nice place." He rubbed his jaw, looking annoyed and vulnerable and a little dismayed, and Candy's lovely outrage faltered. "They have a great bar for—"

"Candy Graham!" Mrs. Abernathy appeared next to Jus-tin and clapped her hands to her cheeks. "How a-dor-able you look! And you, too, my goodness. What's your name, dear?"

"Abigail." Abigail looked as if her morning sickness was about to come back, but not because of the baby.

"I've got to get going." Justin held out the plate. "Nice to meet you, Abigail."

He turned and left abruptly. Mrs. Abernathy frowned at his back. "Friend of yours? He'd adorable, too. I was about to introduce myself."

"He's my neighbor across the street. Come in, Mrs. Aber-nathy." Candy found herself clutching the pie plate in a violent embrace, and made herself release it and close the door, stop-ping to take one more peek at the broad shoulders striding away.

Why did this man have to be so confusing and so, so

delicious? Why couldn't she control her feelings around him? Her head seemed to be totally enslaved to her heart and hormones.

Sighing, she followed Abigail and Mrs. Abernathy into the living room, where an hour later, Mrs. Abernathy had chosen, thank God, the less revealing outfit Abigail was wearing, had approved the final menu, had brought up a thousand logistics Candy had already covered and finally left, proclaiming that the party would be the hit of the year.

Candy and Abigail lost no time in stripping off the costumes and reassuming their mortal forms.

"I should go, too." Abigail pulled her long dark hair back in a ponytail that brought her wide dark eyes and lovely cheekbones into prominence. The same hairstyle made Candy look like a middle-schooler. "But first we're having a sit-down."

"Over what?" Candy looked at her watch, pretending to be worried about time, when she was actually trying to avoid the inevitable continuation of their argument over Justin. Especially since, having met him, Abigail would consider herself an expert. "I have to get my Professor outfit ready for Sam."

"This won't take long." Abigail led the way downstairs and into the kitchen as if she owned it, took down a glass, filled it with water and guzzled half. "We need to talk more about this Justin thing."

Candy slumped onto a stool and groaned, as if she hadn't expected those exact words. "Why?"

"He is gorgeous, Candy. Like oh-my-God gorgeous."

Candy put her hands over her ears. "I do not need to hear this."

"Yes." Abigail reached over the counter and yanked her hands down. "You do."

"Make it quick then, because I have to get ready and I think I'm allergic to your lectures."

"Did you see how he was looking at you?"

"Uh, yeah. He was looking at you, too. Because we

were showing almost as much skin as Vegas showgirls. Exactly what I was telling you about what the guy values in women."

"No. No, honey. This was not the look of a guy into your body. This was the look of a guy into *you*."

"Oh, really." Candy made a sound of derision while her heart did another triple flip.

"Really."

"Then why doesn't he ever pay attention to me when I'm not dressed like a streetwalker? Why did he say no after his party if he thinks I'm that amazing?" The anguish in her voice surprised her.

"I don't know. Maybe he's a virgin. Maybe he was constipated. Maybe he'd just found out his best friend killed someone."

"His best friend was at the party."

"You know what I mean." Abigail put her empty glass into the sink. "The point is, what is so horribly wrong with a man thinking you're hot when you're half-naked?"

"Because that sex kitten part isn't really me."

"Your body isn't you?"

"It's a costume, it's a put-on attitude."

Abigail clutched the sides of her head. "Not this again. Since grade school you've clung to this ridiculous idea that you're not sexy. Sometimes I felt like you were trying to be invisible when we went out."

"No, I was invisible next to you."

"Give me a break. You just wanted to feel that way." She crossed to one of Candy's food cabinets and scanned the contents. "Worse, then you found a guy who made you feel even more invisible and called it love."

Ouch. Candy scowled at her. "Now you're sounding like Justin."

Abigail's head whipped around. "Justin? He said that?"

"Well. Kind of." She sighed and thumped her elbows on the counter. "Yes. He did."

"Oh, my God." Abigail closed the cabinet without having taken anything down, eyes wide with excitement. "This guy is one of the fabled few."

"What are you talking about?"

"A guy who has a clue. Seriously, Candy. He figured out that much about you? It took me years. And for a little comparison, Ron and I had four dates before he stopped talking about himself long enough to notice I was sitting across from him the whole time. Even now, though I really have grown to love him, and I think he'll be a great dad, even now, he doesn't have what it takes to make the kind of observation this guy made on your first meeting."

"Second meeting."

Abigail folded her arms. "You are a moron."

"Don't hold back."

"I'm serious. If you become as determined not to see this guy for what he is as you were determined not to see Chuck…"

Candy found herself trembling, furious and oddly frightened. "I was the only one who knew Chuck."

"Because he barely let you leave the house so the rest of us could get to know him, too."

"That's ridiculous. You can't blame that all on him."

"I don't. Only half. The rest goes on you."

"Abigail." She gasped out her friend's name. "I can't believe you—"

"I have good instincts. And my instincts are telling me that this Justin guy is into you big-time, and not because you've been dressing as Sexy Glamour Girl." She came forward and gripped Candy's arm hard, but her features had gentled. "Don't you see, honey? If you turn your back on Justin now, you're also turning your back on yourself."

11

CANDY SAT OPPOSITE SAM, smiling pure, attentive happiness while inside her stomach felt as if it was trying to form itself into a pretzel. He was such a nice man. Good-looking, in shape, intelligent, opinionated without being obnoxious about it, curious about the world, a reader, a traveler...

But her heart hadn't done a triple flip when she met him in the foyer of the Firefly Café. Not even a gentle somersault. Only a feeling of warmth, like when a good friend walked into a room unexpectedly. Even after a couple of glasses of wine, which could do wonders to expand friendship into attraction, she wasn't able to summon any tingles for him.

"Have you been to Cempazuchi?"

It was all she could do not to jump. "Yes. Once. The food was very good."

"I haven't been. We should go there next time."

"Mmm." She smiled, experiencing a jolt of irritation that he'd take her wanting a third date for granted. And yet, why wouldn't she?

The answer came easily. Because she could envision a line of pleasant evenings stringing out as far as the eye could see, and nothing about it made her jump up and down. His type would be happy to strand her, staying home every night, the way Chuck—

She picked up her glass and took a huge swallow. Since when had the life she had with Chuck seemed anything but idyllic?

Oh, God, what if Abigail and Marie and her brothers and pretty much everyone else she knew who had also known Chuck were right?

A harsh woman's voice sounded from a tiny room off the main bar behind her. Candy had been in there once with Chuck—she'd brought him here for a drink on his birthday one December. There was a fireplace and banquettes lined either side of the narrow space, with four tiny tables for couples who wanted the snug feeling of a private room.

This woman sounded angry. And loud. She was cussing out someone who wasn't answering back.

"Whoa, what's going on in there?" Sam craned his long neck. "Sounds like someone had too many drinks."

"Whaddya mean you won't sleep with me?"

Candy cringed. "Charming."

"I won't take no for an answer. You are much too cute."

Shushing sounds were heard, then a low male voice.

"I don't care if we just met. Or that you're dating someone else."

"Uh-oh." Sam let out a nervous chuckle and adjusted his glasses. "This doesn't sound good."

"One night. Tha's all I want. C'mon. Once you've had me you'll never go back.

Ew. Candy sat, rigid with discomfort. Impossible to make any conversation now. The rest of the bar had grown gradually quieter, but a few giggles were heard after the last outburst, and someone shouted out, "Go for it!"

The male voice swore quietly behind the privacy curtain.

"Come home with me!" She was almost screaming. *"You have to be with me."*

Two burly male restaurant employees crossed the room quickly, flung open the curtain. "What's going on in here?"

"He tried to rape me!"

The crowd started laughing.

"Maybe the other way around!" some guy shouted.

More laughter.

By now Candy was feeling sorry for the guy Psycho-Woman had trapped in there. Sorry until the male voice sounded again.

"I don't know her at all. I came alone tonight."

Candy twisted to stare at the doorway to the little room. No. *No way.*

A shriek, then a scuffle; the man's head showed briefly around the open curtain where he'd apparently been shoved by Ms. Demon Fury.

Justin.

She no longer felt sorry for him. In fact, call her Ms. Demon Fury II.

What the hell? Why was he here when he knew she would be? Had he followed her? Was he spying on her? Was he some weird stalker? Candy would like to think she'd be able to tell if a guy was missing that many screws, but she'd heard some psychopaths appeared normal and trustworthy in every way until it was too late.

She could barely think for the horror and confusion, afraid she was going to be sick. Around her the crowd laughed and jeered, competing with shouted off-color jokes at Justin's expense.

Calm down, Candy, think this through. Stalker-guys usually showed up after women rejected them. But in this case Justin had done the rejecting. So that didn't fit the stereotype at least.

But if Justin didn't want her, why would he follow her here tonight? It couldn't be a coincidence. He'd asked her where she was going on her date; his presence here was deliberate.

Wauwatosa police arrived; the woman, who looked like a man in drag, and Justin were escorted out of the bar. Candy shrank back against the wall as he passed; he barely glanced at her. Conversation gradually returned to normal around them.

Candy didn't think she'd ever return to normal.

How she made it through the rest of the date, she had no idea. She could feel burning spots of color mounting on her cheeks as she drank her third glass of wine and recklessly ordered a fourth. Sam was driving, Sam was paying, who cared if as "the Professor" she shouldn't be much of a drinker? Who cared about anything except how furious she was, and how forcefully she would give it to Justin when she got home. As soon as Sam's car was out of sight, she'd be crossing the street to jab his doorbell all the way back into the woodwork.

An hour later, she was able to attempt exactly that, pushing again and again, so hard she nearly hurt her thumb. The damn thing kept popping back to glowing orange, ding-donging inside as if she were announcing happy news with a pealing of bells.

If he wasn't in jail, if he had the balls to open the door to her, knowing she'd most likely attempt to rip his head off, she was going to…attempt to rip his head off.

The door opened. Justin stood there calmly. A long scratch traveling from his cheek close to the outside of his eye looked as though it would sting and make sleeping difficult.

Stop. She did not care if it hurt him. She did not care if he had trouble sleeping.

"Candy." He spoke quietly, didn't look surprised or guilty. "What are you doing here?"

"It's *my* turn to stalk *you*."

"Come in." He stood back from the door. "I doubt the neighbors want to hear this."

She flounced in, turned to face him with her hands on her hips. No worries about him seducing her tonight. She'd worn her glasses and was covered from under her chin to the tip of her toes in thick, sensible earth colors. "What were you doing at that bar?"

His eyes were almost cold. "I was watching you play with your latest victim."

"My *what?*"

"The guy you were with tonight. Who did he think he was dating?"

"What are you talking about?" This was her rampage to go on, not his. "Sam and I were having a nice time until you and your one-night-stand wannabe hijacked the whole bar."

"I have no idea who that woman was."

"I don't care about your love life. I want to know why you showed up on my date."

"I want to know why you have four profiles up at Milwaukeedates.com."

For a second she was taken aback, but on the way to being ashamed, she stopped herself. She was not in the wrong in this situation. No way was she admitting something that private to Creepy Stalker Guy. "Because I chose to. What's your excuse?"

"I got matched up with you at Milwaukeedates, Candy." His voice was full of contempt, but also pain. "So did Troy. So did quite a few other men. Marie has you working pretty hard."

"Marie is a good friend and she's helping me out. How she does that is none of your business."

"I thought you were doing *her* a favor." He threw her words back at her.

She strode toward him, hardly aware of anything but her desire to strangle him, thinking better of it at the last second, both because she didn't want to spend her life in jail and because he was a lot stronger than she was, and because even now she didn't trust herself to touch him. Instead she stopped an inch away and shot her next words right into his face. "You can think whatever the hell you want."

He didn't back off. If anything, he came closer, pitching his voice to a low taunt. "You need the money that badly?"

"What money?" Despite the fury in her brain, she registered his stubbled jaw, his smooth, firm lips and how close they all were.

Oh, God. She was getting turned on. By her rage, by this man, by his nearness and his power.

This was entirely too twisted.

"There has to be money in it for you." His eyes flicked down to her mouth and back; his tone was slightly less harsh.

"Money in what?"

"Dating men for Marie."

Outrage stole her breath. "You think I am dating men for *money?* Do you know what that's called?"

"Yes."

She couldn't speak for nearly ten seconds, only managed a gasp. "How could you think—"

"I don't. I can't. No matter how much evidence…" He let his head drop back in exasperation. "You're driving me completely insane, Candy."

The way he spoke, in hoarse despair, the way he raised his head and looked directly at her when he said her name, the heat in his eyes, all made it hard to get back her breath. She needed to find her outrage again. He'd practically called her a whore, she should be—

His mouth found hers as if it was made for that purpose. And even though she'd only kissed him a couple of times, even though this savage angry kissing was unlike anything they'd shared, the taste and feel of him was like coming home, and she couldn't even imagine why they hadn't been doing this nonstop since they met.

Except…

She broke the kiss, but didn't step back—not that she could have with his arms holding her tightly. "Wait."

He groaned his protest.

"Why are you kissing me?" She heard the awe in her voice and saw the confusion in his face.

"Because you're the most beautiful, desirable, fun, funny, full-of-life woman I've ever met, and even though I hate what you're doing I can't get you out of my head."

She frowned up at him. This made no sense. "But I'm wearing glasses again. And a turtleneck. And brown pants."

"What the— *Why* are you so obsessed with what you're wearing around me?"

Candy sighed. Abigail was right. It was time the two of them did more talking and less assuming. "For the past couple of weeks the only times you've seemed interested was when I was Sexy Glamour Girl."

"Sexy who whah?"

"Sexy Glamour Girl. One of my profiles. You were hot for her, lukewarm for the others. No, tepid. No, icy."

"Icy?" He slid his hands down to her hips, coming dangerously close to resting them on her rear end. "Candy, I have never felt anything for you but pure, sweet, gentlemanly animal lust."

"What about when I was shoveling?"

"Oh, man, yeah." His features softened into sexy amusement. "You were like a mummy all wrapped up. I wanted to play archeologist and excavate."

Hmph. "You had a strange way of showing it."

"I was half-crazed on no sleep and deadline pressure. And I had no shoes on."

"What about when I showed up with the brownies?"

He started laughing, a low, sexy chuckle that made his eyes glint mischievously. "I was flustered. I'd just had a dream about you that I would very much like to come true someday."

She tried very hard to keep frowning, hands jammed on her hips. "Oh?"

He nestled her snugly against him. "Oh."

"I'm not being paid by Marie for anything, Justin." She whispered the words, head lolling to one side as his mouth explored her throat. "I'm just playing."

His lips stilled. "With men."

"With different parts of my personality. But not with you." She touched his face, hating the scratch now that looked so raw. "Never with you."

His struggle was so obvious now. She'd missed it before. Struggling with whether he could trust her. And all she'd been worrying about was her clothes.

"Tell me about your dream. The one that got you flustered."

"Hmm. One part I'd rather not re-create. No, two parts."

"Tell me."

He sighed with exaggerated resignation. "The part where my old girlfriend shows up."

"I think that woman did a number on you." She couldn't believe her anger had dissipated so quickly into tenderness. What was it about this man that kept her coming around, that kept her wanting things to work out between them. Good instinct or loneliness?

"I'm over it." He started walking her backward toward the stairs.

"Do you want me to do a number on you, Justin?"

"No, thanks."

"Not even a nice number?"

"Such as…"

"Sixty-nine?"

He laughed. "That *is* a nice number."

"What else didn't you want to tell me about from your dream?"

"The black satin jockstrap."

"You've seen me in a tiara and wings. I think I can handle—"

"Oh, that Cupid outfit." He looked like a man reliving one of the best moments of his life. "You were so hot in that, I could barely speak. Maybe you noticed."

"Actually—" she flung him a sheepish glance "—I figured you were overcome with loathing."

"No. No loathing. Frustration, sure, annoyance, yup, but never loathing." They reached the stairs; he looked up the flight, then down at her. "*Lots* of frustration, Candy."

She knew what he was asking. They'd been at this juncture twice before. Once she'd said no, the second time he had. But like it or not, they'd been heading for it since they met. Maybe he trusted her a little more now, maybe she trusted him a little more, too, because she didn't care so much about the whys of his presence in the bar. It had something to do with his misunderstanding of her role at Milwaukeedates. They'd work it out.

"Let me guess." She slid her arms up around his neck. "You have something to show me in your bedroom."

"As a matter of fact, I do." He took her hands down, keeping hold of one, and led her up three steps.

She followed, realizing how much she'd been wanting him and how hard she'd been fighting against that wanting. It was time now. For better or worse, no matter what happened, she needed to do this. "That woman from the bar better not be up there."

"I promise." Three more steps.

"Not your old girlfriend, either."

"I promise again." Three more, step, step, step.

"And you better not lead me on then kick me out."

"I promise that, too." Up at the top of the landing he turned and pulled her close, kissed her as if the interval their lips had been apart while they climbed the stairs had been unbearably long.

Which it had been.

"Answer me something, Candy."

"Mmm?"

"I need to know this." He stroked hair back from her face. "I've met a lot of women since I've been here. Through Troy mostly, but also a couple in bars, one at a Bucks game. Nice women. Beautiful women. Sexy women."

"That's plenty, thanks." She pretended to glare when he chuckled. "What about all these hundreds of gorgeous, perfect women?"

"Not much."

"And your point is…"

"My point is." He rested his forehead against hers. "Why you?"

She had to swallow before she could speak. He felt the pull, too, and was just as confused by it. "You promise it's not my sexy outfits?"

"Again with the promises!" He threw up his hands, let them slap down. "My God, you're demanding."

Candy giggled so hard she made a terrible snorting noise.

"Mmm, do that again," he whispered. "That is soo hot."

"Stop." She got her giggles under control. Barely. "Stop that."

Justin grinned with such tenderness she grew quiet and solemn almost immediately. A crazy hopeful shimmer started in her belly, spread down low and then up to threaten her heart.

He kissed her again, hands cupping her head, sweetly at first, then as their lips clung and parted, clung again, her shimmer turned warm, then hot. She didn't think she'd ever wanted anybody as much as she wanted this man, and if he felt even some of the same way, then she thought she understood what he meant when he asked, why her?

Why him? She didn't understand it either, not fully.

But right now, understanding wasn't as important as feeling. The thick softness of the hair at the nape of his neck, the smooth taut muscle covering his shoulders, the firm pressure of his mouth against her cheek, her temple, her lips, the warmth of his hands sliding under her shirt and exploring the bare skin of her back. He pulled her shirt over her head; she helped him, lifting her arms, dropping them back down to let her bra slide to the floor after he unhooked it with quick fingers.

He steadied her against him, pelvises joined, upper bodies apart. She knew he was looking at her half-nakedness, and she tried not to tense or wait for judgment.

But the way he said her name, with awe and desire, made her bold. She lifted her head and wondered why she'd been denying herself the pleasure of his face. He wasn't ogling or leering, but studying, admiring. He lifted one hand, palm flat, and slowly stroked it across her chest, barely brushing her nipples, the stimulation gentle but wildly arousing for its restraint.

Again, he passed his palm over, then back and again, until a moan broke from her. He smiled, eyes holding hers, his that magical deep brown. His palm curved, molded to her skin, his caresses grew more urgent. Candy moaned again, and arched back, pushing her pelvis against his, the bulge of his erection hard and tantalizing between her legs.

His smile vanished; his eyes glazed. He took her hand and led her over to his bed.

She stood waiting while he took off his shirt, unbuttoned his jeans and stepped out of them. She seemed caught in some spell that made her feel something significant and meaningful was about to happen between them that involved more than sex, which frightened and beckoned her with equal power.

He emerged from his clothes, muscular long thighs, broad chest covered lightly with hair she couldn't wait to touch, penis reaching toward her as if it had a mind of its own. He stood before her, unself-conscious, eyes reading her, still dark but no longer glazed. "You're sure you want this?"

"Oh, yes." She laughed at the understatement. "I'm just, I don't know, trying to take it all in emotionally."

She closed her eyes briefly. Take it all in emotionally? For heaven's sake, he was going to think she expected a ring.

"I know what you mean. Whatever else, it's always intense between us."

"Yes." She reached to trace a line down his arm, a lump in her throat. His beautiful features were too familiar somehow, more than they should be for the short time she'd known him.

He smiled slowly. Reached for her. "Hey, Candy."

"Mmm?"

"Let's make it even more intense."

"Yes." She rubbed her breasts against his chest lightly, loving the coarse tickle on her skin. She took off her glasses, pulled down her sensible professor pants and bent to lower her panties. On the way up to standing, she surprised him by taking the tip of his penis into her mouth, letting her tongue roll around its edges, savoring the baby-smoothness of the skin, the clean male taste and the drop of moisture that told her she was turning him on.

His body froze; his breathing quickened.

Again and again she played his tip with her tongue, then slid her lips the rest of the way down his erection, back out, down again, establishing a firm rhythm then varying the speed and pressure, keeping him off balance.

"Candy." He put a hand to the back of her head, riding on her rhythm. "You have no idea how good that feels and how sexy you look right now."

She twisted, opening her lips, pulling her tongue along the base of his penis, tipping her head back to meet his eye. She felt female and powerful, smiling wickedly at his helpless arousal, thrilled that she could please him this much.

When she was with Justin, she felt as if part of her really was Sexy Glamour Girl.

"Come here." His hands gripped her upper arms; he pulled her to standing. "You're making me feel greedy."

"I want you to feel good."

"I still will." He gestured her onto the mattress, retrieved a condom from his nightstand, tossed it onto the bed and followed. He lay next to her and drew her close, kissed her cheek, her chin, her breasts, briefly taking each nipple into his mouth for a gentle, sexy bite. His next kiss landed on her stomach, he turned on his hands and knees and moved his lips lower on her abdomen, his thigh up next to her shoulder.

Candy opened her legs, breathless with anticipation. She felt his warm breath on her open sex, then the quick playful flick of his tongue, once, twice. Her body shivered, jerked, then he settled into a rhythm that poured heat through her. She reached for his leg, brought his torso over her, and took him back into her mouth. The angle made it easier to draw him in farther; her arousal from his tongue's dance gradually increased the pace of her sucking to a frenzy. She lifted her hips while moving her head up and down, taking him deep, this angle, that one, not able to get enough. This contact, so uninhibited, both of them giving and receiving pleasure was new for her, new and wonderful.

She closed her eyes and disappeared into her other senses: the heat, the male smell and taste, the sounds of their pleasure, the rivers of desire flowing through her, and underneath it all, a glowing warmth.

He broke away suddenly; her eyes narrowed back into relief when she saw him diving for the condom. Impatience she understood—and shared.

Condom on, he climbed over her, positioned his erection at her entrance. She lifted, eager for him, and a shower of electric sparks settled over and through her as he sank slowly inside, the sensations thrilling not only her body but also her heart.

She wrapped her arms around his wide back, lifting against each thrust, panting as the in-and-out rhythm tugged on her clitoris.

There was a hot, animal edge to the way he rode her that surprised her, made her a little uneasy and turned her on beyond all reason. This was not polite I-love-you sex, this was raw and powerful, primal and exciting. He lifted himself onto his arms, changing his angle, and a new burst of lust flooded her. Then he balanced on one arm while the other explored her breasts.

She liked that, too; she liked it a lot, taking in short gasps of surprised pleasure when his rough fingers began to play with the line of pain.

"Am I hurting you?" he whispered. "It is too much?"

She shook her head, unable to believe what he was doing, what she was letting him do, how exciting it was that he had this mastery.

A minute later, when she was about to cry uncle, he rolled to the side, taking her with him, looped her top leg over his hip, gripping her thigh, still pushing into her. He kissed her while his hand traveled over her hip to the crevice between her buttocks and explored there, carefully, gently.

More new territory.

Candy made herself relax. Maybe there were still questions unanswered between them, but there was no doubt she trusted him here, with her body.

His finger slipped inside, kept rhythm with his penis; she gradually accepted the intrusion, then let the new sensations build, closing her eyes, breath stuttering as her body fought for oxygen with her oncoming climax. Her head lifted from the pillow; her cheeks burned. She gasped, gasped again, struggling against something she didn't understand, something bigger than what he was doing to her.

"Candy." His murmur was low, the tone strained. "I will carry the picture of your face right now with me forever."

His finger went deeper; her gasp sounded like a sob. She was so close now. So close.

"Let yourself go," he whispered. "Let me feel you coming. Grip me tighter, let me feel it."

She moaned and let go, the spasm flooding her with ecstasy.

"Yes. Like that." He waited out her pleasure, then rolled her urgently onto her back, put one leg outside hers. "Pull your thighs together."

She obeyed, desire still on high. He rode her again, clutching her legs between his, the friction of his thrusts increasing, building more desire.

"Justin."

His mouth covered hers; their tongues tangled; his breathing changed and she felt a deep satisfaction spreading through her. Her arms enfolded him, hands burying in his thick hair, and she suddenly had the answer to why she hadn't been able to stay away, why he drew her so profoundly: She was falling for him.

A shock burst through her at the same time his accelerated breathing peaked; he thrust in and held, releasing a groan she felt in her chest as keenly as she felt the pulsing inside her.

Falling for him? She barely knew him.

And yet somehow, without even understanding how it could be possible, she knew in her heart it was true.

12

CANDY LAID STILL UNDERNEATH Justin, hardly able to breathe, and not just because he'd gone heavy after his orgasm. She was falling for him. That was what this was all about. That's why after so many times being sure she wasn't going to give the man any more chances, she kept doing it. Because her subconscious knew he was a good thing, and it wouldn't let her give him up.

The subconscious was always supposed to be right, wasn't it?

Justin raised himself, made a quick trip to the bathroom and was back moments later.

"Exhausted?"

"Happy." He pulled her close, grinning. "I needed that."

She laughed, though fear curled her insides. Just the sex? "Me, too."

"Been a while?"

She nodded.

"Same here." He took her hand, laced their fingers, stroking her knuckle with his thumb. "But, boy, was it worth the wait."

Hope rose. With his face and body he'd be able to get lucky

as often as he wanted. "You probably could have gotten some much sooner from the woman in the bar."

The instant horror on his face cracked her up. "Candy, let me make this clear to you."

"Ye-es?"

"That was not going to happen. Ever." He squeezed her hand. "In fact, the second I saw you, however many weeks ago that was, I knew I was doomed. It was going to be you or nobody."

"Nobody?" She turned giddy in an instant. "So if I'd said no tonight, you would have gone the rest of your life without—"

"Geez." He feigned throwing the pillow at her. "Let me have my sentimental hyperbole, okay?"

"Yes." She nodded, her smile fading into tenderness she tried to hide. "Very okay."

"While *you*—" He scowled comically, pretending to be angry, but she felt something real, too "—you were out to get whatever you could from whomever you could all over town."

"No, no. I want to explain about that." She struggled up on her elbow, put her hand to his chest. "Marie pushed me to start dating, only I couldn't fill out the Milwaukeedates form because I felt as if I had a lot of sides to my personality and didn't know how to present myself."

"Go on." He was watching calmly, but he'd let go of her hand.

"So Marie suggested I put up four profiles and see which one felt the most natural. It was supposed to be for fun, not to confuse anyone. You were the only one who even noticed."

He moved restlessly, apparently still processing. "I see."

"You picked Sexy Glamour Girl, so that's who you kept getting. But Marie really thought we'd hit it off, and I really hoped we would, too." She rushed to finish. "That's it. The whole story."

"Okay." He ran his hand over his face. "That explains a lot."

"Now it's your turn." The fear came back, acid in her stomach. "What was going on tonight?"

He positioned a hand under his head and stared at the ceiling. "I had a roommate for a while in California, Bob Rondell. Bob had certain weird paranoias, one of which was that the dating site he signed up for hired hot women to tempt regular guys into keeping up their subscriptions by going out with them a few times, then disappearing and on to the next."

Candy recoiled. "You thought I was doing that?"

"Er. Maybe." He rubbed his chin sheepishly. "I did investigative journalism in California, and thought I was on to another scandal here."

"Oh, for—" She rolled her eyes. "You took *me* for a professional escort?"

"That night after the party you did try to seduce me."

"Argh!" She clapped her hands over her ears. "You thought I was coming on to you because of some financial arrangement?"

"Yes."

Candy didn't pretend to whack him with the pillow, she let him have it. Or tried to. He took one blow, stopped the next and had her on her back a split second later.

"Thought. I thought. Thought is past tense. And no, I could never quite become convinced."

"The subconscious knows, huh?"

"I guess so." Justin smiled lazily into her eyes. "You definitely fascinated me."

"Past tense!"

He kissed her mouth, her chin, her collarbone. "You fa-a-ascinate me."

"So if my seduction made me a pseudo call girl, what were you when you tried to seduce me?"

He pressed his lips together, thinking, then his face cleared. "Horny?"

She pretended to push him off her, giggling.

"No, no, sorry, fa-a-ascinated." He kissed her once more, rolled over and sat up, ran his hand down her thigh then back up. "I would like nothing more than to make love to you again right now, but two things are stopping me."

"One?"

"I'm starving."

"Two?"

"I'm thirsty."

"Me, three."

He climbed off the bed, pulled on boxers and a T-shirt, then threw her a clean one from his drawer. "Wear this? There's nothing sexier than a hot girl wearing only a cool T-shirt."

"Pervert." She pulled it on happily and thumped downstairs into his kitchen, a mirror image of hers, with the same tile and cabinet style. His counters, however, had been modernized to a warm, mottled beige finish that suited the room, and his sink was stainless steel where hers was still the old porcelain. As in the living room, he had plants on nearly every available surface.

She gestured to them. "Antidote to winter?"

"Bingo." He got down two glasses from his cabinet. "Juice? Tea? Coffee? Milk? Beer?"

"Juice sounds good. Orange?"

"Orange." He pulled out a carton and poured. "My mom's house was always full of plants. When we lived with Dad, we had someone care for them. In the house she and I moved to, if I hadn't stepped in they would have died. Mom was big on ideas, not so great on follow-through. I guess I got used to having them around."

"Like pets."

"But quieter. What would you like to eat?" He opened the refrigerator. "I have, let's see, homemade guacamole, tofu, hot dogs, sliced turkey—how about a turkey sandwich with guacamole and chips?"

"That sounds delicious." She sat at his kitchen table, making a mental note to buy plants and find some way to remind herself to take care of them. They were very cheering.

Justin pulled out a bowl of guacamole and set it on the table with a bag of tortilla chips. "Tell me about your family. I've talked about mine already."

She drank juice, loving the special intimacy of conversation after sex. "I grew up in Milwaukee, you knew that. Basic middle-class existence. No golf course near our house, but we did have a park nearby. I am the oldest, two younger brothers who got away with murder while I wasn't allowed to walk down the block without a bodyguard. I told you that already."

"Yup. Daddy's little girl. Mustard on your sandwich?"

"Please. And yes, Dad was over-the-top protective."

"Yellow, brown or Dijon?"

"Dijon."

"Whole grain or regular?"

She raised her brows. "The king of condiments! Regular is fine."

"Go on." He retrieved a jar from the refrigerator. "Dad kept you in chains and your brothers got away with everything."

"Right. Of course, all that did was make me want to get away from my parents and do whatever I wasn't supposed to."

"The paradox of teenagers, the more you control them, the less control you have." He put the mustard back. "Though if you don't try to control them at all, the result is the same, which was the case with me."

"I think when I have teenagers I'll hire someone else to deal with them."

"Oh, now there's a good plan." He put a sandwich down in

front of her, piled high with turkey, swiss cheese and romaine lettuce. "So you were wild, huh?"

She snorted. "Wild for me was telling them I was going over to Abigail's to study and then not studying."

"Whoa." He shook his head over his sandwich. "You're lucky you weren't arrested."

"I'll say. You said you weren't either."

"I came close once. My father intervened. But it scared me into declaring an end to my rebel days."

"How old?"

"Seventeen."

Candy imagined him at seventeen, coming into manhood, still struggling with his parents' divorce, taking out his anger in self-destructive ways until his natural good sense took over from the testosterone. She could still glimpse the juvenile delinquent in him now and then. So different from being with Chuck. Exciting and dangerous in a sexy way that felt safe.

"I don't think I ever really rebelled."

"No time like the present." He winked at her. "If what went on upstairs just now was any indication I'd say you have plenty of wild child in you."

She giggled, torn between embarrassment and pleasure. "I don't know."

"Do you remember when you said you jumped out of that cake with nearly nothing on?"

"God, yes, that was so funny."

"No, Candy." He lowered his sandwich. "That was not funny. I am getting hard again. Like the first time you told me."

She could only stare. She remembered telling him, but it hadn't been sexy at all. "You jumped off the couch like I'd horrified you."

"It was either jumping off the couch or jumping you. And I wasn't quite at the point where I felt comfortable doing that. Which we've already gone into."

"Yes." She squeezed her thighs together under the table. The idea that he'd had to hold himself back from her was very sexy.

"Do you still have the outfit?"

"The pasties? Ugh, yes, I kept them somewhere, hidden well away. I think I brought them out one Valentine's Day, but…" She shrugged. Chuck had been mortified. He wouldn't even look at her in the outfit, said it was cheap and beneath her.

"But what?"

"They didn't have the intended effect." She wasn't going to set Chuck up for anyone else to tear down. "Another Valentine's Day disaster."

"You've had lots?"

"Well not lots, really. My ex wasn't into the holiday. So we never did the roses-and-chocolates-and-fancy-dinner thing, which was always my girlhood fantasy. And disappointments always seemed to plague the day for family and friends, too. What about you? What do you think of Valentine's Day? Silly commercial manipulation or chance for all-out romance?" She waited, hating that his answer already mattered so much.

"I don't think I was ever in a serious relationship on Valentine's Day, so I acknowledged it but never went all out." He frowned and crunched down on a chip. "I can't say I'm against it on principle, but I have to feel love to celebrate it."

"That makes sense." She wished she hadn't brought it up. Valentine's Day was four days away and now they were sort of involved. Would he want to celebrate it with her? She took a bite of sandwich, chewed self-consciously, aware he was studying her, wondering what he was thinking.

"So you still have those pasties, huh?"

Laughter made Candy cover her mouth to keep her sandwich inside. "Mm-hm."

"Wear them for me sometime?"

"The G-string, too?" She wrinkled her nose when he

nodded, though she was happy to hear at least that he was planning to get naked with her again. "They're *so* ridiculous."

"Trust me. On you they would not look ridiculous."

She made a dismissive gesture, but had already started glowing inside. He did that glowing thing to her fairly often. She could get used to it. "You're sweet to—"

"I'm not being sweet." He pushed his plate out of his way, leaned forward on his elbows; the potency in his eyes convinced her. "Tell me what the costume looked like. Exactly."

"Exactly?" Her urge to giggle was incinerated by his gaze. "It was…tiny."

"Tiny." The gaze traveled to her breasts, which tightened under his T-shirt. "How tiny?"

"The top was just hearts. Red ones. Sequined. The size of apricots."

"How did you get them to stick?"

"Double-sided tape. I was too embarrassed to wear only the pasties so I sewed straps to their edges and tied them around my neck and back. It looked like a super-tiny bikini clinging to the tips of my breasts."

He reached down under the table, adjusted, brought his hand back up again. "Tell me more."

"The bottom was another heart. With fabric strings."

"Thong?"

"Yes."

"How many guys were there?"

"About a dozen."

"Tell me what they did when they saw you."

"Shouted a lot. Stared a lot." She didn't tell him she'd been so convinced she looked ridiculous that she'd jumped out of the damn cake nearly in tears, and had been astounded by the roar of approval.

"What did you do?"

"There was loud music. I danced, or more accurately undulated, for a while, kissed the groom, then got the hell out of there."

"Did he touch you?"

"He grabbed my ass when I kissed him. Both cheeks."

"Take off your shirt. Slowly."

She caught her breath, reached down and pulled it off, the warm air of his kitchen teasing her breasts, but not as much as his eyes did. "Will there be anything else, sir?"

"Stand up."

She stood, mutely waiting, getting crazy turned-on.

"Show me where the top was on your body."

She drew hearts around her nipples, taking her time, one breast first, then trailing her finger through the middle of her cleavage moving to the other."

"Now the bottom."

She traced the bottom, heart-shaped over her naked sex, then turned and jutted out her rear, followed the path of the thong.

His breath hissed in sharply; his chair scraped back. Strong hands caught her around the waist and swung her toward the table where she landed bent over, supported on her hands, head tipped so her hair tumbled nearly to the abandoned bag of chips. She swept it away, moved the dishes, felt him parting her legs farther, heard the swish of lowering boxers, the unrolling of another condom. Then the rigid push of his penis inside her, an inch at a time, stopping instantly when she gave a gasp.

"Hurting?"

"No, no, keep going." It did hurt a little, but the pain was part of the pleasure, the thrill of being taken like this by someone she trusted.

She felt again that swell of emotion that she'd fought for so long. Love? Maybe. But wilder and freer than anything she'd felt before. *She* felt wilder and freer than anything she'd felt before.

He started to move; she braced herself against the tabletop, pushing back against him, bumping savagely into his pelvis each time, relishing the grunts and moans, the animal nature of their coupling.

And yet…

His hands were gentle, reverent, stroking her back, long sweeps over her muscles, then under and across to tease her breasts with light caresses. The combination was pure aphrodisiac, everything she could want: passion, lust, but also respect and consideration.

She could only hope more came with that.

But with that hope also came the startling realization that more had already come with that. She liked herself again. The strength she'd been needing to put her relationship with Chuck on the shelf had become part of her. She'd found within herself a solid foundation of sanity and self-reliance. Ironic that by engaging her heart, Justin had also given it freedom and independence.

Whether he ended up falling in love with her or dumping her back onto her single butt—either way, from now on Candy Graham was going to be fine.

MARIE WALKED INTO ROOTS, not sure if she hoped Quinn would be there or not. On the one hand, she did want to see him. She was upset. This guy Troy had shown up at Milwaukeedates.com, and after Marie had done all she could to help him realize what he wanted, and help him see how they could get him there, it turned out he was a friend of Justin's.

Even during their interview something had been nagging her. Only later when she connected him to Justin, did she figure out the parallel. Both had been closed off, analyzing her more than wanting to be analyzed, and only after careful prodding on her part did they reluctantly get to a place where they seemed sincere about wanting to find someone. Troy's last girlfriend was playing manipulative games, so he was obviously drawn to female strength, which was why Marie showed him Candy's Superwoman profile. He needed that female strength to be decent and true, not bullying that covered insecurity.

Marie had sincerely thought Troy might be a good way to get Candy back on the horse, so to speak, and that Candy, hurting from Justin's disinterest, might be just what Troy needed.

But his reaction to seeing Candy's profile had been Marie's next tip-off that something wasn't right. He'd stared at the picture for a few seconds, then fixed Marie with a look that had baffled her at the time. Accusation or contempt, maybe? No reaction she'd ever seen before to a beautiful woman. Then he'd launched into a bizarre rant about how gorgeous she was and how he couldn't wait to go out with her.

Marie was still baffled. Justin got tired of Candy so decided to pass her on to his friend? If that was the case, why go through a dating site? Why not just introduce her to Troy? If Justin found out about the duplicate profiles, why didn't he talk to Candy about it or come to Marie? Why send a friend? Nothing made sense, but whatever Justin was playing at, Marie didn't like it.

Nor did she enjoy the current dilemma: whether to call Candy about all this. That's where she thought Quinn might be able to help her. He knew how men thought—particularly manipulative or predatory men—and might be able to shed some light on what Justin could be thinking, and how much Marie should tell Candy to protect her.

She slid onto a chair at the bar, smiled at Joe and ordered a Prufrock, uncomfortable with her reasoning. If Marie didn't know Quinn, she'd talk the problem over with girlfriends, who would serve her well. She was afraid she was now making up excuses to speak to him. Not good.

Darcy had finally called back with the expected rejection of the idea of meeting Quinn, even for coffee, and Marie had been guiltily relieved. Not good either. Her feelings were confused enough where Quinn was concerned. She couldn't let a silly, unrequited crush get in the way of a match she was convinced would be good both for Darcy and Quinn. She needed to settle herself firmly into the "sister" role he saw her in, and treat him like the brother figure she'd said he was.

Half an hour later, he still hadn't showed. Marie shame-facedly ordered a sandwich and another drink, knowing she should have gone home to prove she hadn't become so hung up on a guy that she'd deliberately change her routine to put herself in his way, a tactic she associated with junior high school. But she'd ordered the sandwich and the second drink, now she was stuck finishing them.

Right. Because it was illegal to order food and leave?

A few bites into the sandwich, Quinn showed up, easing his athletic frame into the seat next to her, causing a rogue blush to climb onto her cheeks and have itself a nice ride around her face.

"Hey, Marie. I'm late tonight, huh?"

"Are you?" She glanced at her watch, hating herself for playing such a silly game. Why couldn't she just say *Yes, I waited for you so long I got hungry?* Friends could say something like that easily. "I guess you are."

Oh, Marie.

"You didn't miss me?"

She made herself smile at him. Deep breath, too. "Of course I did. I waited so long I got hungry."

It didn't work. The words, which were supposed to come out lightly, caught in her throat and sounded like blame. Exactly the way people acted when they started to imagine themselves into more of a relationship than they were in. How often had she counseled clients out of that trap?

"I got tied up at the office."

Classic male cover for "I've been with a woman," though,

ha, the tied-up part could be true. Now he was showing up to chat with his sister-clone with another women's scent still—

Stop. Stop now. Marie pushed away her drink and summoned every ounce of strength she'd developed over the last years as a scorned wife turned entrepreneur. "That's nice. Especially since you don't have an office."

He laughed. "Can't get anything past you."

"Hey, Quinn, the usual?" Joe put a napkin in front of him.

"Yes, thanks." He swiveled his chair so he was half facing Marie. "How've you been since Saturday? We were going to go to dinner sometime. I haven't forgotten."

"I've been okay." She ignored the dinner part. If he wanted to go, he'd have to issue a real invitation, not a general intention. "I have sort of an issue at work right now, with a friend."

"Yeah?" He nodded absently to Joe, pulling the drink toward him, but his attention was all on Marie. "Can you talk about it?"

"I set a friend up with someone I'm discovering might not have the world's best intentions. And I'm not sure what my duty to her is, since it's mostly instinct on my part, nothing really wrong, just a few things that aren't adding up."

"Hmm." He moved his fingers restlessly on the bar. He had fine hands, large and capable-looking. Of course. Couldn't he have a weight problem or a shriveled limb to put him more on her level? "Is she the type men can take advantage of?"

"Can and have."

"Are you close to her?"

"We're friendly. Both members of Women in Power. We have lunch once in a while. But not girlfriend-close, no."

"What's your instinct?"

Marie laughed. "Besides visiting the gentleman in question with a castrating device?"

"Oof." Quinn pressed his legs together. "I like the mama-bear loyalty. The punishment, not so much. So yes, besides that."

"My instinct is to call her and warn her. I don't think they're dating right now, but last I talked to her, she was hurting and likely to crawl back if he beckoned. She really likes him. My other instinct is to mind my own business and let her make her own mistakes. My other *other* instinct is to admit I don't know this guy at all, and trust her to do the right thing."

"Those all sound like good instincts, Marie. The initial one, the other one and even the other *other* one."

"Thanks." She pretended frustration, hiding pleasure at his compliment. "I just don't know which good instinct is the one to listen to."

"Well, if I can offer a suggestion?"

"Please. I'd like your opinion."

"As a man."

She turned away, played with the straw in her drink, then realized she was pulling it up and down suggestively. "As a friend."

"Okay. As a friend."

Was she crazy or did he sound disappointed? She snuck a peek at his smooth, untroubled face.

She was crazy.

"My advice would be to lay the case in front of her without giving judgment or opinion, and let her make her own decision. To hold back feels wrong, and to jump to some conclusion and warn her off without knowing all the facts feels wrong, too. It's a middle-lane approach, and this way you don't risk clouding anything with emotion."

Right. Clouding things with emotion. Good advice. She needed to keep it in mind herself.

"Thanks, Quinn. I think you're right. I'll do that."

"You're welcome. How's that sandwich?"

She relaxed all of a sudden. "Delicious. Want a bite?"

"I was thinking of ordering my own and joining you for dinner."

"By all means." She smiled and raised her glass to him, not even flinching when two young, attractive women sat at the bar and elbowed each other, staring at Quinn.

Friendship was good, dependable and something he'd give her that he'd never give those younger babes. Marie would just concentrate on enjoying it.

13

CANDY CAREFULLY SPREAD buttercream frosting onto another cupcake, butt-boogying in time to Sheryl Crow's "All I Wanna Do" blasting from her iPod in its docking station. She could barely concentrate on what she was doing. Every ten or twenty seconds her body was urging her to break into a giddy dance all around her kitchen, then into the living room, then back. Valentine's Day was a day away and she was finally dating a man who might enjoy celebrating it with her. Worse, February was doing one of those spring-is-coming teases, temperatures nearing fifty, sun pouring over the city, snow shrinking and steaming like the Wicked Witch of the West in her final moments.

Who could work under conditions like this? Completely inhumane to expect it. However, Mrs. Abernathy's party had to go on; she was a good customer who loved to entertain, so Candy would work.

The phone? Candy rushed to turn down the iPod for some quiet. Yes, phone. She shouldn't answer. She should finish the cupcakes so she could take them to Mrs. Abernathy's house and make sure everything was in order for tomorrow, even the tacky Cupid costumes.

What if it was Justin?

She ran for the phone, peered at caller ID. Yes! It was him. Oh, she was weak.

"Hi there." Her voice sounded bubbly and young.

"You been out running?" His voice was deep and male and sent through her body chills that guaranteed her voice would become even more breathless.

"No, I'm…I ran to get the phone." She rolled her eyes. Yeah, for someone who did three miles a day, running several feet would be enough to wind her. "And I'm frantically busy."

"I can call back if you—"

"No!" She'd been trying to explain the breathlessness, not cut the call short. "It's fine. I was needing a break."

"What are you doing?"

"Frosting cupcakes."

"Yum. What kind?"

"Chocolate."

"And the frosting?"

"Buttercream."

"Mmm. That gives me an idea."

She sank onto a stool, her body coming alive at his tone. "What's that, Justin?"

"Why don't you come over with your frosting and find out?"

She closed her eyes, imagining him spreading the creamy softness onto her breasts, his warm tongue licking it off. "Oh, my."

"You'll come?"

"Getting close just thinking about it."

"Same here."

"But…" Candy snapped herself briskly out of the daydream. "I can't."

"Cold water on my hot fantasy!"

"I know, I'm cruel. I have to get these cupcakes done, then

delivered to Mrs. Abernathy, and while I'm there check on the decorations and food and music and…you get the picture."

"It's not as much fun as the other picture I was getting."

"I know." Candy sighed wistfully.

"Can I see you tomorrow night?"

"Well, sure." She tried to sound perky and casual. *Valentine's Day. Of course!* But how would he want to celebrate?

"Restaurants will be jammed, but we can get takeout, maybe hang out and watch a movie?"

"Sure, that sounds great." It would be. She'd tell herself that firmly and mean it. Much too soon in their relationship for her to be expecting him to put on the Ritz. He'd said he only did that if he felt love. Hanging out with her was plenty. Candy was not going to go all spoiled-brat disappointed over this.

"We could watch some classic like…"

In spite of herself, she waited hopefully for a romance title: *Sleepless in Seattle? Casablanca? Romeo and Juliet?*

"One of the early *Star Wars* movies."

Star Wars. Was there any possible way that could be considered romantic?

No.

At least they could have good food. Maybe she could contribute the meal. Smoked oysters or salmon, beef tenderloin, raspberries, some kind of French pastry or—

"With take-out pizza."

That was fine. Pizza was fine. Practical certainly. They could eat it by candlelight maybe.

"I was also thinking…"

"Yes?" She was still hopeful. Ever hopeful.

"…of all the things I'll want to do to you after the movie."

She smiled. Now they were talking. Many guys who couldn't express romantic feelings substituted sexual ones.

This was not a bad thing. And the way her body reacted to him was definitely not a bad thing.

"You mean like…" She pitched her voice into sultry territory. "Make me clean up the kitchen?"

"Oh, *yeah,* that's what I'm talking about."

She clamped down laughter, spirits rising again. "I'll scrape your scraps, boy. Scrub your stubborn spots."

"Mmm, tell me more."

"Then I'll rub down all your surfaces. And if you're really good…"

"Ye-e-es?"

"I'll squeeze your sponges." She had to pull the phone away from her mouth to let out a snort.

"You know you are turning me on, Candy. Even joking around."

"Really?" She returned to her normal voice, or as normal as her voice could get when she was euphoric and turned on herself.

"Really. Want to do me a favor?"

"I probably shouldn't. What is it?"

"Go into your living room and sit on your couch."

"Justin…"

"Hey, bay-bee, you know you want to."

She laughed at the cliché and the grin in his voice. "Tell me you didn't just say that."

"Say what? I didn't say anything." He made a crackly noise. "Bad connection."

"Uh-huh. What will I do on the couch?"

"Show me your beautiful cushions."

She burst into more laughter. When had she ever had this much fun talking to a guy on the phone? "What's in it for me?"

"An orgasm that will bring human sexual consciousness to a new level?"

"My goodness." She shouldn't do this. But she had a feeling she would.

"Seriously, I don't want to bug you, Candy. If you have things you have to do, do them."

"Don't you have a chapter to write?"

"I tried. Believe me. But all I could think about was how you look, how you taste, how you feel around me. It's hopeless."

"Hopeless, huh?" It was anything but.

"And you've been frosting just fine, I suppose."

"Just fine. No problems." She sauntered into her living room, perched on the edge of her sofa. "I seem to be sitting on my couch."

"Yeah? Hmm. I think you're wearing too many clothes."

"How do you know what I'm wearing?"

"I'm at my window. I can see your head and shoulders. White shirt. Long sleeves."

She turned and found him standing at his second-floor window, phone pressed to his ear. He waved. A car passed. Otherwise the block was silent and still.

She took off her shirt.

"You're beautiful."

His voice was low, reverent. She shivered in delight. "Do you get to keep your clothes on?"

"Yes. Keep going."

She unhooked her bra, slid it off, listening to his breathing accelerate slightly. "Done."

"Now pants."

"I'll have to stand up."

"If anyone walks by I'll tell you."

She hesitated only for a second then stood, took down her jeans and stepped out of them.

"Panties. Slowly."

She worked them down. Between the room's cool air and the imagined heat of Justin's gaze, so private in a public venue, she could feel every inch of her skin in sensuous detail.

Panties got twirled around her finger and tossed across the room. He gave a half laugh, half groan. "Perfect. You're perfect."

She kept her back to him, glanced at the street, one way then the other. No one. She turned slowly and stood, feeling stupidly naked and vulnerable until she heard his reaction, a long, low sound that flooded through her body and focused her attention on the way he made her feel—strong, female and powerful, the rest of the block be damned. She wanted him shamelessly, his skin against hers, his tongue and breath and fingers all over her.

"Touch yourself."

"Where?"

"You choose."

"I could be arrested."

"You won't be."

She started shyly, using her finger to draw a line up the middle of her stomach.

"Mmm, yes, like that."

His words gave her courage. She flattened her hand and passed it gently over the tips of her breasts, brushing her nipples the way he had their first night. His low moan made her smile.

"You're watching out for people?"

"No one will see you but me."

A new song started, "It's Only Love." Candy closed her eyes and swayed back and forth, humming softly. *I think I met my match again.*

"You're killing me."

"Yeah?" She cupped her breasts and pushed them up, offering them to him, circling her nipples with her thumbs, enjoying the stimulation, enjoying his pleasure more. She could see him at his window, one arm bent over his head, leaning on the glass, the rest of his body solid and still, broad shoulders tapering to his jeans. She focused on remembering the feel of his erection between her legs, reliving the instant before he slid inside her the first time, so soft and so strong, insistent, unyielding.

The memory sent tingles down between her legs. She sent her fingers after them; the tingles became an unbearable ache. "Justin."

"Mmm."

"I want you inside me."

His breath drew in sharply over the phone. "What about your cupcakes?"

"Screw the cupcakes."

"Tempting as that is…"

"Come over, Justin," she whispered. "I'm naked and wet and I want you."

She disconnected the call; his form disappeared from the window. A few seconds later, he was striding out his back door, down his driveway, a man on a mission. She lay down on the couch, legs open, not a way she'd ever greeted any man before, but it felt completely safe.

Her front door opened. Closed. He appeared around the corner and she caught her breath as she always did. He walked toward her, taking off his shirt. A few more steps and his pants were unbuttoned, unzipped; his cock emerged, fully erect. He put a condom on in record time, knelt between her legs. His palm landed possessively over her sex; she squirmed impatiently against the warm pressure. "Do I need to wait, Candy?"

"No." She shook her head, pulled her knees up to her shoulders, caught in the upsurge of lust and vulnerability that made her feel sexually daring and emotionally shy. "Don't wait."

He broke their gaze to look down, hands on either side of her hips. "You are so beautiful spread for me like that."

"Come inside me."

"Now?" He took hold of his erection, used the tip to rub

against her, up to her clit, around her sex, back up again, teasing her with the promise of his first thrust.

"Please." She tried to wiggle forward but he held her back with a firm hand on her sternum, rubbing, circling, teasing, pushing in an inch, pulling out and circling again. "Justin."

Another inch. She reached between his legs, encircled his penis and tried to pull it farther into her. When he resisted, she reached farther, took his balls in her hand and squeezed gently, manipulated the small pebbles in the larger, softer sac. His body stiffened. He closed his eyes.

She had him, tugging, twisting gently, then skimming the outline of the bundle, making him shudder with pleasure. She took hold again, used her thumb to stroke the sensitive spot on the underside of his penis at the base, where the skin changed texture.

He clenched his jaw; his breathing became labored. When she thought she'd tortured him to the point of desperation, she lay back, knees bent up again, spread wide for him.

"Now, Justin," she whispered.

He plunged to the hilt, where he stayed, arms flung around her, pushing her back against the soft cushions of the couch with his body, keeping her there, still and silent except for their ragged breathing. Candy's body caught fire, nerve endings registering every sensation, from the bulk of his cock filling her to the strength of him pinning her to the couch, to the warmth of his uneven exhale against her cheek.

His hips moved; he pulled slowly, slowly out, tugging deliciously at the walls of her vagina, then reentered, slowly again, still holding her captive.

Again, pull out. Push in. She wanted more, wanted to come; she couldn't bear to be still any longer, yet couldn't bear to move and break the spell. But it wasn't enough, this slow slide; she had to have more.

"Harder," she whispered. "Please, harder."

He wouldn't, the bastard, but kept up the easy slide while

heat built through her, teasing and simmering, still not enough to get to a full boil. Her head fell back in frustration, her lips parted. He took advantage, kissing her, his tongue entering her mouth, withdrawing for a sweeter kiss, then entering again, sending her even higher.

Finally when she was on the brink of clawing and biting, his thrusts began to build in speed and intensity until she *was* clawing and biting, desperate for the release she knew he was about to give her. He pulled away; she protested, missing his warmth and closeness, but his thumb found her clitoris and she gave in to her climb to the top, watching him watching the pleasure on her face, then looking down at their joining, his hard length disappearing, reemerging, disappearing again, his thumb working her.

Candy went over the edge, crying out; he lunged, caught himself bent-armed on the back of the couch, pushed roughly, lost control of his breathing, then gave a hoarse moan and sank into her one more time.

She loved him. This had been raunchy, wonderful sex, not the tender and emotional kind an announcement like that would fit, but she loved him. She wanted to open her mouth and tell him, but fear held her back. Just because her feelings had come rushing up with her orgasm didn't mean he felt it, too. She felt love; he felt pizza and a movie.

"Candy." He helped her put her stiff legs down, gathered her in his arms; she burrowed there, drinking in his scent and proximity. "I don't know if you figured it out yet, but you turn me on."

She swallowed the thickness in her throat and smiled. Yes, she knew she turned him on. But she wanted to do a lot more than that. "It was incredible."

Really incredible. She loved him. Crazy loved him. She couldn't stop thinking it; her heart was bursting with the knowledge.

"I'm sorry I took you away from your cupcakes." His expression turned confused. "Wait, what am I saying? No, I'm not."

She laughed, giving his joke its due, made sure her voice was clear and light when she answered. "I'm not either."

"I suppose you need to get back to them now."

She didn't give a crap about the cupcakes. She wanted to go upstairs with him and lie in bed the rest of the afternoon, the rest of the evening, the rest of her life.

"That's what I thought." He'd mistaken her silence, pulled out of her gently and got to his feet, found her clothes and started putting his on.

She dressed, too: panties, bra, jeans, shirt, socks, slippers, thanks for the afternoon delight and goodbye.

At her front door, he pulled her into his arms. "I hate leaving. I want to stay in bed with you the rest of the day. The rest of the night, in fact."

The rest of our lives? "Me, too."

He kissed her, tenderly, sweetly, lingeringly, put his forehead against hers. "Tomorrow, okay?"

Valentine's Day. "Yes."

"We'll have fun."

"We will."

He kissed her again. "I'm glad I found you, Candy. This feels so good. And so…good."

"Well, good." She grinned up at him. Had he been about to say something else? "That's good."

"Yeah, um, yeah." He rolled his eyes, chuckling. "I'm getting out of here, I promise."

"Bye." She shut the door after him and collapsed against it, momentarily drained. Then, like a smitten teenager, she ran to her living room and peeked through the window to watch him walk home.

When he disappeared from view, she reluctantly returned to the kitchen without paying the slightest attention to what she was doing until she found herself washing the bowl and realized the last dozen or so cupcakes were frosted. Next task: she filled a piping bag with red gel icing and started forming groups of hearts on each.

The phone rang. She started and hurried to check.

Not Justin. Marie.

"Hey, Candy girl, what's going on?"

"Frosting is going on. What's up with you?" More than frosting was going on. Much more. She was falling for a terrific guy and didn't know whether he was falling for her or if he ever would.

"I want to talk to you about Justin."

Now there was a coincidence. Except Marie wasn't sounding happy about the prospect. "What about him?"

"A guy named Troy came into my office the other day."

"I know Troy." Candy picked up her piping bag again. "I recommended he contact you. I'm glad he went. He can't get his old girlfriend out of his system."

"*You* sent him to me?"

"Yes. Did you find someone for him?"

"Uh-huh."

"Oh, good! Tell me about her."

"She's about your height, your body type, your coloring, your personality, your address, your phone number…"

"You matched him up with *me?*" Candy readjusted the phone between her ear and shoulder. "I don't think that's going to work."

"Candy, he was delighted. More than delighted. Euphoric."

"He…was?" She frowned. He hadn't seemed anything more than polite to her at Justin's party. She didn't get an "interested" vibe at all.

"Justin is his friend, right?"

"Yes, they're writing the book together." She started to see what Marie was driving at. "No, no, he seems like a complete sweetheart. Not the type to move in on his friend's love interest."

"I thought you weren't Justin's love interest anymore."

"Oh, um, well. That changed." She couldn't help her smile. "Radically."

"Oh."

Decided lack of enthusiasm.

"It's fine, really, Marie. In fact, it's wonderful. He thought—" Candy sighed. How was she going to explain all this? "He was investigating me. And you."

She managed to get the rest of the story told. But where she expected Marie to laugh with relief that Justin was shooting straight, her friend was oddly quiet.

"So he was dating you only as a means to a story?"

"Not only, but yes. It explains all his cold/hot behavior, everything." For some reason she felt a little sick, and it wasn't from too much frosting on an empty stomach.

"You really like this guy, huh." It wasn't a question.

"I do." Candy had to wipe her eyes with the sleeve of her decorating smock. She couldn't believe she was getting even this close to a second chance after a relationship as special as what she had had with Chuck. She must have felt this alive and exciting and new with Chuck at the beginning, too. Though it seemed most of her memories were of feeling quietly content.

"Can you trust him, Candy?"

"Yes." She answered too quickly, with too much emphasis. "I mean as much as…"

"As much as you can trust anyone who has been manipulating you."

Candy sighed. Why did her friends work so hard to burst all her bubbles? First about Chuck, now about Justin. "I think he's telling the truth this time, Marie. I know he is."

"Okay. It's just that after Chuck…"

"What about Chuck?"

"I'm sorry. I've already said too much."

Candy abandoned her cupcakes. "You don't trust my judgment, is that it?"

"I didn't say that." Marie's voice lacked conviction.

"Not in exact words, no." She banged the piping bag onto the table. Red gel squirted onto her white work surface where it would need to be wiped immediately or it would leave a stain. Her body was shaking—from anger, from fear, or some combination. Which meant her friend had hit a hot button. What? She didn't trust Justin? She didn't trust her own judgment?

"Candy, I am sorry. Truly. I'm butting in once again where I don't belong. I just don't want you to be hurt. Please be careful."

Candy took a deep breath, then another. "I will be."

She ended the call, furious that her beautiful idyllic mood had to be spoiled by anything as ridiculous as caution and maturity and common sense.

Yes, she loved the fantasy of love as much as the next person. Which was probably partly why she'd always wanted an over-the-top Valentine's Day. Maybe she had idealized her relationship with Chuck to a certain extent. Maybe she was in danger of doing it again with Justin.

But she couldn't believe he was manipulating her. Not after what they shared last night and just now.

The phone rang again. Justin this time. It had to be. He'd make her feel better, get rid of this ridiculous self-doubt.

No, an unlisted number. "Hello?"

"Candy Cane. It's me."

Her eyes bugged wide. *Oh, my God.* Not Justin. *Chuck.*

"You there, honey?"

Honey? "I'm here."

"I thought I'd give you a call to say hi. It's been so long, and I've missed you. I wanted to hear how you were doing."

"I—" How to answer that with any honesty and coherence

when Chuck was asking? *Chuck!* Candy couldn't believe she was hearing his voice. And yet, oddly, it had always seemed impossible she never would again. "I'm fine."

"Do you miss me?"

What the hell? If he'd asked her that a month ago, maybe even a couple of weeks ago... "What's going on with Kate?"

"That's over, baby. I was crazy. It's not the same. She wasn't—I made a mistake."

Candy closed her eyes, trying to control her temper. "A mistake? Breaking my heart into tiny splinters and stomping all over them was a *mistake?*"

"It took losing you to realize what we had."

Her temper refused to be held back any longer. "Sounds like it took losing *her* to make you realize what we had. You lonely now, Chuck? Life not as fun as it was?" She thought of all those long nights she'd spent crying in bed, trying to understand why he'd left her, how he could have given up on something so special.

"I don't blame you for being angry. But I'd like to see you." He was clearly off balance, surprised by her reaction. What did he think, that she'd come running back without so much as a second thought? Is that how little he respected her or thought she respected herself? She was shaking with fury; she couldn't believe the clean, hard depth of it.

"I'm really busy, Chuck. I'm sorry."

"Are you seeing someone?"

"Yes. I am."

"It's not like it was with us, is it?"

Candy couldn't respond intelligently. Apples and oranges. Someone solid and dependable she'd known for years, some- one new and exciting she'd only recently met.

"I know how that is, Candy, when someone seems fresh and fascinating. You think it's the real thing so you follow it. But it's not, it's like a soap bubble, enticing for a while, but it doesn't last. I see that clearly now. Candy, honey, what we had was meant to last forever. You told me that when I told you I was leaving, remember?" His voice broke. "I wish I'd listened to you. You were right."

"Chuck…" Her anger started to fizzle out. Deep sadness and regret waited to take its place.

"I need to see you to believe there's no hope for us anymore. If I don't give our relationship this last shot, I'll be wondering for the rest of my life if I should have tried harder."

Candy's heart threatened to thaw like the snow outside. She'd never heard Chuck sounding this emotional, or this humble. Or this wise.

"I'll always be wondering, Candy." His voice slowed. "And so will you. You know it's true."

A prickle of irritation. He'd always defined her emotions for her. She recognized the annoyance immediately but had never understood its source, instead assuming she was annoyed at being caught in the wrong. But she wasn't wrong this time. He'd had his chance with her and she'd been as devoted to him as she knew how until he found his soap bubble and ran. What more was there to say? Candy was starting something with Justin. Chuck had no place here.

"I'm sorry, Chuck. I don't think it's appropriate. I wish you everything wonderful in your life, but I can't be part of it anymore."

"You don't mean that. You told me you'd always love me. Were you lying?"

"No, but…" Candy started to feel desperate and confused. Also a familiar feeling. Now he was telling her what she meant. And accusing her. "Of course I wasn't lying. Not at the time. But you said you'd always love me, too, and then one day you didn't."

"Honey, I explained that to you." His voice gentled. She wanted to sock him through the phone. Justin never made her feel stupid. Only sexy and beautiful and smart.

"I'm sorry, Chuck. The answer is no." She hung up the phone, picked up the piping bag and wiped up the spilled gel, which had left a red stain on her counter, a small misshapen heart.

She finished piping hearts onto the cupcakes, somehow getting them right, even with shaking hands. She went over to Mrs. Abernathy's house and decorated, hearts and tinsel everywhere, red flowers, white lights, silver cupids. She smiled and chatted, mind barely clear enough to function, always churning in the background: Chuck, Justin, Chuck, Justin.

She'd done the right thing rejecting Chuck, hadn't she? The emotional fallout since she'd hung up on him had been considerable. First contact in a year with a man she didn't think she'd ever get over until these powerful feelings had started for Justin. And yet Chuck also had powerful feelings for Kate, powerful enough to sacrifice Candy to them, and here he was again, realizing as she'd always been certain he would, that what Chuck and Candy had had together couldn't be replaced.

Back home she fell into bed early, even knowing she wouldn't be able to sleep, wishing Justin would call and hoping he wouldn't. Too much confusion. Chuck, Justin, Valentine's, *Star Wars*…

The doorbell rang. Justin. She leaped out of bed, then stood frozen for a second, trying to figure out what she'd say to him, how she'd react, whether she should tell him about Chuck.

Argh! She was too exhausted and confused to figure it out. She'd make it up as she went along. Justin would probably help her.

Not bothering to put on a bathrobe, she prowled downstairs in her short cotton nighty, and peered through the peephole before she opened the door, just to be sure.

Not Justin.

Chuck.

14

JUSTIN CAREFULLY ACCEPTED the giant bouquet over the counter from the grinning florist. A dozen red roses, long-stemmed, thorns carefully trimmed, buds velvety soft and vivid against the greenery backdrop, white baby's breath peeping delicately out of the bundle. Had he overdone it? He wasn't sure.

He'd bought flowers for women before on Valentine's Day, but had always avoided red roses, the floral symbol for passionate love. He'd felt passion before, he'd felt love, but nothing like this combination. His feelings for Angie paled in comparison—what he'd mistaken as depth of emotion had merely been jealousy and uncertainty, fear and lust, which produced enough adrenaline and longing to fool him.

What he felt for Candy had a solid foundation holding it steady. They shared personal stories easily, they had similar temperaments, humor and values. He loved her creative spirit, her enthusiasm for finding the fun in any activity. He loved her serious thoughtful side, and yes, no surprise, he loved that she gave him her body in a wild, uninhibited way that would keep him coming back for the rest of time.

But her heart—she was still guarding that. Not that he could blame her. He hadn't been able to express the depth of his feelings either. It was too soon, they'd both been hurt too recently and had a bumpy start to their relationship. He'd let the roses speak for him and cross his fingers she'd welcome such a declaration. Admittedly, he was a little queasy still, even with all the plans in place. More than the flowers, he'd planned fancy chocolates and dinner out at one of Milwaukee's finest, satisfying her Valentine's Day fantasy.

The perfect evening? Or too much too soon? Would she melt in his arms or panic and bolt? Did she really prefer his red-herring plan of *Star Wars* and pizza?

An elderly man wearing a parka so huge it practically swallowed him came into the shop, eyed Justin's roses and winked behind his wire-rimmed glasses. "Ho-ho. There's a lucky girl out there somewhere. Your wife?"

"My girlfriend." He grinned saying the word, not even knowing whether it fitted.

"Hi, Mr. Quigley. Your flowers are ready." The plump, cheerful florist handed him a bouquet with a yellow rose, a blue-and-yellow iris, and another blue-purple flower Justin recognized but didn't know the name of.

"Thank you, Patty." The old man nudged Justin. "These are for my wife. We got married on Valentine's Day. Our wedding bouquet was supposed to look like this, all yellow and blue. But the florist shop burned down that morning and we got nothing. I promised her I'd give her the same flowers every year to make up for it, and I have. Sixty-one bouquets on sixty-one Valentine's Days. Women love flowers. Your girl will, too."

"I hope so."

"I know so! You going to marry her? Nothing like a Valentine's Day proposal. They love those, too, right?" He beamed at Patty, who nodded agreeably.

Justin chuckled and rubbed the back of his neck, oddly excited. "We haven't been dating long."

"Ach, don't give me that 'too soon' crap. You know or you

don't. How did you feel the first time you met her? On your first date? Giddy? Crazy like you drank too much?"

"Yeah." Justin glanced at Patty, who was smirking, but not unkindly.

"Then she's the one!" The man smacked his hand down on the counter. "You young people make everything about love so bloody complicated. Marry her! You won't regret it."

The excitement peaked. What the hell was Justin doing even listening to this guy? "I wasn't really planning to—"

"Trust what you have together." He raised a long, bony finger. "Be honest, play fair and pay attention when she talks. You'll do fine."

Justin started feeling as if he'd landed in some alternate universe. Ask Candy to marry him? When he was nervous even buying her roses? "That's all it takes, huh?"

"Simple, simple." Mr. Quigley's pale eyes gleamed. "Is she beautiful?"

"Very."

"Sweet-tempered?"

"Yes."

"Generous?"

"Absolutely." Justin found himself chuckling. The guy was too much.

"Strong, too? So she won't lean on you all the time?"

"Definitely."

"You know what?" The old guy leaned closer, nudged Justin again with his sharp elbow. "I think *you're* the lucky one."

Justin joined in with the man's wheezy giggle. "I think you might be right. Thank you, sir."

"Ach, you don't need to thank me." He waved Justin away and turned to Patty, digging his wallet out from worn, baggy pants. "Now, what do I owe you?"

Justin left the shop, strangely moved by the encounter. If the way he felt on the first date really was an indication, Justin would have asked Candy to marry him halfway through his appetizer at Cempazuchi. And then had to wait while she laughed herself under the table.

At least tonight would be a memorable evening. He had the flowers and was on his way to Sendik's supermarket for a box of Omanhene dark milk chocolate, made in Milwaukee from beans grown exclusively in Ghana, which Troy told him was some of the best chocolate in town.

Miraculously, he'd called around this afternoon and landed a cancelled reservation at Bartalotta's Lake Park Bistro, one of Milwaukee's finest restaurants.

Take-out pizza and *Star Wars?* Nope. She was getting the works. Minus a ring, which he really thought would be over the top no matter what Mr. Quigley decided.

The only possible flaw was that Candy wasn't likely to dress up enough for the restaurant if she was expecting to hang out at home. Justin didn't care, but she might not like to go to a fancy place in jeans. He'd go over early with the flowers and let her know she should be dressed for another surprise.

Justin grinned and whacked his steering wheel. He couldn't wait. Couldn't wait to see her. Couldn't wait to please her. Couldn't wait to make love to her.

He passed a jewelry store on Silver Spring and, as if it had a mind of its own, his car turned, his foot hit the brake and he pulled into a parking space just vacated outside.

What the hell was he doing here?

Ten minutes later he was still in his front seat, trying to figure it out. Finally, after the third car pulled up next to him and the third driver gave hand signals, asking if he was about to leave, he made it onto the sidewalk, fed the meter and took the ten steps to the store's front window.

Necklaces. Bracelets. Watches. And rings.

Gaudy, most of them, not very subtle. Too big. Too small, too ornate, too spare…

Wow. That one was…wow. Art deco, one diamond in the

middle, a small twist in the white metal on either side, then two more diamonds amid a glittering cascade of chips.

The ring was stunning. It would suit her perfectly.

Justin turned away. This was ridiculous. Utterly ridiculous. He was not going to ask Candy to marry him tonight. That old man must have slipped something into his oxygen.

Back home, he tried six different versions of a card to go with the flowers and finally decided to skip it. Everything sounded either overwrought, clichéd or too casual. And signing his name was superfluous since he'd be standing there with them on her doorstep.

He threw a quick glance in the mirror on his way out, and strode down his driveway, enjoying memories of the last time he'd made this trip, after watching her strip for him through his window. The thaw had held, and his California soul was brimming with relief, though more snow was predicted for early the next week. Tonight, however, it would feel like wonderful warm, romantic spring. Along with the weather, he'd felt a similar awakening from the long nightmare of lust and betrayal that had been his relationship with Angie to the bright sunshine of this wonderful woman. And to love? He was becoming pretty sure, yes.

Grinning like the fool he was, he leaped onto her front step and jammed his finger on the bell, heart thudding. He wasn't planning to say anything right away. Just hand her the flowers and watch her face, which would tell him everything he needed to know.

Footsteps came closer. The handle turned. The door opened.

A man. Younger than Justin by a few years. Good-looking, not as tall as he was, thin but muscled. Light brown hair and eyes, handsome in a bland way. Wearing an undershirt. And pajama bottoms.

His eyes narrowed when he saw Justin behind the gigantic mass of roses. "Who are you?"

Justin swallowed. Please, please tell him this was one of Candy's brothers. "Where's Candy?"

"She's setting up a party still. What's with the flowers?"

"Are you one of her brothers?"

"No, I'm her boyfriend. Who the hell are you?"

Justin stared, heart chilling to ice. He wanted to drop the bouquet and punch this guy in his undershirted gut.

"I'm her neighbor." Instead of the punch, he shoved the flowers over. "Give these to Candy. They were delivered to my house by mistake."

"Who are they from?"

"How the hell should I know?" He turned around, walked as calmly as he could considering he was falling apart, to his house, through the back door and directly to the phone where he made one brief terse call, then dialed Troy.

"Hey, you doing anything tonight?"

"Uh, Valentine's Day? What do *you* think?" Troy's voice dripped sarcasm. "Why? Candy has a hideous best friend who rolled into town and you need to foist her off on someone?"

"No." Justin let his body fall back against the wall next to the phone. "The date is off."

"You're kidding. What happened? You guys fought?"

"Not exactly." He told Troy about meeting Candy's boyfriend.

"What the *hell?*"

"No idea." He heard the misery in his voice and hated himself and all women. No, not all women, just the ones who could get to him like this. "Justin strikes again. Or should I say strikes out again."

"This doesn't make sense."

"Makes perfect sense to me. All her back and forth, this costume and that. The girl's a freak." He didn't believe it. He couldn't. Even with evidence right in his face. Right across the street. Right in pajamas.

"Are you home?"

He laughed bitterly. "I'm sure as hell not out on a date."

"When is your reservation at Lake Park Bistro?"

"Why, you want to go?"

"Uh, no offense, but you're not really my type."

"Ha ha ha. Though maybe I'd be happier if you were. It *was* at eight o'clock. But I cancelled."

"You *cancelled?*" Troy mumbled something about idiots under his breath. "Have you talked to her?"

"To Candy? No, to the boyfriend. Who looked freshly out of bed to me. And was definitely suspicious and hostile of unknown male carrying roses."

"Oh."

Justin laughed bitterly. "Yeah, oh."

"How did she act last time you saw her?"

"Fine. Amazing. Except…I knew she was holding something back. Apparently it was a six-foot man."

"This doesn't—" In the background Dylan barked. "Hang on."

"What's with Dylan?"

"He thinks you should talk to her."

"No, *you* think I should talk to her. Because you and I are so used to being male doormats. I'm telling you, Troy, this is it. I'm not putting up with this push/pull female crap anymore. I'm writing our book, minding my own business. Candy and her man-playground can go on ruining more lives all by themselves."

"Justin, you can't let—"

"Hey, *you* got matched up with her, why don't you get in line, too?"

"Shut up, you're being an asshole."

Justin sighed. "You're right."

"If it felt that good between you, if it felt that right, then it probably was."

Justin made a sound of disgust. "You been talking to Mr. Quigley?"

"Mr. who now?"

"Never mind."

"You know, every time you talked about Angie it was bad. It was always bad, and quite honestly, dude, I couldn't figure out what there was about this woman that had you so hooked. With Candy, I got it. Right away. You clicked, you liked her, you respected her, you had fun together. Is this the first sign of something wrong?"

"No, not the first."

"Then think about it. All the other stuff turned out to have a reasonable explanation, why not this? Maybe he's a jealous ex, maybe he's a friend playing some stupid joke, maybe he's got the wrong house."

Justin let his head drop back against the wall behind him, hating the hope that rose again that it was that Chuck guy who was so bad for her.

Rat-bastard hope. Always leading to disappointment. "Bob Rondell, remember him?"

"Yeah, Big Bob, what does he have to do with it?"

"He had this theory about women and chickens."

"Oh, my God, I do *not* want to hear this. The guy is a complete maniac, Justin."

"He said women find ways to keep us interested by sometimes giving us what we want and other times denying it, so we keep coming around."

"I can see how that would fit Angie. But Candy?"

He was right. Again.

"And excuse me, but Bob is a deeply paranoid, lonely and bitter man who deep down I suspect hates women. Great choice for relationship advice, dude."

Justin slid down to a squat. "Will you stop making sense? You are really screwing up my righteous bad mood here."

"Talk to her. See what she has to say."

Justin made a loud noise of frustration, like a bear woken too early from hibernation. "Okay, I'll talk to her. She'll probably call when she gets back. I left all those damn flowers over there."

Troy chuckled. "Nice one."

"Yeah, the boyfriend will probably tell her they're from him."

"Ouch." Troy sucked in pained air. "Take it easy. Call again if you want company. We can watch a movie or something. Order some pizza."

"Sure, thanks." Justin hung up, wincing at the pizza-and-movie reference and ambled into his living room, feeling as if he had weights dangling from his limbs and a boulder in his stomach. All of which doubled their drag when Candy's car pulled into her driveway and he had to watch her pop out and rush eagerly to her door.

Hi, honey, I'm home.

Couldn't wait to see her man? Though how she could make a date with Justin for Valentine's Day while some other guy...

Justin didn't want to know. Maybe the boyfriend showed up unexpectedly? Maybe it was her ex.

He didn't even know why he was standing here staring. What was he going to do, imagine what was going on inside? A lustful reunion? That was about as much pain as he'd ever felt. The thought of someone else's hands on her...

Candy belonged to him. He'd even wanted to buy her that ring to make it official. The only thing that had stopped him was fear. Fear of rejection. Fear of making the wrong decision. Too much fear.

He and Candy were right together. Justin needed to fight to help her see that, not sit back and let some jerk who denied everything that was most special about her take her away.

Candy's front door opened. Boyfriend emerged, dressed now, holding an overnight bag. Behind him, literally pushing him out the door: Candy. Justin's heart skipped several beats.

The mere sight of her always did that to him, but the sight of her forcibly evicting Dickhead made it even more fun.

Across the street, she crossed her arms, scowled. Boyfriend seemed to be pleading.

Candy's arm pointed to the street, pointed again. Vehemently. She wanted him gone. Maybe Troy was right, and there was a reasonable explanation that had nothing to do with her changing or faking her feelings for Justin.

In which case, Troy was also right: Justin was an asshole.

Candy's fantasy Valentine's Day celebration had been his to give her. Now he'd pissed away the dinner reservation, lost the chance to present her the flowers—*damn,* he'd forgotten to buy the chocolate—and he hadn't had the balls to buy her a ring. All because he refused to trust her feelings or his, even though they'd never felt so true and so strong.

Okay. Start over. He'd find another way. What time was it? He glanced at his watch. Crap, nearly seven. He was due over to her house at seven-thirty.

Never mind. Even if he had to break into stores and rob them, he'd make this a Valentine's Day Candy would never forget.

CANDY PULLED INTO HER driveway, going too fast, having to brake sharply. She threw herself out of the car, glancing at her watch. Mrs. Abernathy had driven her crazy fussing over every last detail even though every last detail was ready. Now Candy had only half an hour to dress before Justin showed up. She was going to wear the red sequined-heart pasties and G-string under baggy sweats and surprise him when they got to the undressing part of the evening.

Seeing Chuck the previous night had changed her life. For the better. She'd spent the first twenty minutes after he walked in feeling as if her life's clock had been spun in reverse, an odd feeling of inevitability. They were together once again in their house and everything about it was familiar and right.

And then another twenty minutes went by and she was filled, instead of with joy and confusion, with rage.

Everything her friends had said about him was right. While trying to insinuate himself back into her life after she'd told him in no uncertain terms that she was not open to him coming back, he'd thought he was being charming and loving while managing to criticize nearly everything about her. What was worse, that criticism felt familiar and almost sweet, and she'd experienced that equally familiar but now creepy urge to surrender to him, to let him decide, to mold herself to what he wanted her to be.

No wonder she'd had to "invent" personalities to be on Milwaukeedates.com. The only personality approved by Mr. Control Freak had been his. He didn't let her be sexy, didn't let her out of the house to pursue her interests. My God, how had she survived five years of suspended animation being his girlfriend? How had she spent the last year slowly coming back to life and still pined to be his puppet again?

How had she missed that Justin made any way she wanted to be okay? That he'd encouraged her to push boundaries, sexually, emotionally, whatever she wanted? Denial was a powerful and dangerous force.

Candy absolutely could not wait for their date.

She hurried up to the front door, wanting to blow a kiss to Justin's house, but afraid the driver of a passing car would think she meant it for him. Key in the lock, she turned, shoved, stumbled in and found herself in Chuck's strong arms, smushed against his chest.

Grrrr.

She pushed as hard as she could and freed herself. "*What* are you still doing here? I said you could spend the night but you had to be *gone* when I got back!"

"Honey." He reached for her again.

She jumped away. "Not 'honey.' Candy. No, Catherine. No, *Ms. Graham*."

"You don't mean this." He smiled pityingly. "I wanted to tell you in person that I'm considering moving back to the neighbor—"

"No."

"We could have a second chance to—"

"No."

"If you'd just let me—"

"Listen." She flashed her hands up, elbows locked straight, stopping him and keeping him at a distance. "I am in love with someone else. In love the way I have always wanted to be in love. The way I kept telling myself I was in love with you, but I was completely deluding myself."

"Candy, that's crazy. I want us to try again."

"You don't want me, Chuck. I'm not the same person. I like to…here." She held up an extra Cupid outfit she brought back from Mrs. Abernathy's. "I like to wear things like this, now. All the time."

"Baby, you don't know what you—" He took in the outfit and his eyes popped. "Really?"

She stuffed it hurriedly back into her bag. Okay, that didn't work. "I have a date in half an hour. You have to go."

His face fell. "You're serious?"

"Hello? Hello? Have you heard a thing I've been saying?" She jammed her hands onto her hips, because otherwise she was going to smack him. "No. You haven't heard me. You never have. It was always about what you wanted for all those years, and I went along with it because it was easier than trying to get through to you. That isn't what I want anymore. I have found a guy who cares about me, who understands who and what I really am, and accepts…"

Chuck's eyes were glazing over. He wasn't listening. He was trying to think of new ways to win the argument. How many times had she lived this exact scene?

She sighed. A lot of the fight went out of her. What was the point? She took his arm and propelled him to the front door. "I'm sorry, Chuck. You need to leave. Now. I have to get dressed."

"In that fake little costume? That's not a real part of you."

Candy laughed bitterly. "This little costume brings out all the very real parts of me you couldn't handle."

That got through. His face darkened. "You'll regret pushing me away someday, Candy. When this little fling blows over, you'll—"

"Maybe. But that's a risk I'm willing to take. Please go."

Finally she got him to the front door, literally had to push him out, then had the immense relief of seeing him head for his car. Relief so immense she even managed some friendly feelings toward him. "Safe travels, Chuck."

The slight change in tone had him turning back. "If you change your mind—"

"No." She pointed emphatically to the road. "No. Go."

"I bought you flowers for Valentine's Day. Roses. The way you always wanted me to. They're in the kitchen."

For one sucker moment she was touched. Then instinct nudged her and she laughed to herself. When she belonged to him he'd never bothered. Only now, to get what he wanted. "That's sweet of you, Chuck."

"A dozen. Because I love you." He took another step toward her, eyes pleading. "I love you, Candy."

"Thank you, Chuck. I loved you, too, but that's over. You need to go."

"Long-stemmed, they're long-stemmed. Red."

"Goodbye, Chuck."

"I didn't write a card, though, I figured I'd get to talk to you when—"

"Goodbye, Chuck."

She waited until his car was out of sight and gave a shudder, of sadness and distaste but also of release. Truly gone. He was truly gone, not only from her house and from her life, but from her heart. And Justin was the reason.

Justin. Oh, my God. She had twenty minutes to get ready.

Back inside, she was on her way to the stairs when a flash of red caught her eye from the kitchen. Flowers. Gorgeous flowers. Entranced in spite of herself, she went over to them, touched a perfect bud, inhaled the rich, sweet scent. Beautiful. They were so beautiful.

And they were from Chuck.

She swept up the vase and headed out her back door to the garbage. No more reminders of that stupid fantasy portion of her life. Outside, she heaved open the trash-can lid and tossed them in headfirst, watching them crush and break at the bottom.

Done. Gone. The jerk was entirely cleansed from her life. The old Candy who cared more about fantasies than what was real—she was also gone.

Now, new Candy wanted nothing more than to get ready for the most romantic date of her life, featuring pizza, *Star Wars* and Justin. Because on Valentine's Day, love was the only thing that mattered.

15

CANDY SAT ON HER KITCHEN STOOL wearing red heart-sequined pasties and G-string under sweatpants, impatiently kicking the rung of the chair next to her. Five to Northern Oriole on the bird clock. Twenty-five minutes after Justin was supposed to come over. Valentine's Day. She'd already gotten rid of the boyfriend she'd thought she wanted, and the roses she'd thought she wanted. All she wanted now was Justin, take-out pizza and a movie, yes, even *Star Wars*. Chuck had been half right: the trappings of Valentine's Day were commercial and silly. But celebrating love on that day wasn't, and she still planned to do exactly that with Justin. If he ever showed up.

No, no worries. Wherever he'd gone, whatever he was doing that had delayed him, he'd be in touch with her at some point and they'd have their celebration. She knew it with every chamber of her heart, and didn't need anyone else to verify it for her. Not Abigail, not Marie, not any of her four personalities. Just herself.

Doorbell. Candy leaped up, nearly tripping, the same way she had before their first date. This had to be him. If it was Chuck, Candy was going to brain him with a crowbar. The fact that she didn't have a crowbar or the capacity for such violence wouldn't stop her.

She peered through the peephole and electricity zapped every nerve ending to full attention. Justin. Looking harried but excited, not miserable, not as if he'd received the worst news of his life or got in a terrible accident or anything dreadful. Thank God.

Candy wrenched open the door. "Hi."

"I'm late. I know. I'm sorry." He was holding a pizza box, grinning as if she was the most wonderful thing he'd ever set eyes on, which was fine by her because she was positive she was grinning the same way. "I should have called but I was... well, it's complicated."

"It's fine. You're okay and you're here, and that's all that matters to me. Come in." She leaned in for a quick kiss as he passed, but the kiss was so delicious and whetted her appetite so thoroughly, she wanted another one, and one more, and by then her desire had risen considerably, though nothing truly sexual had happened yet. Arousal had become a Pavlovian response to any touch from him. She wanted to knock the pizza out of his hands and beg him to take her up against the wall.

"Happy Valentine's Day, Candy."

"Happy Valentine's Day." She managed to break away and close the door behind him, feeling fizzy as always around him, but with a solid-centered core now, no longer splintered into parts. She was only looking forward, to all the places she wanted to go in life, literally and figuratively, hoping most of them included Justin.

"No disasters tonight at the party?" He was looking around.

"No news is good news." She pointed to the kitchen table. "Want to put the pizza there?"

"Um, yeah, sure." He peered into the living room before

walking into the kitchen, craning his neck toward the dining room.

"Looking for something?"

"Oh. I just wondered. The flowers…"

Candy gaped. "How did you know about the flowers?"

He eyed her strangely. "Because I got them for you?"

"You?" She put her hand to her heart, absolutely wretched. She'd thrown away flowers from Justin. She was going to kill Chuck.

"Where are they? Upstairs?"

In the trash. "Oh, God. Justin. I thought they were from Chuck."

"Chuck." He swallowed, holding her eyes. "No, they weren't."

Tears gathered. She felt absolutely sick. This wonderful man had worked to make her dream come true by giving her flowers, and she'd tossed them.

"Justin, I'm so sorry. I threw them away." She spoke quickly to get the horrible confession out.

He blinked. "You *threw them away?"*

"Yes." Her voice barely sounded. She felt as if she'd driven a knife into him, which had also gone into herself.

His frozen face melted into an enormous grin. He burst out laughing. "That is the best news I've heard all day."

"Um." Candy was afraid she'd shoved him over the edge. "It is?"

"I showed up with them earlier because I'd made us a dinner reservation at Lake Park Bistro, and I wanted you to have plenty of time to dress."

"You…" She looked down at her baggy sweats in panic. "For tonight? What time?"

"Don't worry." He shook his head, still chuckling. "Instead of you, Chuck came to the door, practically in his underwear, and told me he was your boyfriend."

"No." She gasped in horror. "That little—"

"This entire pizza and *Star Wars* joke was to make the fancy stuff you'd always wanted a surprise, Candy. But after seeing Chuck I cancelled the reservation and you threw away the flowers." His laughter turned dry.

"Justin, it's fine, at least as far as I'm concerned." She ran over to him and put her hand on his arm, searching his face, wanting to make it all better. "I only *thought* the fancy stuff was what I wanted."

"It wasn't?"

"No. All the trappings were fantasies, the flowers, the fancy dinner, the chocolate—"

"Chocolate!" He smacked himself on the forehead. "I forgot it again!"

She took his shoulders, grinned up at his distress. "I don't care. Really."

"Dinner, flowers, chocolate, strikes one, two, three, but I'm not out?" He pulled her to him.

"No. You're very much in. Because what I always wanted on Valentine's Day and never got wasn't flowers, chocolate or fancy dinners. It was love, and I never had it. Not really. But now…" She kissed him, feeling more fear and vulnerability than she'd ever felt in her life. This wasn't safe the way being around Chuck had felt. This was dangerous and terrifying, but she refused to go back, because it was also real. "I love you, Justin. I know it's soon to say it, I know it's completely crazy, but I don't care. I'm finally trusting what's inside me. And what's inside me is you."

He looked so stunned she was afraid she'd horrified him and her heart nearly stopped.

Then he whispered her name with an intensity that restarted it, and he kissed her, sweetly, passionately, then with desperate intent, backing her up against the kitchen table.

"Wait." She pushed him away, pulled off her sweatshirt, yanked down her sweatpants and stepped out of them in the almost-not-there pasties, feeling absolutely at home as Sexy

Glamour Girl. No. Not Sexy Glamour Girl. Candy. "This is what I got you for Valentine's Day."

He reacted as if she'd banged him over the head, practically staggering under the impact, eyes glazing. She loved that she had that power over him, and that she had that power in herself because of him.

Yet when he kissed her, the lust was muted, controlled, there was more sweetness than desire, and the hands that held her were gentle. For a long time there was nothing but kisses and murmured words, long caresses and exchanged gazes between them.

Candy had never been this purely and deliciously happy. Opening herself up to Justin had not made her more vulnerable as she feared. Instead it had given her more peace than she'd known was possible. Whether he could say the three words back yet, whether he felt them, she knew he was not going to disappear anytime soon. He said as much with every kiss and every look.

Finally, kisses and looks weren't enough; she unfastened his jeans and started to push them down.

"Wait." He put his hands to her wrists. "I know this will sound really kinky and strange, but...I'd really like to make love to you in a bed again."

"A bed?" She twisted her face into disbelief. "Again? We did that already."

He managed to keep a straight face. "Not yours yet."

"Hmm, true." She took his hand and led him upstairs to her room, where the day before she'd thrown away the picture of Chuck at the Brewers game with no regret or sadness, just certainty that it was time.

They took each other's clothes off, silently, calmly, not feeling the need to make undressing a rushed production, not this time, not this night. Then they slid naked under the sheets to lie on their sides, face to face, skin to skin, absorbing each other's warmth.

"This is as good as it gets." She rubbed her face against his smooth shoulder.

"Hmm. If I try very hard, I can think of something else that's just as good. Or maybe better."

She bit his shoulder, used her tongue to soothe the spot and her lips to dry it. "Give me a hint?"

"Here it comes." He rolled her to her back, stroked her stomach, long, slow sweeps that stopped short of her breasts, short of her sex, then circled it around her thighs, occasionally brushing gently across her curling hair, barely touching her clitoris with the tip of a finger.

She lay still, tortured by the teases, her body growing warmer and more impatient for what it ultimately wanted.

Finally his finger did more than brush her, it dipped down slowly, entered her, then settled onto her clitoris. Her hips lifted, tensed. She gripped the sheets with her hands, then reached for him. She wanted them together.

He retrieved a condom and put it on, rolled gently over her, kissing her neck, her collarbone, her mouth.

"Hello." She whispered the word, lying under him, legs parted for him, hands trailing down the muscled slope of his back. "Welcome home."

He smiled at that, pushed slowly into her, holding her gaze, his smile faltering only when the pleasure closed his eyes for a moment. Then he was back with her, moving with her, mouth leisurely exploring her lips. When he spoke it was in a low murmur, without warning.

"I love you."

"Justin." A thrill shot through her, mixing joy with her arousal. She hooked her legs over his, wrapped her arms tightly around him to merge them as closely as possible. They rocked together, a slow steady rhythm that was more about love than orgasms, more about peace than desperation, with nothing of the rough pain/pleasure mix they'd shared before. They let the sensations and emotions build, keeping pace with each other until she shattered into a climax only moments before he did, her heart overflowing with what she felt.

"Happy Valentine's Day." His voice tickled her neck. She smiled lazily.

"Happy Valentine's Day, Justin."

He lifted his head, looked down at her with those intensely brown eyes she hoped to be able to look into for the rest of her life. "Are you ready for some pizza?"

She was startled. Pizza didn't seem quite the logical next step, at least not so immediately, but okay. "You're hungry?"

"Oh, um. Yeah." He slid out of her, sat up and reached for his clothes, looking oddly excited and uneasy. "Yeah, I had an early lunch."

"Sure." She got out of bed and rummaged for nonsequined underwear in her dresser, wondering what was so enticing about pizza when they had each other and a bed and the rest of the weekend to enjoy, but okay. Maybe he was *really* hungry.

"Ready?" He was dressed, standing by the door. She was still half-naked. Hello? Did she *look* ready?

"Not quite. Almost."

She pulled on her sweats, her socks, but decided to skip slippers since he was practically tapping his foot with impatience.

Downstairs, he started opening cupboards. "Plates? Glasses?"

"Here." She took down two of each, got a couple of beers from the refrigerator and sat opposite him, surprised after all that when he didn't dig right in.

"So." He pushed the box toward her. "Ladies first."

She smiled. Ever the gentleman, even when he was near death from starvation. The box opened easily.

"Mmm, veggie pizza, my favor—"

Her mouth refused to finish the word. Taped to the little

three-legged plastic doohickey that kept the box from crushing was a ring. A diamond ring. A stunning diamond ring with a glittering stone, flanked by twisted white gold and more diamonds spilling down steps on its shoulders. And spelled out in sliced black olives on the by-now-tepid pie surface were two words: *Marry Me*.

Candy looked up at Justin, unable to speak. The look on his face—love with a healthy dose of terror—made her laugh, and then she started to cry and stood up, reaching blindly for him.

"Justin." She giggled, sobbed, hiccupped. "I think this p-pizza asked me to m-marry it."

His arms were strong around her. His head bent next to hers. "The pizza is incredibly in love with you, Candy. I have never met a woman like you before. You light up my world, you make me want to live better and I'm sure I will never find anyone like you again. Will you marry me?"

It took her three tries before "yes" came out, even though she was urging it along as hard as she could. Her body was shaking. She'd never felt emotion this powerful.

"Yes. Yes!" Now that she'd said it, she couldn't seem to stop, until his mouth did a good job of cutting her off.

Many kisses later, he was still holding her close, stroking her hair. "Ah, Candy, I was going to do this right tonight. The flowers, the chocolate, a window table at Lake Park Bistro, with the ring in a glass of their best champagne. Instead you got the cheesy pizza proposal."

"But it was *my* cheesy pizza proposal and I wouldn't have wanted it any other way, Justin."

"Guess what?" He grinned at her and winked one of those beautiful brown eyes filled with love. "We have the rest of our lives to get that Valentine's Day celebration perfect."

"No." Candy laughed and shook her head, certain of one thing absolutely. "Tonight we already did."

Epilogue

"On a *pizza*?" Darcy plunked a hand to her chest and burst out laughing. "I think I actually might like this guy."

"Me, too." Kim was grinning. "Especially because he tried so hard to do it by the book, but came up with such a fun and creative Plan B when the first one didn't work out. You'll always remember this, too, because it's so unique. Your kids will love the story."

"Except when they're teenagers, because everything parents do is lame then." Candy made a face that couldn't hide her joy.

"Absolutely, they'll love it." Marie reached over and squeezed Candy's hand. The courtship had been rocky and awfully quick, but now that Justin had come through with a proposal, quieting Marie's unfounded fears, instinct was again telling her this was a good match. Funny how she could have better insight into other people than herself. "I couldn't be happier for you."

"It's wonderful." Kim's eyes were brighter; she looked less weary than at their last Women in Power meeting.

"What's going on with you this month, Kim?" Marie asked.

"I do have a couple of pieces of hopeful news. Finally."

"Tell us!" Candy turned, clearly anxious for happiness to be spread around.

"A friend at my old ad agency told me Carter International, the china and crystal company, is accepting nonagency bids for a new website. I came up with a pretty cool idea, and my friend is putting in a good word for me with her Carter contact, so I thought I'd give it a somewhat desperate shot."

"Oh, Kim!" Candy crossed fingers on both hands. "That would be wonderful. And would really get your business on solid ground."

"I turn thirty in April and that was my deadline. If I can't make Charlotte's Web Design work by then, I'll give up and go back to corporate life."

"Then make this happen." Darcy raised her hand for a high five. "Millions of people see the Carter website every year. You'd be in."

"I know." Kim blew out a shaky breath. "This is my last chance. Scary, but at least it's a big honking last chance."

"It certainly is." Marie applauded, both thrilled and anxious for her. Kim had put in so much hard work and so many long hours to get her company going. It was unthinkable that she'd fail. "What's the second piece of news?"

"I think I'll be able to get help with my rent for a while. Just in time. One of my brother's friends lost his lease because the landlord is selling the building. He's a master's student at UWM School of Architecture. Nice enough guy, and I'd get financial help for a couple of months. When he finishes his thesis he'll find his own place."

"By that time you'll get the Carter account and not have to worry," Darcy said.

"That's the fantasy."

"That's the *plan*." Marie gave her a brilliant smile, heart aching for all Kim had gone through. Thirty might be an arbitrary deadline, but Marie respected her for setting it. Though if Kim didn't get the job the birthday celebration would be more misery than milestone.

Marie stifled a gasp. The perfect idea had just flashed into her brain. Of course! They'd throw Kim a surprise party using Candy's expertise to make it a really special event. They could enlist Kim's brother, Kent, to help them. Or even better, this new roommate, who'd be in a perfect position to inform on Kim's doings, habits and tastes.

The president of Women in Power got up to the podium and called for everyone's attention. The women around the room fell silent, shifting chairs to be able to see better, putting napkins on the table, getting one more cup of coffee to last them the program.

Marie kept her eyes on Kim, mind working overtime. The party was a great idea, but one more piece falling into place would guarantee Kim's thirtieth would be something to celebrate instead of mourn, no matter what happened with Carter International.

Business success or no, Marie was going to find Kim a man.

* * * * *

Dear Reader,

Thank you so much for picking up *The Wild Card*. This is the eighth book in my MEN OUT OF UNIFORM series and I never tire of writing these sinfully wicked, but oh-so-honorable heroes. These guys are all Southern gentlemen—so they know how to treat a lady, particularly when they find the right one— and they're always quick-witted, fearless and lethally charming. An excellent combination, wouldn't you say?

Having made a death-bed promise to his mother to leave the military as soon as his next tour was up, Seth McCutcheon has no intention of going back on his word. He'd promised. He would deliver. Seth has absolutely no idea what he's going to do once he leaves though, and is both relieved and honored when Colonel Carl Garrett makes a recommendation on his behalf to Ranger Security.

But when Seth is tapped to provide security at a high-profile wedding, he soon begins to think that he preferred dodging bullets to dodging angry brides. And the wedding planner he has to pretend to be in love with? Make-believe has never been more fun.

Nothing brings a smile to my face faster than hearing from my readers, so be sure to check out my website at www.ReadRhondaNelson.com

Happy reading!

Rhonda Nelson

THE WILD CARD

BY
RHONDA NELSON

First published in Great Britain 2012
by Mills & Boon, an imprint of Harlequin (UK) Limited,
Eton House, 18-24 Paradise Road, Richmond, Surrey TW9 1SR

© Rhonda Nelson 2011

ISBN: 978 0 263 89364 9

14-0212

Harlequin (UK) policy is to use papers that are natural, renewable and recyclable products and made from wood grown in sustainable forests. The logging and manufacturing processes conform to the legal environmental regulations of the country of origin.

Printed and bound in Spain
by Blackprint CPI, Barcelona

A Waldenbooks bestselling author, two-time RITA® Award nominee and *RT Book Reviews* Reviewers' Choice nominee, **Rhonda Nelson** writes hot romantic comedy for the Blaze® line. With more than twenty-five published books to her credit and many more coming down the pike, she's thrilled with her career and enjoys dreaming up her characters and manipulating the worlds they live in. In addition to a writing career, she has a husband, two adorable kids, a black Lab and a beautiful bichon frisé. She and her family make their chaotic but happy home in a small town in northern Alabama. She loves to hear from her readers, so be sure and check her out at www. readRhondaNelson.com.

For my brother, whose character and
wit is in every hero I write.

1

As an active Ranger in Uncle Sam's service who had performed more tours of duty than he could remember, Seth McCutcheon was used to seeing terrible things. But watching his mother die was definitely the worst.

"Mom, you need to rest," he chided softly, his throat thick. Lamplight glowed against the side of her face, illuminating her smooth cheeks, the faint laugh lines around her eyes. She was fifty-two. Too young to be at the end of her life, a vibrant one that had been spent making sure that he and his little sister had been provided for. His gaze slid to the vase of daisies on her nightstand, her "happy" flowers, and his lips twitched in a weary smile.

"Tired of losing to me, are you?" his mother asked, a weak laugh shaking her unbelievably frail shoulders. She looked up from the cards in her hand and eyed him shrewdly. "You're not letting me win, are you?"

Under the circumstances he would have, but it hadn't been necessary. She'd always been able to beat him at poker, one of the few people who had, if he was quite honest. She'd taught him, after all. It only seemed fitting.

"You know damned well I'm not letting you win," he told her, rolling his shoulders against the ache that had settled there. He'd been sitting at her bedside for hours, afraid to leave, afraid to miss a single second with her in case the next might be her last. "You're trouncing me," he complained good-naturedly. "If I were letting you win, I'd at least put on a good enough show that you wouldn't know it."

She hummed under her breath, consulting her cards. "True enough, I suppose, but I do wish you'd make more of an effort, Seth. I'm about to up the ante in a way that's going to seriously impact your future. You'd do well to get your head in the game." Her tone was deceptively light, but he knew better.

Seth stilled and looked up. "Up the ante? What are you talking about?"

She smiled wearily. "I have little use for money," she said. "Soon enough I'm not going to need it. I—"

"Mom," he interrupted, panic and dread making his heart race.

She set her cards aside, then reached over and took his hand. Her bright blue eyes were soft and full of compassion. Comforting *him,* when it should have been the other way around. *Jeez God, how was he going to get through this?*

"Seth, I know that you don't want to have this conversation, but it's one that has to take place. There are things we have to talk about before I shuffle off this mortal coil," she said in an attempt to season the terrible conversation with humor. "You know that. Please just listen."

She was right. He didn't want to have the conversation, he'd never imagined that they'd be having it so soon. They'd only found the cancer four months ago—in her brain, no less. She'd undergone high doses of chemotherapy, causing her to lose more than twenty pounds and all of her hair. She currently wore an outrageous long blond wig, one that put him in mind of a Barbie doll. He'd been shocked when he'd first seen her in it—the first of many—but she'd merely laughed and said that the good Lord hadn't blessed her with long hair of any sort and that this provided the perfect opportunity to try out different styles. Her glass was firmly half-full, even in the midst of this horrible disease. Seth looked heavenward and gave a grunt, his chest feeling as if it were locked in Satan's vise grip.

Only his mother.

His eyes burned, but he tried for a smile all the same and gave her hand a squeeze. She was right. They couldn't put it off much longer. She was getting weaker every day—in part, he was sure, because she refused to sleep more than a couple of hours at a time. She'd even made both him and his sister promise to wake her. She didn't want to waste whatever time she had left by sleeping, she'd said. Were their positions reversed, Seth knew he'd likely feel the same way. Still…

He finally nodded, silently encouraging her to go on.

"Let's get the grisly part over first, shall we? I don't want a traditional funeral."

He snorted before he could stop himself.

She laughed. "Yes, yes, I know. I'm predictably un-predictable, but I don't care. The idea of all my friends and family gawking over my dead body lying in a cof-fin, talking about how 'good' I look while I'm *dead,* for pity's sake, is just more than I can bear. Cremate me and scatter my ashes among my roses, where I'll do some good."

So that she'd still be useful…and still here. How was he going to get through this? he wondered again. How was the world going to go on when she was no longer a part of it? She'd always been there for him. Bandaging scraped knees, nursing colds, tossing the football with him in the backyard. A constant source of love and encouragement, one he'd realized too late he'd taken for granted.

"My will is in the desk over there," she said, jerking her head in that direction. She picked up her cards once more. "It's simple enough. I don't have much, but what I have is yours and your sister's." She paused. "I want Katie to have the house. Since Rat Bastard left she's been having a hard time making ends meet and I don't want that for her and Mitchell."

Seth was in full agreement there. "Rat Bastard's" real name was actually Michael, and he'd recently left Seth's sister and child and moved in with the girl who worked as the jelly doughnut filler at the local pastry shop. When the time was right, Seth fully intended to pay a visit to Michael and give him a lesson in how to treat a lady, most specifically, his sister.

He'd already given that same lesson to his father, the faithless, miserable, weak-willed son of a bitch.

"I've had the house appraised," his mother continued. "And I've made provisions in the will to offset what your part would have been if I hadn't left the house to Katie."

"Mom, you didn't have to do that. She can have it all. I don't want—"

"Fair is fair," she insisted. "I've been paying those life insurance premiums all these years just in case something happened and it's a comfort for me to know that your sister will have this house and you'll have a little money to put toward your own."

Because he didn't want to upset her, he didn't point out the obvious. Seth didn't need a "home." His home was in the military.

She smiled weakly. "I know what you're thinking, son, and that's where my ante comes in. When I'm gone, your sister and Mitchell aren't going to have anyone—" She swallowed, betraying the first crack in her resolve. That single fissure absolutely shattered him. "And I'd feel a whole lot better if I knew that you'd be coming home when your contract runs out."

"Mom," he said, shaking his head. *Not this, anything but this.* "You know—"

"I *do* know, Seth," she interrupted. "I know that you love your job, that the military has been your life. I do know," she repeated softly. "It pains me to ask and hurts even more that I have to." She swallowed again. "But I also know that if something happened to you, Katie and Mitchell would be completely, utterly alone…and I just can't bear that. And neither could they."

It was a terribly bleak picture, but one that was equally accurate, should the worst happen. He thought of his sister, hardworking and funny. His nephew, only two years old, with curly blond hair and big brown eyes.

"Play me for it," his mother said, glancing shrewdly at him above her cards. "If I win this hand, then you come out as soon as you can. If you win, then you do whatever you feel is right."

A bark of laughter erupted from his thickening throat and he watched her lips twist. "Meaning if I don't come out, then I'm a selfish, uncaring bastard." He shook his head. "Excellent. Great choices there."

His mother chuckled. "I'm being shamelessly manipulative, I know, but…"

He looked up at her. "And you're also holding a winning hand, otherwise you wouldn't have brought it up now."

His mother merely stared at him, betraying nothing. "Are you in or out?"

Seth consulted his own cards. He was pretty confident, not that it would matter. He'd already lost. "In," he said.

"Let's see what you've got," his mother said.

Seth laid his hand down. "Three of a kind, kings high."

His mother quirked a brow. "You and those wild cards," she *tsked,* noticing the one in his hand. "Those one-eyed jacks always find their way to you, don't they?"

Yeah, they did. He'd actually been given the nickname the Wild Card when he'd been in Jump School, and had a tattoo of one on his right shoulder to commemorate the moniker. Of course, considering that Seth's methods were occasionally deemed unorthodox at best and reckless at worst, the name served double duty.

He merely shrugged, smiling. "They do seem to favor me."

His mother's lips lifted in a grin that made a sick feeling in his belly take hold. She laid down her cards. "They favored me with this hand, too," she said, sliding a finger over the edge of the jack of hearts.

Four of a kind, aces high.

Shit.

His lips twisted. "Well played, Mom," he said, mentally watching his future roll out in a direction he had never anticipated, never wanted.

She arched an eyebrow, but the relief in her face was so stark it was painful. "I have your word?"

He nodded, struggling to speak. "Of course."

Seemingly satisfied that she'd completed an important task on her last to-do list, every muscle in her body relaxed and she settled more firmly into her bed. "Good," she said, her voice thin. "Thank you. You're a good man, Seth. My sweet boy," she murmured. Her eyes drifted over his face with affection—a look he'd seen hundreds of times—then fluttered shut.

"You should rest," he chided, his eyes stinging. "I'm tiring you out."

She laced her fingers through his. "I do think I'll take

a little nap. Wake me in two hours," she said, giving his hand a firm squeeze. "Don't forget."

"I won't, Mom."

Exactly one-hundred-and-twenty minutes later, he tried…but didn't succeed.

2

Seven months later...

"PAYNE HAS impeccable taste and Jamie lets his better half dress him, but no one—not even his lovely wife, evidently—can convince Guy McCann that camouflage isn't proper wedding attire," the slim man behind the desk was saying when Seth approached. The office manager, he presumed, held up one finger, indicating that he would only be a moment longer, and shot Seth an apologetic look. The man's gaze dropped down to a photo on his frighteningly immaculate desk and he gave a delicate shudder. "Yes, Terrence, yes. He's wearing *camo pants* and a *black t-shirt*. That's what the cretin wore to the wedding. Tanner gave me a photo this morning. I'm looking at it right now." He exhaled mightily again, as though the camo-wearer's sin against fashion was almost more than he could bear. Seth couldn't quite reconcile this outraged put-upon Latino as an employee of Ranger Security. "You're right, of course, but camo?

At a wedding? Yes, yes. All right. I'll see you later, then."

The man uttered a swift goodbye, then disconnected. His quick gaze snapped up to Seth's. "Sorry about that," he said, his tone immediately professional. "I don't ordinarily take personal phone calls on the job, but in this case I made an exception. You're Seth McCutcheon, correct?"

Seth nodded, making an effort to flatten his twitching lips.

"I'm Juan-Carlos, the office manager here at Ranger Security." He selected a file from the corner of his desk and gestured for Seth to follow him. "Come with me, please. They're waiting for you in the boardroom." The last sentence was delivered with a curiously sarcastic bent.

And thirty seconds later, Seth understood why.

The boardroom, as it were, didn't have the traditional table and rolling executive chairs. Instead, it more resembled a high-tech clubhouse, complete with a pool table, a huge, flat-panel television anchored to the wall and lots of comfortable leather furniture. A stainless steel side-by-side refrigerator stood in the kitchenette and a host of different snacks were lined up in old-fashioned candy jars along the counter. Everything from biscotti to Pixy Stix—his childhood favorite—were represented, bringing a smile to his lips.

Jamie Flanagan and Guy McCann—he recognized them from the research he'd done—were playing a war game on the Xbox and Brian Payne sat in a recliner, perusing a file. He looked up when Juan-Carlos announced Seth and immediately stood.

"Seth," he said, extending his hand. "Brian Payne. It's good to have you here."

McCann and Flanagan immediately put their game on hold, setting their controllers aside to welcome him. Juan-Carlos heaved a long-suffering, but seemingly re-signed, sigh as he looked at McCann. Then, with a tragic baffled shake of his head, he left the room.

As soon as the door shut behind Juan-Carlos, Flanagan and McCann broke into gut-clenching guffaws, while Payne merely chuckled.

"Sorry," Payne told him. "McCann has been play-ing with Photoshop and has been torturing our long-suffering but *irreplaceable* office manager," he said, shooting the other two a dark look.

Ah. Seth inclined his head and smiled, looking at McCann. "So you didn't really wear camo to a wedding?"

Still wheezing with laughter, McCann shook his head. "No, but it's been *huge* fun letting Juan-Carlos think I did."

"I can't believe he fell for it," Jamie remarked. "I mean, I know you're a not a fashion icon—" he glanced meaningfully at the jeans and Alabama T-shirt Guy currently wore "—but the guy should know that even *you* have some sense of propriety."

Still laughing, Guy looked up. "Did he show you the picture?"

Seth shook his head. "No, but he was talking about it to someone on the phone when I came in."

"Sweet," McCann crowed, looking jubilant. "A colleague of ours—and now yours—Tanner Crawford, married in Asheville a while back and the three of us made the drive over to celebrate the nuptials with the happy couple," McCann explained. "Juan-Carlos had been invited, as well—"

"Because he gets pissed off if he isn't included," Jamie interjected.

"—but he'd had tickets to an Elton John concert and didn't want to miss it." McCann grinned. "For kicks, I've been playing around with the wedding photos just to needle him," he said. "It's provided hours of entertainment."

So they were practical jokers? Seth thought, feeling more at ease. He and his friends had been notorious for that, as well. He'd once had an entire eyebrow shaved off after a night of too much alcohol and too little sleep. It had taken much longer than he'd ever imagined to grow it back.

"Would you like something to drink?" Payne offered. "Coffee? Tea? A soda?"

Seth shook his head. "I'm good, thanks."

Flanagan gestured for him to take a seat and they all settled in. The atmosphere was relaxed and warm. The camaraderie between the three men was enviable. These guys weren't just comfortable in their own skins, they were comfortable with each other.

That was one of the things that he'd most hated about leaving the military, Seth thought. Aside from it being his purpose, his way of life, his best friends were there. Finn O'Conner—who had recently become engaged to his childhood sweetheart and planned to move to Tybee Island to run an old motor inn when he came out—and Greer West had been part of his crew since ROTC. And, though he knew they both understood why he'd had to get out, he couldn't help but feel he'd betrayed a trust of sorts. As if his defection had broken something that might not ever be completely repaired. Or maybe that was simply the guilt talking. He felt he'd abandoned them. And leaving the service during a time of war…

That was the worst. Knowing that his country needed him, that his fellow soldiers needed him. And he was here, about to take a cushy job protecting politicians, debutantes, celebrities and people with more money than sense. Where was the honor in that? And better still, how did these guys find it?

"You've reviewed the employment offer?" Payne asked.

Seth nodded. To say that it was generous would be a vast understatement. In addition to the extremely healthy salary, he'd been given an apartment, as well. He had to admit that was a perk he sincerely appreciated. As much as he loved Katie and Mitchell, living with them was another matter altogether. Katie was under the semi-accurate impression that she and Mitch would cramp his dating style. While that was a legitimate concern, it wasn't his primary reason for wanting his own space. He'd given up his career to come back here and be there for them—he didn't think having a little privacy was too much to ask. Besides, being in that house without his mother felt…wrong. He hoped someday it would be a comfort, but right now it was too much of a reminder of his loss.

"Do you have any questions? Any concerns?" Payne asked.

None that he could go into without insulting them, Seth thought. Colonel Carl Garrett had recommended him for this job and, ultimately, he was eternally thankful to have it. He'd be working with former Rangers, men he understood, doing a job he was overqualified for, but equally overpaid. It wasn't their place to make him feel this new direction his life had taken had purpose—that was his own to sort out. Obviously these men had walked the same path—under different, more tragic circumstances, he knew—and they'd found their way.

He would find his. Hopefully sooner rather than later.

And he couldn't find it with better men.

Known in certain circles as the Specialist, Brian Payne was coolly efficient and had strategy down to an art form. With an unmatched attention to detail, there was no such thing as half-assed in his world. He didn't tolerate it.

Jamie Flanagan purportedly sported a genius-level IQ and had been the original player until he met and married Colonel Garrett's granddaughter. That quick brain, combined with a substantial amount of brawn, made him a force to be reckoned with.

And with a lucky streak that bordered on the divine, Guy McCann's ability to skate the thin line between recklessness and perfection was still locker-room lore.

Much like his, Guy's methods were governed more

by his gut than his head and, thus far, his gut hadn't failed him. Had Seth been orchestrating the prank on Juan-Carlos, he would have put the groom in camo, the bride in a Hooter's T-shirt and the pastor in a wife-beater undershirt. He inwardly smiled, wishing he knew them well enough at this point to say so. It would come, he knew, but building those kinds of relationships took time, something he certainly had plenty of now. He mentally grimaced.

Payne and the other two shared a look and Seth got the distinct impression that an entire unspoken conversation had passed between them.

That kind of communication took time, too.

"Listen, Seth," Payne said. "Ordinarily when the Colonel sends us new recruits, we know those guys are getting out because they want to. They've reached a point in their careers where, for whatever reason, they're no longer able or willing to do the job." He paused. "As we understand it, you were not at that point."

To be less than honest wouldn't be fair, but that didn't make him any more eager to have this discussion. Nevertheless, like so many others recently, it was a conversation he would have to have. He swallowed a sigh.

"No, I was not," Seth admitted. "I'd intended to make a full career of the military. It's what I'd envisioned when I went in and an alternate path—or occupation, for that matter—was never in any future I'd planned."

"You were ROTC, right?" Jamie asked. "Through the University of Georgia?"

Seth nodded. Go Dogs. He was still a huge fan and

proud alumnus. Judging from the Alabama memorabilia scattered about the room, so were they. Nick Saban had secured the Tide's thirteenth National Championship, but the perpetually unsmiling coach still had a long way to go before he could ever reach Bear Bryant's legendary status, if you asked him.

Seth released a slow breath, hoping to ease some of the sudden tension from his chest. "But, as I'm sure the colonel told you, I lost my mother seven months ago and I promised her that I would come out as soon as I could. I've got a little sister and a nephew and, without getting into too much family history—" he'd just as soon boil his balls in acid, thank you very much "—I'm the only family they have." And vice versa, of course, he suddenly realized, the thought giving him an odd pause. He blinked, struggling to focus. "She wanted me to be around for them," he finally managed to say. "I made a promise, so I'm here."

"Well, it goes without saying that we're glad you are," Payne said. "We know this will be an adjustment for you, but have every confidence that you'll be up for whatever we throw at you."

"And I am particularly glad you're here," McCann chimed in with a chuckle, popping the top on an energy drink. "Because that means you're going to take my place on Ono Island this weekend." He scratched his chin in apparent bafflement. "Curiously, Julia doesn't like it when I pretend to be in love with another woman."

If he'd been eating something he would have choked. "I'm sorry?"

Before he could recover, Payne opened the file he'd been reading when he came in. He sent a cool stare in Guy's direction, but Guy merely bit the end off a piece of red licorice and grinned unrepentantly.

"Trent McWilliams," Payne said, arching a blond eyebrow. "Does the name ring a bell?"

Seth's jaw nearly unhinged. "As in the quarterback for the Orlando Mustangs? *That* Trent McWilliams?" He was South eastern Conference royalty, was a first-round draft pick and a born-and-bred Alabama boy. He was supposedly good-looking—he'd have to be when one considered he had an entire fan base who'd nicknamed themselves "Trent's Tarts" and hung out with country music superstars and the Hollywood elite. He wasn't just a mega-talented quarterback, he was a star in his own right.

Payne flashed a smile. "That would be the one. Trent's been having some security issues, issues that seem to be escalating the closer it gets to his wedding date, which is this weekend. We've been running point for him for the past several weeks trying to isolate the threat." He grimaced. "So far we haven't had any luck."

Seth found himself more intrigued than he'd expected. He savored the adrenaline that shot into his system. "What sort of threats?"

"Well, you've always got the run-of-the-mill overzealous fans," Jamie drawled, leaning forward. "The ones who have watched all the games, every bit of YouTube footage, have read every interview and believe that they have a *unique* connection to the object of their misplaced attention. You've got the obsessive letter writer who critiques every game and sends his notes and suggestions, the toenail-clipping woman, who mailed her 'collection' as a gift."

They all grimaced.

"Then there's the women," Guy chimed in. "The constant propositioning, the barrage of nude photos."

"And then there's stuff like this," Payne said, his tone subdued, handing Seth a sheet of paper that had been slipped into a page protector. "This was the first."

It was Trent McWilliams's wedding announcement, which had been printed from an online celebrity gossip site. The couple had been circled in red with a slash across the photo as though "banning" the couple. *Not no, but HELL no,* had been written in block-style capital letters across the bottom of the page.

"Initially, that one didn't raise too much concern," Payne told him. "It seemed harmless enough. Trent received dozens of letters from sad women denouncing the impending marriage. But when this one arrived a month later," he said, handing over another sheet, "*then* it became an issue."

Seth inspected the second paper. The same red pen, same barring symbol, but this one was over Trent and Nella's names. More significantly, on their save-the-date announcement. Which someone would have had to have received. Someone who wasn't a run-of-the-mill-psycho fan, but someone who was close…or too close for comfort at the very least. The hair on the back of Seth's neck prickled. *Call it off* was written in the block-style letters, again in red, on the bottom.

Now he understood.

"Ah," Seth murmured, studying the two. "How many people got a notice?"

"One hundred. They're hosting the wedding at Trent's place on Ono Island, so space is an issue. It's three acres max, with the house and guesthouse, various garages and the like. They're keeping it intimate, according to the wedding planner."

Guy snorted. "Intimate is *not* a hundred people. Intimate is five, with two of them being the bride and groom, and one being the preacher."

"Finally, Trent received this one two weeks ago." Payne handed over the last page.

It was the wedding invitation, which left no doubt that the threat was real. Whoever was sending the messages was relatively close to Trent. It was hand lettered, too, leaving no room to speculate that this was a copy. There was the banning symbol again, with *So it's to be death at a wedding, then? So be it,* printed in red along the bottom.

How bizarre, Seth thought. And ambiguous. Whose death? Trent's? His bride's? Or someone else's?

Better still, how was he supposed to protect every single one of the guests? One-hundred people plus the wedding party, not to mention the catering and service crews. Seth considered himself a pretty damned fine soldier, but he'd never quite mastered the handy ability to be everywhere at once. What, precisely, did they expect him to do? He could wing it, of course. He was certain that something would come to him—it always did—but he'd prefer to at least attempt to play by the rules on this first mission. He needed to establish their trust first, so that they wouldn't question him later when he did pull what his previous commanding officer liked to call his "stunts." Stunt or not, he always managed to get the job done.

"Naturally we don't expect you to protect every single person at the event," Payne told him, displaying the unsettling knack of plucking the thoughts right out of his head. "You're going to take over as point on security—"

"Disguised as the wedding planner's boyfriend," Guy interjected.

"—and, if you haven't isolated the threat by the rehearsal, then your purpose will shift to acting as personal bodyguard to Trent McWilliams and his intended bride."

In other words, if he wanted to avoid catastrophe, he needed to apprehend the culprit before someone died or ruined the wedding. Someone who had eluded these guys for several weeks.

Excellent.

Seth was considering his odds of actually keeping this job when something McCann said fully registered. "The wedding planner's boyfriend?" That sounded more ominous than he cared to contemplate. He didn't want to be anyone's boyfriend, pretend or otherwise. A friend with benefits was more to his liking, preferably one with an excellent sense of humor, a nice ass and her own address. Though Seth knew there were people who made the marriage and family plan work, he knew more people who didn't. While he wasn't opposed to taking risks, he nevertheless knew when to heed the odds.

Marriage, or any variation, wasn't for him.

He felt a nudge of dread prod his belly.

The wedding planner was probably going to have a sickeningly different attitude about it. Oh, jeez, he thought, becoming more alarmed by the second. She'd likely be a hopeless romantic bent on trying to convert him and anyone else who had the misguided audacity to want to remain single. No doubt his naked ring finger would be a challenge to her and she'd alternate between fits of perkiness and pity that would drive him insane. *Shit.*

Perky women annoyed him. What the hell did they have to be so happy about anyway? he wondered, his mind quickly calculating how many levels of discomfort he'd have to endure over the course of this assignment. The seventh circle of hell sounded more appealing.

Granted, he had to admit it was a good idea—the wedding planner had access to everything and everyone involved on every level of the event. If he'd been pulling the plan together, he imagined this would have been his solution, too.

But for someone else. Not for *him.*

Payne handed him a photo. "Penelope Hart is the wedding planner. She's based here in Atlanta and was a sorority sister of the bride, Nella Francis."

"And she's—"

"—totally vetted," Payne supplied, anticipating his question.

Seth nodded, glad that they seemed to be thinking along the same lines, at any rate.

"Evidently Ms. Hart is the go-to girl for all fashionable

weddings in the area," Jamie said, his lips twisting with baffled humor. "I'd have married Audrey at a drive-through if she'd been game."

"That would have seriously wounded Juan-Carlos," Seth remarked, his gaze dropping to the image as the other three laughed.

A strange flutter moved through his belly as he looked at the woman in question. Curly black hair hung to her narrow shoulders and framed a face that was more startling than pretty. She had a wide forehead made softer with sleek, dark brows that winged over a pair of very bright blue eyes. Her skin had an olive tone that hinted of Italian origins and, though she was relatively fair in this photo, he could tell she was a girl who tanned easily. Her cheekbones rested high on her face, leaving sultry hollows beneath, and the mouth and chin that tied it altogether were simultaneously charming and sexy.

Pretty definitely didn't fit, Seth thought broodingly as he continued to study the photo. *Compelling* was a more apt description, he decided. She drew the eye and had the power to hold it. And, when it came right down to it, that was probably better than pretty. Pretty got boring.

She, he instinctively knew, would never be boring.

And the same instincts—these of the ball-tightening variety—that told him she wouldn't be boring also told him she'd be trouble.

He mentally swore. He didn't have time for trouble, pretty, interesting or otherwise.

"Penelope has been brought completely up to speed

and is fully willing to cooperate in any way possible," Payne told him.

He would imagine so, Seth thought. He didn't know a whole lot about the wedding planning industry, but he suspected that having a murder take place at one of the events she'd coordinated would be bad for business.

"You'll meet her tomorrow morning. Since parking is at a premium on the island and you're supposed to be a 'couple' anyway, you'll ride down with her. Will Forrester, Tanner Crawford and Lucas Finn will follow and the four of you will coordinate the security. As Ms. Hart's love interest, you'll be in closest proximity to Trent and Nella and, because of that, you'll run point."

That was certainly going to endear him to his fellow security specialists, Seth thought with an inward grimace. *Thanks, boys.* He appreciated *that* target on his back.

"You're also the only single guy here," Jamie told him. "And, as Guy pointed out earlier, women don't typically like it when their significant others pretend to be in love with other women."

Ah, Seth thought as understanding dawned. He didn't get point because of his untested skill—he'd gotten it because none of the rest of them wanted it. He didn't want it either, but as low man on the totem pole, he wasn't going to get a choice. He felt his lips twitch, reluctantly impressed with their plan. It was clever and devious, both traits he happened to admire.

A hint of humor lurked in Payne's cool gaze. "You're still unattached, correct?"

Seth nodded and smiled. And he had every intention of staying that way. Those weren't the kind of odds he liked to play with. What was the point, really? He'd never met a woman who made him want to do anything any different and he'd come to the conclusion that she didn't exist. "Quite happily, with no plans to change the status quo."

"Famous last words," Guy muttered with a significant eye roll.

Before Seth could form a rebuttal, Payne handed him a set of keys. "To your apartment," he told him. "You're on the third floor. It's furnished for now, but we can easily move those things out as you feather your nest, so to speak. Feel free to make any changes you want." Next he handed over a laptop case, a Glock 9 with a permit to carry concealed, a cell phone and the file for his first case. "You'll need to take a look at the file, then you're to meet the others this evening to go over strategy. We can't let anything get by on this one. This is as high profile as anything we've ever done and our reputation is fully on the line here."

No pressure, Seth thought.

"Five o'clock, your place okay?" Payne asked.

Even aware of the especially high stakes, Seth felt more confident with a plan in mind. He nodded. "Sounds good."

"I've told Ms. Hart to expect you at eight tomorrow morning. Her address is in the file. She's in Marietta."

The same as his sister and nephew, Seth thought. Familiar with the drive, he made a mental note to leave in plenty of time to compensate for the heavy morning traffic.

"You've got transportation?" Payne asked.

He did, a new-to-him quad-cab truck. It was midnight-blue with leather interior and a sunroof. When he'd pulled up in the big monster, his sister had merely smiled indulgently, shaken her head and asked if the tank he'd wanted hadn't been available. The smart-ass. Yes, it was big and yes, it wasn't exactly economically friendly, but he'd test driven other vehicles and decided that he'd rather be in something a little more substantial than a soup can. He recycled, dammit. It wasn't like he wasn't doing his part.

At his nod, Payne stood and extended his hand. "All right, then. Welcome aboard."

Seth got to his feet and his palm met Payne's. "Thank you. I appreciate the opportunity." He congratulated himself for the diplomatic response. He couldn't say that he was glad to be here, because that was a lie. He'd rather be with his guys, finishing the job they'd started. An image of his mother suddenly rose in his mind's eye and he swallowed.

But a promise was a promise.

And Seth McCutcheon was a man of his word.

PAYNE WAITED until their newest recruit was safely out of earshot before turning a questioning look at his friends and partners. "Well?"

"I like him," Guy said. "But it's obvious that he doesn't want to be here."

"Did any of us really want to be here to start with?"

Jamie asked. "Had Danny lived, would any of us be doing what we're doing? Or would we still be in the service?"

That was an excellent point, Payne thought. Had their good friend and unit mate Danny Levinson lived— had they not each felt responsible for his death in some way—would they have left the military? Would there even be a Ranger Security?

No, probably not.

But there also wouldn't be any wives and children, no one to go home to at the end of the day, no one to love… and that was a pretty damned miserable thought.

"I guess not," Guy said, suddenly somber. "But it's a damned shame that some sort of tragedy always brings new recruits to our door."

Because they didn't hire anyone without Colonel Carl Garrett's recommendation, as well as extensive background checks on their own, they knew as much as it was possible to know about Seth McCutcheon. So they'd been able to read a lot about his situation and his character simply by looking between the lines. His father had left when he was just five years old—old enough to remember him, but not to actually know him. Seth had been raised by his mother, a high school English teacher who supplemented her income by selling cosmetics on the side. By all accounts, she was highly regarded, deeply loved and, given that Seth had kept his promise to her after her death, even more respected.

Though he'd been voted Class Clown, he'd graduated valedictorian from his high school class, earned the ROTC scholarship, where he got a communications degree, then went through Jump School to complete his Ranger training.

Interviews with fellow soldiers painted the picture of a man very much like Guy, one who didn't always follow the play book, but never failed to get the desired result. He'd been nicknamed Wild Card and, though he'd only spent roughly thirty minutes in Seth's company, Payne could sense the same sort of irreverent energy in him he'd always associated with McCann. There was an intelligence and humor that lurked in his gaze that was unmistakably familiar.

In short, despite the fact that he didn't want to be here, that he'd never planned to leave the military, ultimately Payne thought Seth would eventually come to enjoy this career move. The work was different, certainly, but it was never boring and—his gaze slid to his friends—the company was first-rate.

As for this initial assignment… He chuckled.

Jamie glanced up. "What's so funny?"

"To make sure that our agent is up to speed on his role as her love interest, Penelope Hart sent a 'history' of them over today for Seth to review and learn before they make their debut on Ono Island."

A bark of laughter erupted from Guy's throat. "She did, did she?"

"Did you read it?" Jamie asked.

Payne nodded and released a slow breath. "Yep. And let's just say that if the wedding planning business ever fizzles out for her, then she's got an excellent future writing soap operas."

Guy grinned. "That good, eh?"

Payne lifted a bottle of soda to his lips. "Oh, yeah. I put it in the file."

"I'd like to be a fly on the wall when he reads it," Jamie remarked, chuckling under his breath.

He would, too, Payne thought. He would, too…

3

As a rule, Penelope Hart didn't appreciate it when people showed up unexpectedly on her front doorstep, regardless of whether it was the Girl Scouts, the Jehovah's Witnesses, would-be politicians or cosmetic salesladies. She thought simply dropping by was rude and, though Southerners were famous for it, she still believed it was bad form to appear at another person's home, uninvited, unexpected and otherwise out of the blue.

That opinion was soon going to make her a giant hypocrite. Because she was about to do it herself.

Her would-be victim? The security specialist assigned to keep Trent and Nella safe. Why couldn't she wait until eight o'clock in the morning to meet him as scheduled? Her cheeks puffed as she exhaled mightily.

That was the million-dollar question.

On the drive over, Penelope had been telling herself that she needed to assess him herself, that she needed to make sure that, first, he was capable—as if Ranger Security hadn't already done that themselves she thought with a mental eye roll—and, second, he was believable boyfriend material for her.

If she was honest, that was the real reason she couldn't wait until the morning. She had to see him for herself—meet him for herself—if for no other reason than to make sure she could pull this off. All she knew about Seth McCutcheon was that he was a new hire and, as the only unattached man employed by the security company, he had to be *her* man.

Penelope understood that. Trying to pass him off as one of Trent's best friends or relatives wouldn't work due to the intimate nature of the wedding. The agency was plugging in three other security experts, as well. Each of those men would be going in disguised as service workers.

Since she was the wedding planner and would have access to every part of the event, having Seth working with her was a no-brainer. But putting him in as her boyfriend felt very…weird.

Especially since Penelope hadn't ever had a proper boyfriend.

Had she dated? Certainly. With regularity? Yes. But she never allowed things to progress past the fun stage, past the first blush of new romance. As such, the bloom was never fully off the rose. Meeting someone, that first sizzle of awareness, the prelude to that first kiss… that epitomized romance for her and that was all she was interested in. The minute she felt obligated to do anything—family functions, laundry, errands, what have you—for the guy she was dating, she instantly withdrew from the relationship and moved on to the next guy. She was never invested enough to care about the end of the relationship—translate: she never got hurt—and there were plenty of fish in the sea. Her lips quirked. Luckily, she was a pretty good angler.

As it happened, there was no next guy at the moment. So in that regard, pretending to have a boyfriend wasn't going to be a problem.

She'd be lying, though, if she didn't admit to a little bit of trepidation. Even pretending to be even semicommitted made her skin itch and her chest squeeze. Her friends often teased her about her chosen profession, considering that she never had any intention of getting married herself—her parents had *nine* marriages between the two of them, need she say more?—but it was *the* ultimate party and, when it came to planning, she was a pro. She always had been.

Her degree was actually in communications, but after hosting one party after another throughout college, then baby showers and the weddings of a few friends, she'd found her niche and had never looked back. Despite the fact that she never wanted to have a wedding herself, it was *the* grand event. Everything else—birthday parties, baby showers, etc.—was simply second tier.

Pen didn't do second tier.

Trent and Nella's wedding was her highest profile to date, and it went without saying that having this event go off without a hitch would fully cement her in her field. With that came financial security, something she'd been working toward since she was old enough to get a job. She'd grown up in a feast-or-famine paycheck-to-paycheck world and had hated the uncertainty of it.

As such, Penelope was careful with her purchases, knew when to pay for quality and when to abstain, and she was a saver. In the early days of her business, it had been especially hard. But if this wedding went off the way it should and brought her the recognition she anticipated, every penny she'd banked would be worth it because she'd finally, *blessedly,* be able to spend a bit of it as a down payment on a house.

A place of her own. Once she got into it, she'd never move again. With as many marriages as her parents had had, she'd been moving for what felt like her entire life, yanked from pillar to post, at the new stepparent's whim. She'd hated the packing and unpacking, sleeping in an unfamiliar place, making new friends, leaving old friends. But with her own house, bought and paid for with her own money that she'd earned, she'd never have to worry about that again.

Then again, given the threat aimed at Trent, that was a big if.

In fact, if she could get her hands on the interfering asshole who was making the threats, she'd throttle the culprit herself.

Of course, Trent and Nella's safety had to come before anything else. Still, she couldn't deny that the letter writer was throwing a wrench into more than a year's worth of planning.

It annoyed the hell out of her.

Penelope pulled into a parking space and took a deep cleansing breath, then let it go with a whoosh. It was after business hours, but she'd learned from Guy McCann that Seth McCutcheon had moved into the building today. Luckily, she'd gotten the security code to enter the building the last time she'd been by. She entered it now, then took the elevator to the third floor. To her chagrin, her palms inexplicably began to sweat, and a nervous flutter winged through her belly. She was being ridiculous, Pen told herself. He was only a man. There was no reason for her to be tense.

Her heels clicked in the quiet hallway, punctuating the rapid beat of her heart. She found his door and, after the briefest hesitation, she rang the bell. She heard the soft pad of bare feet over the floor, then the lock tumbled and he opened the door.

Whatever she'd expected, *he* was not it.

Penelope swallowed, blinked, and then attempted to pull *all* of him into focus. It was difficult, for many reasons, but the most pertinent was the fact that he was half-naked. He'd opened his door wearing nothing but a pair of low-slung khaki shorts that were in serious danger of slipping off his lean hips. His massive feet were indeed bare, as were most of his legs, all of his splendidly muscled chest, shoulders, back and neck. She caught a glimpse of a tattoo on his upper arm, but wasn't at an angle to appreciate it. A bottle of beer dangled loosely in one mouthwateringly large hand and the expression on his extraordinarily handsome face was baffled but friendly. A slow smile crept over a very sensual mouth and interest flared in his direct, dark green gaze.

Every cell in her body sizzled so loudly she actually thought she could hear the steam, and a flush of heat rolled over her skin in a long scorching wave that should have made fire flame from her fingertips.

Sweet mercy.

He peered out into the hall, then ducked back in and winced apologetically. "Listen, sweetheart, I'm not sure who sent you, but I don't need any company tonight."

Sent her? Company? It took almost three full seconds for the implication to set in, then another one to make her flush violently with embarrassment.

Another reason not to appear unexpectedly on someone's doorstep, Pen thought.

One might be mistaken for a hooker.

She extended her hand. "Penelope Hart," she said briskly. "I'm the—"

"Wedding planner," he finished, chuckling. "Sorry, I couldn't resist," he said, though she didn't get the impression he was sorry at all.

"That's okay. I get taken for a call girl all the time," she quipped.

He laughed, the sound low and slightly rough. Sexy. "My instructions said to meet you at eight tomorrow morning," he told her, opening the door to allow her in. She slid past him, too close to all that tempting bare masculine flesh, and felt a low throb hum a warning in her belly. She caught a faint whiff of his cologne, something smooth and musky. She licked her lips. "Did I miss a memo?"

"No," she said, turning as he closed the door. He motioned for her to follow him down a small hallway, then gestured for her to take a seat.

"Can I get you something to drink?" he asked. "Tea, soda, beer?"

Truthfully, she could use it—her mouth was bone-dry—but she ultimately refused. "No, thanks."

He excused himself for a minute and she took advantage of that time to take stock of his apartment. It had obviously been decorated by a man, but one with very good and very expensive taste. Heavy leather furniture the color of creamed coffee was positioned around a flat-panel television that hung above a marble fireplace and a large footlocker served as a coffee table. Various pieces of original artwork hung on the walls and a very interesting driftwood piece sat in the corner.

Though he'd supposedly only arrived today, already a few photographs were on the mantel and she resisted the urge to get up and inspect them. From this distance, she could make out one picture in particular—one of a family on a sailboat. She noted the condensation on the coaster on the table next to the recliner, a small bowl of trail mix beside it. The television was tuned into the History channel, a documentary about WWII paused, awaiting his return. A file with Trent McWilliam's name on it sat on the coffee table, along with a laptop, a gun and a set of keys. He might have only been here for twenty-four hours, but she could tell he'd made himself at home. Was he used to adapting quickly to his circumstances or was he happy to be here? she wondered, unreasonably intrigued.

"Sorry about that," he said, returning to the living room. He'd shrugged into a T-shirt, a dark olive that somehow made his eyes appear even greener, and had slipped on a pair of top-Siders.

Impossibly, he was just as good-looking with his shirt on. His hair was a dark brown with natural golden high-lights and a small scar curved like a half-moon on his chin. Irrationally, she wanted to lick it. "No problem," she said, her voice strangely thick.

"Has something happened?" he asked.

She stared dumbly at him.

"With the case?" he prompted, his lips twitching. "Any new threat? Another letter? Anything suspicious going on? I'm assuming that's why you're here."

Yes, well. That was a perfectly logical assumption, but it'd be wrong. Because deciding to come over here was completely illogical. She was a moron, Penelope decided. A complete and utter moron.

"Actually, no," she said, clearing her throat. "I came by because I wanted to talk to you about our cover story."

His eyes twinkled and he passed a large hand over his face to disguise a smile. "Oh, I think you covered that quite well already. I read the dissertation, er, file."

Dissertation? So he was a smart-ass? How unfortu-nate that she liked that about him. "It's important that we have our story down," she said, tucking a strand of hair behind her ear. Jeez, it sounded even lamer when she said it aloud. What the hell had she been thinking?

"It is," he agreed. "Though I think we might have kept it a little simpler." He shrugged. "We met, we clicked, we're dating."

"That's too vague," Penelope told him, determined to

salvage this ill-advised visit. "Some of the women who are going to be at this wedding know me pretty well. We were sorority sisters and they're going to want details. How we met, where we went on our first date—"

"To Piedmont Park for a picnic," he supplied, evidently remembering some of what she'd supplied.

"—and what was it about you, specifically, that has made me want exclusivity rights."

"Nevertheless, I don't know why I had to rescue your puppy from a storm drain, why I'm taking art classes at night or why I have to be anti-meringue," he said. "I happen to like meringue. It's the perfect complement to chocolate pie." A small line emerged between his brows and that keen gaze, which upon first inspection had appeared irreverent, was actually more shrewd than what she'd originally given him credit for. "What do you mean 'make you want exclusivity rights'?"

"Rescuing the dog was noble, an admirable trait," she explained, ignoring his question. If someone rescued her own dog, Byron, she'd certainly find that noble. "You're taking the art classes because you aren't afraid to learn new things and you're anti-meringue, as you put it, because it's an endearing quirk."

"So I'm noble, intrepid and endearing?" he asked, his lips slipping into a wide smile. "Why don't I donate a kidney to a complete stranger so that I can be generous, too?"

"Ooh, that's a good one," she said. "You should write that down."

His expression blanked. "I was kidding."

She knew that, of course. "And you've got an excellent sense of humor, too. We're on a roll."

"You never answered my question."

"Which one?"

"Exclusivity rights? What did you mean?"

Penelope suddenly stood. She'd learned everything she needed to know and even more that she wished she hadn't. Like the fact that he was too damned good-looking for her own good, that he wasn't going to be as easily managed as she'd hoped and that he had enormous feet, which meant that the rest of him was probably proportionate. Heat flashed over her thighs and her lady business sizzled beneath her panties.

"We'll cover that in the morning," she said, slipping her purse over her shoulder. "I should be going. I've still got quite a bit to pull together before we roll out in the morning."

"Er…okay," he said, looking somewhat bemused, evidently unsure what to make of her or her unexpected visit. That was fair enough, she thought, because she was acting like a crazy person.

With a stream of silent obscenities and recriminations slipping through her brain, she retraced her steps to the door. She knew without looking that he was staring at her ass—she could practically feel his gaze—and then abruptly turned to tell him goodbye before reaching for the doorknob. Without warning, he bent down and kissed her. It was bold and brash, a sensual sweep of his lips over hers. Her breath caught in her throat, blood boiled beneath her skin and her heart faltered, then galloped in her chest.

Looking gallingly unaffected, he drew back and winked. "For practice," he said, his eyes twinkling with humor. She had a feeling he was trying to teach her some sort of lesson, but knew that she couldn't have earned a passing mark. Her brain was too scrambled to absorb any kind of message, well-intentioned or otherwise.

"Oh," she said, another brilliant stab at coherent conversation. She bade him a quick good-evening, then made a beeline for the elevator. He was still staring at her, a too-satisfied smile on his sexy lips, when the doors slid shut.

Penelope immediately sagged against the wall and let out a huge breath. Well, this was a fine snag. She'd had come here to find out if she was going to be able to pretend to like her bogus boyfriend and was leaving with the unequivocal assurance that, given the way her nipples were tingling and the breathless anticipation crowding her throat, she was in more danger of liking him *too much*. She smothered a whimper.

Something told her this wasn't going to be a good thing.

WEDDINGS BY HART was located a block off the historic Marietta Square in an old, white brick building with lots of black wrought-iron accessories. Window boxes burst with pink geraniums and an ornate sign with Penelope's logo hung over the door. The windows were loaded with wedding gowns, veils, tiaras and tulle, and just looking at them made Seth want to turn and run in the other direction.

Penelope was standing at the back of a big, white

van, a clipboard in her hand. Black curls spilled out of a ponytail that hung over her shoulder and she was nibbling on the end of a pencil, deep in thought.

He envied the pencil, especially since he knew how soft her mouth was. Kissing her last night had been a spur-of-the-moment decision—they were some of his best ones, if you asked him—and so he'd leaned in, catching her unaware. She'd been warm and responsive and when he'd tasted her sweet gasp, he'd felt something strangely expectant settle in his gut.

He'd done it in part to put her in her place, because he didn't think purposely mistaking her for a hooker had done the trick. Seth grinned, remembering the look on her face. He wanted her to know just exactly who was in charge here. Showing up at his place unannounced to scope him out and take his measure had been a ballsy move, he had to admit, but it had also been a power play. His company had been hired by Trent McWilliams to do a job and he'd been assigned to the case. She was supposed to cooperate with the security team, not try to run it. Undoubtedly, she just couldn't help herself—there was no way she could do her job effectively without being able to organize and delegate, he imagined—but this was *his* area of expertise.

"Morning," he said, handing her a cup of coffee. He stared at her, even more intrigued than he'd been last night. And that was saying something, because he'd gone over the file she'd given him at least half a dozen more times after she'd left his apartment, trying to glean as much as possible from what she'd included about herself.

She looked up and her startled gaze tangled with his. Her eyes were a clear blue, unpolluted and ringed in a slightly darker hue. A self-conscious smile flirted with her especially ripe lips, but never quite made the curl. "Good morning," she said, accepting the drink with a tiny frown.

"Two sugars, one cream, right?"

"Yes," she remarked hesitantly. She glanced at him uncertainly again. "How did you—"

Seth grinned. "You included it in the 'Things I Need To Know' section," he explained. As well as a lot of other interesting tidbits that hadn't seemed particularly pertinent before her visit, but had somehow gained significance. Like the fact that she was double-jointed, knew sign language, could recite "Casey at the Bat" and didn't like sweet potatoes. Why did any of this matter? He was still asking himself that, as well.

She inclined her head. "Ah. Thank you."

He glanced inside the van, where it had been packed with her luggage—purple, her favorite color, he remembered—and various wedding paraphernalia. "All packed up, then?"

"We will be as soon as your stuff is properly loaded."

He slid the duffel bag off his shoulder and directly into the van. "Done."

"What about that other bag?" she asked, nodding to his other arm.

"I need this one." It contained his laptop and files, all of which he needed to consult while they were on the road. He was as up to speed as he could be, but couldn't shake the feeling that he was missing something, that there was a clue hidden there that he just hadn't picked up on yet.

"And the other operatives?"

Operatives? She made them sound like international spies, Seth thought, feeling his lips twitch. "They're going to meet us in Foley and follow us in." Actually, they'd originally planned to meet here, but Forrester had wanted to go to Lambert's Café, "Home of the throwed rolls" and had convinced the other two men to leave a little bit early this morning so that they could have lunch.

"No problem," she said. "I'd actually promised my staff that we'd stop at Lambert's on the way in, so that'll be perfect."

Unable to help himself, he chuckled.

"What's so funny?"

"That's why the other guys left early. They didn't think we'd have time to stop."

She slipped the pencil behind her ear and then closed the van doors. "We always have time to stop for yeast rolls," she said. "I built it into the schedule."

She would. "This must be one helluva restaurant," Seth remarked with a shake of his head.

She arched a brow. "You've never been?"

"No," he said.

Truth be told, he'd never been to the Gulf Shores area at all. Several of the kids from his high school class had gone down after graduation, but he'd already had a job lined up and, even with the ROTC scholarship, still needed every penny he could get. He'd stayed home and his mother had thrown a big party for him. She'd cooked his favorite meal—chicken and dumplings—and they'd had a horror film marathon, then played cards. She'd let him win a hundred bucks from her and wouldn't take it back no matter how hard he'd tried to return it to her. Afterward they'd gone out to Donagan Lake and gone sailing, which had been one of his mother's favorite pastimes. He smiled, remembering, and felt a hollow ache settle around his heart.

Her expression brightened. "Oh well, you're in for a treat then. It's good, old country food and lots of it."

That certainly sounded good to him, Seth thought. He offered to drive, knowing that she would refuse. This was a woman who had written a ten-page history of their *fake* relationship and dropped by his apartment twelve hours before they were supposed to meet just to scope him out. The term "control freak" didn't begin to cover her need to direct, organize and otherwise oversee.

He'd gotten the distinct impression that his way of doing things with a more fluid plan was going to drive her insane.

Perversely, he actually looked forward to that.

"I've got it, thanks," she said, then promptly slid into the driver's seat and waited expectedly on him.

He felt a droll smile roll around his lips as he settled into the passenger seat and watched her drop her sunglasses into place. She picked up a walkie-talkie and told Monica—her good friend and assistant who'd been with her for the past three years—that they were leaving. She waited for a response, then pulled out into traffic. Paul, her other must-have-man on staff, was the official heavy lifter and had only been around for about a year. He'd been in the service, but hadn't re-upped after his first four years. He had to give the guys at Ranger Security credit—they'd left no stone unturned and had thoroughly investigated everyone.

"So you've had a chance to look over everything?" she asked.

"I'd looked over everything before you came by last night to check up on me," Seth told her. "I thought I passed the test last night."

"Who said anything about a test?"

"You didn't have to." He settled his own sunglasses into place and tried not to stare at the sleek expanse of tanned thigh her sundress revealed. "Did I pass muster? Can I be your pretend boyfriend?" he teased.

"We've got a lot riding on whether or not you can act like my boyfriend," she said, not bothering to deny it. "Sorry if my concern annoys you, but I just needed to make sure that you—"

"Would be someone you'd date," he finished, chuckling. "I get it. So?" he prodded, purposely goading her because it was fun. "Are you going to be able to muster the enthusiasm to pretend to like me?"

She flushed, the pink climbing her neck. "I think I can manage." She pulled onto 75 south, competently negotiating the heavy morning traffic. "What about you? Going to have any problem playing the part of Mr. Wedding Planner?"

His gaze lingered over her leg, up over her breasts and settled on her mouth. Given the dream he'd had last night, one that featured the two of them rolling naked in the sand, he didn't think so. "No," he said, his voice strangely hoarse. "I think I can manage it. Granted, it helps that you're attractive." He sighed heavily. "Feigning interest in a dog-pointer would have been a harder sell."

"That's a terrible thing to say," she said, trying to turn a shocked laugh into self-righteous outrage. She didn't succeed and, to his delight, continued to smile.

"Terribly honest," he corrected, pleased that he'd startled a chuckle out of her. He shot her a modest grin. "That's the least you can expect from a noble puppy-rescuer, right?"

"But you never really rescued a puppy."

"Do you want me to get confused? I'm trying to get into character here."

She sighed heavily and bit her lip. "Why do I get the feeling I'm going to bitterly regret coming up with our history?"

Probably because she was, Seth thought. But she couldn't have it both ways. She either wanted him to adhere to the script or she didn't. And, as much as he'd originally dreaded this, he could actually see that pretending to be her boyfriend was going to be the silver lining of this assignment. He was intensely—stupidly—interested in her. For every question she'd answered about herself, he had twenty more.

Starting with the one she hadn't answered last night. He'd been turning that "exclusivity rights" comment of hers over and over again in his mind. The more he thought about it, the more it sounded to him as if she'd never found someone she cared enough about to give them exclusivity. Like she'd never really had a significant other.

But that couldn't be right, Seth thought, shooting her a covert look. She was a wedding planner, for heaven's sake. From death do you part, to love and to cherish, in sickness and in health, I do and I do. She *arranged* romance.

"Back to that exclusivity comment you made last night," Seth persisted, unwilling to let it go. Intuition told him a wealth of information was hidden in that offhand little comment and he wanted to know what it was.

From the corner of his eye he saw her hands tense on the steering wheel and her sleek jaw tighten. She lifted her chin. "What about it?"

"What did you mean? Because unless I'm mistaken, the inference was that you giving exclusivity to someone was a rare occurrence, a phenomenon of sorts. Or did I read that wrong?" He chuckled under his breath. "I mean it almost sounds like you've never had a boyfriend before."

Her cheeks puffed as she exhaled mightily. "That's because I haven't," she said. "By choice. I'm in the business of uniting couples, Mr. McCutcheon. It doesn't mean I'm in the business of *becoming* one."

And with that grim, enigmatic statement, which hadn't been in the file—hers or Ranger Security's— Penelope Hart, the commitment-phobic wedding planner suddenly became the most interesting person Seth had ever met.

4

FROM THE LOOK on his face, she'd thoroughly shocked him, Pen thought and was secretly pleased. For whatever reason, she got the impression that very little surprised Seth McCutcheon. By doing so, she'd accomplished something rare.

Nevertheless, a subject change was in order. She was already at a disadvantage, thanks to the unexpected, unholy attraction tying her middle up in knots. Giving him more personal information about her when she knew so very little about him wasn't prudent. The flow of information hadn't been the least bit equitable and she had no one to blame for that but herself.

In retrospect, coming up with their history and providing him with so much personal information, even if most of it was superficial, had turned out to be one of her less intelligent ideas. She should have met him first, then put together what he would need, not the other way around. But how was she to know that he was going to be the most attractive man she'd ever seen. Or that her loins quivered just by looking at him. Or that he was in possession of a very keen mind and eyes that she suspected never missed a trick?

"So now that you've reviewed the case file, do you have a particular suspect in mind?" she asked. She picked up 285 west and took a sip of her coffee.

"Other than safely assuming it's a woman, no," he admitted.

She thought so, too, but still felt the irrational need to argue. She suspected it was going to become the theme for the weekend. "What makes you so sure it's a woman?"

From the corner of her eye she watched him grin. "I'm not maligning your gender, Penelope," he said, and she loved the way her name came off his lips. "It's just simple deductive reasoning. Trent's a good-looking guy about to go off the market. As you know, he got dozens of letters from disappointed women."

"There were a few from men, too," she retorted. Mostly gay men, she would admit, but still…

"True," he said. "But when you consider the ratios and the whole passive-aggressive nature of the threats…I'm not saying that I don't think it's real or that this person isn't dangerous, because I do." He frowned. "But I'm getting a weird vibe on this, as though there's something I'm missing, a dot I'm not connecting."

"You haven't even really started yet," Pen added.

"I know, but—" He shook his head. "At any rate, my money is on this being a woman. Typically, a man's nature is to confront, put it all out in the open and come to blows if necessary. Women tend to be a bit more… sneaky." He pulled a face. "They'll bake chocolate laxatives into brownies, slash tires, scrub the toilet bowl with a guy's toothbrush. That sort of thing."

She felt a laugh break up in her throat. "Are you speaking from personal experience?"

"No," he said. His expression turned thoughtful. "Though I did once have a girl place an ad for free goats in the local newspaper, using my number for the contact."

She chuckled darkly, admittedly impressed.

He swiveled to look at her, his green eyes crinkling at the corners. Half of his mouth kicked up in a smile that made her pulse jump. Good Lord, he was beautiful. Need warmed in her belly, making her squirm in her seat. "Filing that one away for future use, are you?"

"I have to admit I kind of like it. Little effort for a very annoying payoff." She bit her bottom lip. "What did you do?"

"What do you mean, what did I do?" he asked, shooting her a look. "I told every bleeding caller that I didn't have any free goats, then I started giving them *her* number."

He would, she thought, chuckling. "No, I meant, what did you do to her? The woman who placed the ad?"

He winced. "Oh. I gave her the it's-not-you-it's-me line," he said with a sheepish shrug. "I was just trying to spare her feelings. It would have been unkind to tell her that she was too needy and her laugh made me think of a braying donkey."

She felt her mouth drop open and another burst of laughter rolled off her tongue. "You think?" He was utterly outrageous and equally honest. She found that she liked that about him, that it was, in many ways, very refreshing.

"I was trying to be a gentleman," he said. "It wasn't my fault she went all *Fatal Attraction* on me."

"How long had you been seeing her?"

"About three hours. Dinner and a movie. And at the end of it, rather than lie to her and tell her I'd had a good time or would give her a call, I cut to the chase to keep her from developing any expectations." He shook his head. "I'd have been better off lying to her, but it's not my style. I can't abide a liar."

That sounded personal, Pen thought, noting the grim tone of his voice. That tone piqued her curiosity and she shot him a sidelong glance. "Me, either," she said. She waited a beat and asked the one question that had been burning on her tongue since the minute he'd started this story. "So, you're obviously not married, otherwise your boss wouldn't have paired you up with me. Any close calls?" she asked, purposely making the question light.

He turned to look at her then, a knowing twinkle in his eye. Half of his sinfully wicked mouth cocked up in a smile. "No," he told her. And that was all. He didn't elaborate, didn't offer the first insight into why that was the case.

But considering she hadn't either, she could hardly fault him, could she?

Which was why he was being purposely vague.

Naturally that made her all the more curious about him. But rather than press him for an explanation—

because she knew he'd expect her to return in kind—she merely smiled.

"You've been working with Trent and Nella for more than a year, right?" he asked.

"I have."

"And you're familiar with the guest list and everyone involved on a more personal level with the wedding?"

That would be true also. She nodded. "Yes."

"So have you been getting any weird or negative vibes from anyone? Her mother? His mother? Bridesmaids?"

Though she typically made it a rule not to discuss her opinions of any member of the wedding party or their friends and family—it was a small world, after all, and she'd never wanted to risk saying anything that could potentially harm her business—in this instance, she didn't see how she was going to adhere to that principle.

Still, she hesitated, because it felt like a betrayal of sorts. Her couples came to her, asking her to provide the setting and experience for one of the most monumental events in their lives—their marriage. Admitting that the bride's mother was a total bitch or the groom's father was a skinflint felt wrong, even if the descriptions were true.

"Whatever you say stays with the security team," Seth told her. "It goes no further. But you have the most access and you've more than likely already interacted with the person responsible."

She imagined that was true as well, as unsettling as it was. Penelope released a breath. "Nella's mother is overjoyed, so I think we can safely rule her out. Ordinarily the mother of the bride ends up being a pain in the ass. They have a specific idea of what they want their little girl to look like on her wedding day and are loath to give it up. Very often, I end up having to tangle with the mother on behalf of the bride. It's *her* day. Period. Nella's mother hasn't been like that at all. She's simply wanted whatever is going to make Nella happy." She sighed again. "Trent's mother, on the other hand, doesn't seem as taken with Nella as Nella's mother is with Trent. However, before you make anything out of that, that's typically the case, as well. Have you ever heard the old saying 'A daughter's a daughter for life, but a son is only a son until he takes a wife'?"

He shook his head.

"Well, in my experience that's been pretty true. Even the biggest mama's boy doesn't need her as much after he's married."

"So Trent's a mama's boy?"

"Trent adores his mother and respects her opinion, but he doesn't let her direct him in any way. That bodes well for Nella, because you can tell a lot about how a man is going to treat a wife based on how he treats his mother."

He turned to look at her. "Really?"

"Yes," she said. "It sounds trite, but it's true. A mother is every guy's first frame of reference for a woman. He either loves and respects her—appreciates her—or he doesn't."

"And based on that, you can tell how he's going to treat his wife?"

"Not in all circumstances," she said. "But just as a rule, you know?"

He seemed genuinely intrigued. "And you've seen this?"

"I've coordinated more than two-hundred-fifty weddings over the past five years. I'd say it holds true around ninety percent of the time."

He hummed under his breath. "Impressive odds. So do you think Trent's mother could be behind this, then?"

Penelope took a second to really think about it, to check her gut. In all truth, she couldn't say that she especially liked Trent's mother, who was a little on the chilly side, but did she think she'd risk wrecking Trent's wedding when Trent was so obviously happy? So in love with Nella? Ultimately…no.

She shook her head. "I really don't think so. In the end Trent's happiness is more important to her than anything else. I think she has doubts as to whether Nella will make him happy in the long run, but he believes she will. Mrs. McWilliams is not going to interfere, to risk the rift."

"Do you think Nella will make Trent happy in the long run?"

That was a question she hadn't expected. She turned to look at him, then back to the road. "Does that matter?"

"I'm just curious, that's all. You seem to have a real knack for reading people."

She did, actually, which had helped make her really good at her job. That he'd noticed made her chest swell.

"I think Trent and Nella are going to be very happy for a very long time. There's a mutual respect there, a reverence, even, that I don't often see. They're a nine."

He frowned. "A nine?"

Shit. She shouldn't have said that. "It's nothing," she said, wishing she could cut her own tongue out. "It's just a little scale I use."

"On your couples?" he pressed. "You rate them? On whether or not they're going to live happily ever after?"

She cleared her throat. "As for the rest of the bridal party, all of Nella's bridesmaids are happy for her," she said, trying to get back to their original subject. "She's only got four and, with the exception of Trent's sister, Lucy, she's known all of them since grade school."

"But if you don't think they're going to make it, then how do you give your dead-level best to make it wonderful for them?" he continued, still stuck on her rating system. "Why bother?"

"Because it's *their* day—it's what *they* want—and it's my job. It doesn't matter what I think. It's not about me. It's about them. And really, who am I to judge? To interfere?"

"Especially when you don't want to risk it yourself," he said, nodding sagely, as if he'd just cracked her own secret code. "I get it."

She chuckled darkly and bit the end of her tongue, a forcible reminder to keep her mouth shut. He was trying to goad her, to get her to tell him why she'd never wanted a boyfriend and, by extension, a wedding of her own. Had she ever fantasized about it? Yes, she had. She was a wedding planner, after all. She knew that she'd want a cake covered in fondant, a simple gown and even simpler veil, and lots and lots of calla lilies. She imagined the party—the dancing, the twinkling lights, the food—but she'd never once imagined a groom.

And if that wasn't telling, then she didn't know what was. That was self-preservation in its most potent form, her subconscious telling her that it wasn't meant to be.

She took the exit for 85 south and grimly noted they had another five hours alone in the car before the show would fully commence. He'd probably kiss her again, Pen thought, and felt a thrill whip through her at the mere thought.

And for the first time in her life, Penelope Hart thought she might be in over her head.

It looked like another subject change was in order.

"I UNDERSTAND this is your first assignment for Ranger Security, that you're new to the agency," Penelope said, playing defense again.

He'd give her credit—she was damned good at it.

Every time he tried to edge the needle toward something a little personal, she'd invariably turn the conversation back to him or to the case. But never about herself and her inability or desire to commit. The incongruity was utterly fascinating.

She fascinated him.

He suspected that he couldn't afford to be fascinated by her. Even though he'd found himself staring at her beautiful mouth and imagining the depraved things she could do with it to him, he seriously needed to keep his priorities in check.

He was here to catch an instigator, to possibly prevent a murder. He'd do well to remember that.

"That's right," Seth told her. He didn't elaborate. If she wanted to know more, she was going to have to ask. He suspected this was going to be the pattern for both of them and smiled at the thought. He'd bet she was damned good at chess.

He watched her release a small sigh, her lips twitching with put-upon humor. "And what were you doing before you became a security expert."

Was it terrible of him to enjoy this so much? He cocked his head thoughtfully. "I guess you could say I was in a similar field."

He could sense her frustration building. "And who was your previous employer?"

"Uncle Sam."

She aahed knowingly. "You were in the military?"

"Yes."

"What branch?"

"Army."

Something clicked in her quick little brain and he watched her smile. "A Ranger?"

"That's right."

"How long did you serve?"

"Eight years."

She gave a slow nod. "Thank you for your service."

He hadn't expected that. The surprise comment left him momentarily at a loss. He swallowed. "You're welcome," he finally managed to say.

"One of my stepdads was in the military," she explained. "He was in the army, too. A warrant officer. I never fully understood the sacrifice, both for the soldiers and their families until then. It gave me a whole new understanding and appreciation for our men and women in uniform."

One of her stepdads? How many had she had? he wondered, suspecting that this little tidbit was somehow vitally important. His own mother had never remarried after his father had walked out—bastard, Seth thought. He hadn't been joking when he said he couldn't abide a liar.

Though he'd only been five when his father had left, Seth distinctly remembered her believing that the man was going to come back. He remembered her worrying about his father, convinced that he'd been in an accident, that he'd been hurt. She'd walked the floor, called the police and filed a missing person's report as soon as they'd let her. The bastard had told her he was going to the store for gallon of ice cream—it had been unbearably hot that summer—and he'd simply never come back. He hadn't written, hadn't called, hadn't made any sort of contact with them ever again.

Seth had waited until he'd graduated from college before tracking the man down. He'd found him some fifty miles away, shacked up with a girl half his age in a ratty little trailer park. "Do you know who I am?" he'd asked his father, rage boiling up inside of him. He hadn't gone there with the express intention of hurting him, but he'd taken one look at the man who'd abandoned his family and hurt his mother and an anger like he'd never known had rolled through him and he'd…snapped. "I'm your son," he'd told him, then proceeded to beat the living hell out of him. The girlfriend had called the police and, rather than let his mother post bail, Seth had spent the night in jail. Had he cared?

Not in the slightest.

A man was supposed to keep his word, to keep his promises.

"You were in Iraq?" Penelope asked, yanking him away from his thoughts.

He gave himself a mental shake. "I've been there, too, but up until two weeks ago, I was in Afghanistan," he said, letting go a small breath. It still felt wrong being here, Seth thought. As though this was not his real life and he was merely standing in for someone else. It felt odd living alone, waking up in the morning without a specific purpose and plan for the day. Granted the plan might change at the drop of a hat, especially if he was in charge, but the purpose never did.

And it was too damned quiet. It had bugged him so much he'd started leaving the television on all the time, just to simulate conversation. He'd gotten a call from Finn a couple of nights ago and just hearing his friend's voice, listening to the sound of rowdy soldiers in the background, had made his throat go tight.

But he'd promised.

Because he didn't want the burden of his unhappiness hanging over his sister's head, he'd never confided the circumstances of his return, though he knew she suspected. She called every day and always put Mitchell on the phone to relay some sort of gooey greeting. Did he think they needed him? Yes, he actually did. His sister had had a hard row to hoe since Rat Bastard had left her and he imagined the betrayal was especially painful in light of her son. Coupled with the loss of their mother—their constant—it had been especially terrible for her.

He knew Katie was second-guessing her choices and was having trouble making decisions, fearing to make the wrong one again. He hated seeing his otherwise happy, confident little sister reduced to this tired, chronic uncertainty, but other than being available when she wanted to talk, he didn't know what else he could do for her. His mother thought being there would be enough—and she would know after his own father's desertion. He certainly hoped she'd been right.

Because she was going to miss so many milestones, his mother had written letters to each of her children and to Mitchell to be opened upon the occasions she'd indicated. She'd given Katie's letters to him and his letters to Katie.

She'd handed him the first when he'd arrived home.

It had been simple enough. A thank-you for coming out of the military, an apology for forcing his hand, an order to take care of his sister and Mitchell, an assurance that all would ultimately be well. "I know it doesn't feel like it now," she'd written. "But this will be good. You'll find your rudder…and I hope she initially mops the deck with you."

His gaze slid to the woman sitting in the driver's seat and he felt a curious whirring sensation bolt through his chest. If he let her close enough, he knew beyond a shadow of a doubt that the woman seated next to him could do that, Seth thought. He didn't know where the assurance came from but felt it all the same. How bizarre, particularly when he'd never had this sort of reaction to a woman before. He'd never felt anything remotely resembling this intense curiosity, hellfire attraction and certain inexplicable knowledge that she was different, dangerous even, if he let her get too close.

The picture of efficiency, Penelope was dressed in a sleeveless pale green dress that accentuated her curvy frame and contrasted well with her dark hair. She wore a pair of dangly silver earrings, a silver necklace with a single *P* charm and sparkly silver flip-flops on her small feet. Pale pink nail polish decorated her toes, along with what looked like little palm trees painted on each of her big toes. She looked relaxed yet competent, but that self-assuredness was only a small part of her appeal. She was effortlessly sexy and fresh, interesting and smart, and he wanted to lick her up like an ice-cream cone while she melted all over him.

Though he imagined he could kiss her again as part of the ruse—and he fully intended to—he seriously doubted he'd be able to justify any further salacious contact. Pity, that, he thought, feeling his dick twitch in his pants.

He wanted her.

It was inconvenient, foolhardy, utterly inappropriate and damned poor timing, but there it was.

"What made you decide to leave the military?" she finally asked, evidently unable to help herself.

"What makes you think the decision was mine?"

"Are you saying it wasn't?"

He chuckled and looked out the window, watching the passing landscape with more fascination than was warranted.

"You can always tell me it's none of my business," she said, a smile in her voice. "I'm just curious. Typically you Special Forces guys don't go in with the intent to come out until you retire. You've had too much training, too much of your life assigned to a particular purpose. You're what? Thirty-two?"

"Yes."

"Aha!" she chortled, as though this was a contest. "Got you to answer one directly." She gave a little fist pump that made him grin.

"I'll answer as directly as you like, so long as the favor is returned in kind." He purposely let his gaze linger along her neck, waiting for it to pinken. It did. "And I think you have more to hide."

"I don't have anything to hide," she said, immediately refuting his charge.

"So you're purposely mysterious?"

Her eyes widened and she smothered another laugh. "Purposely mysterious? I think you're giving me too much credit. I seriously doubt I'm that interesting."

That's where she'd be wrong. She was fascinating. "I'd have to disagree with you on that one," he said, and had the pleasure of watching her swallow. The tops of her ears turned red.

She snorted. "You'd disagree with me if I said the sky was blue if it meant you wouldn't have to answer a direct question."

"Hi, Pot. Meet Kettle," he said in a deadpan tone.

She merely chuckled. "Diverted again. But I still haven't forgotten what I asked you."

She wouldn't. He released a small sigh. "You want to know why I came out of the military?"

"That's what I've been asking."

"The short answer is I lost a bet in a card game."

She mulled that over. "That's definitely a short answer. You're not the type to bet your future on a card game."

"How do you know?"

"Intuition," she said. "You'd lose money before you'd lose control. Are you going to tell me the long story?"

She'd known him less than twelve hours and had pegged that right already. What else was she going to correctly guess before this assignment was over? Seth wondered, feeling a bit unnerved. What other truths had her keen mind already deduced? He waited a beat, debating. "It's a sad one," he finally told her.

She instantly winced and muttered a low oath. "I'm sorry," she said, immediately contrite. "I had no right to pry."

"The question was reasonable," he said, sensing her discomfort. "I'm working on a case with you that impacts your future and the future of your clients. I'm untested. An unknown quantity." He laughed softly. "If I were you, I'd have questions, too."

She shook her head. "Nevertheless, I shouldn't have pressed it. You don't owe me an explanation. Trent's people have hired you and they're confident that you'll take care of him. That's good enough for me. I was just more curious than anything. We're going to be spending a great deal of time together over the next three days and I just thought it would be better if we knew a little bit about each other. I—"

"I kept a promise," he finally told her. "And so I'm here."

She looked strangely moved. She swallowed, then gave a jerky nod and managed a magnanimous smile. "Well, that's even better than saving a puppy from a storm drain."

Seth chuckled, thankful that the moment had passed. "I'm glad you approve."

And he was, which was clue enough that her opinion already mattered more to him than it should.

5

AFTER WHAT HAD FELT like the longest car ride in the history of the world, Penelope was still feeling strangely fidgety and out of sorts hours later. Despite the fact that she'd been putting out fires most of the day and was completely in her element doing so, she'd nevertheless been keenly aware of *him*. She didn't have to look to know that he was talking with another one of the Ranger Security guys—Will Forrester, if memory served, another tall drink of water.

She could *feel* him there, ten feet to her left.

To make matters worse, she could feel it even more when he looked at her. It was as though a mere glance in her direction raised some sort of supersensory perception in her brain and, when that purely masculine gaze roamed over her, whether long and lingering or short and fleeting, she could feel that, too.

It was disconcerting to say the least.

"I think every guest should get a matching tattoo, don't you? How about little dolphins jumping through wedding bands? Wouldn't that be adorable? I'll line someone up to take care of that *tout de suite*."

Pen blinked and looked at her friend and assistant, Monica. The petite blonde had come to work for her fresh out of college and had quickly proven herself to be not only a good friend, but an invaluable asset to her business. She was a little mouthy and even more opinionated and she didn't always have the best judgment in men, but she was a hard worker who never failed to give Penelope more than one-hundred-and-ten percent.

"What?" Pen asked, trying at least that hard to focus.

Monica heaved an exasperated sigh, her spiky blond curls quivering in irritation. "You haven't been listening to a word I've said!" she accused. "You didn't bat a lash when I mentioned squirting disappearing ink all over Nella's gown or clubbing Trent over the head with a candelabra and dragging him off for myself. What's wrong with you?" She gasped and her gaze turned annoyingly shrewd. "Oh, never mind. It's your *boyfriend*," she drawled with enough innuendo to make Penelope blush.

"Pretend boyfriend," she corrected. She bit her bottom lip. "He is a bit more distracting than I'd anticipated," she admitted.

Monica glanced over and slid Seth an appraising look, one that unreasonably irritated Pen. "I'll say," her assistant breathed. "Pity he's the only single one, isn't it? They're all damned fine."

It was true, she had to admit. She couldn't imagine that being handsome was prerequisite to landing a job with the elite firm, but if not, then they'd gotten terribly lucky. All four of the guys representing Ranger Security were unbelievably attractive and, in some sort of bizarre twist of irony, Seth McCutcheon was the one who appealed to her the most.

There was something about the shape of his smile, the hint of perpetual laughter and irreverence lurking in his dark green gaze that made him especially attractive. She liked the way the sun glinted off the golden hairs on his beautifully muscled forearms and the competent strength in his hands. He was loose and easy in his own skin and had an effortless self-assurance that was as inherent as breathing. It was hard to be unmoved by that sort of confidence and she was anything but unmoved.

In fact, if she had to sum up her present state in one word it would be *hot*.

Of course, it would have helped if he hadn't slipped so easily into character the instant they'd arrived on the island. The minute they'd gotten out of the car, he'd immediately taken her hand, threading his fingers through hers, and the feel of his rough palm against hers—the mere strength in his fingers—had sent a knife of desire right through her. The lust alone she could deal with. It was familiar, even if this was a more concentrated form of it. But it was the sudden longing, this strange sense of something more… That completely unnerving awareness was making her feel she could vibrate out of her own skin.

It wasn't exactly what one could call an altogether pleasant sensation.

And, thanks to the red-letter terrorist—her own personal nickname for the thoughtless asshole casting a pall on the wedding preparations—there wasn't truly an end in sight.

In order to keep Seth as close to Trent and Nella as possible without actually raising suspicions, she and Seth had been given the guesthouse at the back of the property. In just a few short minutes, they were going to be alone together for the rest of the night. If she didn't get herself under control, self-combustion was going to become a legitimate concern.

"So what do you think, boss? Can we call it a day?"

No doubt her intrepid assistant and the rest of her crew were eager to scope out the local nightlife. Under ordinary circumstances she might have been, too, but Penelope had too much riding on the outcome of this wedding to muck it up with some premature partying. She was keen to find out what Seth had learned since he'd gotten here, to see if anything else had happened. His comment on the drive down that she'd probably already interacted with the perpetrator had given her a lot to think about today.

Pen consulted her clipboard and ultimately nodded her consent. "I think we've got everything under control," she said.

"We're prowling for good seafood and margaritas," Monica told her, and jerked her head in Seth's direction. "You and Mr. Gorgeous are welcome to join us."

"He's got to stay close to Trent and Nella," Pen reminded her. Monica was the only staff member that she'd confided in regarding the threat to the bride and groom. While the others suspected something strange was going on, they hadn't been brought into the loop. In fact, even Trent and Nella's families had been left in the dark. The less said, the less likely the real letter-writer would be tipped off to Ranger Security's presence.

"And you've got to stay close to him," she said, nodding sagely. "Poor you."

"Shut up," Pen hissed, shooting a covert look at Seth. "What's everyone saying?"

"About him and your sudden penchant for bringing boyfriends to work? Not a lot, actually," she said. "They don't completely buy the Seth's-a-big-Trent-McWilliams-fan line, but they have too much respect for you to call you an outright liar, either."

That was good, she supposed, Pen thought.

"Paul was the most surprised. He didn't think Seth was your type."

Penelope couldn't imagine Seth not being anyone's type.

She frowned, momentarily sidetracked. Paul, a friend of Monica's, had been working for her for a little less than a year. He was hardworking and funny and, though she wished he wouldn't smoke, provided endless entertainment. "Paul thinks I have a type?"

"Yep. He calls them the E.D.'s."

"The Erectile Dysfunctions?" She grimaced. "That's rather harsh."

Monica snickered. "Not Erectile Dysfunctions," she said, laughing softly. "The Easily Directed. Paul says the only kind of man you ever date is the kind you can boss around. Somehow he doesn't think your current 'boyfriend' fits the mold."

That's because Seth McCutcheon was more accustomed to giving orders than taking them, Pen thought, releasing a shaky breath. "I don't only date men I can boss around," she said, because at the very least, she needed to refute the charge.

"Yes, you do," Monica told her. "But that's just because you're smarter than the rest of us." She nudged her shoulder indulgently. "See you in the morning."

And with that parting comment, her assistant made her exit.

Seconds later, Nella joined her. Looking more relaxed than any bride she'd ever known, her former sorority sister surveyed the scene and a dimple winked in her cheek. "I know I don't have to ask, but how is everything coming together?"

Pen smiled. "Perfectly," she said, though that wasn't exactly true. Somehow or another, when she'd called to double-check the times with the caterer, she'd been told that their order had been canceled. Er…no. "You have absolutely nothing to worry about."

"Apart from the whole someone wanting to commit murder—possibly mine or my future husband's—you mean?" she teased.

"Apart from that, yes," Pen said, glad her friend could find a bit of humor in the situation. But that was Nella. She'd always been able to find a laugh in just about anything. It was no small part of her friend's charm.

"It's beautiful here," Nella sighed, looking out toward the bay. "Trent's sister tried every way in the world to convince us to marry in a church or a hotel—anywhere with air-conditioning—but this is Trent's favorite place on earth. He says he feels more grounded and content here than he does anywhere else. When he first told me about the house, I'd imagined a huge mansion dwarfing the trees and lots of modern art, compliments of his interior decorator." She gave a grin. "Instead, it's more cottage than mansion, with local art on the walls and more screened-in porches and deck than house. I absolutely love it here," she said. "Probably not more than Trent does," she confided. "But just as much." She slid Penelope a sly look. "Can I tell you a secret?"

"Of course."

"Greece is a ruse."

"What?"

She looked around to make sure no one was eavesdropping, then leaned in closer. "We're not going to Greece for our honeymoon."

"You're not?"

"No. We're coming back here. We're simply leaving long enough for everyone else to clear out, then we're honeymooning here, in the place we're going to call home. We haven't—" Nella faltered. "We've waited," she said, blushing to the roots of her hair. "And when we finally…well…we want to be here, at home." She smiled self-consciously. "Sounds bizarre, doesn't it? I'm marrying a man who can afford to take me all over the world and the only place I care about being with him is home."

For whatever reason, Penelope's throat grew tight and her gaze inexplicably drifted to Seth. She made herself look away. "I don't think it sounds bizarre at all," she said. "It sounds like the two of you can't wait to start your life together and what better place than where you'll have your happiest moments? You're making this about what you want, not what everyone expects, and that's wonderful, Nella. I'm so incredibly happy for you."

"Do you think Seth is going to be able to prevent a tragedy here, if it comes to that?" she asked, betraying the first bit of nerves.

"Without a doubt," Pen told her. She didn't know where her sense of certainty came from, but she knew it all the same. She'd known Seth less than twenty-four hours but she would have had the same conviction had it only been twenty-four seconds. He inspired that kind of confidence, that kind of unquestioning regard. He'd signed on to neutralize the threat and protect Trent and Nella at all costs and she instinctively knew he'd put himself in harm's way before he'd let something happen to them.

I kept a promise, he'd said.

Four simple words, but the intent and act behind them spoke volumes about his character. Seth McCutcheon was one of those rare men who actually did what he said he was going to do. He was a man of his word and, in a world where lies were more common than the truth, where everyone was content to do the right thing until it became uncomfortable, that was a very, very admirable quality.

She suspected it was just the first of many she was going to discover about her *pretend* boyfriend.

But if she had to have a pretend boyfriend, she could certainly do a lot worse.

SHE WAS LOOKING at him again, Seth thought, feeling a telltale twitch in his pants. He'd been semiaroused since the instant he'd seen her nibbling on the end of that pencil this morning and, predictably, five hours in the car hadn't helped matters. He didn't know what sort of perfume she was wearing—something musky with a hint of exotic spice—but it was absolutely driving him crazy. Every once in a while he'd catch a whiff of it and it would sort of stun him, leaving him momentarily dazed and out of sorts.

He wasn't accustomed to feeling either of those things, especially where a woman was concerned.

That this one was poised to knock him off his game was irritating at best and downright stupid at worst. He couldn't afford to be anything short of one-hundred-percent focused. Trent and Nella's safety depended on his attention to every detail, to not missing a single nuance of what was happening around him. It was a skill that had served him well in the military and would no doubt be helpful on this mission, as well. Like now, for instance.

There were three men installing the dance floor beneath the largest tent, which was currently being festooned with little white lights. Twenty feet northeast of where he stood, Trent, his mother and sister were talking and, though he couldn't hear a word, a quick read of the body language told him Trent's mother was trying to direct. Trent was standing firm with an eye toward his future bride and his sister was twirling her hair around her finger as though merely clocking time. Ten feet to his right, Penelope and Nella were chatting amiably about something that was making Nella smile. From the corner of his eye, he couldn't discern the exact look on Pen's face, but it was one that was hauntingly puzzling, a combination of surprise and wistfulness.

He was entirely too interested in what had caused that expression, Seth realized, muttering a hot curse under his breath.

Acting as one of the tent company's crew, Tanner made his way over. "We're going to head out," he said, shooting a look down toward the water. The sun was sinking low on the bay, casting orange iridescent shadows on the waves, and a line of squawking seagulls sat perched along the end of the pier. The salty breeze ruffled through the palms and stirred the Spanish moss dripping from the live oaks. It was a beautiful close to a long day though Seth suspected the coming evening was going to test limits he hadn't known were there.

Seth nodded. "You guys were lucky to have been able to rent a house just a couple of doors down," he remarked, thankful that the security team would be on the island instead of having to move off-site like the rest of the wedding crew.

Tanner merely grinned. "Lucky to have a boss with friends in high places."

Given the fact that Payne owned the building in which the agency was currently housed, Seth suspected their boss had lots of friends in high places. "There is that," he said, nodding.

"What's your gut saying on this?" Tanner asked him. "Any thoughts?"

Seth released a slow breath and rubbed his hand over

the back of his neck. His gut was sending him mixed signals, which was a first. He suspected that the threats were merely a stall tactic, but he couldn't shake the sensation that there really was something brewing here, something more sinister. But were they related? That was the million-dollar question.

"Well, given what we know regarding the people who sent the save-the-date and wedding invitations, it's someone who is close. Probably closer than we realize," he said. "They've made threats but no other overt action that we know of." He winced. "Intuition tells me that there's no real threat to Trent and Nella, that the irrational tone of the notes was to postpone the wedding, to keep Trent on the market a little longer. But…I don't know. Something feels off to me, but I can't put my finger on what." He could practically taste the malice in the air. It was the same sort of premonition he'd had when doing patrol. The certain expectancy of an ambush, of a roadside bomb. They'd known it was there, whether they could see it or not.

Tanner nodded and sent him a shrewd look. "I'm getting the same vibe," he said. "Like there's a secondary element that we're missing."

"Exactly," Seth told him. "I've been through the file half-a-dozen times since yesterday, have practically memorized the information we have on everyone, hoping that something will jump out at me." He shook his head. "So far, nothing."

"We'll catch it," Tanner said. "I'll run first circuit and let you know how it goes." He jerked his head toward

Penelope and his lips twitched with poorly disguised humor. "How's it going with your girlfriend?"

"We're in love," Seth said in a deadpan voice, taking an instant liking to his new colleague. "She's looking at china patterns and I'm sizing my ankle for a ball and chain."

Tanner chuckled. "She looks easy enough to drag around. She's cooperating, then?"

"Fully," he told him.

"Good. That'll make your job easier."

He didn't know about that, Seth thought. But rather than comment, he merely grunted. It would have made his job easier...if he hadn't taken an immediate interest in her. If he hadn't been studying every nuance of her character since meeting her last night, from the way she cocked her head when she was thinking about something, to the backward way she stirred her tea. Counterclockwise. Who did that? It also would have been easier if he hadn't found his loins consigned to the fiery hell of the damned every time he watched her absently lick her lips or smile or...hell, *breathe* for that matter.

Clearly he should have taken the time to get laid before embarking on this first assignment, Seth thought, giving himself a mental shake.

Intuition told him it wouldn't have mattered. He'd have still wanted her.

Because he'd been entirely too interested in what would happen when he touched her, under the guise of going into character, Seth had taken her hand as soon as they'd gotten out of the car. He'd been breathing the same air with her for several hours, had been studying every inch of exposed flesh, had been watching the way her mouth moved when she spoke and had been utterly enchanted with her.

He'd rationalized this behavior by telling himself that it was important that he knew who she was, what made her tick, what made her *her*, so that he could better play his part. So he wouldn't bungle this mission up right out of the gate because he wasn't properly prepared for his role.

He didn't know what he expected to happen when he touched her, but the burst of warmth, breathlessness and tingly sensation that followed certainly hadn't been it. The hair on his arms had stood on end and he'd felt that seemingly innocuous contact all the way down to the soles of his feet.

Bizarre. Unsettling.

He'd probably have a heart attack if he bedded her, Seth thought, shooting a look in her direction. His gaze drifted over her face and settled on her mouth, particularly the plumper lower lip. He went painfully hard again.

He made a mental note to pick up a bottle of aspirin—better safe than sorry—and while he was thinking about preventive measures, he imagined a box of condoms wouldn't be remiss, either.

Because before the weekend was out, they were going to need them.

6

CERTAIN THAT she'd put off the inevitable for as long as possible, Penelope started toward Seth, who was standing just outside of the tent. Seemingly aware that she'd moved, he turned to look at her. The instant that dark green gaze connected with hers, her heart gave a jolt and warmth puddled in her belly.

Even though she knew an unattractive man wouldn't have made for a believable "boyfriend," she almost wished Seth had been a "dog-pointer" as he'd so eloquently put it. The fact that he was six-and-a-half feet of pure masculine beauty—the worst kind of temptation—made her all too aware of him, and it was that attraction that made her all the more aware of certain parts of her own anatomy.

Parts she'd like to feel all over him, preferably naked, if she were completely honest.

Wondering when she'd become so shallow, Pen pasted a smile onto her face and bravely continued on. "I'm ready to wrap up for the day," she said. She lowered her voice. "How's everything going?"

"Nothing new to report," he said, slinging an arm over her shoulder. She repressed a full-body shiver and resisted the urge to melt into him. "The rest of the team is staying on the island and we're going to take turns running surveillance."

"Is there anything I can do to help?"

"You could start by looking up at me like you adore me. You're supposed to be my girlfriend, after all."

She chuckled and did as he asked. "Is that what your other girlfriends have done? Adored you? Worshipped the ground you walked on? Tattooed your name across their lower backs? Tramp-stamping their eternal devotion?"

He grinned. "I don't expect you to get a tattoo," he said with a humble nod. "But if you wanted to build a spectacular shrine in my honor, then I'd be cool with that."

Penelope laughed and, smiling, continued to stare up at him. She didn't have a choice. He was at least a foot taller than she was. For whatever reason, she found that especially thrilling. "A spectacular shrine? Is that all you expect of me?" She chuckled again. "Lucky me. I'll, uh… I'll get right on that."

"See that you do," he said with a grave nod. "I don't know how we'll be able to convince everyone that we're an item if you don't." He placed a mouthwateringly large hand over his heart. "I need to feel the love if I'm going to completely get into character."

He was doing a pretty damned fine job of getting into character if you asked her. He certainly didn't have any problem touching her, that was for sure. In fact, if she wasn't careful, she'd be in more danger of actually believing the ruse.

And that would be utterly disastrous. Stupidity and self-destruction in their most basic forms.

"Penelope!"

Pen turned and saw Nella's maid of honor—another former sorority sister—Patrice Anderson, hurrying toward her. Evidently Patrice had arrived early, as moral support for Nella she supposed. Pen absently wondered where Patrice was staying. She wasn't sure there was room left in the house.

"Patrice," Pen returned, giving her a small hug.

"I've only just arrived," Patrice said, sliding a covert look at Seth. Tall and willowy with exotic gray eyes and long brown hair, Patrice had always been unfairly pretty. Strangely, Pen had never hated her for it until right now. "I was able to get away a day early and wanted to see if I could do anything to help," she said.

Patrice was one of Nella's closest friends so this made perfect sense, and yet something about it felt odd to her. Evidently sensing that as well, Seth moved closer to her and seemed to be watching the exchange with more interest. The fact that he could pick up on the subtle shift in her mood when she knew she hadn't betrayed a hint of her unease made her equally unnerved and delighted.

"Not that I can think of," Pen told her. "I'm sure Nella will be glad that you're here."

Patrice looked back over her shoulder. "I haven't gone into the house yet," she said. "I saw the two of you—" once again her gaze drifted annoyingly to Seth "—and I wanted to come down and say hi." She nodded in Seth's direction. "I'm Patrice Anderson."

"Seth McCutcheon, Pen's significant other," he said, giving Penelope a gentle squeeze. His scorching gaze slid over her face with fondness and Pen felt a warm blush scald her cheeks.

Clearly he'd missed his calling—he could surely find a home on the stage.

"You're the maid of honor, right?" he said to Patrice, then looked down at Penelope. "Another of your sorority sisters? I'm glad that I'm getting to meet so many of your friends."

Patrice's gaze bounced between the two of them and her grin grew wider. "It's so nice to meet you, Seth. So how long have the two of you been dating?" Pen's short-lived romances were well-known. No doubt Patrice was asking so that she could determine the expiration date and see when Seth would be officially back on the market.

"Four months," Pen told her, smiling tightly.

Patrice's eyebrows winged up her forehead. "Four months?" she repeated. "Wow, Pen. That's a bit of a record for you, isn't it?" She glanced at Seth again and rocked back on her heels. "You must be quite special."

Seth merely chuckled and tried to look humble. "I like to think so."

"He is," Pen confirmed with an awkward nod.

"So how did the two of you meet?" Patrice asked.

"Now that's a funny story," Seth told her, shooting a look at Pen. "Why don't you tell her, baby. You're so much better at it than I am," he demurred.

The wicked twinkle in those dark green eyes told her he not only sensed her discomfort, but was enjoying it, as well. Wretch. "Er…okay." She glanced at Patrice, to find her waiting patiently. "It's quite heroic, actually," Pen told her. "He helped rescue my puppy from a storm drain."

Patrice clasped her hands to her chest and gazed at Seth as if he was a saint. "Aww," she said. "That's wonderful. So you're a fireman?"

"I am," Seth lied smoothly, to her immense shock. Just as well, though, Pen decided. In her quest to outline their relationship, she'd completely forgotten to come up with an alternate line of employment.

"Done any calendars?" Patrice quipped, flirting outrageously right in front of her.

"No," he said, laughing softly. "I—"

"He's actually going to do some boudoir photos for me while we're down here, aren't you, darling?"

His smile froze.

Pen put her hand on his chest and leaned toward Patrice as though she were sharing an intimate secret. "They're an early birthday present for me," she said. "The wedding photographer is a friend of mine and she's going to take a few shots down at the beach." She smiled up at him. "Don't worry, honey. I have every intention of applying the oil myself."

Patrice whooped and gave Pen a you-sly-dog look. "When is that particular photo shoot?" she asked.

"Not until after the wedding," Pen said, savoring a wicked thrill. She could improvise, too. "We're staying on for a couple of days. We'll stroll the beach, eat too much seafood, that sort of thing."

"I'm envious," Patrice told them. "I'll have to get on the road as soon as the ceremony is over. Mom's sixtieth birthday is on Sunday," she confided. "But it sounds like the two of you will have a wonderful time."

"Better than I imagined," Seth muttered. Pen gave him a little jab with her elbow.

"It's good to see you, Patrice," Pen said, hoping the woman would take the hint and leave before this became any more uncomfortable.

"You too." She turned to go. "Let me know if you can put me to work, Pen. I'll pitch in wherever I'm needed."

"Thanks." She breathed a silent sigh of relief as Patrice finally made her way to the house and then turned to face Seth. She chewed the inside of both cheeks— she was saving her tongue—before trusting herself to speak.

"You're a fireman? When were you planning on letting me in on that little tidbit?"

"What was I supposed to say when she asked?" His lips twisted with droll humor. "You left that out of our 'history' and I couldn't very well tell her the truth, could I?"

She supposed not. Still, she had a horrible suspicion that he was going to be dropping these little bombs on her the rest of the weekend and she was going to be powerless to keep him from doing it. One explosion after the other.

"Furthermore, I can't believe you have the nerve to

complain after your little 'boudoir photos' revelation." He chuckled low. "That was devious," he said, and to her pleased astonishment, he looked impressed.

She hadn't liked the way Patrice had been looking at him. Initially it had been quite flattering. He was pretending to be her boyfriend, after all, so she could claim temporary ownership. But even after Pen had made it clear that Seth was hers, Patrice hadn't backed off. Instead, she'd stared at Seth as though he were the last ham on the shelf on Christmas Eve.

It irritated the hell out of her.

How had this happened? Pen wondered. Had she simply been a serial dater so long that no one thought anything about making a play for a guy she was involved with because they knew he'd be history soon enough? And if so, how was she going to change that perception, particularly when she had no intention of changing her modus operandi?

Better still, why was she worried about this with a fake boyfriend? One she wasn't even really dating? Good grief, she was losing her mind. And, irrationally, she thought it was his fault.

Unfortunately, she couldn't argue with her feelings. Patrice's drooling over her guy, real or not, had supremely ticked her off. Patrice had thought he was genuinely hers, but that hadn't kept her from blatantly flirting with him right in front of her.

Clearly they were going to have to work on their performance.

And, more specifically, she was going to have to post a No Fishing sign.

"WHY FOUR MONTHS?"

Seemingly preoccupied with some thoughts that were making her forehead wrinkle, Penelope blinked and looked up at him. "What?"

"Why four months?" He'd noticed it in the file of their fake relationship. At the time, he'd thought it was an odd choice for the amount of time they'd been dating, but he'd forgotten to ask her about its significance. Given Patrice's wide-eyed astonishment when Pen had told her, there was obviously something else to it.

"Nella made sure that Trent's staff outfitted the guest-house with a few groceries for us," she said, dodging the question altogether. She turned and started in that direction, leaving him no choice but to follow. "I'm not a gourmet chef by any stretch of the imagination, but I can probably knock up something decent. Are you hungry?"

"Yes, but that's not what I asked you," he persisted. "Why four months? What's the significance?"

"Who said it was significant?"

"Nobody had to," he said, reaching out and taking her hand. "We're supposed to be a couple, remember? Come on, Penelope. I'm not going to let it go."

She heaved an exasperated sigh and seemed to be inspecting the ground for a hole she could conveniently fall into. "Because I have a three-month rule."

"A three-month rule?"

"Yes," she admitted reluctantly. "I don't date a man beyond ninety days. Anyone who knows me well, knows that. In college, it became the source of endless entertainment and betting. I had to tell her I'd been seeing you for at least four months in order to let her, or anyone else who would know better, see that it's serious. Otherwise I wouldn't have brought you along with me, see? I've never brought anyone with me to a wedding before," she said, as though the idea were so far out of the realm of possibility, it might as well be nonexistent. She suddenly stopped and looked up at him. "Why does this matter?" she asked, exasperated. "Why do you care?"

"If we were dating in real life and I'd surpassed your ninety-day cutoff, would I know why? Would you tell me that I was special?"

She opened her mouth, closed it, then ultimately released a defeated sigh. "I suppose," she admitted grudgingly.

"*That's* why I need to know. You've given me lots of little insignificant tidbits, like your favorite color, your favorite movie, the one book you'd have to have if you were stranded on a desert island—*Pride and Prejudice*. But you've left out all the important stuff, the things that make you tick. You've given me trivia, but nothing significant."

"I've given you a hell of a lot more than you've given me," she said, arching a pointed brow.

Oh, hell, Seth thought. This wasn't going exactly the way he'd planned. Why ninety days exactly? He'd wanted to continue to grill her about her ninety-day rule and find out what had put that pucker in the middle of her forehead a minute ago. He wanted to know what had given her pause when Patrice had unexpectedly shown up. It had been a subtle shift, just the slightest tension in her small frame, but he'd caught it.

"Are you telling me that you never date anyone longer than three months, that even if it's going great and every aspect of the relationship is firing on all four cylinders, you break it off? You let the relationship *expire?*"

He didn't know why this was so important for him to understand, but he couldn't seem to keep from pressing her about it. He *had* to know how she ticked, what made her do the things she did. Should it matter? No. Was it really as relevant to what they were doing as he was making out? Also no. But that didn't change the fact that he desperately wanted to understand her. To know her. In less than twenty-four hours, this had gone beyond mere intrigue, fascination or interest. He wasn't sure he could label it at all, but if he had to try, "obsessed" probably came closer to the mark than anything else.

Penelope inserted the key into the lock and pushed open the door. Long black curly tendrils escaped her ponytail and clung to the back of her swanlike neck and he was suddenly hit with the insane urge to sweep them aside and press a kiss against her nape and breathe her in.

He was losing his damned mind, Seth decided.

She continued on into the house—he noted lots of blues, reds, and white beadboard—and set her clipboard on the bar. With a reluctant sigh, she turned to face him.

"Look, Seth, my reasons for staying single are my own. And, quite frankly, they aren't any of your business. You know what you need to know."

True, he supposed, however unpalatable. He blew out a breath and nodded.

Seemingly satisfied that the subject was closed, she relaxed enough for her shoulders to sag. "So," she said, glancing determinedly toward the kitchen. "Dinner."

Seth merely smiled. He wasn't the only one who preferred to have a purpose, he thought, following her into the kitchen. She was peering into the fridge, a thoughtful look upon her increasingly interesting face. "Hmm," she murmured. "How do you feel about a dressed-up hot ham and cheese?"

"Sounds good," Seth said. "What can I do to help?"

She nodded toward the wine refrigerator. "You can start by pouring me a glass of whatever you're having."

He chuckled and took a couple of glasses down from the rack, then inspected the various bottles. He finally settled on a nice chardonnay. "Here," he said, handing her a glass. She stopped slicing sweet peppers and onions long enough to take a grateful sip.

"Ah," she said, a slow smile spreading across her ripe lips. "Better already."

"Should I see about getting you a flask?" he teased.

She grimaced and set back to work. "I might need one by the time this weekend is over."

Working with him was that stressful, was it? He didn't know whether to be annoyed or pleased. He watched her drizzle some olive oil into a pan and dump the vegetables in. Dressed-up ham and cheese, indeed, Seth thought as she buttered four slices of Texas toast and piled them high with thick-cut ham and a couple of different kinds of cheeses. When the veggies were done, she added those as well, then transferred the sandwiches back into the pan for toasting.

Rather than stand there and watch her work, he pulled plates down from the cabinets, snagged some cutlery and set the table. He'd just finished adding pita chips to each of their plates when she made her way over. She'd halved the sandwiches and had only kept one wedge for herself.

"You didn't have to share," he said. "One would have been plenty for me."

"You're a big guy," she said, her gaze quickly skimming over him. The tops of her ears turned pink. "And I'm a little woman and want to keep it that way." She grinned at him. "Eat up."

He did and hummed with pleasure. "This is delicious. Thank you."

She popped a chip into her mouth and appeared pleased. "You're welcome. Though I'm not as good at it as I'd like to be, I enjoy cooking. One of my stepmothers had a little diner and she'd let me play around in the kitchen. I learned a lot from her."

Another stepparent, Seth thought. How many had she had? he wondered. But after her recent none-of-your-business comment, he had no intention of asking her.

He could ask her something else though.

"So what's the deal with Patrice?"

She took a sip of wine and her gaze tangled with his. "What do you mean?"

"You tensed up when you were talking to her. Was that because we were officially 'on' or because something about her arriving early rang an alarm bell?"

"Both, actually, but more so the latter." She frowned thoughtfully. "It's not like Patrice to be on time for anything, much less early," she said. "I don't know if this whole situation is making me paranoid or what. It just struck me as a little odd."

Patrice obviously hadn't called ahead to let Pen know that she was coming. "Do you think Nella knew she was on her way down?"

She hesitated. "I don't think so," she said. "That wasn't the impression I'd gotten. And Nella didn't say a word when I was talking to her." She shrugged. "Then again, maybe it's not a big deal. Nella's had a lot on her mind and if Patrice is here to help lighten her load, then that's wonderful. I'm probably just pissed because she was flirting with you," she admitted, to his astonishment.

"You think?"

"Probably." She nodded. "It's bad form to flirt with your friend's guy, especially when she knows that you're special."

He couldn't help the grin that spread across his lips and laughed out loud when she looked up, an expression of mortified horror on her face. "I'm special, am I?"

"You know what I mean," she said, taking another drink of wine. "I'm talking about that three-month rule."

Rather than needle her any more, he reluctantly turned the conversation back to business. "So did you notice anything bizarre today? Anything strike you as odd?"

"No," she said. "Though it was the day from hell.

Evidently our caterer was under the impression that we'd canceled our entire order, which would have been a disaster of epic proportions. And when I called to confirm the rehearsal time with the pastor who is marrying Trent and Nella, he seemed completely baffled. Evidently he'd been told the service had been moved to Sunday."

Seth's antennae twitched. "By whom?"

She shrugged. "I don't know and neither does he. His secretary took the call."

"Has anything like this ever happened before?"

She looked offended. "To me? No," she said. "I don't just double-check—I quadruple-check," she told him. "People make mistakes all the time and the wrong stroke of a key when confirming a time for the food, the pastor, the band, anything…can ruin a wedding. I—" She stopped and her eyes widened. "This isn't a coincidence, is it?" she asked, turning a bit green.

He didn't think so. "Probably not," Seth said. "Who would have access to these details, the caterer being used, the person officiating at the ceremony?"

"The usual suspects," Pen told him. "Anyone close to Trent and Nella. Any member of the wedding party."

"And members of your staff," he added.

"No," she said flatly. "I trust each one of them implicitly. Furthermore, Monica is the only one who has been brought up to speed on stuff."

She could trust them all she wanted to, but it was his job not to trust anybody. And right now, with the exception of her, everyone was a suspect. Canceling the food and trying to put off the pastor were simple attempts at stopping the wedding, but they spelled trouble. Those attempts took guts because the person behind them ran the risk of getting caught, being remembered. It was amateurish, yes, but it was also reckless. And a reckless person could be dangerous.

As for Trent and Nella, he'd met with the couple earlier and had been extremely impressed with both of them. He'd been following Trent's career for years and was unbelievably pleased with the man's down-to-earth attitude. Nella quite obviously adored him and Seth had gotten the overwhelming impression that the sentiment was returned. No wonder Pen had rated them a nine, Seth thought. Hell, he would have given them a ten.

"Would Patrice have any reason to want to sabotage the wedding? Any grudge?" he asked, wondering again about her interesting timing.

Penelope shook her head. "None that I can think of. She squealed along with the rest of us when Nella told us about the proposal. She hosted a wedding shower and even tried to throw the bachelorette party, only Nella didn't want one," she confided. "Overall, she seems to be quite happy for her." She paused, as if searching her memory. "Patrice is a bit of a prophet of doom. Her marriage only lasted a few months, so she's not exactly enamored with the institution."

"She's divorced?"

She nodded.

"Did you plan her wedding, as well?"

Another small nod. "Yes," she said on a sigh.

"What happened?"

"Affair."

"Guilty party?"

"Him."

Seth winced. He'd only just met Patrice and could imagine how well that had gone over. Honestly, why bother? Why say *I do* when you know *you won't?* "So she'd have reason to want to save her friend the same kind of heartache. Would she do that? Would that be enough?"

"I don't know," Pen admitted. "She and Nella are close, obviously. But Patrice hasn't said a negative word to me about Nella tying the knot."

"How long has it been?"

"Since Patrice's wedding?"

"Yeah."

"It was a Christmas wedding," she said. "So around eighteen months."

Seth mulled that over. "We definitely need to keep an eye on her," he told her. "From what you've observed, it's out of character for her to arrive early and she has more than enough reason to think marriage on the whole is a bad idea, particularly for a good friend."

Penelope released a breath. "I suppose so."

Seth's cell phone suddenly sounded at his waist. He unclipped it from his side and checked the display. Katie. She'd worry if he didn't answer, and if he sent her to voice mail she'd just call back. He looked up at Penelope, shooting her an apologetic smile. "I need to take this."

Looking intensely curious, she merely nodded. "Sure."

He stood and backed away from the table. "Leave the dishes," he instructed her. "You cooked. I'll clean."

She made a moue of pleasure and nodded, then helped herself to another glass of wine. "That's fair," she said. "No objection from me."

That was novel, Seth thought. He wondered if the same sentiment would hold true when he kissed her. Because he fully intended to do so the instant the opportunity presented itself.

7

THOUGH SHE KNEW it was impolite to eavesdrop, there was nothing wrong with Pen's hearing. And since Seth had only moved into the living room, she couldn't help but hear virtually every word he was saying. She'd known from the instant he'd looked at the display that this was a personal call, not business related. She'd seen the slightest upturn of his mouth, the faintest smile that made her long to know who had put it there.

Aha, Pen thought, cocking an ear toward the living room. It was someone named Katie. An irrational stab of jealousy momentarily pierced her. Of course it was a woman, she thought with a fatalistic sigh. Just because he wasn't married, that didn't mean that he was completely unattached. He could still have a girlfriend. Or maybe someone who hadn't quite made the upgrade to girlfriend status. Hell, for all she knew, this was a friend-with-benefits relationship, where they simply got together when the mood struck for a little recreational no-strings sex.

Her eye began to twitch.

"Yeah, it's beautiful down here. Very peaceful. Has Mitch ever been to the beach?"

Mitch? Who was Mitch?

"We need to plan a trip this summer. Bring him down and let him play in the sand." He chuckled. "He'd love it. Yeah, sure. It'd be great. Maybe come down in October when the bulk of the tourists more or less clear out and the kids are back in school."

So he was planning a vacation with this Katie person and her child? A young child by the sounds of it. Her eyes widened. Could it be *his* child? she wondered and gasped. Was Katie his baby mama?

She tossed back the rest of her wine.

He laughed again and a smile entered his voice. "Yeah, I hear him. Put the little rug rat on the phone." Another pause, then, "Hey, buddy. Are you being good for mama? You are? Good. What was that? You want to ride in my truck? Sure, bud. I'll take you for a spin when I get back, okay? Okay," he said, his voice full of fondness. "Let me talk to mama again, okay? Love you, buddy."

Aww, Pen thought. *How sweet.* She didn't know for sure who this little boy was, but he was lucky that Seth was in his life.

"Yeah, he told me," he said. "I told him I'd take him for a ride again when I got back." He laughed, the sound soft and slightly rough. "Hey, I can make anything look cool, little sister. Even a car seat."

Little sister?

"You know it," he laughed. "Right. I'll talk to ya'll tomorrow, sis. Love you, too. Bye."

Seth walked back into the kitchen and held up his phone. "My sister," he explained with a sheepish smile.

"I heard, sorry. I wasn't trying to listen, but…" She shrugged. "And a nephew?"

He nodded and started clearing the table. "Mitchell. He's two and half. Adorable."

"They typically are at that age," she said. "They call them the terrible twos, but in my experience it's not until they hit around three to three and a half that the true tantrums set in."

He filled the sink with soapy water. "Your experience? You've got nieces and nephews?"

"Oodles of them," she sighed, feeling warm and pleasant from the alcohol currently moving through her system. Honestly, with all her half siblings combined, they could have their own football team. There were some she was closer to than others, some that she'd bonded with and continued to keep in touch with after their parents had broken things off. Her family tree was mangled all to hell and back, Pen thought with an inward snort. She only had one true sibling, her younger sister Phoebe, who was currently in England on a student exchange program. As an English Lit major, nothing could have been more fitting. She got the occasional postcard rhapsodizing clotted cream and scones and bemoaning the lack of ice in her drinks, but overall she knew her sister was having the time of her life.

As for her parents, her mother and husband number four were panning for gold in Alaska—Geoff was the quintessential mountain man—and her father, who had just recently divorced wife number five, was on a spiritual retreat in Sedona, looking for his "true" self via vortexes and a self-proclaimed shaman. Honestly, she didn't mind that either of her parents danced to the beat of their own drums, it was just remarkable to her that they both had no trouble finding someone to do that dancing with them. She'd seen them both utterly euphoric, blissfully content, mildly dissatisfied and completely miserable—all on account of love.

No, thank you. Pen didn't want any part of it, other than the business that enabled her to earn a living. The rest—the romance—she could live without. And she fully intended to. Her gaze slid to Seth, who was standing at the kitchen sink washing dishes, and her heart gave an unexpected and odd pang. Only he could make the domesticated chore look sexy. She loved the way the hair around the nape of his neck curled. Muscles rippled beneath the thin black T-shirt and she could just make out the fluted hollow of his spine. Her gaze slid lower and she felt her nipples bead behind her bra.

He had the best ass she'd ever, *ever* seen. In all honesty, she thought there was something pretty ridiculous-looking about a man's penis—not that she couldn't appreciate one when it was being properly utilized, but a bit funny all the same. But a man's ass... Now that was the money shot.

And his was priceless.

"Mitch is all I've got," Seth told her, interrupting her blatant ogling. "He kind of got the shaft in the father department, so I'm trying to make up for that as best I can."

They really needed to abandon the rescuing the puppy from the storm drain aspect of their history, Pen decided. Seth McCutcheon didn't need the artifice. He was one of those rare guys who actually did the right thing.

"I'm sure your sister appreciates that."

He dried a plate and put it away. "She does. It hasn't been easy for her, I know."

Was that the reason he came out of the military? Pen wondered. Had he promised his sister that he would? He hadn't said a word about his own parents and she couldn't think of a reason to ask without it coming off as prying. Which is exactly what it would be. But the more he revealed about himself, the more he was going to expect of her. And her parents and their marathon of marriages wasn't a topic she wished to discuss with him or anyone else for that matter.

Moving methodically around the kitchen, he quickly wiped everything down, then rinsed out the sink. When he pulled a broom and dustpan from the pantry and proceeded to sweep the kitchen floor, she found herself smiling.

He caught her. "Is something funny?"

"Not at all," she said. "I'm just amazed at your thoroughness, that's all." She'd be willing to bet every one of his coat hangers were the same color, shape and size and were properly spaced on the closet rod. She'd noticed that he'd been tidy at his new apartment, but had wondered if that was the case only because he hadn't been there long enough to make a real mess.

Evidently not.

"There's not much point in doing something if you aren't going to do it right," he said. He looked up and his gaze lingered over her breasts, up her neck, and settled long enough on her mouth to make her breathing go shallow. "Being meticulous typically pays off." His gaze met hers. "Surely given your line of work, you of all people understand that, right?"

Her mouth had gone dry and her glass was empty. Damn. She cleared her throat. "Yes, of course," she said, her voice a bit strangled.

"You need a refill?" he asked solicitously, his lips twitching.

"Nope," she said, standing up. "I've had two glasses already and that's my limit." Any more and she'd be in danger of losing her self-control or common sense, both of which seemed to be in short supply whenever she was within a few feet of him.

He nodded, then glanced at the clock on the microwave. "I need to take a walk around the property," he said. "Why don't you come with me?"

"I think I'd better stay here." She needed some much needed distance and knew she wasn't going to be getting any of that over the next couple of days.

"It's going to look like I'm skulking around if I'm alone. Whereas if you were with me, it would look like we were taking a romantic evening stroll."

That made perfect sense and yet she was getting the distinct impression that she was being manipulated, that he actually wanted her company. Dangerous, Pen thought. She should stay right here, take a cold shower and count the many reasons why genuinely liking Seth was a bad idea. She should and yet…

"Skulking," she remarked. "Now there's a word you don't often hear."

"Do you need a definition?" he asked, shooting her an innocent look.

She smirked. "No, smart-ass, I do not."

A surprised laugh rumbled up his throat as they got ready to leave. "Are you sure you won't have another glass of wine? I think your tongue needs loosening up a little bit more."

Any more wine and it would come unhinged altogether. He fell in behind her and then, ever the gentleman, reached around her and opened the door. A soft breeze blew in off the water, lifting her hair. Half the sun had dipped below the horizon, painting the sky and water in beautiful warm tones, a few pinks and purples thrown in for good measure.

Though she'd expected it, the feel of his big hand finding hers was still a bit of a lovely shock. "Keeping up appearances," he said, giving her fingers a slight squeeze.

Right, Penelope thought, releasing a slow breath.

"Where exactly are we going?"

"We're just going to walk along the perimeter of Trent's estate."

"To make sure nobody's lurking in the bushes?"

He was scanning the area, doing an admirable job of make the intense scrutiny look casual. She knew better, of course. Had she asked him, she knew he could tell her exactly how many blooms were on the bushes close to the house and which shades were drawn on the windows and which weren't. He didn't miss a trick, she was certain. "Something like that."

"What would you do if you actually found some-one?"

"Whatever's necessary."

That covered a lot of ground, Pen thought, as goose bumps skittered over her skin.

"Don't look, but someone's watching from the win-dow in the cupola."

Even though he'd told her not to look, her head inex-plicably turned in that direction. Then to her immense surprise, which instantly turned to delight, he caught it with his mouth.

There was something to be said for a man who was naturally thorough, Pen thought dizzily as her hand landed on his chest and fisted in his shirt. Her entire body felt as if it had been doused in gasoline and then set ablaze. She savored the burn, reveled in it even as her insides melted and her blood scorched through her veins.

His lips were warm and soft and firm and moved over hers with a lazy purposefulness that told her that kissing wasn't merely the appetizer before the main course. He obviously enjoyed the taste of her, the feel of her against his mouth.

Though she knew he was merely doing this as a pre-ventive measure that he'd improvised to keep her from blowing their cover, she nevertheless could appreciate his expertise...and he was definitely an expert. Last night's kamikaze kiss had been nothing compared to this slow exploration of her mouth. Still, she wasn't sure which one she like better—they both left her breathless.

He groaned low in his throat, the sound reverberating off her own tongue and dragged her closer to him, fitting her body more closely to his. He was big and warm and wonderful and she loved the way her own body felt when it was next to his—enervated, alive and on fire. Like she was plugged into his energy, was feeding off of it. She needed it, craved it….

And that was the danger, Pen realized foggily, as his tongue tangled skillfully around hers. She couldn't afford to need anyone…least of all a pretend boyfriend she suspected could do the one thing no other guy had ever managed.

He could steal her heart.

And then he'd have the power to break it.

SETH KNEW he was taking extreme liberties with his stealth kiss, but hadn't been able to resist the opportunity. He'd told her not to look, knowing that she'd try, and had easily captured her mouth under the guise of maintaining their cover.

He was a self-serving opportunistic bastard, Seth thought, molding her small womanly body closer to his, and he'd never been less ashamed of himself. Who had time to feel remorse—who would even bother?—when she felt like this against him? When she tasted like wine and cheese, and her mouth was plum soft and juicy and her sweet body was pressed so closely against his own.

He'd tasted her startled breath, then the following

sigh. Even though he'd suspected that she'd wanted it as much as he had, savoring those two things against his tongue were all the proof he needed that the desire was mutual.

Seth McCutcheon had been stealing kisses since kindergarten. He regularly found third base in junior high and lost his virginity to an *older woman,* a sophomore, the summer before his freshman year of high school. He knew when a girl was into him. He recognized the tells—the fluttering heartbeat at the base of the throat, the sidelong glances, the lingering attention on his ass. Gratifyingly Pen, in particular, seemed to like his ass. He could read the body language, the certain way a woman cocked her head, the unconscious lean in, the unwitting need to get closer, to breathe and smell a person in.

He'd watched Penelope's eyes widen and darken last night when she'd unexpectedly dropped by his place. He'd recognized that instant flash of awareness, because he'd felt it himself and known that they were going to be in serious trouble.

While Seth was aware that he was only supposed to be pretending that he and Penelope were an item, and he further suspected that he wasn't supposed to allow, much less encourage, things to go beyond simple playacting, he couldn't seem to help himself. She obliterated his self-control, beckoned his wilder tendencies.

Though he could think of at least half-a-dozen reasons off the top of his head why they shouldn't do this—the most significant being that he imagined Ranger Security would disapprove—he knew he wasn't going to heed a single one of them.

He wanted her.

And from the tension and desperation in her touch, she wanted him as well.

He had a feeling his bogus fling was going to be anything but fake. Something about that unexplainable premonition gave him the briefest pause, made the nape of his neck tingle with…expectation?

With difficulty, he reluctantly ended the kiss. Pen's lashes fluttered and she looked up at him, still seemingly dazed. Something in his chest shifted and he smiled down at her. "I thought I told you not to look."

She blinked and drew back, a faint blush coloring her cheeks. "Sorry," she murmured.

He took her hand once more, noting the shadow in the window was still there. Trent's sister, he thought, but couldn't be sure. Furthermore, Paul, who was part of Pen's crew, was having an evening smoke down by the pier and seemed to be looking up at the house. He noticed Seth and lifted his hand in a casual wave.

A droll smile slid over her lips. "You just played me, didn't you?"

"Sorry?"

She jabbed him with her elbow, shook her head and laughed. "No you're not," she said. "Well done, Mr. McCutcheon." She faked a couple of coughs and lifted her hand to her mouth, pretended to spit something into her palm and toss it on the ground.

He frowned down at her. "Are you all right?"

"Fine," she said. "Just trying to hack up that hook, line and sinker."

Seth felt a laugh break up in his throat. "I didn't plan it exactly," he lied. "But I will admit to taking unfair advantage. And I'll also admit I'm not sorry." He paused. "You?"

The crash of the surf and night sounds settled around them and the wind was warm and easy. "Nah," she said. "I'm only sorry I enjoyed it as much as I did."

He chuckled again, surprised at her honesty. "That's a hell of a thing to be sorry about," he said. "But it's a compliment...I think."

"It is," she confirmed, then merely shrugged. "But it's a bad idea."

They were talking bigger picture here, not just the kiss, and he knew it. "Probably," he agreed. "But I have to admit I like it."

She inclined her head. "Then I'll take that as a compliment."

"It's definitely intended to be one. You're a good kisser," he remarked. "If you were trying to discourage me, you should have botched it," he told her, shooting her a smile. "Remember that next time."

He felt her laugh before he heard it. "Next time?"

"It could happen again." In fact, he fully intended to make sure that it did. Stupid? Reckless? Foolhardy? Yes, yes and yes, but unavoidable all the same. Seth wasn't in the habit of lying, least of all to himself. What was the point? He could go through a laundry list of reasons why he shouldn't make a play for Penelope Hart, but ultimately none of those reasons was going to matter.

He wanted her. She wanted him.

In fact, in so many ways, she was the perfect woman. She wasn't looking for a long-term commitment—was actively avoiding it, in fact—and wouldn't expect a declaration of love or any of the other sticky wickets that generally came up when dealing with the fairer sex. They could engage in a little mutually satisfying phenomenal sex, and given the way his dick was trying to come out of his shorts, he knew the sex would be better than spectacular. Then they could part as friends, both of them satisfied and happy.

Win, win.

And if he was simplifying this a little too much or was mildly certain that it wouldn't go off completely the way he was envisioning it, then he was going to ignore those thoughts altogether and pretend he wasn't having them. He knew he'd have to deal with the consequences of these actions at some point, but by the time that inevitability rolled around, he would have already gotten what he wanted.

Her.

"You're awfully quiet," he remarked, intrigued by what her continued silence meant. Like him, was she ready to say to hell with everything and go for it? Or was she trying to figure out a way to get him to back off, to keep things on the level they were supposed to be playing?

"Who was looking out the window?" she asked. Or maybe she wasn't thinking about him at all, Seth realized, the thought pricking his ego.

"I'm not sure, but I think it was Trent's sister."

"Lucy?" She hummed thoughtfully under her breath. "She's a sweet girl," Pen said. "I think she's really looking forward to having Nella in the family. Their mother can be a bit…stern," she said, taking the diplomatic approach.

"Is that code for a real bitch?"

She smiled at him. "I would never say that."

"But you'd think it," he said, laughing. "So you don't think Lucy could be behind this?"

She paused, seeming to be giving his question serious thought before answering. "I really don't," she said. "But honestly it's hard for me to imagine any of the women who are here deliberately trying to sabotage Trent and Nella's wedding."

Be that as it may, the fact remained that it was most likely a woman making the threats, definitely someone who was close enough to receive the necessary invitations, and there were only so many women in Trent's circle. That significantly narrowed the pool of suspects, if you asked Seth.

Improbable or not, someone they trusted was behind this. And that made that person all the more dangerous. But the same instincts that told him there was a missing element here also told him that he could handle it, that he would succeed. Arrogance? No. Arrogance could get you killed.

Confidence, on the other hand, was invaluable.

His gaze slid to Pen, who seemed to be deep in thought. Probably second-guessing her staff, he imagined, since it would be been extremely easy for someone in her circle to cancel the caterer and attempt to postpone the pastor. Then again, why would they bother, knowing how manically prepared she was? Knowing that she'd catch it? No matter how he tried to put it all together, the pieces didn't fit. But he had every intention of making sure they did before the weekend was out.

In the meantime, they had the rest of the night to get through…and he was hoping they were going to get to work on authenticating their performance a little more.

Preferably in bed.

8

"OKAY, WHAT HAPPENED?" Monica demanded first thing the next morning.

Pen feigned interest in watching the rental company unload the chairs. "I don't know what you mean."

"Yes, you do. Someone said they saw you and Mr. Gorgeous in a lip-lock last night and that was in *plain view*. I want to know what happened behind closed doors."

Someone saw them, huh? She knew exactly who'd seen them—Paul, she was sure. Her official heavy lifter was smirking at her when they'd made the return circuit to the guesthouse. She knew exactly what had put that knowing smile on Paul's face and congratulated herself for further perpetuating the idea that they were really a couple.

Despite the fact that Paul didn't think Seth was her type, she knew she had him fooled, at least. No doubt he'd been catching a smoke before going out with the others, she thought and made a mental note to make sure that he hadn't left any unsightly cigarette butts behind.

He typically didn't, but she liked to be certain. She never wanted to give any of her clients a reason to complain. Being courteous was just as important as orchestrating the perfect wedding.

As for what had happened behind closed doors… Pen's cheeks puffed as she exhaled mightily.

Absolutely nothing.

She'd cited being tired and having a lot to do the next morning. Then she'd made some sort of awkward gesture with her thumb and hastily retreated to her bedroom. Thankfully, both guest rooms had been outfitted with en suite facilities and she'd run herself a bubble bath and tried not to think about the six-and-a-half feet of masculine temptation that would be literally ready for action if she so much as crooked her finger.

It had been hard.

And he'd been hard, too, when they'd been kissing, so she knew exactly what she was missing.

Oy.

Suffice it to say that Seth McCutcheon was an extremely large man and, given the way a certain part of him had been nudging high on her belly, the rest of him was definitely proportionate.

Her mouth watered anew, her breasts tingled and a hot snake of heat coiled low in her belly, making her resist the urge to squirm. She felt she'd been resisting that urge for a damned eternity instead of a mere twenty-four hours, and didn't have any idea how on earth she was going to hold out for another night.

"Why are you turning red?" Monica demanded, her voice full of insinuation. "If nothing happened, then why do you look like you let Raggedy Ann apply your blush?"

"Because it's hotter than four hundred hells out here," Pen complained good-naturedly, which was the truth.

Though she would never admit it to Nella, she had to agree with Lucy when it came to the whole issue of holding the wedding outside. Early morning would have offered the best temperature, but who held a wedding at seven in the morning? Two o'clock was the norm and two o'clock here, particularly beneath the tents containing the food and dance floor, would be utterly stifling.

As such, they'd opted for an evening wedding. The festivities would begin at seven o'clock, the actual service over by seven-thirty, and then the cooler evening breezes would keep the icing from melting off the cake and the dancers from expiring in the heat.

Provided everyone lived through it, which was where Seth and his team came in. He'd been floating around today helping out as needed and seemed to be paying particular attention to the women around the house. She knew Seth wasn't flirting, which would be bad form considering he was supposed to be here as her boyfriend, but had been chatting with them all quite a bit. Even Monica, who thankfully didn't realize that he'd moved her onto the official suspect list. The same held true for Patrice. But in that case, Patrice was the one who was laughing a little too loudly and standing a little too close. Gratifyingly, Seth always moved back, lengthening the distance between them.

He was faithful, her pretend boyfriend, she thought, and squashed another smile.

No doubt he would be equally faithful to a real girlfriend. Granted she hadn't known him long, but in her line of work, she could typically spot the cheaters of both the male and female varieties, and Seth just didn't seem the type. No, he was a guy who would tell a woman the truth at the end of the evening to prevent her from waiting on a call that was never going to come. He was the kind of guy who put more stock in honesty than diplomacy. He spoke his mind and didn't waste time.

Honestly, if she didn't know any better, she'd think he was perfect. Or at least as close to perfect as a man could get.

"Are you telling me nothing happened?" Monica persisted. "Absolutely nothing?"

"I'm not going to tell you anything," Pen said, counting pedestals as they came off the truck. She was supposed to have twenty, ten on each side. "Because it's none of your business."

Monica stuck her tongue out at her. "Boo hiss. You know I want details." Her gaze drifted to Seth once more. "That man is one long, tall drink of water."

Yes, Pen thought, grinding her teeth. *She knew.*

Monica blinked innocently. "You look pissed," she remarked. She studied Penelope thoughtfully for a moment, then she gasped and her eyes widened. "Wait a minute," she breathed, as though she'd just unlocked some secret compartment inside Pen's brain. "That's not pissed. That's jealous. Oh my God! You're *jealous!*" She gave a little bouncy squeal. "You don't like it when

I drool over your pretend boyfriend. Oh, oh, this is epic! This is—ow!"

"Cut it out," Pen told her, not the least bit sorry that she'd whacked her friend with her trusty clipboard. "I am not jealous," she said, enunciating every word, trying to make the lie more believable. "I'm annoyed. I've got a wedding to pull off and a crazy person doing their best to ruin it. But all you can talk about is the guy who is supposed to be making sure that nothing goes horribly, heinously wrong. Unless you've forgotten, we're talking about a potential *murder* here," she reminded Monica in her stiffest, most stuffy tone. "Death at a wedding, then, remember?" Penelope quoted. "Someone dies here, they not only lose their lives, but I lose my business. Have you thought of that? Who'd hire me after that?"

She hated that she sounded so self-serving and mercenary…but she couldn't help it. Naturally she didn't want anyone to get hurt, but she'd be a fool not to consider what would happen to her business if someone did.

She'd be ruined.

She'd have to start over in another field and she could kiss goodbye the house she wanted. Her little plot of permanence, some place of her own that she desperately needed. She'd actually taken a home buyer's guide into the tub with her last night and looked at what was currently on the market. She'd been too afraid of getting her hopes up. It was the first time she'd allowed herself the luxury. She'd found a lovely antebellum a few blocks from her shop that she'd instantly fallen in love with. It was in her price range and she could even walk to work.

It had lots of stained glass and flowers and a whimsical turret on the second story.

She'd melted when she saw it, much the same way she'd melted the first time she'd laid eyes on Seth McCutcheon.

There was a frightening insight in that, but Pen refused to excavate the emotional territory enough to unearth its meaning. Some things were better left alone. She instinctively knew this was one of them.

Monica's face fell. "Goodness," she said. "I'm sorry, Pen. I hadn't even thought… I hadn't considered…"

"It's all right, Mon. I *have* to consider. It's my business."

She grimaced. "Yeah, but if you go under, then we're all unemployed."

Pen grinned. "There is that."

"So has anything else happened?" Monica asked, thankfully onto a new topic. "Any more letters or threats?"

She didn't tell her what Seth thought of the cancellations yesterday. No need to worry her further. "Not as of yet, no."

"Do you think the person might have just been bluffing? If they're close, then they know that the wedding is going off anyway, right? They have to know that Trent and Nella haven't called anything off."

"True," Pen conceded. "But it may just mean that they're biding their time, waiting for the perfect moment to sabotage everything."

"Well, if that's the case, then they're leaving it to the last minute, aren't they?" She looked around, evidently considering everyone as a possible suspect now. "I mean, the rehearsal is tonight. Besides, they're going to have a hard time getting anything past those Ranger Security boys," she said.

Pen knew that was right. Using Trent's celebrity status as an excuse, they were ferrying guests over in vans from a nearby marina and were wanding everyone for possible weapons. Purses and bags would be searched and nothing was coming onto the island without being checked first. In addition to that precaution, Trent's regular security contingent would be circling the island in patrol boats, making sure that no one attempted to come ashore via a different route.

"Unless the person is already here," Monica murmured, her eyes narrowed shrewdly. "In which case, how will we know who is behind it? We can't very well go up and start accusing everyone, can we?"

"Seth's on it," Pen told her. "We need to leave the sleuthing to the professionals and do our dead level best to make sure that Trent and Nella's wedding goes off without a hitch. That's our job," she said to Monica, but the reminder was as much for herself as anyone.

Monica suddenly smiled. "I rather think I'd prefer to be a detective."

Pen chuckled, not the least bit surprised. "In that case why don't you hit Paul on the walkie-talkie and find out why it's taking him so long to get those runners up here?" Paul wasn't what one would call a self-starter, but did as he was told and, at the moment, he seemed to be under the delusional impression that this was a beach vacation instead of a wedding.

Monica heaved a put-upon sigh. "That wasn't exactly the kind of detecting I meant."

"But that is the kind you're getting paid for. Scoot," she shooed her. "Get moving. We've got more to do today than we can conceivably handle."

Her assistant heaved a breath. "You say that every time."

"Because it's always the truth."

Nella suddenly burst out of the house, her face white, tears streaming over her cheeks. "Pen!"

Pen's heart stopped. "Nella?"

Nella's face crumpled as she hurried toward her. "Pen, my d-dress," she sobbed. "It's ruined!"

SETH WATCHED silently as Penelope inspected Nella's gown. Trent, his mother and Patrice attempted to comfort the crying bride-to-be, while Lucy, Trent's sister, stood nearby and looked on awkwardly. She was pale, but that could be said for the rest of the women as well.

Because she knew that Seth couldn't ask any questions in front of anyone without possibly tipping their hand, Pen did her best to ask the questions he would most want to know. That she had the presence of mind to do this despite what could only be described as a potentially show-stopping disaster showed him a lot about her character.

"Nella, when were the alterations on the dress complete?"

"Last week," she sniffed. "I went in and tried it on, everything fit perfectly."

"They stored it in the bag and you took it home?"

She nodded.

"Has it been out of the bag since? Have you shown it to anyone at all?"

"I showed it to Lucy yesterday," she said.

"Did you take it out of the bag?"

"No," she said, looking thoughtful. Her gaze tangled with Pen's. "I didn't. It…it could have been like this yesterday and I wouldn't have known," she told her, seemingly horrified all over again.

That's because the damage to the dress had been done on the back, where it wouldn't have shown had she only unzipped the front of the bag and moved the plastic aside to show off the front. He and Pen shared a look. Which meant this could have been done in the store before Nella brought it home or at any time over the past week while it was still at her house. Or it could have been done here.

It really was a shame, too, Seth thought, feeling sorry for Nella. The entire back of the dress looked like someone had taken a box cutter and sliced it to ribbons. It was definitely beyond repair and he wasn't sure what would happen now. Though he had little experience with weddings, it was his understanding that, for the bride, the dress was the pièce de résistance. Furthermore, that dress had probably cost as much as a compact car and now it was utterly ruined.

Well, at least one thing was certain. Whoever was making the threats was close enough to Nella to have the time and the opportunity to destroy her dress. And that was too close for Seth's liking.

Pen inspected the back of the dress, fingered the

shredded satin. Finally, she looked up and sighed. "I don't see how this can be repaired, at least not in time for the wedding tomorrow."

Nella nodded, dabbing at her eyes.

Pen leaned over and took Nella's hand. "Nella, I know that this is heartbreaking and I can't imagine what would possess someone to do something like this to your dress," she added, her voice throbbing with anger. "This was an heirloom, something that you'd intended to preserve and pass onto your own daughter and—" She couldn't finish. "I know that this is a blow. But after the wedding, we'll find someone to fix it as best they can. It won't look exactly like the dress you'd wanted, but it will be close enough to serve its purpose."

Trent's mother spoke up for the first time. "Elise Martine can repair it, dear," she said, laying a hand on Nella's shoulder. "As Penelope says, it's not ever going to be the same dress again, but it can be salvaged."

"In the interim, we're going to have to go to Plan B," Penelope said.

"Do we have a Plan B?" Nella asked, her voice still thick with unshed tears.

Pen smiled. "We do now. You're going to have to go get another dress today," she said. "I'll make some calls, find the best boutiques and—" she nodded toward Lucy and Patrice "—you'll need a couple of pairs of eyes to make sure that you make the best choice."

Brilliant, Seth thought. No doubt she would find something else to occupy Trent's mother's time and that would free up him and his team to do a little recon through the women's things. In particular, Trent would be looking for a sharp instrument... and a red pen.

"Of course we'll help, won't we, Lucy?" Patrice chimed in. Honestly she was almost too happy. On the other end of the spectrum, Lucy looked like she'd prefer a colonic cleanse. He couldn't imagine why either one of them would have any reason to sabotage Trent and Nella like this, but common sense said that one of them was the guilty party. Evidently, Pen thought so, too.

Armed with a plan, Nella stood and turned directly into Trent's arms. "It'll be all right, sweetheart," he told her, pressing a kiss onto the top of her head. "You could wear a potato sack and I'd still think you were the most beautiful bride on the planet."

Sincerity rang so strongly in his voice that Seth didn't doubt for an instant that Trent was making a true statement. For one terrifying moment, he wondered what it would feel like to be that tied to another person, that invested. And for reasons he couldn't explain, his gaze drifted to Penelope.

Nella smiled up at Trent. "Are you thinking we should start a new tradition? The potato sack wedding dress?"

"It's got a certain cachet," he said.

She hesitated, then patted him on the arm. "I'll go see what I can find."

"I'll get the phone book," Trent's mother said, seemingly desperate to be helpful. Her mouth had formed a grim line and, when she'd seen the back of the dress, Seth had noticed that her eyes had watered with unshed tears. She looked at her son. "Trent, I'd like a word later, please."

No doubt that was going to be the what-the-hell-are-you-not-telling-me? conversation, because after this incident, she was shrewd enough to understand that something was amiss. Though he wasn't comfortable ruling anyone out completely, like Pen, he didn't think Trent's mother was behind any of this either.

Trent's mother hurried out of the room after the other three, leaving the rest of them alone. He and Trent helped Pen put the ruined dress back into the bag and then Trent looked at Seth. "It has to be someone close," he said, his voice low and sick. "Someone we trust, obviously, which makes me feel a little foolish, but..." He shrugged helplessly and gave a humorless laugh. "What can I do?" Trent asked.

"Occupy your mother," Seth told him. "Honestly, I don't think that she's involved, but while I'm in the house looking through Patrice and Lucy's things, I want to go ahead and do a thorough search so that we can completely rule her out. Also, make sure that Nella goes in her car and that the other two leave their vehicles here. You can tell them that we might need to move them or something—make up some story—but I want to sweep the cars as well."

"You think it could be one of them?" Trent asked.

"No one else has had the kind of access required to pull this off," Pen piped up. She gestured to the bag. "This wasn't done at the boutique—the owner is meticulous about inspecting everything that leaves the store. So that means this was done either at Nella's house or here. And both Lucy and Patrice have been both places."

"I don't know if Lucy has been to Nella's in the past week," Trent said, looking thoughtful.

"Check with Nella," Seth told him. "Also find out if Nella has a Hide-A-Key and who would know about it if she did."

Trent nodded and set off.

Pen and Seth shared a look. "This is bad, isn't it?" she said.

"It's bad for the dress, but it's actually not bad for the case. We've narrowed our suspects down to two and, despite what's happened to the dress, I don't think Lucy or Patrice is likely to try to kill anyone. I think the whole 'murder' aspect of the threat was for dramatic effect. They're sabotaging—being hurtful, certainly—but they aren't hurting *anybody* and that's what's important." And even if they were planning on hurting someone, Seth would make sure that he stopped them first. Something still wasn't quite right, but at least now they were on the right path. They had a direction, even if it wasn't one they'd wanted to take.

Pen chuckled grimly. "True, but Trent might hurt someone when he finds out who's behind this. Nella's gown was custom-made. She had more than eighteen months invested in it. The lace on the front was actually from her mother's wedding dress and the veil had been her grandmother's. They'd added a few things to make it coordinate with Nella's dress, but both were heirloom pieces."

"The veil was untouched?"

"Yes, thank God, though I think we should probably move it down to the guesthouse with us."

He nodded. "When is Nella's mother supposed to arrive?"

"This afternoon," Pen said. She massaged the bridge of her nose. "She'll be relieved that the front of the dress wasn't ruined."

"Was it common knowledge that the lace was from her mother's gown?"

Pen frowned, her brow wrinkling adorably. "I think so," she said. Her eyes widened significantly. "Oh, I see," she said. "You think destroying the back of the dress wasn't just to avoid detection? That whoever did it knew the lace on the front had special significance?"

"More than likely," Seth said. But anyone who'd spare heirloom lace certainly wasn't going to kill anyone. So why make that threat? The first two letters had expressed a desire to stop the wedding. The last had escalated to a full-on threat.

The hair on the back of his neck prickled and his palms tingled. That was the piece he'd been missing, Seth suddenly realized. Now he suspected that the last letter was written by someone else...someone who was in on the original plan but had a different agenda altogether.

The question, of course, was...who?

9

WITH THE REHEARSAL a mere eight hours away, the bride still in town searching for a new dress that didn't need much alteration, the culprits still at large, and Seth and his crew sweeping the house, Pen took a moment to do something she'd never done when she was officially at work.

She had a stiff shot of liquor.

Paul came around the corner, saw her with the bottle—who had time for a glass?—and skidded to a stop. "Whoa," he said, his eyes rounded. "It's not like you to hit the hard stuff," he said, giving his head a shake. "What's happened, Pen?"

Because they seriously didn't have a prayer in hell of keeping the destroyed dress a secret, Pen told him. She didn't, however, confide the original threat. Nor was she quite ready to confess that Seth wasn't really her boyfriend. Rather than explore the reasons behind that little nugget of unwanted insight, Pen merely ignored it.

"Her dress was destroyed? On purpose?" Paul repeated, evidently as shocked as she had been. "But why?" he asked, a perplexed scowl sliding over his face. "Why would anyone want to do that?"

"My guess is someone is trying to sabotage the wedding, keep it from happening," Pen said. Actually that wasn't a guess since she knew it for a fact, but she still didn't think she needed to tell Paul that.

Paul took the bottle from her hand and took a giant swig, wincing when it burned. "I don't blame you for drinking," he said. "So what are you going to do?"

"Carry on as usual. Trent's security team is on it," she said, hoping he wouldn't ask where Seth was. "In the interim, Nella is scouring the local area boutiques for another gown and we're going to move forward."

Paul's gaze turned speculative. "Bet you'd like to smack someone upside the head right now, wouldn't you?"

She grinned. "Are you volunteering?"

"Nope," he said, rocking back on his heels. He looked at the various tents, the white lights, the runners and pedestals that would hold the flowers when they arrived tomorrow. "It's a shame," he said. "I think this is one of the nicest shows you've ever put on."

She actually agreed. In keeping with the island theme they'd used a lot of shell colors and pale turquoise. Large fountains were erected on either side of the massive arbor, which had been built specifically for the nuptials. When the wedding was over, Trent had said he planned to put a porch swing there so that they could sit together and look out over the ocean. The property really was remarkable, Pen thought, loving the salty scent of the breeze and the live oaks, Spanish moss and oleander that littered the landscape. It was lovely and relaxing, a homey kind of paradise.

"So where's the boyfriend?" Paul finally asked. "Out fishing?"

The only person fishing around here was Paul. She felt her lips twitch. "I couldn't tell you," Pen said. "He pretty much does his own thing and let's me do mine. It's wonderful, really."

"Forward thinking, is he?" Paul remarked, clearly not buying it.

Pen suppressed a chuckle. Actually, if they'd been in a real relationship, she imagined that Seth would be a little bit old-fashioned. Despite the fact that he seemed every bit as protective of his single status as she, he nevertheless struck her as a bit traditional, for lack of a better description. He'd pulled out her chair at dinner, stood when she did and held open doors. She'd heard him use a "yes ma'am" with Trent's mother and it was as natural to him as breathing. His mother had done well with him, Pen thought. He was just reckless and irreverent enough to be utterly charming—irresistible, really—but the core values were equally evident, making him a man who was damned hard to resist.

And after that kiss last night, Pen would be the biggest kind of liar if she said she wanted to resist.

She didn't.

In fact, though she would have to worry about her equally weak flesh and moral fiber at some point in the near future, she very much wished she hadn't resisted last night. And that was a first for her. She'd met guys who'd lit her up before and, if the fire was still burning when she figured out whether or not they were worthy of sharing her body, then she typically indulged. She might be a champion dater, but she'd always been quite selective when it came to picking bed partners. It required a certain level of trust that sometimes simply never materialized.

With Seth, it had been there from the beginning. That, combined with all the other particularly compelling things about him, had made her more than a little nervous. She'd never hopped right into bed with anyone, had never had one of those all-consuming I-have-to-have-you-right-now-or-I'll-die kinds of experiences. The fact that she'd felt that kind of attraction to Seth had sent a dart of panic directly into her lust-ridden breast.

Furthermore, there wouldn't have been a bed required. She'd have been happy with a quick tumble against the wall.

Last night, rather than act on her irrational impulses, she'd played it safe and hidden in her room. And she'd been sorry all day. Why had she done that? Why had she held back when chances were that nothing like this would ever happen to her again? What were the odds that she'd ever *want* someone as much as she did right now? She knew it was her self-preservation kicking in, knew that the power that made him so appealing made him equally dangerous.

Clearly her subconscious was trying to tell her something and even more clearly, a part of her trusted him more than she trusted herself. This, she instinctively knew, was a once-in-a-lifetime opportunity and she had every intention of taking advantage of it.

After tomorrow night, whether they'd discovered who was trying to sabotage Trent and Nella's wedding or not, she'd likely never see Seth McCutcheon again. A pinprick of pain nicked her heart, making her inwardly wince with regret. She stilled as that unhappy thought wrapped itself around her chest and squeezed. A strange kind of panic sent her pulse to racing and she took the bottle of whiskey back from Paul and determinedly took another sip.

It was ridiculous, she thought, shaking off the bizarre sensation. She barely knew him. It was insane to get this worked up over someone who was as permanent as a henna tattoo.

She only regretted that she wouldn't have the time to get to know him better, Pen told herself. That was what was making her anxious. There were still so many things she didn't know about him, so many things she longed to learn. And really, considering that she'd given him so much information about herself, it hardly seemed fair that she wouldn't get at least a few answers to her questions. It was an inequitable exchange of information and the injustice irritated her, dammit. Fair was fair.

Yes, probably what she most wanted to know was none of her business, but that didn't make her any less curious. And what she wanted to know more than any-thing was who he'd kept his promise to. Why had their wishes been so important? Important enough for him to give up a career she instinctively knew he'd loved.

He was a walking puzzle and she longed to make the pieces fit.

Preferably his pieces into hers.

"That was a quick recovery," Paul remarked, staring at her with an uncomfortable amount of shrewdness. "A minute ago you looked like someone had kicked your dog. Now you're smiling." He nodded to the bottle and quirked a brow. "That must be magic liquor."

"I don't know about that, but it's good."

Paul frowned. "Where'd you get it?"

"From my secret stash."

"Which is?"

"Secret," Pen told him. "Now get to work. We've got a wedding to pull off."

Grumbling good-naturedly about whip-wielding bosses, Paul went over and started helping the caterer move the tables into place. She'd provided a diagram, of course, but her attention to detail was one of the main things that had contributed to her success. Typically people did what they said they were going to do, but invariably mistakes were made. It was her job to fix them before they became major problems.

The fact that she wasn't doing anything to help Trent and Nella find out who was behind the threats had weighed on her more than she'd like to admit. Feeling useless wasn't a problem she was used to having. Her gaze stole to the house, where Seth and the other Ranger Security guys were busy doing their part and an idea suddenly struck.

The cars.

She could do a little recon of her own. Under the

guise of letting Pen know whether or not Nella had found a replacement dress, Nella was supposed to give her an estimated time of arrival. With any luck, Nella and her bridesmaids would be gone long enough for Seth and his men to do a thorough search of the house and the vehicles.

She was going to help them out with those.

Though she knew no one was watching her, she nevertheless peeked around and then quickly made her way to the driveway. Thankfully, Lucy had driven, her mother with her, and she could take a quick peek inside to see if anything looked suspicious. Crouching low, she carefully opened the door of the sporty sedan and slid into the passenger seat. She looked around, noting the overall tidiness of the interior—no straw wrappers or stray French fries here, she thought—and decided to start with the glove compartment. Insurance papers, tag receipts, air freshener and a few pens. Nothing damning whatsoever.

She moved to the console and found a lot of CDs— Lucy was a Lady Gaga fan, evidently—and a small sewing kit, first-aid kit and mini-digital recorder. The latter was intriguing but, while she was intensely curious about what might be on the device, she simply couldn't justify playing it. She was looking for a red permanent marker and a sharp instrument. Deliberately listening to the recording without just cause felt more like spying and less like being helpful. She spent a few more minutes checking the side pockets and underneath the seats, but didn't find anything.

Dejected, she quietly slipped out of the car and headed over to Patrice's SUV.

AFTER AN ULTIMATELY futile search, Seth met Will, Tanner and Huck in the foyer of Trent's house. All four of them were frustrated and, like Seth, knew that time was running out. If they didn't figure out who was behind this at some point before the wedding, then in all likelihood, there *wouldn't* be a wedding.

Because he'd lost all perspective, he was actually more concerned about the consequences to Pen's business than Trent and Nella's marital plans. If push came to shove, Trent and Nella could always go to the courthouse and get married. But Pen's career would go into a tailspin. Everything she'd worked for, all the successful events she'd competently hosted would be largely forgotten in the wake of a high-profile mishap.

That was simply unacceptable.

Even though he knew that he was technically working for Trent, Seth found himself more aligned with protecting Pen's interests than those of his employer. It was a good damned thing that they weren't mutually exclusive, he thought, trying to ignore the significance of that particular revelation.

"You know what the problem is, don't you?" Huck asked them. "It's women. Women are diabolical," he told them, his face twisting with equal parts admiration and disgust. "Which, admittedly can be attractive in a weird sort of way, but in this instance, it's proving to be damned inconvenient."

"Damned straight," Tanner agreed. "I can't believe

we've put the man-hours into this that we have, only to narrow it down to a couple of amateur females who are, quite honestly, getting the better of us." He grinned. "Not that I could share that opinion in front of my wife, mind you. She'd accuse me of being sexist. Which I'm not…really," he qualified with a sheepish smile.

"Sexist or not, we're former military," Will chimed in. "Official badasses and look at us," he said, gesturing to the lot of them. "Bested by a chick with a red pen and a razor. It's despicable."

Tanner chuckled. "Given the choice between tangling with a woman or an insurgent, I'd take the insurgent any day."

A low laugh rumbled up Seth's throat. "I think that's a choice we'd all make," he said. "But unfortunately that's not the option we're presented with." He looked at Will. "Will, I want you to run a check on the cell phones and see if you find anything that looks suspicious."

Will nodded. "On it."

He looked at Tanner and Huck. "Both women have laptops and we're rapidly running out of time. Can you—"

"Of course," Huck said, nodding decisively.

Tanner quirked a brow. "What about the mother's?"

Seth did another gut check. "I think she's clear, but better safe than sorry. Do Patrice's first," he said, thinking that hers was the most likely hit. "I'm going to go out and check the cars. Let me know if you find anything, anything at all, regardless how insignificant it might seem. If it gives you pause, I want to know. Let's meet back down at the pier in an hour. We'll pretend to be admiring the boat."

"I won't have to pretend," he heard Will say as he walked away. "That baby is beautiful."

Smiling, Seth made his way outside and around to the parking area. The sedan belonged to Lucy and the SUV to Patrice. Thinking that the SUV would take longer, Seth decided to work that one first. He opened the door and a woman screamed, frightening him more thoroughly than he'd ever admit. Damned rookie mistake. He should have looked first. But he'd had no reason to. Or so he'd thought. He swore and climbed quickly into the backseat of the vehicle where the windows were better tinted.

"What the hell are you doing?" he whispered furiously at Pen.

"You scared the hell out of me!" She had a hand pressed to her heart and she was struggling to get her breathing under control. Once she did, she looked at him and evidently found something incredibly funny. Because she started laughing and couldn't stop. "You should have seen the l-look on your f-face," she wheezed. "I think I scared you as much as you scared me."

He'd risk dismemberment before he'd admit it, but chuckled despite himself. Then he glared at her and tried to look formidable. "I think you're mistaken."

"And I think you're full of shit."

He felt his eyes widen and a laugh rumbled up his throat. "I can see no way of responding to that without being crude, so I won't." He stared at her, trying hard to ignore the way her breasts strained against the filmy sundress she currently wore and the way her hair was spilling over her creamy shoulders. Whatever perfume she was wearing was doubly intoxicating in the warm car—thank God it had been parked in the shade—and he could feel it curling around his senses, playing hell with his brain.

"What are you doing out here?" he asked, struggling to focus.

She swallowed, the fine muscles in her throat moving deliciously. He was suddenly hit with the urge to lick the hollow in her neck, slide his tongue along the sleek indentations of her collarbone. It was finely made, like delicate wings spanning shoulder to shoulder.

"I had a few minutes and wanted to help," she said. "You'd mentioned searching the cars, so…"

He was torn between being impressed with her dedication to her couple and furious over the fact that she'd interfered. You didn't see him trying to help her plan the wedding, did you? He almost pointed that out, but admiration won out and he merely sighed. "Look, Pen, I appreciate it, but you really need to leave this to me and my team."

She hesitated. "We're running out of time," she said. "If we don't get to the bottom of this tonight, then I'm afraid that something truly horrible is going to happen. That someone will call the pastor and tell him the wedding is off again, that someone will ruin the cake, or cut up Trent's tux or spray weed killer all over the flowers. There are so many things that could go wrong between now and I-do time and I—" She looked away and her hands fisted tightly in her lap. "I'm not trying to step on your toes, Seth," she said, shooting him a look. "I know I'm a control freak. I know that I tend to go a wee bit overboard on things—"

He snorted before he could help himself and she punched him playfully in the arm.

"But I just can't sit around and do nothing. Not when I see an opportunity to be useful."

He stilled and continued to stare at her, then his throat grew tight. He knew someone else who always had a need to be useful, Seth thought. And his mother would have loved Penelope. She would have admired her wit, her work ethic and her sense of humor.

She studied him and her smile slowly capsized. "Did I say something wrong?"

"No," he said, looking away. "And I do understand that you want to help, but…"

She grinned. "But you don't need my help."

"I didn't say that." And he wouldn't, because it would be unkind and, really, not altogether true. At this point he should be willing to take all the help he could get. "So have you found anything?" he asked.

"Not yet," she admitted. "I went through Lucy's car first and, other than a digital voice recorder in the console, I didn't find anything interesting at all."

"A digital voice recorder?" he said. "Lucy isn't a doctor, right? She's a massage therapist, isn't she?" Why would she need a voice recorder? Seth wondered.

"Right."

"Did you listen to it?"

"No," she said, wincing regretfully. "I just couldn't

bring myself to do it. It seems like such an invasion of privacy."

That wasn't a problem for him, Seth thought. Given what had been going on and that his gut was telling him Trent's sister was somehow involved, he didn't have a problem crossing that line. In fact, given the stakes, as far as he was concerned there was no line.

"What about in here?" he asked.

"Nothing so far," she said, moistening her lips. Her gaze dropped to his mouth, then found his eyes again. "We should probably start looking."

If they didn't, he was going to start something else. And, though there was a condom in his wallet, there was precious little room back here. Still…

He nodded, trying to focus on something besides the sweet plumpness of her breasts swelling beneath the fabric of her dress, the teeny bit of cleavage visible when she moved just so. His mouth watered.

They shared a long look, then both of them bolted into action, leaning toward the front of the car at the same time.

Her "ow" was met with his "damn" and they fell back and looked at each other, then started laughing again. He loved that she laughed so easily, so open and honest and unrestrained. She rubbed her temple and he moved her hand so that he could take a look. "Sorry about that," he said, still chuckling.

She was fine—no blood and no bump—but this close he could smell her shampoo and he was loath to move away from her.

"You have a hard head," she said, laughing softly.

That wasn't the only thing that was hard at the moment. "So I've been told," he murmured, drawing back to better look at her. He paused and gave her a significant look. He was quickly losing what little grip he'd managed to keep on his self-control. "One of us is going to have to get out of the car," he said. "Otherwise I'm going to start something and I'm not going to want to stop."

She swallowed. "Is that a warning?"

"It's a fact," he said, laying it all out on the line for her. He wanted her more than he'd ever wanted another woman in his life. He wanted to eat her up and breathe her in and taste every single inch of her. He wanted to fill his mouth with her breasts and feel her small hands sliding over his bare back. He wanted to slip that dress out of the way and pull her into his lap and settle her down on top of him. He wanted to take her hard and fast and slake a bit of his lust and then take her again and savor her slowly.

Every muscle in his body was aching with pent-up need and he was rapidly losing the ability to keep himself away from her, to keep from merely touching his lips to hers—a single touch was all he needed—and then doing exactly what he wanted to do with her.

And the kicker? The cherry on top? What lit him up more than anything else?

She wanted it, too. He could her feel the tension, her need rebounding off his own. It was a damned miracle the heat between them hadn't set the car ablaze.

She looked up at him from beneath a sweep of sooty lashes, her blue eyes dark with desire and the thrill of a challenge. She quirked a sleek brow and her voice, when she spoke, was throaty and low. "What makes you think I'm going to ask you to stop?"

10

IT WAS THE RAW NEED in the warning that ultimately did it for her, Pen thought. His bold green gaze raked over her as though she was a feast for the senses—*his,* in particular—and he was a starving man.

Which was fine with her, because she was starving too. Her body was too sensitive, too tight and too damned hot. The pure desire pumping through her veins was unlike anything she'd ever experienced before. She couldn't believe they were about to do it in a car, particularly one that didn't belong to either of them, but ultimately, she didn't care. Nothing mattered, least of all propriety. Her hands craved him, her very skin ached for his touch, and the low, steady throb hitting her womb with every beat of her heart all but had her squirming in the seat.

She wanted. *Him.*

He chuckled low and his gaze drifted over her face, then settled on her mouth. "Well, in that case," he murmured silkily, his voice rough like velvet against satin as he pushed his big hand into her hair, cupped the back of her neck and brought her mouth to his.

She simultaneously sighed and burned, and a long tremor of anticipation resonated down her spine.

This, she knew, was going to be beyond good.

He kissed her, softly at first, just a mere brush of his lips against hers. His other hand found her face, cupping her jaw. The strength and desire and something else not altogether readable, but profound nonetheless, made her insides quiver and melt.

His tongue tangled around hers, stroking the soft recesses of her mouth, his lips molding perfectly to her own, creating the perfect amount of moisture between them. An elusive trick that, Pen thought dimly as her aching breasts brushed against his magnificent chest. A dry kiss was awkward and too much spit made her gag, but he… She pulled him closer to her, desperate to be nearer. He knew what he was doing.

Pen cradled his face between her hands and savored the feel of his jaw against her palms. Seeing good bone structure and masculine skin was no substitute for actually touching it. Feeling the curve of a jaw, the delicious prick of stubble beneath her hand…wonderful.

He gently tugged her closer, shifting her until she straddled him and the first bit of pressure against her sex had her squirming shamelessly against him. Breathing raggedly, he tore his mouth away from hers and licked a path down her throat, causing a wave of gooseflesh to skitter over her arms. His mouth followed the line along her shoulder and she gasped and held him closer, pushing her hands into his hair, along the strangely soft skin behind his ears.

She felt his big hands slide down her back, along the edge of her spine. They settled possessively on her rump and gave a gentle squeeze. She shifted against him, aligning herself more firmly against the thick ridge straining against his shorts. Her sex wept, readying for him, and he pushed up, nudging her swollen clit. She gasped and he used the distraction to his advantage, slipping her breast from the built-in cup of her sundress.

"No bra," he murmured against her nipple before laving it and pulling it into his hot mouth.

"No need," Pen managed, the breath thinning in her lungs as pleasure arced through her. "It's part of the dress."

He freed her other breast. "Ingenious," he said, then pulled the bud into his mouth, flattening the sensitive crown against the roof of his mouth. His hands slipped her dress out of the way, putting skin against skin, and the first touch of those greedy palms against her bare rear made a shudder rip through her.

He drew back, his eyes heavy lidded and sexy, and he grinned, seemingly impressed. "No panties, either?"

"Thong," she said, chuckling.

"An itty-bitty thong," he remarked, his hands sliding higher until he found the minuscule straps. "Ah," he sighed knowingly. "This is almost indecent," he murmured. His green eyes twinkled with admiration. "I like that in a woman."

"You know what I like in a pretend boyfriend?"

"I hate to disappoint you, baby, but I don't wear thongs," he said, kissing her again.

She chuckled against his mouth and shifted so that she could find the snap of his shorts. His zipper whined and, with the smallest amount of maneuvering, he sprang free right into her waiting hand.

She'd been right. He was *definitely* well proportioned.

He was hot and hard and thick. Her mouth watered and her feminine muscles clenched in anticipation of feeling him there, deep within her, pushing and pulsing and taking her to the top of Orgasm Mountain and then shoving her off, so that she could free-fall through the sensation. That's what she wanted, what she needed. She—

Her cell phone suddenly sounded, the tune of "Going to the Chapel" echoing like a gunshot in the hot SUV.

Seth swore. "What the fu—"

Pen scrambled for her phone and checked the display. "It's a text from Nella," she said. "She found a dress and they'll be here in about thirty minutes. They ended up in Foley."

Seth leaned forward and kissed her again, pushing up against her once more, snatching the breath from her lungs. Her eyes practically rolled back in her head. "Then I guess we'd better hurry," he said. "But give me five seconds." He called Will and gave him Nella's ETA. Once that little bit of business was concluded, he found his wallet and drew a condom out. He tore the package open with his teeth, then quickly withdrew the protection. She took it from him and rolled it into place.

It was a tight fit.

Sweet mercy... He was magnificent.

"I like it when your eyes go all sleepy," he told her as she leaned forward and felt him nudge her entrance. He swept her panties aside, moving them out of the way. Every vital organ in her body shook from that small contact and she dimly wondered what would happen when he was inside her. If she'd simply fly apart on the inside, her skin the only thing holding her together.

He framed her face with his hands and bent forward and kissed her again. Then he moved his hands down, lingering over her rear and sliding up her back, his thumbs skimming her spine. Though, at five-two, Pen was used to feeling small, he made her feel positively dainty and breakable. The need and reverence in his touch was something she'd never felt before, a lethal combo that could truly screw up her heart if she wasn't careful.

But it was a little late for being careful, Pen thought, sliding slowly down onto him. Her eyes fluttered shut and her breath, when it finally returned, leaked weakly out of her lungs. He was... She could...

Oh, my.

She looked at Seth and his teeth were bared in a primal sort of smile, one that sent a thrill through her. She tightened around him, then lifted up once more and moaned on the way back down.

He made a low masculine growl in the back of his throat and then bent forward and licked a path between her breasts. Then he moved over and wrapped his lips around her nipple, laving it with his tongue.

She inexplicably tightened around him, and repeated the process over again. Up and then down, slowly undulating her hips so that she took all of him inside her, feeling every long, hot inch of him deep in her core.

He was like a drug winding through her blood, Pen thought, her entire body simultaneously energized and languid, the poison and the antidote. And as much as she'd like to draw this out, to milk every bit of sensation slowly and thoroughly from their bodies, she could feel the quickening in her sex, the tingling herald of impending orgasm. She upped her tempo, riding him harder, her hands anchored on his shoulders. She should have taken his shirt off, Pen thought, absently and made a mental note for next time. She wanted to taste that bare skin, feel it beneath her tongue.

Recognizing her intent—what she needed—Seth arched up beneath her. He caught her rhythm and pounded into her, his hands on either side of her hips, holding her while he made her his. With each flex of his hips, she felt him claiming her, branding her, marking his territory…ruining her for anyone else.

That terrifying thought echoed through her head at the exact moment the orgasm finally crested and she free-fell through the exquisite sensation. Her breath caught in her throat, her mouth opened in a soundless scream, and every muscle in her body tightened as the pleasure exploded inside her.

She happened to look down at him, saw the satisfied gleam in his eye, the masculine pleasure, and the crooked grin on his beautiful lips and knew she was in terrible, terrible trouble.

Because though she was resistant to the idea, she had the horrible suspicion that she was falling for her pretend boyfriend.

Thankfully, he wasn't finished yet, so the worry fled as quickly as it had come. And then he kissed her again and she stopped thinking altogether.

BLACK CURLS spilling around her creamy shoulders, plump breasts tipped with pouty pale pink nipples, her teeth sunk into that full bottom lip as she rose and fell on top of him, his dick surrounded by her tight warmth…

He'd died and gone to heaven, Seth thought. Or he'd been transported to paradise, because she was the most responsive, most beautiful creature he'd ever had the pleasure to take to bed.

Or take in the car, actually, he thought, wishing they had a lot more room and a limitless amount of time to explore and play, to sample and taste.

Honestly, when she'd looked at him and said "What makes you think I'm going to ask you to stop?" he'd gone from being painfully hard to near immaculate ejaculation. He could feel the desperation in her touch, her desire mingling with his own and there was nothing— *nothing*—more attractive than a woman who wanted you, who wanted to get beneath your skin, who genuinely with-every-fiber-of-her-being *had to have* you.

He'd been getting that vibe from Penelope from the instant she'd appeared on his doorstep. And, though he wished they could have done this last night like he'd wanted to, he damned sure wasn't going to complain.

How could he, when she was riding him like this? When she'd just come for him and, with any luck, he was going to make her do it again. He thrust up into her, over and over again, taking her harder and faster, her sweet channel squeezing him, seemingly trying to keep him inside of her body. Her heavy breasts bounced on her chest, her nipples pearled tight, begging for his kiss.

He bent forward and drew one into his mouth, raked the hard tip against his tongue and felt her shudder. He could feel his own release building in the back of his loins, gathering force with every delicious draw and drag between their joined bodies.

"Seth," she gasped, and he loved the way his name came off her lips, all breathy and feminine and low.

"Pen," he returned, kissing the underside of her jaw. She smelled like ginger, he realized, finally isolating the scent. Ginger and musk and cloves. It was earthy and provocative and he enjoyed how it rose off her skin and slid into his lungs.

"I don't know if I can—" She moaned and clung to him, her breath hitching. "I… Please… Now—"

And there we go, Seth thought, the moment he'd been waiting for. He pushed high and angled deep, then reached between them and stroked the nub nestled at the top of her slippery sex.

She shattered around him, her feminine muscles clenching tight once more. That was all it took to send him hurtling over the edge. He let go and came hard and when he would have quit, she kept going, kept squeezing, kept rocking above him, pulling every bit of sensation from him that she could.

She was thorough, his pretend girlfriend, Seth thought, and every muscle in his body went limp.

Best. Orgasm. Ever.

Ever.

She handed him a tissue—thankfully Patrice had a box on hand—and he quickly disposed of the condom. Or disposed of it as best he could until he could find a garbage can. He couldn't very well leave it in the car, Seth thought, stifling a smile. That would be bad form. Evidently reading his thoughts, Pen grabbed another handful of tissues, wrapped up the evidence and, grimacing slightly, stowed it in her purse.

She rested her forehead against his, heaved a big sigh and smiled. "I'm glad we got that out of the way," she said, much to his surprise.

A startled laugh rumbled from his chest. "You make me sound like something on your to-do list."

Her smile turned wicked. "You were and I just did you, so…" She lifted a shoulder in a little shrug.

Feigning outrage, he wrapped a black curl around his finger and tugged. "Where is this damned list?" he asked her. "I need to make sure that I'm penciled in a few more times."

She chuckled. "Oh, I think that can be arranged."

He grinned, pleased. "After the rehearsal dinner tonight?"

She grimaced. "Provided there is a rehearsal dinner. Did you find anything in the house?" she asked.

He shook his head. "Not yet. We're still checking a

few things like the computers and cell records, but so far, we haven't come across anything that's going to be solid evidence."

A worried frown worked its way across her brow and he slid a finger over the line, smoothing it away.

She smiled and something about that grin made his chest constrict, made his heart skip a beat, and the prelude to something he didn't fully understand yawned before him. *One of these days you're going to find your rudder...and I hope she initially mops the deck with you.* Nah, Seth told himself. He was being ridiculous. He'd just met Penelope, they barely knew each other. He couldn't—

"I guess we'd better get back to work," she said, reluctantly climbing off him.

Still trying to recover from that bizarre premonition, Seth buttoned his shorts and made an effort to focus. It took more concentration than he was accustomed to, which only served to rattle him further. "Right," he said. "So where have you looked?"

"In the glove box, the side pockets and console," she said.

He smiled at her. "Are you going to be insulted if I go behind you?"

She rolled her eyes. "And people call *me* a control freak."

"You are a control freak," he said, slipping into the front seat so that he could better search.

"And you're not?"

"Nope. I'm a perfectionist. There's a difference."

She snorted. "You're so full of—"

"Hey," he interrupted, shooting her a look as he closed the glove box. As she'd said, it had yielded nothing. "I didn't say it was a bad thing. In fact, I happen to think it's one of those endearing quirks you mentioned before."

She looked momentarily startled, then she smiled. "Er…thanks. I think."

He chuckled and moved to the console. Several CDs, a few pens, a package of cigarettes that smelled curiously like vanilla, a notebook that revealed only the odd address, phone number and grocery list. Nothing that said, *I'm guilty!* unfortunately.

Pen had practically turned herself upside down to look under the backseat and he chuckled softly, admiring the view. "Anything under there?"

"Only some loose change and a flashlight," came her slightly muffled reply.

Seth checked the passenger-side door compartment and found a lone French fry and a packet of salt, then moved to the driver's side. There was an atlas, more CD cases, a receipt from Starbucks and a Jolly Rancher candy. That was it. Getting more and more frustrated and less and less confident of actually being able to catch either Patrice, Lucy or even Nella's mother, for that matter, Seth swore.

"It's looking bad, isn't it?" she said, righting herself. Her pink cheeks puffed as she exhaled heavily, her lips still swollen from his kisses.

He'd been better off not to notice that, because it just made him want to kiss her again. Sadly, though, they really didn't have the time. The clock was ticking and they were no closer to outing the villain than they'd been when Nella and the others left.

Pen's phone rang again, this time to the tune of the theme music from *Jaws.* "Monica," she explained with a wry smile in answer to his questioning gaze.

The *Jaws* theme music? he thought, smothering another laugh. Did she have a special ring tone for everyone? he wondered. If so, what would she choose for him?

"Yes, Mon?" She looked at him and grinned. "Where am I? I'm here. Where are you?" A pause then, "Er...no. Is there a problem? No? Then why are you—" Another pause. "I'm not AWOL, dammit. I'm helping Seth." He could hear Monica's laugh over the phone and he had the pleasure of watching Pen blush to the roots of her hair. "Monica, we're quite busy right now, so—" She moaned and snapped the phone shut. "Nosy help," she muttered. "*I'm* the boss here," she ranted quietly. "A fact she frequently forgets."

"She seems to have a great deal of admiration for you," Seth said. Her entire staff did, in fact, as well as anyone else he'd met who'd worked with her in any capacity.

"But a little too much familiarity for my liking," she said, shooting him a smile.

Seth climbed back over to where she was sitting, then leaned over that seat as well and inspected the cargo area. To his delight, he could feel her gaze on his ass.

"You can touch it if you want," he told her.

"Sorry?"

Rather than tease her, he lifted the small hold in

the bottom of the cargo area and shook his head when there was nothing there. He'd still sweep Lucy's car but felt certain he wasn't going to find anything of significance.

He hauled himself back over and settled heavily into the seat, then muttered a low curse under his breath. Okay, Seth told himself. Time to move on to something else, to check in and see if the others had found anything at all. He leaned over and kissed Pen again and it took more strength than he'd guessed to pull away. His will was getting weaker and weaker where she was concerned.

Gratifyingly, her eyes were dark with longing when he drew back.

"We'd better get moving," he said.

She nodded, then leaned forward to put the tissue box back where they'd found it. An odd look passed over her face when she picked it up and, rather than set it down, she brought it closer and gave it a shake.

Something rattled from inside the box and they shared a look.

She reached in and withdrew a slim X-Acto knife, the kind with the retractable blade. White fibers had been caught between the casing and the knife when the blade had been pulled into the safety position.

She inhaled sharply. "Patrice," she breathed, clearly stunned.

The smoking gun that wasn't, Seth thought.

But it was all the evidence they needed.

To nail her, anyway.

11

STILL REELING from the fact that Patrice was obviously behind everything, Pen scrambled out of the car, both hot and heartsick. How could Patrice do this? What on earth would possess her to try to ruin her friend's wedding? She'd hosted Nella's shower, for heaven's sake! She'd helped pick out the bridesmaids' dresses and put together the menu. What would make her *destroy* Nella's dress? The letters she could almost see. If she was simply trying to stop the wedding, then the threats were an annoyance, but not destructive or malicious.

Ripping the back of that dress to ribbons was both.

She could personally throttle Patrice with *both* hands as well.

Seth immediately got on his cell phone. "I've got an X-Acto knife with white fibers attached," he said. "We found it in Patrice's car."

She liked that he'd included her in that, Pen thought, wishing that she had more time to linger over the fact that they'd had the most amazing sex of her life. Unfortunately, when this weekend was over, she'd have plenty of time. But for the moment, Trent and Nella's wedding had to come first.

"You did," she heard him say. "Well, that's an interesting development," he said, shooting her an enigmatic look. Good grief, he was unbelievably good-looking. She knew it was an inopportune moment to be thinking that, but she couldn't seem to help herself.

What? she mouthed, hating being left out of the loop, even for an instant.

"Right. In the laptop case. Anything on the computer?" A pause then. "No shit," he breathed, looking utterly blindsided. "Wow. I, uh…I certainly hadn't seen that coming, had you?"

"What?" Pen asked more loudly. The suspense was killing her. They rounded the corner and came face-to-face with the other security agents, all of them looking slightly bemused.

Seth and Will snapped their phones shut. "We've got about ten minutes before they arrive," Will said, and looked to Seth. "How are we going to handle this?"

"First order of business is to tell Trent," Seth said. "We need to brief him completely and then see what he thinks about Lucy's involvement."

Pen gasped. "Lucy?"

"Will found a red marker in her laptop bag and a few of the wedding invitations and save-the-date announcements she'd practiced on first."

Oh, no, Pen thought. Poor Trent! Poor Nella! One of her best friends and her future sister-in-law. "Were they acting independently, or were they in it together?" Pen asked.

"One of them was acting independently," Seth said. "The other one was being coerced." She watched him glance significantly to the other men. "And there's still one unaccounted for."

She was developing a terrible headache and felt slightly sick to her stomach. "Please tell me Lucy was the one being coerced." Friends were hard to lose, but marrying into a family where the association would be constant, the betrayal always fresh…that would be utterly terrible. And one unaccounted for? What was he talking about? They'd found the pen and invitations in Lucy's bag and the knife in Patrice's car. That was everything, wasn't it?

"Lucy was being coerced," Seth confirmed. "But the circumstances are…not good," he finished. That sounded exceedingly ominous, Pen thought. "What do you mean one is still unaccounted for?"

"I don't think Lucy wrote the third note," he said, looking at Tanner. "Think about it. The first two were simply instructions to call it off, expressing displeasure. The last one was written in the same style—so this person knew it was happening—but it had a completely different tone. I think we're dealing with someone else here."

Tanner winced and the rest of the them shared a look. "Good spot," he told Seth. "I think you're right."

"Anyone who would spare the lace on the front of the dress isn't going to kill someone," Seth continued. "So that rules out Patrice. Did you find anything at all on the computers?"

"Other than what we told you on the phone, no," Huck told him.

Pen's head was spinning. Everything Seth had said made perfect sense. Something else was going on, something worse than what Lucy and Patrice had done. But who was responsible? And what was their motive?

Having been for a walk down along the beach, Trent and his mother strolled into view and both of them looked up when they saw everyone gathered in front of the house. Trent put a hand to his mother's elbow and they hurried forward.

"Trent, I need a word," Seth told him.

Trent's mother lifted her chin. "I will not be left in the dark anymore," she said. "My son has filled me in, quite reluctantly," she added, shooting him a pointed glare which displayed her displeasure. "But that is done. Whatever you say to him, you can say in front of me, right, Trent?"

Penelope could tell that Seth did not want to share his news in front of Trent's mother. Especially if it involved Lucy.

Trent finally nodded, though a muscle worked in his jaw. "Go ahead," he said. "I've told her everything else."

And he'd caught hell for keeping it from her, if Pen had to guess.

Seth held up the knife with the white threads caught in the case and Trent's eyes widened. "We found this hidden in a box of tissues in Patrice's SUV," he said.

"Patrice?" his mother breathed, obviously stunned. "Patrice did that?"

Will held up the red marker and winced. "And we found this in your sister's laptop case, along with these," he added, showing the trial efforts Lucy had made on their wedding announcements.

Trent's mother blanched and for a moment, she looked as if she was going to faint. Pen hurried forward and slid an arm around the women's waist. "Are you all right, Mrs. McWilliams?"

"Lucy," she said faintly. Her brow furrowed and for the first time, she looked older than her years. "Lucy is involved in this?" She looked at Trent. "But she loves Nella. She's been looking forward to finally having a sister. Why?" she asked. "It makes no sense. Are you certain? Could they have been planted there?"

Seth winced and shook his head. "She was co-erced."

Trent's shrewd gaze narrowed. "Coerced? You mean blackmailed?"

Seth nodded again, looking even grimmer than he had before, if that was possible, and Pen knew the "not good" he'd alluded to earlier was going to be revealed soon. Much as she wanted to know, there was a part of her that was dreading it as well. She tightened her grip on Mrs. McWilliams.

"By Patrice?" Trent asked.

"Yes," Seth told him. "Patrice's former husband was a—" he struggled for moment "—*client* of your sister, and Patrice found out."

Both Pen and Mrs. McWilliams caught on before Trent did and Mrs. McWilliams sagged against her. "Oh, dear God. You don't mean…please don't tell me…"

Lucy was a call girl? Quiet, unassuming Lucy? Timid Lucy who always kowtowed to her mother was a *call girl?*

Trent's eyes suddenly widened with comprehension and then his jaw went slack. "What do you mean when you say *client?*"

Seth coughed uncomfortably. "I mean she was giving more than the traditional massage to certain customers."

Trent looked stunned.

His mother's mind was a lot quicker.

"Are you obligated to report this to the authorities?" she asked, looking directly at Seth.

"No," Seth told her. He didn't look to the others, and for whatever reason, she got the distinct impression that he'd made that call on his own.

"I still don't understand why Patrice would have objected to the wedding?" Trent said, still obviously struggling with the fact that his little sister had become a hooker. "Why should she care whether or not Nella and I get married?"

"According to the emails I found on Lucy's computer, Patrice was merely trying to save Nella future heartache," Will told him. "She doesn't believe any man is capable of being faithful. She enlisted your sister's help as payback and has been threatening to out her if she didn't cooperate. Lucy chose the lesser of two evils and aligned herself with Patrice."

By the look on Trent's mother's face, that was going to be a move Lucy would live to regret.

Seth looked at Trent. "They'll be here in a minute. How do you want to handle this?"

"Does Patrice have actual proof of Lucy's…indiscretions?"

Will shook his head. "I don't think so. I think her ex-husband admitted it, but I don't think she has anything concrete."

And Patrice's ex certainly wasn't going to give her proof, Pen thought.

Trent nodded. "Then I want Patrice escorted off the island with express instructions never to contact myself or my wife again," he said. "If she does, there will be consequences."

"Trent, Nella—"

"I'll talk to Nella, Mom," he said.

"But what if Nella wants to confront her?"

Trent merely smiled and shook his head. "Believe me, when I tell her what Patrice has done, Nella's not going to ever want to talk to her again." He glanced at Pen. "You know Nella, Penelope. What do you think?"

"I think you've got her figured out pretty good," Pen said. And he was right. Nella would absolutely wash her hands of Patrice after this. She wouldn't waste her time listening to any excuses. There was nothing that could be said that would exonerate the behavior.

"And Lucy?" Seth asked.

"I'll take care of her," Mrs. McWilliams said, her voice filled with significantly ominous undertones.

Seth nodded. "All right. We'll look after Patrice, then," he assured Trent.

Trent looked up and cast his gaze around the group.

"Listen, thanks guys. I know this has been a pain in the ass, but I really appreciate the work you've done here."

"You're more than welcome," Seth told him. "But we're not done," he said. He recounted his suspicion that the third note was done by someone else. "We've still got to nail that person—which we will—then see you safely married, without interruption from any crazed fans."

"I'm nervous about those twins," Tanner piped up. It was common knowledge that a pair of identical twins from Miami somehow managed to streak naked across the field during a playoff game. Of course, if you asked Pen, security had been purposely lax on that because the girls were quite pretty.

Trent's mother gave a disgusted grunt. "Harlots," she said, her nose wrinkling in distaste. "If they even think about streaking through this wedding, I'll personally take a birch to them."

Seth's lips twitched and the other three managed to turn their laughs into semiconvincing coughs. "We'll see to it that nothing happens, Mrs. McWilliams."

She nodded, seemingly satisfied.

"All right, then," Seth said. "I think we should be waiting with Patrice's things and vehicle at the security gate." He glanced at Huck. "Can you get clean out her room?"

Huck nodded and hurried inside. After a moment, the other two followed him. "I'll meet you at her car in two," Seth hollered over his shoulder.

"Are you going to tell Nella about Lucy's part in this?" Trent's mother asked her son.

"Of course," he said. "She's my going to be my wife. I can't keep this from her."

"But—"

"Nella comes first, Mom. Lucy should have thought about that before she allowed herself to be maneuvered into this."

"But this will hurt Nella, too," his mother argued.

"It will," he admitted. "And that makes me even angrier at Lucy."

With that comment, he turned and walked into the house.

Penelope had met many couples and had been blown away before by their devotion, but she'd never seen anything as honorable as what she'd just witnessed. He was standing by his bride, his soon-to-be wife, and nothing was going to prevent him from doing what was right by her, even if it meant hurting her in the process.

That took guts. And a helluva lot of love.

For the first time, Mrs. McWilliams seemed to truly accept the change coming into their lives. Trent's father had died when Trent was in his teens and since then, Trent had been the head of the family. And he'd just let his mother know that he would still be the head of the family. Only Nella would be his second in command, not his mother or his sister.

Evidently needing a moment to herself, Mrs. McWilliams turned and made her way back toward the beach.

Seth turned to Penelope, his expression one that was

hard to read. Relief, but with a little regret, no doubt on Trent's behalf, thrown in for good measure. "Well," he said. "This has been quite a day."

She smiled and crossed her arms over her chest. "It certainly has." She paused. "You know what this means, don't you?"

He arched a brow. "Am I supposed to?"

"It means that I'm down at least one, potentially *two*, bridesmaids."

Seth chuckled and slid a finger down the side of her cheek. "I have every confidence that you'll take care of that."

"Should I wait for Nella?"

Seth shook his head. "Let Trent handle it. Once she's absorbed everything, she'll come to you."

The other three Rangers came back outside and they headed off to Patrice's car. As if on cue, Pen's cell phone played the *Jaws* music again.

What a friggin' day. And it wasn't even half over yet.

DESPITE THE FACT that they'd successfully solved part of the problem, Seth couldn't shake the sensation that the other shoe was about to drop, that something terrible was in the works. He scanned the crowd gathered for the rehearsal, searching for anything that looked suspect or out of place. All of these people were supposed to be here. Nevertheless, one of them was still a threat.

Though he didn't want to trod on his new coworkers' toes, a part of him wanted to scan the house again, to look with his own eyes. He particularly wanted to look at Patrice's cell records and to do another scan of Lucy's laptop. Something was bothering him, but he couldn't put his finger on what.

He strolled over to Tanner. "Can you watch things for a minute," he said. "I want to go check something out."

Tanner nodded. "Sure. We'll cover."

Making sure that Lucy, who looked completely miserable, was safely out of the way, Seth made his way back to her car and pulled the digital recorder out of the console. He hit Play and recognized Patrice's voice at once. "You'll do as I say, Lucy, you miserable home-wrecking whore, or I'll make you pay." She chuckled softly. "Or rather *he* will."

He? Who was he?

"Patrice, I've already told you I was sorry. I don't know what else to do. I don't know how to make this right."

"You can't make it right. You've ruined my life. But *he* understands and he's willing to love me, even though he knows I can't love him as much in return. And he blames you, Lucy. He blames *you*." Another eerie laugh. "I'd watch my back if I were you."

He? Seth wondered again. Who in the hell had she been talking about? Furthermore, why hadn't Lucy mentioned this to any of them? When confronted, she'd only said that Patrice had been threatening her and they just assumed that, based on the emails, that it was only in regard to the call girl service. But obviously, it had been more.

Significantly more, based on what he'd just heard.

A terrible sense of unease washing over him, Seth rounded the corner and almost walked into Paul, who was leaning against the house smoking another cigarette.

The scent of vanilla hit him, triggering a memory from Patrice's car. Suddenly, Seth knew he had him.

So did Paul and, with a muttered curse, he took off.

Shouting a loud "Get him!", Seth ran after him. The Ranger Security men were the only ones who didn't react with complete confusion. They took off after Paul as well. But like them, their suspect was fit and former military and he was damned light on his feet. He hurried through the crowd like a seasoned running back and then grabbed Lucy, whirling her around, putting her in a choke hold. He withdrew a knife from his front pocket and pressed it against her throat.

"Paul!" Pen shouted. "What the hell do you think you're doing? Let her go!"

"Pen, stay out of this please," Seth said, trying to keep her out of harm's way. He looked at Paul, who was slowly backing toward the water, Lucy in tow. His men fanned out around Paul, cutting off all lines of escape— on land, at any rate. Paul was making for the boat.

Shit.

"Paul, be reasonable," Seth said. "You know this isn't going to end well."

"That's right. It's going to end with this one dead." He tightened his hold on Lucy and she gasped. "This little tramp hurt Patrice," he said. "*My* Patrice. She can't trust me because of her," he said, obviously completely irrational.

"She can't trust you because her ex-husband was unfaithful," Seth told him. "He made the decision to betray Patrice, not Lucy."

"It's her fault!" he insisted, his eyes wild.

Huck, Tanner and Will moved closer, and Seth gained ground as well, but Paul continued to move toward the boat.

"Stay back," he said. "I'll cut her. You know I will."

Lucy's eyes were wide with fear.

Unfortunately, Seth was pretty sure Paul was capable of doing just that, so he didn't dare rush him the way he normally would have.

From the corner of his eye, Seth saw Trent move in behind a tree and he caught a glimpse of something in his hand. He had to flatten his lips to keep from smiling.

Brilliant.

He knew Trent wasn't going to be in a good position…but Seth was. And Trent knew that, too. He wasn't a star quarterback for nothing.

"Paul, put the knife down," Seth said again. "Let her go. You don't want to do this, man. You don't want to hurt her."

"Patrice is gone," he said. "You made her leave. Everything is ruined."

Evidently picking up on Trent's plan, Will got in on the action. "Paul, you didn't strike me as stupid and this is stupid."

"Shut up," Paul told him. "What do you know?"

"Hey, Paul," Tanner called loudly.

When the man turned his head, Trent drew back and threw the football to Seth. Then Seth quickly turned and drilled Paul right in the side of the head with it. Paul immediately dropped the knife and his hands darted to his face. Meanwhile the four of them had rushed forward and Lucy had taken advantage of Paul's pain to get away from him.

A collective cheer went through the crowd when Ranger Security had Paul safely in hand.

"Get him out of here," Trent said, immediately going to Nella and his sister.

Seth nodded.

Tanner said grimly, "I'll do the honors."

Penelope hurried forward, a look of utter horror on her face. "I can't believe… I just don't know— *Paul?*"

"Patrice was the one who introduced me to him," Monica said. "He'd been looking for a job and we'd just lost Andrew to college. I never dreamed that… They set this up from the start," she murmured. "They've been planning this for almost a year."

It boggled the mind. But then, people could be crazy and Paul was definitely off his rocker.

"Are you all right?" Seth asked, slipping a finger down Pen's cheek. She was still somewhat in shock, her skin pale beneath her light tan.

She nodded and when she looked up at him, he saw gratitude and admiration. "You were great," she said. "Nailing him with the football was a nice touch."

He merely shrugged. "Hey, I'm no Trent McWilliams, but I've spent a little time playing with the pigskin."

"And Trent knew?"

He nodded. "I'd mentioned it in passing and he knew I had a better vantage point."

"What tipped you off? What outed him?"

"The cigarette smoke. It smells like vanilla. I remembered seeing and, more importantly, smelling them in Patrice's car.

She nodded, her lips forming a soft smile. "Well done." She looked up at him. "Is everything okay now? No more surprises?"

Despite the fact that they no longer had to pretend, Seth drew her close and hugged her. No doubt she was second-guessing her instincts. After all, she'd worked with Paul for almost a year and had trusted him. "No more bad surprises," he said.

She leaned back and looked up at him. "That sounds promising."

"Good. Because it is."

"PEN, I'M SO SORRY," Monica repeated for the hundredth time. "I didn't know. He just seemed like a good guy. I never dreamed—"

"Mon, stop it. I didn't know either." Which was actually quite terrifying when it came right down to it. She'd trusted Paul, had even counted him as sort of a friend. He'd been to her house, he'd been entrusted with deposits for the bank. She'd never once looked at him and thought, *Wow, he might be crazy.*

When Paul had come racing around that corner and dragged Lucy with him, Pen's heart had practically landed in her throat. She'd been afraid for Lucy, but more telling, she'd been afraid for Seth, because she knew Seth was going to have to risk his life to take Paul down.

While she was certain that he was competent and she'd never doubted him, the terror that had sent her heart rate toward stroke level was wholly unexpected… and even more telling.

He was supposed to be her pretend boyfriend, completely fabricated and fake, and yet nothing had ever felt further from counterfeit in her life.

And the genuineness of the feelings she was experiencing as a result of this revelation scared the hell out of her.

12

CONFIDENT NOW that everything had been done to the best of his ability, Seth hung back and simply watched Penelope do her job. She was a maestro, he thought, continually amazed at how smoothly everything went. She'd changed clothes for the rehearsal and had swept her hair up into a messy updo that somehow managed to look both effortless and chic. She'd donned a silver sheath dress that moved like liquid over her curves and a pair of strappy silver rhinestone sandals. Gray pearls dangled from her ears and her eye makeup had been applied with a heavier hand, giving her a smoky look.

In short, she looked hot as hell.

And he'd willingly, gladly and hastily throw himself into the fire after her.

Strictly speaking, he knew that sleeping with her in the car today was probably not what Ranger Security had in mind when they'd suggested he pretend to be her boyfriend. Because he worked with other security agents who didn't miss a trick or a half-zipped zipper, as it turned out, he thought with remembered embarrassment, they'd known exactly what had happened. Thankfully, they'd had a pretty blasé attitude about it.

In fact, it seemed like they'd almost expected it, which should have alarmed him, particularly when he'd learned that each and every one of them had met their wives while working for the company.

Evidently he'd either lost his mind or lost the ability to care. Penelope was an amazing girl, very different, very exotic, very intriguing and so sexy she made him habitually hard. He wasn't a bad-looking guy, if he did say so himself, and the chemistry between them had been phenomenal. Beyond anything in his experience. He'd like to think—no, he knew actually—that if they'd met under different circumstances, they would have hooked up. They would be taking the same path they were on right now.

The one that would ultimately end tomorrow, he thought suddenly, a prickle of dread nudging his belly.

Or in three months, whichever came first.

The nudge turned into a kick.

Would she have kicked him to the curb? Seth wondered. Would she have really bailed on a relationship with him? Especially if things had continued to develop between them as well as they already had? Would he have cared?

Much as he was loath to admit it, he cared now. And it was more than pride talking. He liked her, dammit. She was funny and witty and gorgeous and intriguing… special.

Though she hadn't said a word—in fact, she *still* hadn't told him why she'd instigated a three-month rule—he suspected that she'd had to be the strong one in her family, the one who made things right when everything else went wrong.

When his father had walked out, Seth had felt the same way. He'd only been five, but the sensation had been there all the same. And it had only worsened the older he'd gotten. To be fair to his mother, she'd never put any sort of pressure on him to be the leader of their family. She'd done that herself, though during her illness she had certainly looked more to him than his sister. But that had been because he was the older child, not because he'd been a man. Furthermore, he knew she would have made the same request of his sister had she been the one in the military, their positions been reversed. She wanted them to be there for each other, wanted Mitchell to have Seth in his life and vice versa.

And, as much as it pained him to admit it…she'd been right.

Had he ever wanted to come out of the military? No. Had he planned on making a career out of it? Yes.

And then he would have missed everything.

He'd have missed Pen.

And somehow, that seemed like a terrible tragedy to him. His gaze slid to her again, where she was busy making sure everyone was standing where they were supposed to be and he smiled, unable to help himself. She was remarkable, his pretend girlfriend.

He could smell the scent of steaks on the grill, the spicy crab boil going on in the caterer's pots and the evening breeze as it drifted warmly over his skin. Rather than go off-site for the after-rehearsal dinner, Trent and

Nella had arranged for a meal here instead. Because the actual wedding party was small, and even smaller now that Patrice had left, it had been simple enough to arrange.

"All right," Pen finally called, clapping her hands together. "That's a wrap, people." She walked over to Nella and gave her a bracing squeeze. Though Seth couldn't hear what she was saying to her friend from here, he saw Nella smile and knew that whatever it was had been the right thing.

Trent cleared his throat. "The wedding planner says we can eat!" he called, then gave a little fist pump. Trent's gaze caught Seth's and he gestured to a plate, giving him the universal ya'll-help-yourselves gesture.

Excellent, Seth thought. Pen was a good cook, but he'd be lying if he said he wouldn't rather have a steak, particularly since he'd been smelling the meat on the grill for the past hour. He gestured to the others, then fell into line behind Pen's crew, who'd also been invited.

Because Monica had been giving him the I-know-what-you-did eye, even though he was certain she didn't, Seth decided to rib her a little.

"You know what your ring tone is on Pen's phone?" he asked.

"Sure. It's Randy Newman's 'You've Got A Friend In Me.' From *Toy Story*, remember?"

"Nope."

She looked up at him. "Nope you don't remember or nope that's not right?"

"Nope, that's not right." He looked ahead. "It's the theme song to *Jaws*."

She gasped, her eyes narrowed and then she whirled around. "That's all right," she finally said. "Mine for her is 'Beast of Burden.'"

Seth guffawed, which naturally drew Pen's attention. Evidently suspecting something was amiss, she walked over. "What's so funny?" she asked suspiciously.

"Nothing," he lied.

"*Jaws,* Penelope? Seriously?"

Pen gasped and glared up at Seth, then whacked him on the arm. "Snitch," she hissed.

"She says yours is 'Beast of Burden,'" he remarked mildly, then waited for the fallout.

To his surprise, Monica turned around and whacked him, too. He laughed even harder.

"He might be good-looking," Monica said to Pen, "but looks aren't everything."

"Er…I'm standing right here."

"I know," Monica drawled. "I'm freezing in your shadow, Sasquatch."

Pen snickered and shot Monica a look of admiration. "That was good."

"Thanks," she said, displaying what he imagined was a rare bit of modesty.

"Right here," he reminded them again.

Monica shivered dramatically and hurried forward, leaving them to themselves.

"You all right?" he asked, inspecting her face for traces of residual stress.

"I will be, once it all goes off without a hitch," she said, allowing the server to fill her plate with shrimp, sausage and potatoes.

They each got a drink, then Seth jerked his head toward the pier. "Wanna go down there and sit on the dock?" he asked.

She hesitated and he knew she was thinking about her crew.

"I'm still your pretend boyfriend, you know," he told her, smiling down at her.

At least until tomorrow night, anyway, Seth thought.

"Sure," she said and, without prompting, put her hand in his.

He grinned.

"OUR FEET AREN'T shark bait here, are they?" Pen asked, dangling her bare toes into the water.

Seth chuckled, the sound intimate and easy. "I don't think so." He popped a bite of shrimp into his mouth and made a sound of pleasure. "This is excellent."

"It doesn't get any better than fresh," she said. She really should have avoided the corn on the cob, Pen thought, because it invariably got stuck in her teeth and she ended up with butter running down her chin. But it smelled too good to resist. She looked over at him.

"I'm going to eat this corn," she warned him. If she was less attractive as a result of it, he'd just have to get over it.

He blinked, evidently baffled. "Okay. Are you allergic or something? Is there a reason I need to know this?"

"None, other than the fact that it's probably going to get stuck in my teeth and drip down my chin." And wouldn't that be sexy?

Another chuckle, this one louder, rumbled from deep in his chest. He gestured to the corn on his own plate. "Is it going to disgust you if I eat mine?"

"Not at all. I just thought I should give you fair warning. And by all means, please tell me if it does get stuck in my teeth. Don't let me sit here looking like a moron when you can help me out."

"Do I strike you as the kind of man who would let you look a moron?"

She chewed the inside of her cheek. "Not particularly."

He grunted and took a deliberate bite of his own corn. "Good."

She laughed, then helped herself as well and they ate in companionable silence for a while. Trent and Nella's favorite country music song drifted down to them along with the sound of laughter and happy people. This was what a wedding was supposed to be about, Pen thought. This was the reason she did what she did. She worked hard to create the perfect atmosphere, the perfect backdrop for her couple's nuptials and nothing made her prouder than when they drove away, thrilled with the promise of a new beginning together and completely blissed out over the sheer magnificence of their wedding.

"How's Nella?" Seth asked. "I haven't had a chance to talk to Trent since he told her everything."

"She's hurt," Pen told him. "She knew that Patrice had turned against marriage after her divorce, but she hadn't realized that the craziness of her hatred had poisoned her so much that she'd destroy Nella's wedding gown."

Honestly, there was a part of Pen that thought that, secretly, Patrice had known that Trent would never betray Nella the way that Alex had betrayed her. Pen was certain that Patrice resented Nella for her happiness, happiness that Patrice thought should have been hers.

"And Lucy?"

Pen took a sip of her wine, enjoying the warmth of the alcohol moving through her. "You know, Nella's actually relieved to know the truth. She said that she and Lucy had always gotten along fine until she and Trent had become engaged. Then Lucy had basically turned on her."

"Because Patrice turned on her, right?"

"Exactly. She said she just liked knowing that, ultimately, they were going to be okay."

"I noticed that she's still in the wedding party," Seth remarked. He wiped his mouth with a napkin and carved off a bit of steak.

"Yes," she said. "Because they are going to be sisters."

"And you simply eliminated one of the groomsmen?"

"Yes," Pen said. "It was the simplest solution. Trent promised his friend Tuck that he could still wear the tux so that the girls would be into him."

Seth's laugh echoed over the water and he shook his head. "Why do I get the impression this is not the strangest thing you've ever heard?"

"Because it's not. Those groomsmen always score big with the women. Haven't you ever been to a wedding?"

"Only one," he said. "My sister's. And we know how that turned out."

She winced. "I'm sorry," she said. "Have you talked to her again?"

"I checked in a little while ago. She's fine," he said. "Or as fine as she can be when she doubts every decision she makes."

"It happens, unfortunately," Pen said. "But she'll find someone better next time." She grinned and rolled her eyes. "Honestly, if she comes from your gene pool, then she's got to be beautiful."

He turned to look at her, his grin endearingly crooked, those dark green eyes twinkling with satisfaction and humor. "She is, thanks."

"Does she have green eyes, too?"

He nodded and though he didn't do anything to indicate something had shifted, she felt a wall go up all the same. "We both do."

She was treading into dangerous territory, she knew, but couldn't stop herself. "And is this a trait you inherited from your mother or your father?"

"My mother," he said, looking away. "With luck, we didn't inherit anything at all from our father."

Pay dirt. "That bad, was he?"

"Good? Bad?" He shrugged. "I wouldn't know. He didn't hang around long enough for me to form an opinion. He split when I was five and by the time I found out what a faithless bastard he was, I was old enough to kick his ass."

She tried not to betray the shock she felt and busied herself with another sip of wine. "Did you?"

"Not until he called my mother a nagging bitch," Seth said quite matter-of-factly, as though it was nothing. "Then I pummeled the hell out of him."

She'd just bet he did. And who could blame him? She certainly didn't. "I'm sorry, Seth," she said, laying a hand on his arm.

"Don't be," he told her. "I'm not."

"Did your mother ever remarry?"

He shook his head and something about the question made him smile. "No. She had a 'friend'—" he slid her a look "—but she said she'd had all of marriage she wanted and she'd leave it to the young and the stupid."

Penelope felt her eyes widen and a laugh bubble up in her throat. "She sounds like a really interesting woman," she said, and meant it.

Seth sighed, a smile still on his lips, but it had turned sad. "She was," he said softly.

Was? Oh, hell.

"Cancer is a miserable bitch of a disease," he muttered, tossing back the rest of his wine.

"Yes, it is. How long ago?"

"Seven months. And there's not a day that goes by that I don't miss her, that I don't expect a phone call, that I don't think about her," he confessed.

Because he was essentially orphaned or because he'd loved her that much? Somehow she knew it was the latter. And, though he hadn't admitted it, she also instinctively knew that his mother was the person to whom he'd kept his promise.

That's why he'd come out of the military.

Because his sister and nephew were alone and their country was fighting wars in two different countries. His mother must have been terrified that he wouldn't come back, that his sister and little Mitch would lose the only person they had left. So she'd asked him to come home.

And he'd done it.

Her eyes watered.

He'd promised to give up his career…and he had. She swallowed, moved and awed.

"She must have been something else to earn that kind of regard," Pen finally said.

"She was," he confirmed, giving her a smile. He nudged her shoulder. "She would have liked you."

"No doubt I would have liked her as well." She cleared her throat, tucked a loose strand of hair behind her ear. "How are your sister and Mitch coping?"

He kicked a bit at the water around his feet. "Like me, Katie has her good days and bad days, but the good days are getting more and more frequent," he said. "Mitch asks for Mom every once in a while, but not nearly as often as he did in the beginning. It's not that I think he's forgotten her—he still points to her picture and says her name—but he's getting used to her not being around." He grimaced. "And to me, that's actually worse."

She winced and laid a hand on his thigh. "I'm sorry, Seth. My mother and father both drive me crazy, but they're still around. I can't imagine a world without them in it, even though I know it's one I'll have to face someday."

He wiped a bit of butter off her chin and, though she should have been embarrassed, she wasn't. In fact, she found it strangely romantic. "You've probably worked it out for yourself," he said. "But Mom's the one I made the promise to. When we knew she wasn't going to get better."

"I thought you said you lost a bet."

He laughed. "I did. To her. We played poker for it."

She blinked at him, certain she'd misunderstood. "Poker? Seriously?"

He nodded. "She taught me. She was a helluva player, too."

She studied him with new appreciation. "Did you let her win?"

"I would have, but I didn't have to. She'd have won anyway. Four of a kind, aces high with a one-eyed jack."

"A wild card."

"Not just any wild card, *my* wild card, the one that invariably winds up in my hand," he told her. He slid his sleeve up and showed her a tattoo on his left shoulder. It was a perfect replica of a jack of hearts.

She smiled and shook her head. "I really hate that I never got to meet your mother."

"I do, too," he said, studying her thoughtfully.

"Would she have cheated?" Pen asked.

"At that point, possibly, but I don't think she did." He shrugged. "She knew I'd do whatever she asked. Playing the game was just for old time's sake."

Pen was quiet for a moment. "You're a good son."

He looked back out over the water again. "She was a good mother."

IF SHE THOUGHT he was going to bare his soul and expect nothing in return, then she'd better think again, Seth thought as he watched Penelope out of the corner of his eye. She knew it, too, Seth thought. She hadn't moved a muscle or even batted a lash, but he felt her tense up all the same. It was bizarre being this tuned into someone, this aware of her every mood, but he couldn't say that he didn't like it.

In fact, there were times when it came in handy. Like when they were in the backseat of a borrowed SUV.

She smiled and shook her head. "You're just going to wait me out, aren't you?"

He blinked innocently. "I don't know what you mean."

"Liar."

She heaved an exasperated, resigned sigh. "Go ahead and ask whatever you want to ask," she said. "And I will try to answer as honestly as possible."

"What's your favorite flavor of ice cream?" he asked, just to throw her off.

She frowned. "Didn't I include that in the file?"

He chuckled. "It was one of the few things you left out."

She glared at him, but her lips fought back a smile. "You're never going to let me live that down, are you? I told you I liked to be thorough," she said, drying her fingers with a napkin. "Some of this stuff could come up. We still have tomorrow to get through," she reminded him. "When someone asks you how I like my pancakes—"

"With peanut butter instead of syrup," he supplied, remembering that odd little insight.

"—then you're going to be glad you know," she finished.

He shot her a wry grin. "I'm sure that's going to be one of the first things I'm asked about you. But you never answered the question I just asked."

She inclined her head. "Ah. Favorite ice cream. Definitely butter pecan. And, incidentally, my favorite holiday dessert is pecan pie."

His was, too. His mother had made two different varieties, one just a simple pie, the other with chocolate chips and hot fudge. That had always been Katie's favorite. Would she make them this year for the holidays? Seth wondered. Had his mother shared the recipes? Or had they been lost along with her?

"What's yours?" she asked.

"Favorite ice cream or favorite dessert?"

"Both."

"I thought it was my turn to ask some questions?" he groused good-naturedly.

"You'll get your chance," she said.

"You're just delaying the inevitable, you know," he told her.

She merely smiled.

Seth looked away and released a breath. "My favorite ice cream is vanilla," he said. "I know it's very boring, but it's also very good, There's a lot to be said for things that aren't complicated and are still worth having."

She inclined her head and something unreadable shifted behind her too perceptive gaze. He knew he'd just given her a little insight, but he had no idea what it was. "I agree."

"As for my favorite pie—" He shrugged. "Like you, it's pecan." He grimaced. "I've never been a big pumpkin fan."

She nodded knowingly. "Anti-pumpkin, not anti-meringue. Noted."

He searched her gaze, waiting to see if she'd volunteer the information she knew he wanted before he had to ask. "Is it really so hard to tell me?"

She smiled and shook her head, evidently resigned at last. "What do you want to know first? Why I don't ever want to get married? Why I'm the commitment-phobic wedding planner?" she joked. "Or why I won't date anyone longer than three months?"

"Considering I think the two are related, then you choose."

She braced her arms on the pier and leaned back, letting her feet dangle freely. Though she was trying to look calm and relaxed, he knew better. Her jaw was flexed tight and her spine was utterly rigid.

"My parents have nine marriages between the two of them and my mother's fourth is on the rocks."

Nine? Damn. He had already suspected some broken marriages based on the casual references she'd made to "a stepdad" or "a stepmom," but nothing on that scale.

Her lips twisted with droll humor. "I've shocked you, haven't I?"

No point in lying. "Yes," he admitted. "Yes, you have."

"There you go."

"What do you mean, there you go?"

"That's my reason. I've seen them say 'I do' *nine* times and each time, it's been a lie." She shook her head, drew her legs up and wrapped her arms around them. "I don't want that. I don't want to want it. I don't want to believe it and then have it not be true." A bark of laughter slipped between her lips, but there was no humor in the sound. "To tell you the truth, I don't think I *could* believe it. I think I'd always be waiting for the other shoe to drop, for the man I chose to make his exit scene."

Seth took a moment to absorb her words. "So you're saying you don't think you're a better judge of character than either one of your parents?"

"I'm saying that it doesn't matter how good a judge of character you are, people can change. Love makes you stupid." She grinned at him. "I'm in your mother's camp on that one. I don't want to be stupid. I want to date and enjoy that first thrill of a new romance, then move on before it gets all complicated. Before any expectations are made."

His eyes widened and he laughed, then shook his head. "Oh, man, if I didn't have carnal knowledge of you, I'd think you were a guy."

She grinned. "Nope. I'm just a girl with a guy's commitment to self-preservation."

That was one way of looking at it, he supposed. Honestly, he didn't know what he'd truly expected her to say when he'd forced her to have this conversation. But now that he'd had it with her, he felt a bit…used.

Which was ridiculous considering that he'd gone into the relationship with no intention of taking it to the next level, of letting this be anything more than a casual, mutually satisfying fling. He'd had the same intentions she'd had and yet now that she'd admitted hers, he felt differently?

What the hell was wrong with him?

Come tomorrow, they were going to go their separate ways. She'd head back to Marietta and continue with her busy wedding season and he'd go back to Atlanta and Ranger Security would send him on to his next job. But he was going to make damned sure it didn't involve another woman. And it damned sure wouldn't require him to sign on as another pretend boyfriend.

Because at some point over the weekend, he'd stopped pretending. He'd started thinking about seeing her beyond the weekend.

But clearly not past three months.

And he had entirely too much pride to follow her along for the next ninety days, then let her kick his ass to the curb when their expiration date hit.

"I shouldn't have told you," Pen said, studying him thoughtfully.

"Why?" Better that she had, really.

She slid a finger along his jaw. "Because you look like you wished I hadn't."

He did, but he'd asked. "Nah," he said. "I just think it's a little sad, that's all."

"How so?"

He made himself grin. "Always the wedding planner, never the bride," he improvised.

She nodded once. "I'm good with that."

He sincerely doubted it, but he wasn't going to argue with her. She didn't want to risk getting hurt, not because she was afraid of the outcome, but because she was afraid it wouldn't be worth it, because she was afraid of being wrong.

And, truthfully, in her shoes, he'd probably feel the same way. Hell, he'd decided to remain single for less reason than that. He'd just never liked the odds.

Of course, he'd never met anyone who made him want to defy them—until now.

The irony wasn't lost on him and he chuckled softly.

"What's funny?"

"Us," he said, shooting her a look. "We've got less than a dozen good hours left in this bogus relationship of ours and instead of spending them in bed like proper hedonists, we're out here on the pier baring our souls."

She leaned over and kissed him, just the sweetest caress against his lips. "I've rather liked it."

He nodded. "I have, too," he admitted.

She shook her head. "You sound surprised."

"That's because I am." He slid a thumb over the soft slope of her cheek. "But you're easy to talk to."

"And there were things you wanted to know in return," she added knowingly.

He grinned and nodded without hesitation. "There is that."

"There was more than one condom in your wallet, right?" she asked, her lids dropping to half-mast. Her voice had taken on that husky quality that he loved, the low-pitched tones that called to his penis like a snake charmer. Not the best analogy, he imagined, but definitely the most accurate.

"No, but there's an entire box in the cabinet beneath the sink in my bathroom."

"Did an inventory, did you?"

He stood and pulled her to her feet, then slung an arm over her shoulder. "You're not the only one who likes to be thorough."

13

HE WAS RIGHT, PEN thought as she and Seth made their way back to the guesthouse. They did only have a few hours left to make the most of being together. And though sitting outside and talking to him had been more wonderful and cathartic than she'd ever imagined—hell, she'd told him more than she'd ever told any of her closest friends—there were definitely better ways they could be spending their time.

The second he closed the door behind them, she fastened her arms around his neck, then leaped up and wrapped her legs around his waist. He kissed her again, the same slow, thorough excavation of her mouth that he'd done before, but there was an urgency in his touch, a need to possess that she not only understood but felt as well.

He growled low in his throat, a masculine purr that reverberated deep in her womb. Then he promptly carried her into his bedroom, momentarily bypassing the bed to get the condoms. He carefully laid her down and followed her onto the mattress. She leaned up so that he could unzip her dress, then quickly dragged it out of the way. To her vast relief, he finally removed his shirt and she was able to feast her eyes on the beautiful perfection of his chest. Tawny hairs dusted his skin in whorls of gold and then formed a thin line which disappeared below his shorts. She was suddenly hit with the urge lick that line, to see if it tasted as delicious as it looked.

And then she decided that she would.

She rolled him onto his back and started at a flat crown of a nipple, then on to the middle of his chest and lower. He chuckled darkly and made quick work of releasing the back clasp of her bra. Her breasts slid free and he tossed the bra aside and palmed her, his big hands feeling wonderful against her aching flesh. He thumbed a nipple and she gasped, then slipped the button lose from its closure on his shorts.

He sucked in a harsh breath when she took him in hand and began to slide her palm over the slippery skin, working him gently. *Hers, all hers, at least for tonight,* Pen thought. Before she could consider any further depraved things she could do to him, he pulled her up, rolled her over and settled between her legs.

He was hot and heavy and hard and she instantly arched up, licking a path up his throat. He reciprocated in kind, tasting the skin between her breasts before slowly circling each globe with his mouth, building the anticipation of when he'd finally take her nipple. He did and she moaned, pushing her hands into his hair and over his wonderful shoulders and sleek, muscled back. He was utterly gorgeous, a work of art, a masterpiece built for her pleasure.

"Another thong," he breathed, slipping a hand down her belly, into the moist curls between her legs.

"It's the only kind of panties I have," she said as his fingers parted her and stroked. She inhaled sharply. "No p-panty lines," she explained.

"I like them," he told her. "They're indecent. And sexy."

Right now, though, they were in the way. She wished he'd take them off her so that he could replace those fingers with something a little more substantial. She arched against him, silently begging him for more.

He slipped a finger deep inside and then used this thumb to massage her clit. Pleasure raced through her and her muscle clenched around him, a silent plea for more, more, please God, more.

She reached blindly over to the nightstand and fumbled with the box of condoms, almost sending the entire package to the floor. She swore and he laughed.

"Impatient, are we?"

"I want you inside me," she said. "I want to feel you above me. Your strength and your weight. I want to kiss your shoulders and lick your neck and when you're as far into me as you can go, I want to grab your ass and make you go farther," she said, her voice getting louder, stronger and more agitated with every second that passed and he wasn't between her legs, rocking above her.

He stilled and looked at her, his eyes dark and heavy lidded. "Will you not take me seriously if I say that I love you?"

She chuckled. "Get a damned condom on, Seth, or I'm going to totally believe you."

Five seconds later he was fully protected and nudging her entrance. She sighed happily, tilted her hips and beckoned him inside. He pushed slowly, determinedly, with mind-numbing, back-clawing, breath-stealing precision. And when he was fully seated inside of her, she released the breath she'd been holding.

Ah, Pen thought. *That was better.*

She looked up and her gaze tangled with his. She read something there that she knew she wasn't supposed to see, something that she wasn't altogether sure she wanted to see. Then he blinked and the moment passed as he bent forward and kissed her again, threading his hands through hers.

Pen met his kiss, sucked his tongue into her mouth and rocked beneath him. It was slow and thorough, brilliant and perfect and if he made love to her all night like this, it wouldn't be long enough.

He pumped into her, the long hard length of him hitting the sweet spot with every determined thrust. She could feel the tension building in her womb, could feel the orgasm slowly circling in on itself, getting closer and closer. She drew her legs back and anchored them on either side of his hips and rocked beneath him. He sprinkled kisses along her jawline, slid his tongue down her throat and then back up again to her ear. His hot breath fanned against her.

"Come for me, baby," he said, his voice throaty and raw with need.

She thrashed beneath him, rocked harder and felt the

clenching in her belly hit a fever pitch. He bent his head and took her breast into his mouth, giving it a long tug. Something about that determined drag made the taut line between her sex and nipple snap and she came so hard her vision went from color to black and white, then back to color, and the sound that escaped her mouth was like nothing she'd ever heard before—part keening cry, part scream. And the symphony happening in her sex was something she knew would never be repeated, music that couldn't possibly make an encore performance.

Before she could savor, commit the moment to memory, Seth promptly rolled her onto her belly, grabbed her hips and held her up, then pushed into her from behind. He pounded hard, angled deep, and her knees wobbled he felt so good.

"Seth, I— Please, I—"

He reached around her and fingered her clit, stroked it in time to his thrusts. Then his thumb pressed against the rosebud of her bottom and that slightest pressure, the barest hint of sensation, was all it took to send her hurtling over the edge again. She screamed this time, but no sound emerged. Her throat was raw. His tautened balls slapped against her weeping flesh as he pistoned in and out of her, harder and harder and faster still. He showed her no mercy, gave her no quarter and she didn't want it—she only wanted him.

It was the basest, purest, most moving sex she'd ever had in her entire life and she knew that when she left here tomorrow, she'd never be the same. He'd done something to her, Pen realized. She didn't know what, but she felt the shift all the same.

He'd ruined her, Pen thought. But if this was her downfall, then she'd gladly pay the price.

SETH DIDN'T KNOW what had come over him. One minute he'd been content to simply make love to her, to take his time and make the most of it…but then the meaning of making the most of it changed and he couldn't get his mouth on her enough, couldn't touch her enough, couldn't get into her enough. He'd gone from simply wanting to take her to making her his in every sense of the word, to making her want to rethink their pretend status and consider giving him more than a ninety-day trial period.

And then he'd decided that she was literally driving him crazy, because he was an idiot to think those things, to even consider that he could be the one to change her mind. He wished he could say he just wanted the challenge of being the only exception to her rule, but he knew better. He knew in his heart what his mind didn't want to accept. She was special.

She utterly did it for him, in every sense of the word. He wanted to listen to her talk and laugh, he wanted to learn everything about her, the things that mattered and the things that didn't. He wanted to look at the world the way she saw it and notice what the differences were. He wanted to watch her wake up in the morning when the first light of dawn touched her face and those amazing eyes fluttered open, and he wanted to spoon her in bed every night before they fell asleep. He wanted to hold her hand and kiss her fingers and walk the world with her.

In the military, he'd been lucky enough to do a bit of traveling. He'd love to walk the Great Wall of China with her, show her the headwaters of the Nile, paddle through Alaska's Inside Passage and tromp through ruined castles in Scotland. He wanted to hold her hand on the streets of New York and put his arm around her as they stared out over the Grand Canyon. Did she want to do any of these things?

He had no freaking idea. And he was rapidly running out of time to find out.

It was that time or the lack thereof that made him crazy, that made him flip her over onto her belly, then take her hard from behind. He drove into her, pounding harder and harder, her sweet rump the perfect cradle for his sex. *Narrow waist, womanly hips, the sleek swell of her bottom.*

He growled low in his throat and pushed harder, her breasts bouncing on her chest, absorbing his frantic, desperate thrusts.

Another keening cry ripped from her throat and he knew that she was close again. He reached around her and stroked her clit and he felt her tighten around him again.

"Do it again," he told her.

"Seth, dammit. I—"

He smiled as she tightened again, fisted harder around him. He pushed and pulled, stroked and played, then bent forward and nipped playfully where her neck met her shoulder.

She shattered around him once more.

Seth smiled with victory and then raced toward his

own release. The sensation built and built and then, to his astonishment, she reached back and stroked his tightened balls. That one touch sent him into oblivion. Light faded, sound receded, a long growl broke loose from his throat and he shuddered behind her, emptying his seed into the end of the condom.

Breathing heavily, he carefully withdrew, disposed of the protection, then followed her down onto the bed, dragging her to him so that he could feel her against his side. She cuddled in, slinging a leg over his, an arm around his waist, her head resting on his still racing heart.

"Wow," she said, her lips pressing against his chest in a reverent kiss. "That was—"

"Beyond description," he supplied when she couldn't finish.

She nodded, her silky hair tickling his side. "That too," she said.

"Too?"

"I was going to say 'freaking awesome' but your description is more poetic."

He chuckled, tracing circles on her upper arm. He wanted to do more of this, too, Seth thought. He'd never expected to enjoy pillow talk, but imagined it would depend on whether you liked the person you were sharing the pillow with.

"I don't believe I've ever been accused of being poetic," he said, laughing.

"Bet you've been accused of being a lot of other things though, haven't you?" she teased.

"Most recently I was accused of being a smart-ass,

but that was by a mouthy little commitment-phobic wedding planner, so I didn't listen."

She playfully punched him on the chest. "You should," she quipped. "She sounds like a remarkable woman."

"She is," he admitted. "But she's awfully full of herself."

"What?" she gasped, whacking him again.

"How many more times are you going to hit me?" Seth asked. "Am I going to have file domestic abuse charges against you?"

She snorted. "I dare you. A big guy like you filing charges against a little thing like me? They'd laugh you out of the police station."

"Huck was right," Seth muttered, looking thoughtfully at the ceiling in the darkness. "Women are diabolical."

"Ha," she harrumphed. "Only out of necessity," she said. "If men weren't such know-it-alls, women wouldn't have to be diabolical."

He laughed. "I didn't say I didn't like it."

She stilled and a little gasp slipped through her lips. "You think it's sexy, don't you?"

"When it's the right woman," he said, pressing a kiss to the top of her head.

"You probably find it so attractive because you recognize it in yourself," she told him. "Like is attuned to like."

"Do you think we're alike?" he asked. For whatever reason, her answer was more important than it should have been.

She hummed under her breath for a moment, truly considering the question before answering. "Yes," she finally admitted. "I do think we're a lot alike. We both come from broken families, mine more shattered than yours in some ways, and we're both very purpose-driven. You need to have something to do, the same desire to be useful as I have, if not more," she said, displaying a keen bit of insight. "And we're both determined to meet the world on our own terms." She sighed. "And we both keep our promises. You kept yours to your mother and I keep mine to my clients. Being truthful is important, a lost art, even, and it takes courage to be honest when it would be easier to bow to diplomacy." He felt her grimace. "I would have made a piss-poor diplomat."

He laughed and hugged her tighter. "Oh, I don't know about that. You handle your team and your clients with a certain amount of diplomacy. For instance, when Nella's mother arrived with that god-awful blue rhinestone-encrusted hat she intended to wear tomorrow, you told her that the rhinestones would cast little blue glares all around the tent, possibly even against Nella's dress, making it look stained. That was pretty damned diplomatic."

She'd begun to chuckle halfway through his comment and was now struggling to stop. "Oh, jeez, did you see that thing? What the hell was she thinking? It looked like something The Little Mermaid would wear. It was ghastly." Her laughter finally tittered off. "Okay, I suppose I'm better at diplomacy than I thought I was."

He knew it, Seth thought, and fully imagined he'd

be getting a very diplomatic kiss-off tomorrow, when their pretend relationship was over.

The thought was more depressing than he would have ever imagined. He pulled her closer, kissing her once again, and beat back melancholy with the best thing available, the only known cure. God help him…

Her.

14

AH, PEN THOUGHT, the moment she'd been waiting for, the one that made every wedding worthwhile, the minute that Trent and Nella raced through a shower of birdseed and well-wishers on their way to their new life together.

Pen hung back and watched it all unfold and, to her surprise, Nella's gaze sought hers out. Her old friend blew her a kiss and mouthed a watery thank-you. Trent sent a deferential nod in her direction and the thoughtful gesture from the famous quarterback was one she'd always appreciate. Monica slid in beside her. "Well done, boss," she said. "Disaster averted, business and jobs intact, no bloodshed, all's well that ends well."

Pen repressed the unreasonable urge to cry. Something wasn't going to end well and that was her relationship with her pretend boyfriend, the sexy man who'd somehow managed to carve a place in her heart over the past three days.

It was insane.

Great sex and a few laughs did not a relationship

make, Pen told herself. And she didn't want a relationship anyway, dammit. It's what she'd been avoiding her entire adult life. She'd made a career out of attaching people, not getting attached herself.

The minute Trent and Nella were officially gone, the guys from Ranger Security would pack up their big SUV and leave, Seth with them. He wouldn't ride back with her, she knew, because there would be no need. Furthermore, his job was done and hers was not. She had to make sure that the various rental companies quickly arrived to reclaim their things and that the house and grounds were put to rights as soon as possible, especially considering that Trent and Nella actually planned to honeymoon here.

"You're awfully quiet," Monica said, studying her thoughtfully.

"Just tired," Pen said, which was, in part, the truth.

"You look like someone stole your puppy."

She managed a weak laugh. Yeah, the person who saved it from the storm drain to start with, Pen thought.

"I'll be fine," she said.

Monica nodded toward Seth. "It's him, isn't it? You like him."

If by like, Monica meant that Pen wanted to spend every minute of every day, possibly for the rest of her stupid misbegotten life, with him, then yes, that was an accurate description.

How had this happened? Pen wondered furiously. How had she let herself care for him so much? Why did he have to be the one that mattered?

This morning they'd showered together and he'd made love to her, reverently stroking and memorizing every inch of her skin. She'd caught him looking at her with this sort of furious despair, then he'd open his mouth and close it again, never saying a word. He'd made her an omelet and gotten it perfect, too, with no runny bits or crispy edges. He'd prepared her tea the way she liked it. He'd been thoughtful and courteous and utterly easy company. And for the briefest, most terrifying moment, she'd known what it would be like to be with him all the time, to go to bed with him at night and wake up with him in the morning. It would be so easy....

Too easy to believe it was true and too much of a stretch to believe it could last.

Call her a coward, call her selfish, call her whatever you wanted, Pen just couldn't bring herself to take the risk and she didn't blame him for not asking her to. There was no room for misinterpretation between them. They'd been too honest, and now she was boxed into that truth, whether she liked it or not.

He turned to look at her and a tentative smile moved over his lips. But it wasn't the genuine one she'd become used to seeing. Her heart gave a lurch as he started toward her.

Monica moved away. "I'm going to...go do something," she finished lamely, unable to come up with a good excuse to leave.

Seth took her hand in his again, causing warmth to seep into her suddenly chilled fingers. "Looks like you can make an offer on that house you wanted," he said, giving her hand a squeeze.

Whatever she'd thought he would say, that was not it. She chuckled with relief. "Yeah, I think so."

When she'd brought everything into the living room this morning, he'd seen the real estate guide lying on top of her bag and noticed the turned-down page. He'd loved it, and even knew where it was because he'd grown up in Marietta. His sister and nephew were currently living in his mother's old house only a few blocks away. He said it suited her and as far as Pen was concerned, his opinion was the only one that mattered. She planned to call her agent on the drive home today and schedule an appointment to look at the house. She wished he could go with her but knew that was something she couldn't ask.

"Everything was wonderful," he told her. "You've given Trent and Nella a memorable start to an incredible life together. You should be proud."

"I am," she said, nodding once. "Drama notwithstanding, this was one of my favorite weddings."

If he didn't leave soon she was going to lose it, Pen thought. Her heart had begun to pound, her hands were shaking and though she had never been the weepy type, her eyes were watering dangerously.

He hesitated, looked at her, then seemed to steel himself. "Trent's security team has officially taken over, so Ranger Security is finished here."

Just as she suspected. "You've done a great job," she said, managing a mangled smile. "Not bad for your first job, huh?"

He nodded, then rubbed the back of his neck.

"It's been an experience," he said. His gaze tangled meaningfully with hers. "A good one."

"Thanks," she said, her throat getting thicker by the second.

"You've been a wonderful pretend girlfriend."

He was killing her. Another horrible laugh managed to make its way past her lips. "And you've been a kick-ass pretend boyfriend."

He stared at her for a moment longer, his gaze tracing her face, lingering on her mouth. He bent forward and pressed a kiss to her forehead. It was sweet and reverent and heartbreaking and she was falling apart on the inside. "Bye, Pen," he said, his voice rough with an unnamed emotion. Then he turned and walked away.

Pen took a deep, bracing breath, then turned abruptly and headed for the beach. She was going to need a few minutes to pull herself together.

"Pen," Monica called.

She held up her hand, silently warning her assistant off, and walked faster. By the time she reached the surf, she was hyperventilating and her sides ached from trying to hold herself together.

Shake it off, Pen, she told herself. *You can do this.* Better broken now than shattered later. Better to let him go while it was her choice, than to watch him leave or wait until he grew tired of her. How many times had she watched this with her parents? Didn't she know the inevitable outcome?

Yes, she did, she thought. This way was better.

If she said it enough, maybe she'd start to believe it.

SETH SLID into the backseat of the SUV. Will and Huck shared a look he wished he hadn't seen.

They knew.

Of course, they knew, he thought. How could they not know? How could they miss the fact that he'd fallen for the wedding planner, the woman he was supposed to pretend to be in love with. *Pretend* being the operative word there. Sheesh, Lord, he'd lost his ever-loving mind, Seth thought, resisting the urge to tear out his hair. Walking away from her had been like lopping off an appendage, abandoning a part of himself he wasn't altogether sure he was ever going to get back.

How had he allowed this to happen? How in the hell had she gone from merely orbiting through his universe to becoming his whole world in a mere three days?

You'll find your rudder...and I hope she initially mops the deck with you, his mother, evidently a prophet, had said. And that was it, he realized. She *was* his rudder, a strong force in a tiny package. Aside from the maniacal sexual urges she brought out in him, hadn't he felt more grounded, more at peace, when he was with her? Hadn't he practically opened a vein and told her more than he'd ever told another living soul? Hell, even his best friends didn't know about his dad, about how he'd decked him when he'd spoken ill of his mother. And yet he'd told her, a virtual stranger.

No, not a stranger, he realized. Because in some bizarre fashion he had no way of explaining, he *knew* her. His soul had recognized hers.

He'd been done the instant she'd shown up at his door. He'd just been too dumb to realize it.

"So?" Huck finally asked when it was evident that Seth wasn't going to share.

Seth shrugged and blew out a breath. "So…mission accomplished. We're done."

"But I thought—" Will started, but stopped when Tanner punched him.

"She's a pretty opinionated woman," Will remarked with a glare at Tanner. "Reminds me a lot of Rhiannon."

"Oh?" Seth added, just to be polite. He couldn't very well tell his coworkers to shut the fuck up like he really wanted to do. It would be a piss-poor way to repay their friendship, which they'd offered in good faith.

"Yeah. Rhi knows her own mind, but sometimes it takes her mind a little while to catch up with her other feelings."

Dammit to hell, he really didn't want to talk about *feelings.*

"Jeez, Will," Huck complained, grimacing. "We all know how attuned you are to your feelings, thanks to your wife. But if it's all the same to you, we'd like to keep ours to ourselves."

That's right, Seth remembered. Will's wife was an empath and practiced emotional intelligence. She was supposedly able to pick up on other people's emotions, read them and feel them, even.

But he was thankful to Huck all the same.

"I wasn't going to talk about my feelings, jackass," Will said, thumping Huck on the back of the head. "I was merely trying to make a point."

"And that is?" Tanner asked pointedly, with a get-to-it gesture.

"A woman who knows her own mind will ultimately make the right move." He grinned, obviously remembering something pleasant. "I know mine certainly did." Will turned to look at Seth. "Let her stew for a while," he told Seth, then nodded as though he was in possession of some knowledge Seth wasn't. "She'll come around."

Seth found himself strangely heartened by Will's assertion and gave a nod in thanks, once again grateful that Garrett had recommended him for this job. No, he wasn't doing what he'd always planned to do. But he knew he was going to be happy here. His feet were on the right path.

He only wished Pen's were there with him.

PEN KNEW she was going to be in for a miserable conversation when a determined Monica burst into her office. "I know you told me to leave you alone, but I can't."

"Monica—"

"Look, Pen, you've been mopey and bitchy for a whole week! Enough is enough. Do you want to die old and alone, with nothing but a vibrator and porn to comfort you in your old age?"

"Yes," Pen said, just to irritate her. What kind of question was that anyway?

"Pen, I can't let you screw this up. I wouldn't be a good friend if I didn't." She leveled her gaze at Pen and took a step forward. "Pen, you are miserable without him and you know it. You—"

"I am n—"

Monica shushed her. "You *are,*" she insisted. "There's no point in denying it. The truth is written in those ugly bags beneath your eyes. You look haggard and unhappy and have developed an unsightly sallow tone to your skin."

Great, Pen thought. With a friend like Monica, who needed enemies?

"And, honestly, I think it's a bit…stupid of you to continue on this way, in this self-imposed hell of your own making, just because you're too much of a coward to take a chance."

Okay, that was enough. "I am not a coward," she said, sending her assistant a warning glance. "I am *careful.* There's a difference."

"Not in this case, there's not," Monica said, undeterred. "If you'd seen the way he looked at you, you would know that you don't have to be careful with him, sweetheart. The man adores you. He's nothing like those other easily directed—Paul had had that right and you know it—pretty boys you've dated in the past, the kind who were content with the superficial relationship you were willing to offer because you were too afraid of—"

"I'm not afraid," she repeated again. But suddenly she knew in her heart it was a lie. She *was* afraid. She was terrified that she'd let her own happiness become so invested in his that she'd lose herself—that he'd leave and take that part of her with him and she'd never get it back, never get herself back.

"You are," Monica insisted. "We all are," she added more gently. "But you don't have to be afraid with him, Pen. He loves you."

Penelope's chest constricted. "He does not," she scoffed, not daring to believe. "He doesn't know me well enough to love me." She didn't know him well enough to love him either, and yet she was relatively certain she did. It would be horrible to be in this much misery over someone she wasn't in love with, that was for sure.

"I don't agree, but if he doesn't yet, then he will." She handed Pen her purse. "Go to him, Pen. Give him a chance to be different. Because he is," she added. "Abnormal size aside, he's pretty damned spectacular."

"He's not abnormally sized," she said, her throat tight. "He's perfect."

"Exactly," Monica told her. "For you."

Making a split decision, Pen grabbed her purse and headed out of the office. She considered turning around half-a-dozen times before she finally found herself standing outside Seth's apartment door, but she knew that if she didn't give this a shot, she'd regret it for the rest of her life.

She'd been regretting it forever since she'd gotten home. And it had only worsened with every day that had gone by. She'd dreamed about him, scoured wedding pictures for a glimpse of him, played Solitaire and burst into tears when she'd seen the jack of hearts.

She took a bracing breath, then lifted her hand and

knocked. Once again she heard the pad of bare feet against the floor, but unlike the last time, she knew exactly what was waiting for her.

He blinked when he saw her. "Pen?"

He was shirtless again, damn him. Didn't he know how much she loved his chest. Low-slung shorts—that's what happened when a man had virtually no hips, she thought—and bare legs and feet. She had to cross her arms over her chest to keep from leaping into his arms, from crawling all over him like a spider monkey. A strangled laugh broke in her throat, which no doubt made her look a little crazy. Which she was.

About him.

"Is this a bad time? I should have called first, but I—"

"No, no," he assured her. "Come on in. Can I get you anything?"

"A drink would be nice," she said, a departure from the last time she'd arrived on his doorstep, uninvited. She had a feeling he wasn't going to make this easy on her and she knew she was going to need a little alcohol to get her through it.

"Sure," he said, strolling into the kitchen. "A beer okay?"

"Yes, thanks." She sat on the edge of the sofa and tried to pretend her heart wasn't about to pop out of her chest, that what she was about to say really didn't matter.

He returned and handed it to her. She took a grateful sip, then looked up at him once more. He merely stared at her, quite hungrily, which was nice. But he didn't say anything.

She'd been right. He was going to make her beg.

And it was a sad testament to her current state that she'd do it.

"How've you been?" she asked.

"Pretty damned miserable," he admitted affably. "You?"

"The same."

He nodded. "I've been having a hard time seeing the point."

She hesitated. "That's why I'm here. I've been struggling with that, too. I was kind of wondering if you'd like to stop being my pretend boyfriend—"

"I thought I had."

"—and start being my real one," she finished quietly.

He stared at her, his expression unreadable. "Your real one?"

"Yes."

"Your *real* boyfriend?" he repeated, evidently because he enjoyed torturing her.

"Mmm-hmm." She waited.

"Are you going to kick my besotted ass to the curb in three months?"

Besotted? Truly? Her heart leaped and a smile slid slowly over her lips. "That's not my intent, no," she said.

"So if we're still happy in three months, you're going to let our relationship continue to grow and develop?"

"Yes."

He passed a hand over his face to hide a smile. "You're going to do my laundry and darn my socks?"

"No," she said, biting her lip to keep from laughing. Only Seth, she thought. "I will not do those things." She didn't even do her own laundry—she dropped it off at the cleaner's. And she wouldn't know how to darn a sock if her life depended on it.

"Will you occasionally fetch me a beer and scratch my back?"

Her lips twitched. "Yes. Occasionally."

"And when is this relationship supposed to start?"

"Now, preferably."

He stood and offered her his hand. When she put hers in his, he yanked her quickly forward and wrapped his arms around her. "It took you long enough," he said. "I've been sitting here all week."

"Shirtless?"

"Yes."

"Damn," she said, wincing. "If I'd have known that, I would have been here sooner."

"I had no idea you were so shallow," he teased, kissing her. Sweet emotion bolted through her.

"And I had no idea I was such a coward. I'm sorry, Seth. I was just afraid. I—"

He shushed her. "You're not a coward. You're careful. And I happen to admire that about you." He grinned down at her. "It means that I'm ultimately going to be more special than everyone else."

He already was, Pen thought as she pressed her lips to his once more.

Epilogue

Three months later...

"YOU DID WHAT?" MONICA screamed into her ear.

Pen chuckled and squeezed Seth's hand. "We just got married in Vegas," she said. "At a drive-through wedding chapel."

Evidently Jamie had put the idea into Seth's head several months ago. When he'd popped the question this morning, he hadn't wanted to wait so he'd called the airline and booked the tickets, then called his sister and shared the news. She'd been ecstatic and had happily welcomed Pen into their family.

"Pen, I'm going to kill you," Monica said. "You can't be serious. You're a wedding planner, one of Atlanta's *premier* wedding planners! How do you think this is going to affect your reputation? You—"

"See you in a couple of weeks," Pen told her, not caring in the least. "We're honeymooning in Alaska." And when they came home, it would be to the house she'd bought in Marietta. The place where they would build their family. The very idea made her throat tighten.

She snapped the phone shut and looked at her newly minted husband. Desire slid through her, making her belly go all warm and tingly. They were going to need to stop soon and consummate this marriage, Pen thought. She couldn't wait until they got to the other side of the road, much less Sitka. "She's freaking out," she said.

Seth grinned. "You knew she would."

True. And if anyone had told her three months ago that she'd be married, or that she would have done the deed in the same way a person could buy doughnuts, she would have told them they were crazy.

Turns out she was the crazy one.

Because Pen didn't care about the wedding. She only cared about the marriage…and she knew that it was going to be as strong as it possibly could be.

Seth gave her that assurance in the little ways he loved her every day. From making sure that her car was serviced to sneaking a kiss on the back of her neck when she wasn't looking, she always felt loved. And she knew she always would.

Because he'd just promised to love her until death they did part. And she knew Seth was a man who kept his promises…

* * * * *

Read on for a sneak preview of Carol Marinelli's
PUTTING ALICE BACK TOGETHER!

Hugh hired bikes!

You know that saying: 'It's like riding a bike, you never forget'?

I'd never learnt in the first place.

I never got past training wheels.

'You've got limited upper-body strength?' He stopped and looked at me.

I had been explaining to him as I wobbled along and tried to stay up that I really had no centre of balance. I mean *really* had no centre of balance. And when we decided, fairly quickly, that a bike ride along the Yarra perhaps, after all, wasn't the best activity (he'd kept insisting I'd be fine once I was on, that you never forget), I threw in too my other disability. I told him about my limited upper-body strength, just in case he took me to an indoor rock-climbing centre next. I'd honestly forgotten he was a doctor, and he seemed worried, like I'd had a mini-stroke in the past or had mild cerebral palsy or something.

'God, Alice, I'm sorry—you should have said. What happened?'

And then I had had to tell him that it was a self-diagnosis. 'Well, I could never get up the ropes at the gym at school.' We were pushing our bikes back. 'I can't blow-dry the back of my hair...' He started laughing.

Not like Lisa who was laughing at me—he was just laughing and so was I. We got a full refund because we'd only been on our bikes ten minutes, but I hadn't failed. If anything, we were getting on better.

And better.

We went to St Kilda to the lovely bitty shops and I found these miniature Russian dolls. They were tiny, made of tin or something, the biggest no bigger than my thumbnail. Every time we opened them, there was another tiny one, and then another, all reds and yellows and greens.

They were divine.

We were facing each other, looking down at the palm of my hand, and our heads touched.

If I put my hand up now, I can feel where our heads touched.

I remember that moment.

I remember it a lot.

Our heads connected for a second and it was alchemic; it was as if our minds kissed hello.

I just have to touch my head, just there at the very spot and I can, whenever I want to, relive that moment.

So many times I do.

'Get them.' Hugh said, and I would have, except that little bit of tin cost more than a hundred dollars and, though that usually wouldn't have stopped me, I wasn't about to have my card declined in front of him.

I put them back.

'Nope.' I gave him a smile. 'Gotta stop the impulse

spending.'

We had lunch.

Out on the pavement and I can't remember what we ate, I just remember being happy. Actually, I can remember: I had Caesar salad because it was the lowest carb thing I could find. We drank water and I *do* remember not giving it a thought.

I was just thirsty.

And happy.

He went to the loo and I chatted to a girl at the next table, just chatted away. Hugh was gone for ages and I was glad I hadn't demanded Dan from the universe, because I would have been worried about how long he was taking.

Do I go on about the universe too much? I don't know, but what I do know is that something *was* looking out for me, helping me to be my best, not to **** this up as I usually do. You see, we walked on the beach, we went for another coffee and by that time it was evening and we went home and he gave me a present.

Those Russian dolls.

I held them in my palm, and it was the nicest thing he could have done for me.

They are absolutely my favourite thing and I've just stopped to look at them now. I've just stopped to take them apart and then put them all back together again and I can still feel the wonder I felt on that day.

He was the only man who had bought something for me, I mean something truly special. Something beautiful, something thoughtful, something just for me.

© Carol Marinelli 2012
Available at millsandboon.co.uk

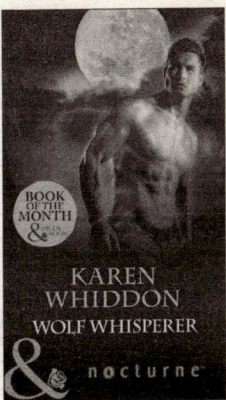